THE LATE MRS. NULL

Frank R. Stockton

THE LATE MRS. NULL

BY

FRANK R. STOCKTON

ILLUSTRATED

WILDSIDE PRESS

ILLUSTRATIONS

THE LATE MRS. NULL

THE LATE MRS. NULL

CHAPTER I

THERE was a wide entrance-gate to the old family mansion of Midbranch, but it was never opened to admit the family or visitors; although occasionally a load of wood, drawn by two horses and two mules, came between its tall chestnut posts, and was taken by a roundabout way among the trees to a spot at the back of the house, where the chips of several generations of sturdy wood-choppers had formed a ligneous soil deeper than the arable surface of any portion of the nine hundred and fifty acres which formed the farm of Midbranch. This seldom-opened gate was in a corner of the lawn, and the driving of carriages, or the riding of horses through it to the porch at the front of the house would have been the ruin of the short, thick grass which had covered that lawn, it was generally believed, ever since Virginia became a State.

But there had to be some way for people who came in carriages or on horseback to get into the house, and therefore the fence at the bottom of the lawn, at a point directly in front of the porch, was crossed by a set of broad wooden steps, five outside and five inside, with a platform at the top. These stairs were wide

3

enough to accommodate eight people abreast; so that if a large carriage-load of visitors arrived, none of them need delay in crossing the fence. At the outside of the steps ran the narrow road which entered the plantation a quarter of a mile away, and passed around the lawn and the garden to the barns and stables at the back.

On the other side of the road, undivided from it by hedge or fence, stretched, like a sea gently moved by a ground-swell, a vast field, sometimes planted in tobacco, and sometimes in wheat. In the midst of this field stood a tall persimmon-tree which yearly dropped its half-candied fruit upon the first light snow of the winter. It is true that persimmons, quite fit to eat, were to be found on this tree at an earlier period than this, but such fruit was never noticed by the people in those parts, who would not rudely wrench from Jack Frost his one little claim to rivalry with the sun as a fruit-ripener. To the right of the field was a wide extent of pasture-land, running down to a small stream, or "branch," which, flowing between two other streams of the same kind a mile or two on either side of it, had given its name to the place. In front, to the left, lay a great forest of chestnut, oak, sassafras, and sweet-gum, with here and there a clump of tall pines, standing up straight and stiff with an air of Puritanic condemnation of the changing fashions of the foliage about them.

On one side of the platform of the broad stile, which has been mentioned, sat, one summer afternoon, the lady of the house. She was a young woman, and although her face was a good deal shadowed by her far-spreading hat, it was easy to perceive that she was a handsome one. She was the niece of Mr. Robert

4

THE LATE MRS. NULL

Brandon, the elderly bachelor who owned Midbranch, and her mother, long since dead, had called her Roberta, which was as near as she could come to the name of her only brother.

Miss Roberta's father was a man whose mind and time were entirely given up to railroads; and although he nominally lived in New York, he was, for the greater part of the year, engaged in endeavors to forward his interests somewhere west of the Mississippi. Two or three months of the winter were generally spent in his city home. At these times he had his daughter with him, but the rest of the year she lived with her uncle, whose household she directed with much good will and judgment. The old gentleman did not keep her all the summer at Midbranch. He knew what was necessary for a young lady who had been educated in Germany and Switzerland, and who had afterwards made a very favorable impression in Paris and London; and so, during the hot weather, he took her with him to one of the fashionable Southern resorts, where they always stayed exactly six weeks.

The gentleman who was sitting on the other side of the platform, with his face turned towards her, had known Miss Roberta for a year or more, having met her at the North, and also in the Virginia mountains; and being now on a visit to the Green Sulphur Springs, about four miles from Midbranch, he rode over to see her nearly every day. There was nothing surprising in this, because the Green Sulphur, once a much-frequented resort, had seen great changes, and now, although the end of the regular season had not arrived, it had Mr. Lawrence Croft for its only guest. There was a spacious hotel there; there was a village

5

of cottages of varying sizes; there were buildings for servants and managers; there was a tenpin-alley and a quoit-ground; there were arbors and swings; and a square hole in a stone slab, through which a little pool of greenish water could be seen, with a tin cup, somewhat rusty, lying by it. But all was quiet and deserted, except one cottage, in which the man lived who had charge of the place, and where Mr. Croft boarded. It was very pleasant for him to ride over to Midbranch and take a walk with Miss Roberta; and this was what they had been doing to-day.

Horseback rides had been suggested, but Mr. Brandon objected to these. He knew Mr. Croft to be a young man of good family and very comfortable fortune, and he liked him very much when he had him there to dinner, but he did not wish his niece to go galloping around the country with him. To quiet walks in the woods, and through the meadows, he could, of course, have no objection. A good many of Mr. Brandon's principles, like certain of his books, were kept upon a top shelf, but Miss Roberta always liked to humor the few which the old gentleman was wont to have within easy reach.

This afternoon they had rambled through the woods, where the hard, smooth road wound picturesquely through the places in which it had been easiest to make a road, and where the great trunks of the trees were partly covered by clinging vines, which Miss Roberta knew to be either Virginia creeper or poison-oak, although she did not remember which of these had clusters of five leaves, and which of three.

The horse on which Mr. Croft had ridden over from

the Springs was tied to a fence near by, and he now seemed to indicate by his restless movements that it was quite time for the gentleman to go home; but with this opinion Mr. Croft decidedly differed. He had had a long walk with the lady, and plenty of opportunities to say anything that he might choose, but still there was something very important which had not been said, and which Mr. Croft very much wished to say before he left Miss Roberta that afternoon. His only reason for hesitation was the fact that he did not know what he wished to say.

He was a man who always kept a lookout on the bows of his daily action; in storm or in calm, in fog or in bright sunshine, that lookout must be at his post; and upon his reports it depended whether Mr. Croft set more sail, put on more steam, reversed his engine, or anchored his vessel. A report from this lookout was what he hoped to elicit by the remark which he wished to make. He desired greatly to know whether Miss Roberta March looked upon him in the light of a lover, or in that of an intimate acquaintance, whose present intimacy depended a good deal upon the propinquity of Midbranch and the Green Sulphur Springs. He had endeavored to produce upon her mind the latter impression. If he ever wished her to regard him as a lover he could do this in the easiest and most straightforward way, but the other procedure was much more difficult, and he was not certain that he had succeeded in it. How to find out in what light she viewed him without allowing the lady to perceive his purpose was a very delicate operation.

"I wish," said Miss Roberta, poking with the end of her parasol at some half-withered wild flowers which

7

lay on the steps beneath her, "that you would change your mind, and take supper with us."

Mr. Croft's mind was very busy endeavoring to think of some casual remark, some observation regarding man, nature, or society, or even an anecdote or historical incident, which, if brought into the conversation, might produce upon the lady's countenance some shade of expression, or some variation in her tone or words, which would give him the information he sought for. But what he said was: "Are they really suppers that you have, or are they only teas?"

"Now I know," said the lady, "why you have some-times taken dinner with us, but never supper. You were afraid that it would be a tea."

Lawrence Croft was thinking that if this girl believed that he was in love with her, it would make a great deal of difference in his present course of action. If such were the case, he ought not to come here so often, or, in fact, he ought not to come at all, until he had decided for himself what he was going to do. But what could he say that would cause her, for the briefest moment, to unveil her idea of himself. "I never could endure," he said, "those meals which consist of thin shavings of bread with thick plasters of butter, aided and abetted by sweet cakes, preserves, and tea."

"You should have reserved those remarks," she said, "until you had found out what sort of evening meal we have."

He could certainly say something, he thought. Perhaps it might be some little fanciful story which would call up in her mind, without his appearing to intend it, some thought of his relationship to her as a lover—that is, if she had ever had such a notion. If

THE LATE MRS. NULL

this could be done, her face would betray the fact.
But, not being ready to make such a remark, he said :
"I beg your pardon, but do you really have suppers in
the English fashion?"

"Oh, no," answered Miss Roberta, "we don't have a
great cold joint, with old cheese, and pitchers of brown
stout and ale, but neither do we content ourselves with
thin bread and butter, and preserves. We have coffee
as well as tea, hot rolls, fleecy and light, hot batter
bread made of our finest corn meal, hot biscuits and
stewed fruit, with plenty of sweet milk and buttermilk ;
and, if anybody wants it, he can always have a slice
of cold ham."

"If I could only feel sure," thought Mr. Croft, "that
she looked upon me merely as an acquaintance, I would
cease to trouble my mind on this subject, and let everything go on as before. But I am not sure, and I would
rather not come here again until I am." "And at
what hour," he asked, "do you partake of a meal like
that?"

"In summer-time," said Miss Roberta, "we have
supper when it is dark enough to light the lamps. My
uncle dislikes very much to be deprived, by the advent
of a meal, of the outdoor enjoyment of a late afternoon, or, as we call it down here, the evening."

"It would be easy enough," thought Mr. Croft, "for
me to say something about my being suddenly obliged
to go away, and then notice its effect upon her. But,
apart from the fact that I would not do anything so
vulgar and commonplace, it would not advantage me
in the slightest degree. She would see through the
flimsiness of my purpose, and, no matter how she
looked upon me, would show nothing but a well-bred

9

regret that I should be obliged to go away at such a pleasant season." "I think the hour for your supper," said he, "is a very suitable one, but I am not sure that such a variety of hot bread would agree with me."

"Did you ever see more healthy-looking ladies and gentlemen than you find in Virginia?" asked Miss March.

"It is not that I want to know if she looks favorably upon me," said Lawrence Croft to himself, "for when I wish to discover that, I shall simply ask her. What I wish now to know is whether or not she considers me at all as a lover. There surely must be something I can say which will give me a clew." "The Virginians, as a rule," he replied, "are certainly a very well-grown and vigorous race."

"In spite of the hot bread," she said with a smile.

Just then Mr. Croft believed himself struck by a happy thought. "You are not prepared, I suppose, to say, in consequence of it; and that recalls the fact that so much in this world happens in spite of things, instead of in consequence of them."

"I don't know that I exactly understand," said Miss Roberta.

"Well, for instance," said Mr. Croft, "take the case of marriage. Don't you think that a man is more apt to marry in spite of his belief that he would be much better off as a bachelor, than in consequence of a conviction that a benedict's life would suit him better?"

"That," said she, "depends a good deal on the woman."

As she said this Lawrence glanced quickly at her to

10

observe the expression of her countenance. The countenance plainly indicated that its owner had suddenly been made aware that the afternoon was slipping away, and that she had forgotten certain household duties that devolved upon her.

"Here comes Peggy," she said, "and I must go into the house and give out supper. Don't you now think it would be well for you to follow our discussion of a Virginia supper by eating one?"

At this moment there arrived at the bottom of the inside steps a small girl, very black, very solemn, and very erect, with her hands folded in front of her very straight up-and-down calico frock, her features expressive of a wooden stolidity which nothing but a hammer or chisel could alter, and with large eyes fixed upon a far-away, which, apparently, had disappeared, leaving the eyes in a condition of idle outgo.

"Miss Rob," said this wooden Peggy, "Aun' Judy says it's more'n time to come housekeep."

"Which means," said Miss Roberta, rising, "that I must go and get my key-basket, and descend into the store-room. Won't you come in? We shall find uncle on the back porch."

Mr. Croft declined with thanks, and took his leave, and the lady walked across the smooth grass to the house, followed by the rigid Peggy.

The young man approached his impatient horse, and, not without some difficulty, got himself mounted. He had not that facility of sympathetically combining his own will and that of his horse which comes to men who, from their early boyhood, are wont to consider horses as objects quite as necessary to locomotion as shoes and stockings. But Lawrence Croft was a fair graduate of a riding-school, and he went away in very good style to his cottage at the Green Sulphur Springs. "I believe," he said to himself as he rode through the woods, "that Miss March expects no more of me than she would expect of any very intimate friend. I shall feel perfectly free, therefore, to continue my investigations regarding two points: First, is she worth having? Second, will she have me? And I must be very careful not to get the position of these points reversed."

When Miss Roberta went into the store-room, it was Peggy who, under the supervision of her mistress, measured out the fine white flour for the biscuits for supper. Peggy was being educated to do these things properly, and she knew exactly how many times the tin scoop must fill itself in the barrel for the ordinary needs of the family. Miss Roberta stood, her eyes contemplatively raised to the narrow window, through which she could see a flush of sunset mingling itself with the outer air; and Peggy scooped once, twice, thrice, four times; then she stopped, and, raising her head, there came into the far-away gloom of her eyes a quick sparkle like a flash of black lightning. She made another and entirely supplementary scoop, and then she stopped, and let the tin utensil fall into the barrel with a gentle thud.

"That will do," said Miss Roberta.

That night, when she should have been in her bed, Peggy sat alone by the hearth in Aunt Judy's cabin, baking a cake. It was a peculiar cake, for she could get no sugar for it, but she had supplied this deficiency with molasses. It was made of Miss Roberta's finest white flour, and there were eggs in it and butter, and it contained, besides, three raisins, an olive, and a prune. When the outside of the cake had been sufficiently baked, and every portion of it had been scrupulously eaten, the good little Peggy murmured to herself: "It's pow'ful comfortin' for Miss Rob to have sumfin' on her min'."

CHAPTER II

ABOUT a week after Mr. Lawrence Croft had had his
conversation with Miss March on the stile steps at
Midbranch, he was obliged to return to his home in
New York. He was not a man of business, but he
had business ; and, besides this, he considered if he continued much longer to reside in the utterly attraction-
less cottage at the Green Sulphur Springs, and rode
over every day to the very attractive house at Midbranch, that the points mentioned in the previous
chapter might get themselves reversed. He was a
man who was proud of being, under all circumstances,
frank and honest with himself. He did not wish, if it
could be avoided, to deceive other people, but he was
prudent and careful about exhibiting his motives and
intended course of action to his associates. Himself,
however, he took into his strictest confidence. He was
fond of the idea that he went into the battle of life
covered and protected by a great shield, but that the
inside of the shield was a mirror in which he could
always see himself. Looking into this mirror, he now
saw that, if he did not soon get away from Miss Roberta, he would lay down his shield and surrender,
and it was his intent that this should not happen
until he wished it to happen.

14

THE LATE MRS. NULL

It was very natural, when Lawrence reached New York, that he should take pleasure in talking about Miss Roberta March and her family with any one who knew them. He was particularly anxious, if he could do so delicately and without exciting any suspicion of his object, to know as much as possible about Sylvester March, the lady's father. In doing this, he did not feel that he was prying into the affairs of others, but he could not be true to himself unless he looked well in advance before he made the step on which his mind was set. It was in this way that he happened to learn that, about two years before, Miss March had been engaged to be married, but that the engagement had been broken off for reasons not known to his informants, and he could find out nothing about the gentleman, except that his name was Junius Keswick.

The fact that the lady had had a lover put her in a new light before Lawrence Croft. He had had an idea, suggested by the very friendly nature of their intercourse, that she was a woman whose mind did not run out to love or marriage, but now that he knew that she was susceptible of being wooed and won, because these things had actually happened to her, he was very glad that he had come away from Midbranch.

The impression soon became very strong upon the mind of Lawrence that he would like to know what kind of man was this former lover. He had known Miss March about a year, and at the time of his first acquaintance with her she must have come very fresh from this engagement. To study the man to whom Roberta March had been willing to engage herself was, to Lawrence's mode of thinking, if not a pre-

15

requisite procedure in his contemplated course of action, at least a very desirable one.

But he was rather surprised to find that no one knew much about Mr. Junius Keswick, or could give him any account of his present whereabouts, although he had been, at the time when his engagement was in force, a resident of New York. To consult a directory was, therefore, an obvious first step in the affair; and, with this intent, Mr. Croft entered, one morning, an apothecary's shop in a street which, though a busy one, was in a rather out-of-the-way part of the city.

"We haven't any directory, sir," said the clerk, "but if you will step across the street you can find one at that little shop with the green door. Everybody goes there to look at the directory."

The green door on the opposite side of the street, approached by a single flat step of stone, had a tin sign upon it, on which was painted:

"INFORMATION
OF EVERY VARIETY
FURNISHED WITHIN."

Pushing open the door, Lawrence entered a long, narrow room, not very well lighted, with a short counter on one side, and some desks, partially screened by a curtain, at the farther end. A boy was behind the counter, and to him Lawrence addressed himself, asking permission to look at a city directory.

"One cent, if you look yourself; three cents, if we look," said the boy, producing a thick volume from beneath the counter.

"One cent?" said Lawrence, smiling at the oddity

of this charge, as he opened the book and turned to the letter K.

"Yes," said the boy, "and if the fine print hurts your eyes, we'll look for three cents."

At this moment a man came from one of the desks at the other end of the room, and handed the boy a letter, with which that young person immediately departed. The new-comer, a smooth-shaven man of about thirty, with the air of the proprietor or head manager very strong upon him, took the boy's position behind the counter, and remarked to Lawrence: "Most people, when they first come here, think it rather queer to pay for looking at the directory, but you see we don't keep a directory to coax people to come in to buy medicines or anything else. We sell nothing but information, and part of our stock is what you get out of a directory. But it's the best plan all round, for we can afford to give you a clean, good book instead of one all jagged and worn; and as you pay your money, you feel you can look as long as you like, and come when you please."

"It is a very good plan," said Lawrence, closing the book, "but the name I want is not here."

"Perhaps it is in last year's directory," said the man, producing another volume from under the counter.

"That wouldn't do me much good," said Lawrence. "I want to know where some one resides this year."

"It will do a great deal of good," said the other, "for if we know where a person has lived, inquiries can be made there as to where he has gone. Sometimes we go back three or four years, and when we have once found a man's name, we follow him up from place to place until we can give the inquirer his pres-

ent address.   What is the name you wanted, sir?
You were looking in the K's."

"Keswick," said Lawrence, "Junius Keswick."

The man ran his finger and his eyes down a column,
and remarked: "There is Keswick, but it is Peter,
laborer; I suppose that isn't the party."

Lawrence smiled, and shook his head.

"We will take the year before that," said the man,
with cheerful alacrity, heaving up another volume.
"Here's two Keswicks," he said in a moment, "one
John, and the other Stephen W.   Neither of them
right?"

"No," said Lawrence; "my man is Junius; and we
need not go any farther back.   I am afraid the person
I am looking for was only a sojourner in the city, and
that his name did not get into the directory.   I know
that he was here year before last."

"All right, sir," said the other, pushing aside the
volume he had been consulting.   "We'll find the man
for you from the hotel books, and what is more, we
can see those two Keswicks that I found last.   Perhaps they were relations of his, and he was staying
with them.   If you put the matter in our hands, we'll
give you the address to-morrow night, provided it's
an ordinary case.   But if he has gone to Australia or
Japan, of course it'll take longer.   Is it crime or
relationship?"

"Neither," replied Lawrence.

"It is generally one of them," said the man, "and if
it's crime we carry it on to a certain point, and then
put it into the hands of the detectives, for we've
nothing to do with police business, private or otherwise.   But if it's relationship, we'll go right through

with it to the end. Any kind of information you may want we'll give you here ; scientific, biographical, business, healthfulness of localities, genuineness of antiquities, age and standing of individuals, purity of liquors or teas from sample, Bible items localized, china verified ; in fact, anything you want to know we can tell you. Of course we don't pretend that we know all these things, but we know the people who do know, or who can find them out. By coming to us, and paying a small sum, the most valuable information, which it would take you years to find out, can be secured with certainty, and generally in a few days. We know what to do, and where to go, and that's the point. If it's a new bug or a microscope insect, we put it into the hands of a man who knows just what high scientific authority to apply to ; if it's the middle name of your next-door neighbor we'll give it to you from his baptismal record. I'm getting up a pamphlet-circular which will be ready in about a week, and which will fully explain our methods of business, with the charges for the different items, etc."

"Well," said Lawrence, taking out his pocket-book, "I want the address of Junius Keswick, and I think I will let you look it up for me. What is your charge ? "

"It will be two dollars," said the man, "ordinary ; and if we find inquiries run into other countries we will make special terms. And then there's seven cents, one for your look, and two threes for ours. You shall hear from us to-morrow night at your hotel or residence, unless you prefer to call here."

"I will call the day after to-morrow," said Lawrence, producing a five-dollar note.

"Very good," replied the proprietor. "Will you

please pay the cashier?" pointing at the same time to a desk behind Lawrence which the latter had not noticed.

Approaching this desk, the top of which, except for a small space in front, was surrounded by short curtains, he saw a young girl busily engaged in reading a book. He proffered her the note, the proprietor at the same time calling out: "Two, seven."

The girl turned the book down to keep the place; then she took the note, and opened a small drawer, in which she fumbled for some moments. Closing the drawer, she rose to her feet and waved the note over the curtain to her right.

"Haven't any change, eh?" said the man, coming from behind the counter, and putting on his hat. "As the boy's not here, I'll step out and get it."

The girl turned up her book, and began to read again, and Lawrence stood and looked at her, wondering what need there was of a cashier in a place like this. She appeared to be under twenty, rather thin-faced, and was plainly dressed. In a few moments she raised her eyes from her book, and said: "Won't you sit down, sir? I am sorry you have to wait, but we are short of change to-day, and sometimes it is hard to get it in this neighborhood."

Lawrence declined to be seated, but was very willing to talk. "Was it the proprietor of this establishment," he asked, "who went out to get the money changed?"

"Yes, sir," she answered. "That is Mr. Candy."

"A queer name," said Lawrence, smiling.

The girl looked up at him, and smiled in return. There was a very perceptible twinkle in her eyes, which seemed to be eyes that would like to be merry ones, and a slight movement of the corners of her mouth which indicated a desire to say something in reply, but, restrained probably by loyalty to her employer, or by prudent discretion regarding conversation with strangers, she was silent.

Lawrence, however, continued his remarks. "The whole business seems to me very odd. Suppose I were to come here and ask for information as to where I could get a five-dollar note changed; would Mr. Candy be able to tell me?"

"He would do in that case just as he does in all others," she said; "first, he would go and find out, and then he would let you know. Giving information is only half the business; finding things out is the other half. That's what he's doing now."

"So, when he comes back," said Lawrence, "he'll have a new bit of information to add to his stock on hand, which must be a very peculiar one, I fancy."

The cashier smiled. "Yes," she said, "and a very useful one, too, if people only knew it."

"Don't they know it?" asked Lawrence. "Don't you have plenty of custom?"

At this moment the door opened, Mr. Candy entered, and the conversation stopped.

"Sorry to keep you waiting, sir," said the proprietor, passing some money to the cashier over the curtain, who thereupon handed two dollars and ninety-three cents to Lawrence through the little opening in front.

"If you call the day after to-morrow, the information will be ready for you," said Mr. Candy, as the gentleman departed.

On the appointed day, Lawrence came again, and

found nobody in the place but the cashier, who handed him a note.

"Mr. Candy left this for you, in case he should not be in when you called," she said.

The note stated that the search for the address of Junius Keswick had opened very encouragingly, but as it was quite evident that said person was not now in the city, the investigations would have to be carried on on a more extended scale, and a deposit of three dollars would be necessary to meet expenses.

Lawrence looked from the note to the cashier, who had been watching him as he read. "Does Mr. Candy want me to leave three dollars with you?" he asked.

"That's what he said, sir."

"Well," said Lawrence, "I don't care about paying for unlimited investigation in this way. If the gentleman I am in search of has left the city, and Mr. Candy has been able to find out to what place he went, he should have told me that, and I would have decided whether or not I wanted him to do anything more."

The face of the cashier appeared troubled. "I think, sir," she said, "that if you leave the money, Mr. Candy will do all he can to discover what you wish to know, and that it will not be very long before you have the address of the person you are seeking."

"Do you really think he has any clew?" asked Lawrence.

This question did not seem to please the cashier, and she answered gravely, though without any show of resentment: "That is a strange question after I advised you to leave the money."

Lawrence had a kind heart, and it reproached him. "I beg your pardon," said he. "I will leave the money with you, but 1 desire that Mr. Candy will, in his next communication, give me all the information he has acquired up to the moment of writing, and then I will decide whether it is worth while to go on with the matter, or not."

He thereupon took out his pocket-book and handed three dollars to the cashier, who, with an air of deliberate thoughtfulness, smoothed out the two notes, and placed them in her drawer. Then she said : " If you will leave your address, sir, I will see that you receive your information as soon as possible. That will be better than for you to call, because I can't tell you when to come."

"Very well," said Lawrence, "and I will be obliged to you if you will hurry up Mr. Candy as much as you can." And, handing her his card, he went his way.

The way of Lawrence Croft was generally a very pleasant one, for the fortunate conditions of his life made it possible for him to go around most of the rough places which might lie in it. His family was an old one, and a good one, but there was very little of it left, and of its scattered remnants he was the most important member. But although circumstances did not force him to do anything in particular, he liked to believe that he was a rigid master to himself, and whatever he did was always done with a purpose. When he travelled he had an object in view ; when he stayed at home the case was the same.

His present purpose was the most serious one of his life : he wished to marry ; and, if she should prove to be the proper person, he wished to marry Roberta March ; and, as a preliminary step in the carrying out of his purpose, he wanted very much to know what sort of man Miss March had once been willing to marry.

When five days had elapsed without his hearing from Mr. Candy, he became impatient and betook himself to the green door with the tin sign. Entering, he found only the boy and the cashier. Addressing himself to the latter, he asked if anything had been done in his business.

"Yes, sir," she said, "and I hoped Mr. Candy would write you a letter this morning before he went out, but he didn't. He traced the gentleman to Niagara Falls, and I think you'll hear something very soon."

"If inquiries have to be carried on outside of the city," said Lawrence, "they will probably cost a good deal, and come to nothing. I think I will drop the matter as far as Mr. Candy is concerned."

"I wish you would give us a little more time," said the girl. "I am sure you will hear something in a few days, and you need not be afraid there will be anything more to pay unless you are satisfied that you have received the full worth of the money."

Lawrence reflected for a few moments, and then concluded to let the matter go on. "Tell Mr. Candy to keep me frequently informed of the progress of the affair," said he, "and if he is really of any service to me I am willing to pay him, but not otherwise."

"That will be all right," said the cashier, "and if Mr. Candy is—is prevented from doing it, I'll write to you myself, and keep you posted."

As soon as the customer had gone, the boy, who had been sitting on the counter, thus spoke to the cashier : "You know very well that old Mintstick has given that thing up !"

"I know he has," said the girl, "but I have not."

"You haven't anything to do with it," said the boy.

"Yes, I have," she answered. "I advised that gentleman to pay his money, and I'm not going to see him cheated out of it. Of course, Mr. Candy doesn't mean to cheat him, but he has gone into that business about the origin of the tame blackberry, and there's no knowing when he'll get back to this thing, which is not in his line, anyway."

"I should say it wasn't!" exclaimed the boy, with a loud laugh. "Sendin' me to look up them two Keswicks, who was both put down as cordwainers in year before last's directory, and askin' 'em if there was any Juniuses in their families."

"Junius Keswick, did you say? Is that the name of the gentleman Mr. Candy was looking for?"

"Yes," said the boy.

Presently the cashier remarked : "I am going to look at the books." And she betook herself to the desk at the back part of the shop.

In about half an hour she returned and handed to the boy a memorandum upon a scrap of paper. "You go out now to your lunch," she said, "and while you are out, stop at the St. Winifred Hotel, where Mr. Candy found the name of Junius Keswick, and see if it is not down again not long after the date which I have put on this slip of paper. I think if a person went to Niagara Falls he'd be just as likely to make a little trip of it and come back again as to keep travelling on, which Mr. Candy supposes he did. If you find the name again, put down the date of arrival on this, and see if there was any memorandum about forwarding letters."

"All right," said the boy. "But I'll be gone an hour and a half. Can't cut into my lunch-time."

In the course of a few days Lawrence Croft received a note signed Candy & Co. "per" some illegible initials, which stated that Mr. Junius Keswick had been traced to a boarding-house in the city, but as the establishment had been broken up for some time, endeavors were now being made to find the lady who had kept the house, and when this was done it would most likely be possible to discover from her where Mr. Keswick had gone.

Lawrence waited a few days and then called at the Information Shop. Again was Mr. Candy absent; and so was the boy. The cashier informed him that she had found,—that is, that the lady who kept the boarding-house had been found,—and she thought she remembered the gentleman in question, and promised, as soon as she could, to look through a book in which she used to keep directions for the forwarding of letters, and in this way another clew might soon be expected.

"This seems to be going on better," said Lawrence, "but Mr. Candy doesn't show much in the affair. Who is managing it? You?"

The girl blushed and then laughed, a little confusedly. "I am only the cashier," she said.

"And the laborious duties of your position would, of course, give you no time for anything else," remarked Lawrence.

"Oh, well," said the girl, "of course it is easy enough for any one to see that I haven't much to do as cashier, but the boy and Mr. Candy are nearly always out, looking up things, and I have to do other business besides attending to cash."

"If you are attending to my business," said Lawrence, "I am very glad, especially now that it has reached the boarding-house stage, where I think a woman will be better able to work than a man. Are you doing this entirely independent of Mr. Candy?"

"Well, sir," said the cashier, with an honest, straightforward look from her gray eyes that pleased Lawrence, "I may as well confess that I am. But there's nothing mean about it. He has all the same as given it up, for he's waiting to hear from a man in Niagara, who will never write to him, and probably hasn't anything to write, and as I advised you to pay the money I feel bound in honor to see that the business is done, if it can be done."

"Have you a brother or a husband to help you in these investigations and searches?" asked Lawrence.

"No," said the cashier, with a smile. "Sometimes I send our boy, and as to boarding-houses, I can go to them myself after we shut up here."

"I wish," said Lawrence, "that you were married, and that you had a husband who would not interfere in this matter at all, but who would go about with you, and so enable you to follow up your clew thoroughly. You take up the business in the right spirit, and I believe you would succeed in finding Mr. Keswick, but I don't like the idea of sending you about by yourself."

"I won't deny," said the cashier, "that since I have begun this affair I would like very much to carry it out; so, if you don't object, I won't give it up just yet, and as soon as anything happens I'll let you know."

CHAPTER III

AUTUMN in Virginia, especially if one is not too near the mountains, is a season in which greenness sails very close to Christmas, although generally veering away in time to prevent its verdant hues from tingeing that happy day with the gloomy influence of the prophetic proverb about churchyards. Long after the time when the people of the regions watered by the Hudson and the Merrimac are beginning to button up their overcoats, and to think of weather-strips for their window-sashes, the dwellers in the land through which flow the Appomattox and the James may sit upon their broad piazzas, and watch the growing glories of the forests, where the crimson stars of the sweet-gum blaze among the rich yellows of the chestnuts, the lingering green of the oaks, and the enduring verdure of the pines. The insects still hum in the sunny air, and the sun is now a genial orb whose warm rays cheer but not excoriate.

The orb just mentioned was approaching the horizon, when, in an adjoining county to that in which was situated the hospitable mansion of Midbranch, a little negro boy about ten years old was driving some cows through a gateway that opened on a public road. The cows, as they were going homeward, filed willingly through the gateway, which led into a field, at the far end of which might be dimly discerned a house behind a mass of foliage; but the boy, whose head and voice were entirely too big for the rest of him, assailed them with all manner of reproaches and impellent adjectives, addressing each cow in turn as: "You, sah!" When the compliant beasts had hustled through, the youngster got upon the gate, and giving it a push with one bare foot, he swung upon it as far as it would go; then lifting the end from the surface of the ground he shut it with a bang, fastened it with a hook, and ran after the cows, his wild provocatives to bovine haste ringing high into the evening air.

This youth was known as Plez, his whole name being Pleasant Valley, an inspiration to his mother from the label on a grape-box, which had drifted into that region from the North. He had just stooped to pick up a clod of earth with which to accentuate his vociferations, when, on rising, he was astounded by the apparition of an elderly woman wearing a purple sunbonnet, and carrying a furled umbrella of the same color. Behind the spectacles, which were fixed upon him, blazed a pair of fiery eyes, and the soul of Plez shrivelled and curled up within him. His downcast eyes were bent upon his upturned toes, the clod dropped from his limp fingers, and his mouth, which had been opened for a yell, remained open, but the yell had apparently swooned.

The words of the old lady were brief, but her umbrella was full of jerky menace, and when she left him, and passed on towards the outer gate, Plez followed the cows to the house with the meekness of a suspected sheep-dog.

THE LATE MRS. NULL

The cows had been milked, some by a rotund black woman named Letty, and some, much to their discomfort, by Plez himself, and it was beginning to grow dark, when an open spring-wagon driven by a colored man, and with a white man on the back seat, came along the road, and stopped at the gate. The driver, having passed the reins to the occupant on the back seat, got down, opened the gate, and stood holding it while the other drove the horse into the road which ran by the side of the field to the house behind the trees. At this time a passer-by, if there had been one, might have observed, partly protruding from behind some bushes on the other side of the public road, and at a little distance from the gate, the lower portion of a purple umbrella. As the spring-wagon approached, and during the time that it was turning into the gate, and while it was waiting for the driver to resume his seat, this umbrella was considerably agitated, so much so indeed as to cause a little rustling among the leaves. When the gate had been shut, and the wagon had passed on towards the house, the end of the umbrella disappeared, and then, on the other side of the bush, there came into view a sunbonnet of the same color as the umbrella. This surmounted the form of an old lady, who stepped into the pathway by the side of the road, and walked away with a quick, active step which betokened both energy and purpose.

The house, before which, not many minutes later, this spring-wagon stopped, was not a fine old family mansion like that of Midbranch, but it was a comfortable dwelling, though an unpretending one. The gentleman on the back seat, and the driver, who was an elderly negro, both turned toward the hall door, which was open and lighted by a lamp within, as if they expected some one to come out on the porch. But nobody came, and, after a moment's hesitation, the gentleman got down, and taking a valise from the back of the wagon, mounted the steps of the porch. While he was doing this the face of the negro man, which could be plainly seen in the light from the hall door, grew anxious and troubled. When the gentleman set his valise on the porch, and stood by it without making any attempt to enter, the old man put down the reins, and quickly descending from his seat, hurried up the steps.

"Dunno whar ole miss is, but I reckon she done gone to look after de tukkies. She dreffle keerful dat dey all go to roos' ebery night. Walk right in, Mahs' Junius." And, taking up the valise, he followed the gentleman into the hall.

There, near the back door, stood the rotund black woman, and, behind her, Plez. "Look h'yar, Letty," said the negro man, "whar ole miss?"

"Dunno," said the woman. "She done gib out supper, an' I ain't seed her sence. Is dis Mahs' Junius? Reckon you don' 'member Letty?"

"Yes, I do," said the gentleman, shaking hands with her; "but the Letty I remember was a rather slim young woman."

"Dat's so," said Letty, with a respectful laugh, "but, shuh 'nuf, my food's been blessed to me, Mahs' Junius."

"But whar's ole miss?" persisted the old man. "You, Letty, can't you go look her up?"

Now was heard the voice of Plez, who meekly emerged from the shade of Letty. "Ole miss done

31

gone out to de road gate," said he. "I seen her when I brung de cows."

"Bress my soul!" ejaculated Letty. "Out to de road gate! An' 'spectin' you too, Mahs' Junius!"

"Didn't she say nuffin to you?" said the old man, addressing Plez.

"She didn't say nuffin to me, Uncle Isham," answered the boy, "'cept if I didn't quit skeerin' dem cows, an' makin' 'em run wid froin' rocks till dey ain't got a drip drap o' milk lef' in 'em, she'd whang me ober de head wid her umbril."

"'Tain't easy to tell whar she done gone from dat," said Letty.

The face of Uncle Isham grew more troubled. "Walk in de parlor, Mahs' Junius," he said, "an' make yo'se'f comf'ble. Ole miss boun' to be back d'reckly. I'll go put up de hoss."

As the old man went heavily down the porch steps he muttered to himself: "I was feared o' sumfin like dis; I done feel it in my bones."

The gentleman took a seat in the parlor where Letty had preceded him with a lamp. "Reckon ole miss didn't 'spec' you quite so soon, Mahs' Junius, cos de sorrel hoss is pow'ful slow, an' Uncle Isham is mighty keerful ob rocks in de road. Reckon she's done gone ober to see ole Aun' Patsy, who's gwine to die in two or free days, to take her some red an' yaller pieces fur a crazy-quilt. I know she's got some pieces fur her."

"Aunt Patsy alive yet?" exclaimed Master Junius. "But if she's about to die, what does she want with a crazy-quilt?"

"Dat's fur she shroud," said Letty. "She 'tends to go to glory all wrap' up in a crazy-quilt, jus' chock-full

32

ob all de colors ob de rainbow. Aun' Patsy neber did 'tend to have a shroud o' bleached domestic like common folks. She wants to cut a shine 'mong de angels, an' her quilt's 'most done, jus' one corner ob it lef'. Reckon ole miss done gone to carry her de pieces fur dat corner. Dere ain't much time lef', fur Aun' Patsy is pretty nigh dead now. She's ober two hunnerd years ole."

"What!" exclaimed Master Junius, "two hundred?"

"Yes, sah," answered Letty. "Doctor Peter's ole Jim was more'n a hunnerd when he died, an' we-all knows Aun' Patsy is twice as ole as ole Jim."

"I'll wait here," said Master Junius, taking up a book. "I suppose she will be back before long."

In about half an hour Uncle Isham came into the kitchen, his appearance indicating that he had had a hurried walk, and told Letty that she had better give Master Junius his supper without waiting any longer for her mistress. "She ain't at Aun' Patsy's," said the old man, "an' she's jus' done gone somewhar else, an' she'll come back when she's a mind to, an' dar ain't nuffin else to say 'bout it."

Supper was eaten ; a pipe was smoked on the porch ; and Master Junius went to bed in a room which had been carefully prepared for him under the supervision of the mistress ; but the purple sunbonnet and the umbrella of the same color did not return to the house that night.

Master Junius was a quiet man, and fond of walking ; and the next day he devoted to long rambles, sometimes on the roads, sometimes over the fields, and sometimes through the woods ; but in none of his walks, nor when he came back to dinner and supper, did he meet the elderly mistress of the house to which he had come. That evening, as he sat on the top step of the porch with his pipe, he summoned to him Uncle Isham, and thus addressed the old man:

"I think it is impossible, Isham, that your mistress started out to meet me, and that an accident happened to her. I have walked all over this neighborhood, and I know that no accident could have occurred without my seeing or hearing something of it."

Uncle Isham stood on the ground, his feet close to the bottom step; his hat was in his hand, and his up-turned face wore an expression of earnestness which seemed to set uncomfortably upon it. "Mahs' Junius," said he, "dar ain't no acciden' come to ole miss; she's done gone cos she wanted to, an' she ain't come back cos she didn't want to. Dat's ole miss, right fru."

"I suppose," said the young man, "that as she went away on foot she must be staying with some of the neighbors. If we were to make inquiries, it certainly would not be difficult to find out where she is."

"Mahs' Junius," said Uncle Isham, his black eyes shining brighter and brighter as he spoke, "dar's cullud people, an' white folks too, in dis yere county who'd put on der bes' clothes an' black der shoes, an' skip off wid alacrousness, to do de wus kin' o' sin, dat dey knowed fur sartin would send 'em down to de deepes' an' hottes' gullies ob de lower regions, but nuffin in dis worl' could make one o' dem people go 'quirin' 'bout ole miss when she didn't want to be 'quired about."

The smoker put down his pipe on the top step beside him, and sat for a few moments in thought. Then he spoke. "Isham," he began, "I want you to tell me if you have any notion or idea—"

"Mahs' Junius," exclaimed the old negro, "'scuse me fur int'ruptin', but I can't help it. Don' you go an' ax an ole man like me if I t'inks dat ole miss went away cos you was comin' an' if it's my true b'lief dat she'll neber come back while you is h'yar. Don' ask me nuffin like dat, Mahs' Junius. I'se libed in dis place all my bawn days, an' I ain't neber done nuffin to you, Mahs' Junius, 'cept keepin' you from breakin' yo' neck when yo' was too little to know better. I neber 'jected to yo' marryin' any lady yo' like bes', an' 'tain't fa'r, Mahs' Junius, now I'se ole an' gittin' on de careen, fur you to ax me wot I t'inks about ole miss gwine away an' comin' back. I begs you, Mahs' Junius, don' ax me dat."

Master Junius rose to his feet. "All right, Isham," he said; "I shall not worry your good old heart with questions." And he went into the house.

The next day this quiet gentleman and good walker went to see old Aunt Patsy, who had apparently consented to live a day or two longer; gave her a little money in lieu of pieces for her crazy-bedquilt; and told her he was going away to stay. He told Uncle Isham he was going away to stay away; and he said the same thing to Letty, and to Plez, and to two colored women of the neighborhood whom he happened to see. Then he took his valise, which was not a very large one, and departed. He refused to be conveyed to the distant station in the spring-wagon, saying that he much preferred to walk. Uncle Isham took leave of him with much sadness, but did not ask him to stay; and Letty and Plez looked after him wistfully, still holding in their hands the coins he had placed there. With the exception of these coins, the only thing he left behind him was a sealed letter on the parlor table, addressed to the mistress of the house.

Toward the end of that afternoon, two women came along the public road which passed the outer gate. One came from the south, and rode in an open carriage, evidently hired at the railroad-station; the other was on foot, and came from the north; she wore a purple sunbonnet, and carried an umbrella of the same color. When this latter individual caught sight of the approaching carriage, then at some distance, she stopped short and gazed at it. She did not retire behind a bush, as she had done on a former occasion, but she stood in the shade of a tree on the side of the road, and waited. As the carriage came nearer to the gate the surprise upon her face became rapidly mingled with indignation. The driver had checked the speed of his horses, and, without doubt, intended to stop at the gate. This might not have been sufficient to excite her emotions, but she now saw clearly, having not been quite certain of it before, that the occupant of the carriage was a lady, and, apparently, a young one, for she wore in her hat some bright-colored flowers. The driver stopped, got down, opened the gate, and then, mounting to his seat, drove through, leaving the gate standing wide open.

This contempt of ordinary proprietary requirements made the old lady spring out from the shelter of the shade. Brandishing her umbrella, she was about to cry out to the man to stop and shut the gate, but she restrained herself. The distance was too great, and, besides, she thought better of it. She went again into

THE LATE MRS. NULL

the shade, and waited. In about ten minutes the carriage came back, but without the lady. This time the driver got down, shut the gate after him, and drove rapidly away.

If blazing eyes could crack glass, the spectacles of the old lady would have been splintered into many pieces as she stood by the roadside, the end of her umbrella jabbed an inch or two into the ground. After standing thus for some five minutes, she suddenly turned and walked vigorously away in the direction from which she had come.

Uncle Isham, Letty, and the boy Plez were very much surprised at the arrival of the lady in the carriage. She had asked for the mistress of the house, and on being assured that she was expected to return very soon, had alighted, paid and dismissed her driver, and had taken a seat in the parlor. Her valise, rather larger than that of the previous visitor, was brought in and put in the hall. She waited for an hour or two, during which time Letty made several attempts to account for the non-appearance of her mistress, who, she said, was away on a visit, but was expected back every minute; and when supper was ready she partook of that meal alone, and after a short evening spent in reading she went to bed in the chamber which Letty prepared for her.

Before she retired, Letty, who had shown herself a very capable attendant, said to her: "Wot's your name, miss? I allus likes to know the names o' ladies I waits on."

"My name," said the lady, "is Mrs. Null."

CHAPTER IV

THE autumn sun was shining very pleasantly when, about nine o'clock in the morning, Mrs. Null came out on the porch, and, standing at the top of the steps, looked about her. She had on her hat with the red flowers, and she wore a short jacket, into the pockets of which her hands were thrust with an air which indicated satisfaction with the circumstances surrounding her. The old dog, lying on the grass at the bottom of the steps, looked up at her and flopped his tail upon the ground. Mrs. Null called to him in a cheerful tone, and the dog arose and, hesitatingly, put his fore feet on the bottom step; then, when she held out her hand and spoke to him again, he determined that, come what might, he would go up those forbidden steps and let her pat his head. This he did, and after looking about him to assure himself that this was reality and not a dog-dream, he lay down upon the door-mat, and, with a sigh of relief, composed himself to sleep. A black turkey-gobbler, who looked as if he had been charred in a fire, followed by five turkey-hens, also suggesting the idea that water had been thrown over them before anything but their surfaces had been burnt, came timidly around the house and stopped before venturing upon the greensward in front

38

of the porch; then, seeing nobody but Mrs. Null, they advanced with bobbing heads and swaying bodies to look into the resources of this seldom-explored region. Plez, who was coming from the spring with a pail of water on his head, saw the dog on the porch and the turkeys on the grass, and stopped to regard the spectacle. He looked at them, and he looked at Mrs. Null, and a grin of amused interest spread itself over his face.

Mrs. Null went down the steps and approached the boy. "Plez," said she, "if your mistress, or anybody, should come here this morning, you must run over to Pine Top Hill and call me. I'm going there to read."

"Don' you want me to go wid you, an' show you de way, Miss Null?" asked Plez, preparing to set down his pail.

"Oh, no," said she; "I know the way." And with her hands still in her pockets, from one of which protruded a rolled-up novel, she walked down to the little stream which ran from the spring, crossed the plank, and took the path which led by the side of the vineyard to Pine Top Hill.

This lady visitor had now been here two days waiting for the return of the mistress of the little estate; and the sojourn had evidently been of benefit to her. Good air, the good meals with which Letty had provided her, and a sort of sympathy which had sprung up in a very sudden way between her and everything on the place, had given brightness to her eyes. She even looked a little plumper than when she came, and certainly very pretty. She climbed Pine Top Hill without making any mistake as to the best path, and went directly to a low piece of sun-warmed rock which cropped out from the ground not far from the bases of the cluster of pines which gave the name to the hill. An extended and very pretty view could be had from this spot, and Mrs. Null seemed to enjoy it, looking about her with quick turns of the head as if she wanted to satisfy herself that all of the scenery was there. Apparently satisfied that it was, she stretched out her feet, withdrew her gaze from the surrounding country, and regarded the toes of her boots. Now she smiled a little and began to speak.

"Freddy," said she, "I must think over matters, and have a talk with you about them. Nothing could be more proper than this, since we are on our wedding-tour. You keep beautifully in the background, which is very nice of you, for that's what I married you for. But we must have a talk now, for we haven't said a word to each other, nor, perhaps, thought of each other, during the whole three nights and two days that we have been here. I expect these people think it very queer that I should keep on waiting for their mistress to come back, but I can't help it; I must stay till she comes, or he comes, and they must continue to think it funny. And as for Mr. Croft, I suppose I should get a letter from him if he knew where to write, but you know, Freddy, we are travelling about on this wedding-tour without letting anybody, especially Mr. Croft, know exactly where we are. He must think it an awfully wonderful piece of good luck that a young married couple should happen to be journeying in the very direction taken by a gentleman whom he wants to find, and that they are willing to look for the gentleman without charging anything but the extra expenses to which they may be put. We wouldn't charge him a cent, you know, Freddy Null, but for the fear that he would think we would not truly act as his agents if we were not paid, and so would employ somebody else. We don't want him to employ anybody else. We want to find Junius Keswick before he does, and then maybe we won't want Mr. Croft to find him at all. But I hope it will not turn out that way. He said it was neither crime nor relationship, and, of course, it couldn't be. What I hope is that it is good fortune; but that's doubtful. At any rate, I must see Junius first, if I can possibly manage it. If she would only come back and open her letter, there might be no more trouble about it, for I don't believe he would go away without leaving her his address. Isn't all this charming, Freddy? And don't you feel glad that we came here for our wedding-tour? Of course you don't enjoy it as much as I do, for it can't seem so natural to you; but you are bound to like it. The very fact of my being here should make the place delightful in your eyes, Mr. Null, even if I have forgotten all about you ever since I came."

That afternoon, as Mrs. Null was occupying some of her continuous leisure in feeding the turkeys at the back of the house, she noticed two colored men in earnest conversation with Isham. When they had gone she called to the old man. "Uncle Isham," she said, "what did those men want?"

"Tell you what 'tis, Miss Null," said Isham, removing his shapeless felt hat, "dis yere place is gittin' wus an' wus on de careen, an' wot's gwine to happen if ole miss don' come back is more'n I kin tell. Dar's no groun' ploughed yit for wheat, an' dem two han's been 'gaged to come do it, an' dey put it off, an' put it off, till ole miss got as mad as hot coals, an' now at las' dey've come, an' she's not h'yar, an' nuffin can be done. De wheat'll be free inches high on ebery oder farm 'fore ole miss git dem plough-han's ag'in."

"That is too bad, Uncle Isham," said Mrs. Null. "When land that ought to be ploughed isn't ploughed, it all grows up in old-field pines, don't it?"

"It don' do dat straight off, Miss Null," said the old negro, his gray face relaxing into a smile.

"No, I suppose not," said she. "I have heard that it takes thirty years for a whole forest of old-field pines to grow up. But they will do it if the land isn't ploughed. Now, Uncle Isham, I don't intend to let everything be at a standstill here just because your mistress is away. That is one reason why I feed the turkeys. If they died, or the farm all went wrong, I should feel that it was partly my fault."

"Yaas'm," said Uncle Isham, passing his hat from one hand to the other, as he delivered himself a little hesitatingly,—"yaas'm; if you wasn't h'yar p'r'aps ole miss mought come back."

"Now, Uncle Isham," said Mrs. Null, "you mustn't think your mistress is staying away on account of me. She left home, as Letty has told me over and over, because your Master Junius came. Of course she thinks he's here yet, and she don't know anything about me. But if her affairs should go to rack and ruin while I am here and able to prevent it, I should think it was my fault. That's what I mean, Uncle Isham. And now this is what I want you to do. I want you to go right after those men, and tell them to come here as soon as they can, and begin to plough. Do you know where the ploughing is to be done?"

THE LATE MRS. NULL

"Oh, yaas'm," said Uncle Isham; "dar ain't on'y one place fur dat. It's de clober-fiel', ober dar on de oder side ob de gyarden."

"And what is to be planted in it?" asked Mrs. Null.

"Ob course dey's gwine to plough fur wheat," answered Uncle Isham, a little surprised at the question.

"I don't altogether like that," said Mrs. Null, her brows slightly contracting. "I've read a great deal about the foolishness of Southern people planting wheat. They can't compete with the great wheat-farms of the West, which sometimes cover a whole county, and, of course, having so much, they can afford to sell it a great deal cheaper than you can here. And yet you go on, year after year, paying every cent you can rake and scrape for fertilizing drugs, and getting about a teacupful of wheat—that is, proportionately speaking. I don't think this sort of thing should continue, Uncle Isham. It would be a great deal better to plough that field for pickles. Now there is a steady market for pickles, and, so far as I know, there are no pickle-farms in the West."

"Pickles!" ejaculated the astonished Isham. "Do you mean, Miss Null, to put dat fiel' down in kukumbers at dis time o' yeah?"

"Well," said Mrs. Null, thoughtfully, "I don't know that I feel authorized to make the change at present, but I do know that the things that pay most are small fruits, and if you people down here would pay more attention to them you would make more money. But the land must be ploughed, and then we'll see about planting it afterwards; your mistress will, probably, be home in time for that. You go after the men, and tell them I shall expect them to begin the first thing

43

in the morning. And if there is anything else to be done on the farm, you come and tell me about it to-morrow. I'm going to take the responsibility on myself to see that matters go on properly until your mistress returns."

Letty and her son Plez occupied a cabin not far from the house, while Uncle Isham lived alone in a much smaller tenement, near the barn and chicken-house. That evening he went over to Letty's, taking with him, as a burnt-offering, a partially consumed and still glowing log of hickory wood from his own hearth-stone. "Jes lemme tell you dis h'yar, Letty," said he, after making up the fire and seating himself on a stool near by : "ef you want to see ole miss come back r'arin' an' chargin', jes you let her know dat Miss Null is gwine ter plough de clober-fiel' fur pickles."

"Wot's dat fool talk?" asked Letty.

"Miss Null's gwine ter boss dis farm, dat's all," said Isham. "She tole me so herse'f; an' ef she's lef' alone she's gwine ter do it city fashion. But one thing's sartin shuh, Letty : if ole miss do fin' out wot's gwine on, she'll be back h'yar in no time ! She know well 'nuf dat dat Miss Null ain't got no right ter come an' boss dis h'yar farm. Who's she, anyway?"

"Dunno," answered Letty. "I done ax her six or seben time, but 'pears like I dunno wot she mean when she tell me. P'r'aps she's one o' ole miss' little gal babies growed up. I tell you, Uncle Isham, she know dis place jes as ef she bawn h'yar."

Uncle Isham looked steadily into the fire, and rubbed the sides of his head with his big black fingers. "Ole miss nebber had no gal baby 'cept one, an' dat died when 'twas mighty little."

THE LATE MRS. NULL

"Does you reckon she kill her ef she come back an' fin' her no kin?" asked Letty.

Uncle Isham pushed his stool back and started to his feet with a noise which woke Plez, who had been soundly sleeping on the other side of the fireplace; and striding to the door, the old man went out into the open air. Returning in less than a minute, he put his head into the doorway and addressed the astonished woman, who had turned around to look after him. "Look h'yar, you Letty, I don' want to hear no sech fool talk 'bout ole miss. You dunno ole miss, nohow. You only come h'yar seben year ago, when dat Plez was trottin' roun' wid nuffin but a little meal-bag fur clothes. Mahs' John had been dead a long time den. You nebber knowed Mahs' John. You nebber was woke up at two o'clock in de mawnin' wid de crack ob a pistol, an' run out 'spectin' 'twas somebody stealin' chickens an' Mahs' John firin' at 'em, an' see ole miss a-cuttin' fur de road gate wid her white night-gown a-floppin' in de win' behind her, an' when we got out to de gate, dar we see Mahs' John a-stan'in' up ag'in' de pos', not de pos' wid de hinges on, but de pos' wid de hook on, an' a hole in de top ob de head which he made hese'f wid de pistol. One-eyed Jim see de whole thing. He war stealin' cohn in de fiel' on de oder side de road. He see Mahs' John come out wid de pistol, an' he lay low. Not dat it war Mahs' John's cohn dat he was stealin', but he knowed well 'nuf dat Mahs' John take jes as much car' o' he neighbus' cohn as he own. An' den he see Mahs' John stan' up ag'in' de pos' an' shoot de pistol, an' he see Mahs' John's soul come right out de hole in de top ob his head an' go straight up to heben like a sky-racket."

THE LATE MRS. NULL

"Wid a whiz?" asked the open-eyed Letty.

"Like a sky-racket, I tell you," continued the old man; "an' den me an' ole miss come up. She jes tuk one look at him, an' den she said in a wice, not like she own wice, but like Mahs' John's wice, wot had done gone forebber: 'You Jim, come out o' dat cohn an' help carry him in!' An' we free carried him in. An' you dunno ole miss, nohow, an' I don' want to hear no fool talk from you, Letty, 'bout her. Jes you 'member dat!"

And with this Uncle Isham betook himself to the solitude of his own cabin.

"Well," said Letty to herself, as she rose and approached the bed in the corner of the room, "I'se pow'ful glad dat somebody's gwine to take de key-bahsket, for I nebber goes inter dat sto'-room by myse'f widout tremblin' all froo my backbone fear ole miss come back, an' fin' me dar 'lone."

CHAPTER V

WHEN Lawrence Croft now took his afternoon walks in the city, he was very glad to wear a light overcoat, and to button it, too. But, although the air was getting a little nipping in New York, he knew that it must still be balmy and enjoyable in Virginia. He had never been down there at this season, but he had heard about the Virginia autumns, and besides, he had seen a lady who had had a letter from Roberta March. In this letter Miss March had written that as her father intended making a trip to Texas, and therefore would not come to New York as early as usual, she would stay at least a month longer with her Uncle Brandon; and she was glad to do it, for the weather was perfectly lovely, and she could stay out of doors all day if she wanted to.

Lawrence's walks, although very invigorating on account of the fine, sharp air, were not entirely cheering, for they gave him an opportunity to think that he was making no progress whatever in his attempt to study the character of Junius Keswick. He had intrusted the search for that gentleman's address to Mr. Candy's cashier, who had informed him, most opportunely, that she was about to set out on a wedding-tour, and that she had possessed herself of clews of

47

much value which could be readily followed up in connection with the projected journey. But a fortnight or more had elapsed without his hearing anything from her, and he had come to the conclusion that hymeneal joys must have driven all thoughts of business out of her little head.

After hearing that Roberta March intended protracting her stay in the country, the desire came to him to go down there himself. He would like to have the novel experience of that region in autumn, and he would like to see Roberta, but he could not help acknowledging to himself that the proceeding would scarcely be a wise one, especially as he must go without the desired safeguard of knowing what kind of man Miss March had once been willing to accept. He felt that if he went down to the neighborhood of Midbranch one of the battles of his life would begin, and that when he held up before him his figurative shield, he would see in its inner mirror that, on account of his own disposition towards the lady, he was in a condition of great peril. But, for all that, he wanted very much to go, and no one will be surprised to learn that he did go.

He was a little embarrassed at first in regard to the pretext which he should make to himself for such a journey. Whatever satisfactory excuse he could make to himself in this case would, of course, do for other people. Although he was not prone to make excuses for his conduct to other people in general, he knew he would have to give some reason to Mr. Brandon and Miss Roberta for his return to Virginia so soon after having left it. He determined to make a visit to the mountains of North Carolina, and as Midbranch would

48

lie in his way, of course he would stop there. This he assured himself was not a subterfuge. It was a very sensible thing to do. He had a good deal of time on his hands before the city season, at least for him, would begin, and he had read that the autumn was an admirable time to visit the country of the French Broad. How long a stop he would make at Midbranch would be determined by circumstances. He was sorry that he would not be able to look upon Miss Roberta with the advantage of knowing her former lover, but it was something to know that she had had a lover. With this fact in his mind he would be able to form a better estimate of her than he had formed before.

The man who lived in the cottage at the Green Sulphur Springs was somewhat surprised when Mr. Croft arrived there, and desired to make arrangements, as before, for board, and the use of a saddle-horse. But, although it was not generally conceded, this man knew very well that there was no water in the world so suitable to remedy the wear and tear of a city life as that of the Green Sulphur Springs, and therefore nobody could consider the young gentleman foolish for coming back again while the season permitted.

Lawrence arrived at his cottage in the morning; and early in the afternoon of the same day he rode over to Midbranch. He found the country a good deal changed, and he did not like the changes. His road, which ran for much of its distance through the woods, was covered with leaves, some green, and some red and yellow, and he did not fancy the peculiar smell of these leaves, which reminded him, in some way, of that gathering together of the characters in old-fashioned comedies shortly before the fall of the curtain.

THE LATE MRS. NULL

In many places where there used to be a thick shade
the foliage was now quite thin, and through it he
could see a good deal of the sky. The Virginia
creepers, or poison-oaks, whichever they were, were
growing red upon the trunks of the trees, as if they
had been at table too long and showed it, and when
he rode out of the woods he saw that the fields, which
he remembered as wide, swelling slopes of green, with
cattle and colts feeding here and there, were now being
ploughed into corrugated stretches of monotonous drab
and brown. If he had been there through all the
gradual changes of the season, he, probably, would
have enjoyed them as much as people ordinarily do ;
but coming back in this way, the altered landscape
slightly shocked him.

When he had turned into the Midbranch gate, but
was still a considerable distance from the house, he
involuntarily stopped his horse. He could see the
broad steps which crossed the fence of the lawn, and
on one side of the platform on the top sat a lady whom
he instantly recognized as Miss Roberta ; and on the
other side of the platform sat a gentleman. These two
occupied very much the same positions as Lawrence
himself and Miss March had occupied when we first
became acquainted with them. Lawrence looked very
sharply and earnestly at the gentleman. Could it be
Mr. Brandon ? No, it was a much younger person.

His first impulse was to turn and ride away, but this
would be silly and unmanly, and he continued his way
to the stile. His disposition to treat the matter with
contempt made him feel how important the matter
was to him. The gentleman on the platform first saw
Lawrence, and announced to the lady that some one

50

was coming. Miss March turned around, and then rose to her feet.

"Upon my word!" she exclaimed, elevating her eyebrows a good deal more than was usual with her, "if that isn't Mr. Croft!"

"Who is he?" asked the other, also rising.

"He is a New York gentleman whom I know very well. He was down here last summer, but I can't imagine what brings him here again."

Lawrence dismounted, tied his horse, and approached the steps. Miss Roberta welcomed him cordially, coming down a little way to shake hands with him. Then she introduced the two gentlemen.

"Mr. Croft," she said, "let me make you acquainted with Mr. Keswick."

The afternoon, or the portion of it that was left, was spent on the porch, Mr. Brandon joining the party. It was to him that Lawrence chiefly talked, for the most part about the game and scenery of North Carolina, with which the old gentleman was quite familiar. But Lawrence had sufficient regard for himself and his position in the eyes of this family to help make a good deal of general conversation. What he said or heard, however, occupied only the extreme corners of his mind, the main portion of which was entirely filled with the chilling fear that that man might be the Keswick he was looking for. Of course, there was a bare chance that it was not, for there might be a numerous family, but even this little stupid glimmer of comfort was extinguished when Mr. Brandon familiarly addressed the gentleman as "Junius."

Lawrence took a good look at the man he was

anxious to study, and as far as outward appearances were concerned he could find no fault with Roberta for having accepted him. He was taller than Croft, and not so correctly dressed. He seemed to be a person whom one would select as a companion for a hunt, a sail, or a talk upon political economy. There was about him an air of present laziness, but it was also evident that this was a disposition that could easily be thrown off.

Lawrence's mind was not only very much occupied, but very much perturbed. It must have been all a mistake about the engagement having been broken off. If this had been the case, the easy friendliness of the relations between Keswick and the old gentleman and his niece would have been impossible. Once or twice the thought came to Lawrence that he should congratulate himself for not having avowed his feelings towards Miss Roberta when he had an opportunity of doing so; but his predominant emotion was one of disgust with his previous mode of action. If he had not weighed and considered the matter so carefully, and had been willing to take his chances as other men take them, he would, at least, have known in what relation he stood to Roberta, and would not have occupied the ridiculous position in which he now felt himself to be.

When he took his leave, Roberta went with him to the stile. As they walked together across the smooth, short grass, a new set of emotions arose in Lawrence's mind which drove out every other. They were grief, chagrin, and even rage, at not having won this woman. As to actual speech, there was nothing he could say, although his soul boiled and bubbled within him in his desire to speak. But if he had anything to say, now was his chance, for he had told them that he would proceed with his journey the next day.

Miss Roberta had a way of looking up and looking down at the same time, particularly when she had asked a question and was waiting for the answer. Her face would be turned a little down, but her eyes would look up and give a very charming expression to those upturned eyes; and if she happened to allow the smile with which she ceased speaking to remain upon her pretty lips, she generally had an answer of some sort very soon. If for no other reason, it would be given that she might ask another question. It was in this manner she said to Lawrence: "Do you really go away from us to-morrow?"

"Yes," said he, "I shall push on."

"Do you not find the country very beautiful at this season?" asked Miss Roberta, after a few steps in silence.

"I don't like autumn," answered Lawrence. "Everything is drying up and dying. I would rather see things dead."

Roberta looked at him without turning her head. "But it will be just as bad in North Carolina," she said.

"There is an autumn in ourselves," he answered, "just as much as there is in nature. I won't see so much of that down there."

"In some cases," said Roberta, slowly, "autumn is impossible."

They had reached the bottom of the steps, and Lawrence turned and looked towards her. "Do you mean," he asked, "when there has been no real summer?"

Roberta laughed. "Of course," said she, "if there

has been no summer there can be no autumn. But you know there are places where it is summer all the time. Would you like to live in such a clime?"

Lawrence Croft put one foot on the step, and then he drew it back. "Miss March," said he, "my train does not leave until the afternoon, and I am coming over here in the morning to have one more walk in the woods with you. May I?"

"Certainly," she said; "I shall be delighted; that is, if you can overlook the fact that it is autumn."

When Miss Roberta returned to the house she found Junius Keswick sitting on a bench on the porch. She went over to him, and took a seat at the other end of the bench.

"So your gentleman is gone," he said.

"Yes," she answered, "but only for the present. He is coming back in the morning."

"What for?" asked Keswick, a little abruptly.

Miss Roberta took off her hat, for there was no need of a hat on a shaded porch, and holding it by the ribbons, she let it gently slide down towards her feet. "He is coming," she said, speaking rather slowly, "to take a walk with me, and I know very well that when we have reached some place where he is sure there is no one to hear him, he is going to tell me that he loves me; that he did not intend to speak quite so soon, but that circumstances have made it impossible for him to restrain himself any longer, and he will ask me to be his wife."

"And what are you going to say to him?" asked Keswick.

"I don't know," replied Roberta, her eyes fixed upon the hat, which she still held by its long ribbons.

THE LATE MRS. NULL

The next morning Junius Keswick, who had been up a long, long time before breakfast, sat, after that meal, looking at Roberta, who was reading a book in the parlor. "She is a strange girl," thought he. "I cannot understand her. How is it possible that she can sit there so placidly reading that volume of Huxley, which I know she never saw before and which she has opened just about the middle, on a morning when she is expecting a man who will say things to her which may change her whole life? I could almost imagine that she has forgotten all about it."

Peggy, who had just entered the room to inform her mistress that Aunt Judy was ready for her, stood in rigid uprightness, her torpid eyes settled upon the lady. "I reckon," so ran the thought within the mazes of her dark little interior, "dat Miss Rob's wus disgruntled dan she was dat ebenin' when I make my cake, fur she got two dif'ent kinds o' shoes on."

The morning went on, and Keswick found that he must go out again for a walk, although he had rambled several miles before breakfast. After her household duties had been completed, Miss Roberta took her book out to the porch; and about noon, when her uncle came out and made some remarks upon the beauty of the day, she turned over the page at which she had opened the volume just after breakfast. An hour later Peggy brought her some luncheon, and felt it to be her duty to inform Miss Rob that she still wore one old boot and a new one. When Roberta returned to the porch after making a suitable change, she found Keswick there, looking a little tired.

"Has your friend gone?" he asked, in a very quiet tone.

"He has not come yet," she answered.

"Not come!" exclaimed Keswick. "That's odd! However, there are two hours yet before dinner."

The two hours passed and no Lawrence Croft appeared; nor came he at all that day. About dusk the man at the Green Sulphur Springs rode over with a note from Mr. Croft. The note was to Miss March, of course, and it simply stated that the writer was very sorry he could not keep the appointment he had made with her, but that it had suddenly become necessary for him to return to the North without continuing the journey he had planned; that he was much grieved to be deprived of the opportunity of seeing her again; but that he would give himself the pleasure, at the earliest possible moment, of calling on Miss March when she arrived in New York.

When Miss Roberta had read this note she handed it to Keswick, who, when he returned it, asked: "Does that suit you?"

"No," said she, "it does not suit me at all."

CHAPTER VI

IT was mail-day at the very small village known as Howlett's, and to the fence in front of the post-office were attached three mules and a horse. Inside the yard, tied to the low bough of a tree, was a very lean and melancholy horse, on which had lately arrived Wesley Green, the negro man who, twice a week, brought the mail from Pocahontas, a railway-station twenty miles away. There was a station not six miles from Howlett's, but, for some reason, the mail-bag was always brought from and carried to Pocahontas; Wesley Green requiring a whole day for a deliberate transit between the two points.

In the post-office, which was the front room of a small wooden house approached by a high flight of steps, was the postmistress, Miss Harriet Corvey, who sat on the floor in one corner, while before her extended a semicircle of men and boys. In this little assemblage certain elderly men occupied seats which were considered to belong to them quite as much as if they had been hired pews in a church, and behind them stood up a row of tall young men and barefooted boys of the neighborhood, while farthest in the rear were some quiet little darkies with mailbags slung across their shoulders.

THE LATE MRS. NULL

On a chair to the right, and most convenient to Miss Harriet, sat old Madison Chalkley, the biggest and most venerable citizen of the neighborhood. Mr. Chalkley never, by any chance, got a letter, the only mail-matter he received being the "Southern Baptist Recorder," which came on Saturdays, but, like most of the people present, he was at the post-office every mail-day to see who got anything. Next to him sat Colonel Iston, a tall, lean, quiet old gentleman, who had, for a long series of years, occupied the position of a last apple on a tree. He had no relatives, no friends with whom he corresponded, no business that was not conducted by word of mouth. In the last fifteen years he had received but one letter, and that had so surprised him that he carried it about with him three days before he opened it, and then he found that it was really intended for a gentleman of the same name in another county. And yet everybody knew that if Colonel Iston failed to appear in his place on mail-day, it would be because he was dead or prostrated by sickness.

With the mail-bag on the floor at her left, Miss Harriet, totally oblivious of any law forbidding the opening of the mails in public, would put her hand into its open mouth, draw forth a letter or a paper, hold it up in front of her spectacles, and call out the name of its owner. Most of the letters went to the black boys with the mail-bags who came from country houses in the neighborhood, but whoever received letter, journal, or agricultural circular, received also at the same time the earnest gaze of everybody else in the room. Sometimes there was a letter for which there was no applicant present, and then Miss Harriet would say: "Is anybody going past Mrs. Willis Summerses?" And if anybody was, he would take the letter, and it is to be hoped he remembered to deliver it in the course of a week.

In spite of the precautions of the postmistress, un-called·for letters would gradually accumulate, and there was a little bundle of these in one of the few pigeonholes in a small desk in the corner of the room, in the drawer of which the postage-stamps were kept. Now and then a registered letter would arrive, and this always created considerable sensation in the room, and if the legal recipient did not happen to be present, Miss Harriet never breathed a quiet breath until he or she had been sent for, had taken the letter, and given her a receipt. Sometimes she sat up as late as eleven o'clock at night on mail-days, hoping that some one who had been sent for would arrive to relieve her of a registered letter.

All the mail-matter had been distributed, everybody but Mr. Madison Chalkley had left the room ; and when the old gentleman, as was his wont on the first day of the month, had gone up to the desk, untied the bundle of uncalled-for letters, the outer ones permanently rounded by the tightness of the cord, and after care-fully looking over them, one by one, had made his usual remark about the folly of people who wouldn't stay in a place until their letters could get to them, had tied up the bundle and taken his departure ; then Miss Harriet put the empty mail-bag under the desk, and went up-stairs, where an old lady sat by the win-dow, sewing in the fading light.

"No letters for you to-day, Mrs. Keswick," said she.

"Of course not," was the answer; "I didn't expect any."

THE LATE MRS. NULL

"Don't you think," said Miss Harriet, taking a seat opposite the old lady, "that it is about time for you to go home and attend to your affairs?"

"Well, upon my word!" said Mrs. Keswick, letting her hands and her work fall in her lap, "that's truly hospitable. I didn't expect it of you, Harriet Corvey."

"I wouldn't have said it," returned the postmistress, "if I hadn't felt dead certain that you knew you were always welcome here. But Tony Miles told me, just before the mail came in, that the lady who's at your place is running it herself, and that she's going to use pickle brine for a fertilizer."

"Very likely," said Mrs. Keswick, her face totally unmoved by this intelligence,—"very likely. That's the way they used to do in ancient times, or something of the same kind. They used to sow salt over their enemy's land so that nothing would ever grow there. That woman's family has sowed salt over the lands of me and mine for three generations, and it's quite natural she should come here to finish up."

There was a little silence after this, and then Miss Harriet remarked : "Your people must know where you are. Why don't they come and tell you about these things?"

"They know better," answered Mrs. Keswick, with a grim smile. "I went away once before, and Uncle Isham hunted me up, and he got a lesson that he'll never forget. When I want them to know where I am, I'll tell them."

"But really and truly," said Miss Harriet,—"and you know I only speak to you for your own good, for you pay your board here, and if you didn't you'd be just as welcome,—do you intend to keep away from your own house as long as that lady chooses to stay there?"

"Exactly so long," answered the old lady. "I shall not keep them out of my house if they choose to come to it. No member of my family ever did that. There is the house, and they are free to enter it, but they shall not find me there. If there was any reason to believe that everything was dropped and done with, I would be as glad to see him as anybody could be, but I knew from his letter just what he was going to say when he came, and as things have turned out, I see that it was all worse than I expected. He and Roberta March were both coming, and they thought that together they could talk me down, and make me forgive and be happy, and all that stuff. But as I wasn't there, of course he wouldn't stay, and so there she is now by herself. She thinks I must come home after a while, and the minute I do that, back he'll come, and then they'll have just what they want. But I reckon she'll find that I can stick it out just as long as she can. If Roberta March turns things upside down there, it'll be because she can't keep her hands out of mischief, and that proves that she belongs to her own family. If there's any harm done, it don't matter so much to me, and it will be worse for him in the end. And now, Harriet Corvey, if you've got to make up the mail to go away early in the morning, you'd better have supper over and get about it."

Meanwhile, at Mrs. Keswick's house Mrs. Null was acting just as conscientiously as she knew how. She had had some conversations with Freddy on the subject, and she had assured him, and at the same time herself, that what she was doing was the only thing that could be done. "It was dreadfully hard for me to get the money to come down here," she said to him, —"you not helping me a bit, as ordinary husbands do, —and I can't afford to go back until I have accomplished something. It's very strange that she stays away so long, without telling anybody where she has gone to, but I know she is queer, and I suppose she has her own reasons for what she does. She can't be staying away on my account, for she doesn't know who I am, and wouldn't have any objections to me if she did know. I suspect it is something about Junius which keeps her away, and I suppose she thinks he is still here. But one of them must soon come back, and if I can see him, or find out from her where he is, it will be all right. It seems to me, Freddy, that if I could have a good talk with Junius things would begin to look better for you and me. And then I want to put him on his guard about this gentleman who is looking for him. By the way, I suppose I ought to write a letter to Mr. Croft, or he'll think I have given up the job, and will set somebody else on the track, and that is what I don't want him to do. I can't say that I have positively anything to report, but I can say that I have strong hopes of success, considering where I am. As soon as I found that Junius had really left the North, I concluded that this would be the best place to come to for him. And now, Freddy, there's nothing for us to do but to wait, and if we can make ourselves useful here I'm sure we will be glad to do it. We both hate being lazy, and a little housekeeping and farm-managing will be good practice for us during our honeymoon."

THE LATE MRS. NULL

Putting on her hat, she went down into the garden where Uncle Isham was at work. She could find little to do there, for he was merely pulling turnips, and she could see nothing to suggest in regard to his method of work. She had found, too, that the old negro had not much respect for her agricultural opinions. He attended to his work as if his mistress had been at home, and although, in regard to the ploughing, he had carried out the orders of Mrs. Null, he had done it because it ought to be done, and because he was very glad for some one else to take the responsibility.

"Uncle Isham," said she, after she had watched the process of turnip-pulling for a few minutes, "if you haven't anything else to do when you get through with this, you might come up to the house, and I will talk to you about the flower-beds. I suppose they ought to be made ready for the winter."

"Miss Null," said the old man, slowly unbending his back, and getting himself upright, "dar's allus sumfin else to do. Ebber sence I was fus' bawn dar was sumfin else to do, an' I 'spec's it'll keep on dat ar way till de day I dies."

"Of course there will be nothing else to do then but to die," observed Mrs. Null; "but I hope that day is far off, Uncle Isham."

"Dunno 'bout dat, Miss Null," said he. "But den some people do lib dreffle long. Look at ole Aun' Patsy. I'se got to lib a long time afore I'se as ole as Aun' Patsy is now."

"You don't mean to say," exclaimed Mrs. Null, "that Aunt Patsy is alive yet!"

"Ob course she is, Miss Null," said Uncle Isham. "If she'd died sence you've been here we'd 'a' tole you, sartin. She was gwine to die las' week, but two or free days don' make much dif'rence to Aun' Patsy, she done lib so long anyhow."

"Aunt Patsy alive!" exclaimed Mrs. Null again. "I'm going straight off to see her."

When she had reached the house, and had informed Letty where she was going, the rotund maid expressed high approbation of the visit, and offered to send Plez to show Mrs. Null the way.

"I don't need any one to go with me," said that lady, and away she started.

"She don' nebber want nobody to show her nowhar," said Plez, returning with looks of much disapprobation to his business of peeling potatoes for dinner.

When Mrs. Null reached the cabin of Aunt Patsy, after about fifteen minutes' walk, she entered without ceremony, and found the old woman sitting on a very low chair by the window, with the much-talked-of, many-colored quilt in her lap. Her white woolly head was partially covered with a red-and-yellow handkerchief, and an immense pair of iron-bound spectacles obstructed the view of her small black face, lined and seamed in such a way that it appeared to have shrunk to half its former size. In her long, bony fingers, rusty black on the outside and a very pale tan on the inside, she held a coarse needle and thread and a corner of the quilt. Near by, in front of a brick-paved fireplace, was one of her great-granddaughters, a girl about eighteen years old, who was down upon her hands and knees, engaged with lungs, more powerful than ordinary bellows, in blowing into flame a coal upon the hearth.

"How d'ye, Aunt Patsy?" said Mrs. Null. "I didn't expect to see you looking so well."

THE LATE MRS. NULL

"Dat's Miss Null," said the girl, raising her eyes from the fire, and addressing her ancestor.

The old woman stuck her needle into the quilt, and reached out her hand to her visitor, who took it cordially.

"How d'ye, miss?" said Aunt Patsy, in a thin but quite firm voice, while the young woman got up and brought Mrs. Null a chair, very short in the legs, very high in the back, and with its split-oak bottom very much sunken.

"How are you feeling to-day, Aunt Patsy?" asked Mrs. Null, gazing with much interest on the aged face.

"'Bout as common," replied the old woman. "I didn't 'spec' to be libin' dis week, but I ain't got my quilt done yit, an' I can't go 'mong de angels wrop in a shroud wid one corner off."

"Certainly not," answered Mrs. Null. "Haven't you pieces enough to finish it?"

"Oh, yaas, I got bits enough, but de trouble is to sew 'em up. I can't sew very fas' nowadays."

"It's a pity for you to have to do it yourself," said Mrs. Null. "Can't this young person, your daughter, do it for you?"

"Dat's not my darter," said the old woman. "Dat's my son Tom's yaller boy Bob's chile. Bob's dead. She can't do no sewin' for me. I'm not gwine ter hab folks sayin' Aun' Patsy done got so ole she can't do her own sewin'."

"If you are not going to die till you get your quilt finished, Aunt Patsy," said Mrs. Null, "I hope it won't be done for a long time."

"Don' do to be waitin' too long, miss. De fus' thing

65

you know some oder cullud pusson'll be dyin' wrop up in a quilt like dis, and git dar fus'."

Mrs. Null now looked about her with much interest, and asked many questions in regard to the old woman's comfort and ailments. To these the answers, though on the whole satisfactory, were quite short, Aunt Patsy, apparently, much preferring to look at her visitor than to talk to her. And a very pretty young woman she was to look at, with a face which had grown brighter and plumper during every day of her country sojourn.

When Mrs. Null had gone, promising to send Aunt Patsy something nice to eat, the old woman turned to her great-granddaughter, and said: "Did anybody come wid her?"

"Nobody comed," said the girl. "Reckon she done git herse'f los' some o' dese days."

The old woman made no answer, but folding up the maniac coverlet, she handed it to the girl, and told her to put it away.

That night Uncle Isham, by Mrs. Null's orders, carried to Aunt Patsy a basket containing various good things considered suitable for an aged colored woman without teeth.

"Miss Annie sen' dese h'yar?" asked the old woman, taking the basket and lifting the lid.

"Miss Annie!" exclaimed Uncle Isham. "Who she?"

"Git out, Uncle Isham!" said Aunt Patsy, somewhat impatiently. "She was h'yar dis mawnin'."

"Dat was Miss Null," said Isham.

"Miss Annie all de same," said Aunt Patsy, "on'y growed up an' married. D'ye mean to stan' dar, Uncle Isham, an' tell me you don' know de little gal

THE LATE MRS. NULL

wot Mahs' John use ter carry in he arms ter feed de tukkies?"

"She and she mudder dead long ago," said Isham. "You is pow'ful ole, Aun' Patsy, an' you done forgit dese things."

"Done forgit nuffin," curtly replied the old woman. "Don' tell me no mo' fool stuff. Dat Miss Annie, growed up an' married."

"Did she tell you dat?" asked Isham.

"She didn't tell me nuffin. She kep' her mouf shet 'bout dat, an' I kep' my mouf shet. Don' talk to me! Dat's Miss Annie, shuh as shootin'. Ef she hadn't fotch nuffin 'long wid her but her eyes I'd 'a' knowed dem; same ole eyes dey all had. An', 'sides dat, you fool Isham, ef she not Miss Annie, wot she come down h'yar fur?"

"Nebber thinked o' dat!" said Uncle Isham, reflectively. "Ef you's so pow'ful shuh, Aun' Patsy, I reckon dat *is* Miss Annie. Couldn't 'spec' me to 'member her. I wasn't much up at de house in dem times, an' she was took away 'fore I give much 'tention ter her."

"Don' ole miss know she dar?" asked Aunt Patsy.

"She dunno nuffin 'bout it," answered Isham. "She's stayin' away cos she think Mahs' Junius dar yit."

"Why don' you tell her, now you knows it's Miss Annie wot's dar?"

"You don' ketch me tellin' her nuffin," replied the old man, shaking his head. "Wish you was spry 'nuf ter go, Aun' Patsy. She'd b'lieve you; an' she couldn't r'ar an' charge inter a ole pusson like you, nohow."

"Ain't dar nobody else in dis h'yar place to go tell her?" asked Aunt Patsy.

"Not a pusson," was Isham's decided answer.

"Well, den, I *is* spry 'nuf!" exclaimed Aunt Patsy, .rith a vigorous nod of her head which sent her spec- tacles down to her mouth, displaying a pair of little eyes sparkling with a fire long thought to be extinct. "Ef you'll carry me dar, to Miss Harriet Corvey's, I'll tell ole miss myse'f. I didn't 'spec' to go out dat dohr till de fun'ral, but I'll go dis time. I 'spected dar was sumfin crooked when Miss Annie didn't tole me who she was. I'se not 'feared to tell ole miss, an' you jes carry me up dar, Uncle Isham."

"I'll do dat," said the old man, much delighted with the idea of doing something which he supposed would remove the clouds which overhung the household of his mistress. "I'll fotch de hoss an' de spring-waggin, an' dribe you ober dar."

"No, you don' do no sech thing!" exclaimed Aunt Patsy, angrily. "I ain't gwine to hab no hosses to run away an' chuck me out on de road. Ef you kin fotch de oxen an' de cart, I go 'long wid you, but I don' want no hosses."

"Dat's fus'-rate," said Isham. "I'll fotch de ox-cart, an' carry you ober. When you want ter go?"

"Dunno jes now," said Aunt Patsy, pushing away a block of wood which served for a footstool, and mak- ing elaborate preparations to rise from her chair. "I'll sen' fur you when I'se ready."

The next morning was a very busy one for Aunt Patsy's son Tom's yellow boy Bob's child; and by afternoon it was necessary to send for two colored women from a neighboring cabin to assist in the prep- arations which Aunt Patsy was making for her pro- jected visit. An old hair-covered trunk, which had not been opened for many years, was brought out, and the contents exposed to the unaccustomed light of day; two coarse cotton petticoats were exhumed and ordered to be bleached and ironed; a yellow-flannel garment of the same nature was put aside to be mended with some red pieces which were rolled up in it; out of several yarn stockings of various ages and lengths two were selected as being pretty much alike, and laid by to be darned; an old black frock with full "bishop sleeves," a good deal mended and dreadfully wrinkled, was given to one of the neighbors, expert in such matters, to be ironed; and the propriety of making use of various other ancient duds was eagerly and earnestly discussed. Aunt Patsy, whose vitality had been wonderfully aroused, now that there was some opportunity for making use of it, spent nearly two hours turning over, examining, and reflecting upon a pair of old-fashioned corsets, which, although they had been long cherished, she had never worn. She now hoped that the occasion for their use had at last arrived, but the utter impossibility of getting herself into them was finally made apparent to her, and she mournfully returned them to the trunk.

Washing, starching, ironing, darning, patching, and an immense deal of talk and consultation, occupied that and a good deal of the following day, the rest of which was given up to the repairing of an immense pair of green-baize shoes, without which Aunt Patsy could not be persuaded to go into the outer air. It was Saturday morning when she began to dress for the trip, and although Isham, wearing a high silk hat, and a long black coat which had once belonged to a clergy-man, arrived with the ox-cart about noon, the old woman was not ready to start till two or three hours afterwards. Her assistants, who had increased in number, were active and assiduous. Aunt Patsy was very particular as to the manner of her garbing, and gave them a great deal of trouble. It had been fifteen years since she had set foot outside of her house, and ten more since she had ridden in any kind of vehicle. This was a great occasion, and nothing concerning it was to be considered lightly.

"'Tain't right," she said to Uncle Isham, when he arrived, "fur a pow'ful ole pusson like me to set out on a jarney ob dis kin' 'thout 'ligious sarvices. 'Tain't 'spectable."

Uncle Isham rubbed his head a good deal at this remark. "Dunno wot we gwine to do 'bout dat," he said. "Brudder Jeemes lib free miles off, an' mos' like he's out ditchin'. Couldn't git him h'yar dis ebenin', nohow."

"Well, den," said Aunt Patsy, "you conduc' sarvices yourse'f, Uncle Isham, an' we kin have pra'r-meetin', anyhow."

Uncle Isham having consented to this, he put his oxen under the care of a small boy, and collecting in Aunt Patsy's room the five colored women and girls who were in attendance upon her, he conducted "pra'rs," making an extemporaneous petition which comprehended all the probable contingencies of the journey, even to the accident of the right wheel of the cart coming off, which the old man very reverently asserted he would have linched with a regular pin instead of a broken poker-handle, if he could have found one. After the prayer, with which Aunt Patsy signified her entire satisfaction by frequent amens, the company joined in the vigorous singing of a hymn, in which they stated that they were "gwine down to Jurdun, an' though the road is rough, when once we shuh we git dar, we all be glad enough; de rocks an' de stones, an' de jolts to de bones, will be nuffin to de glory an' de j'y."

The hymn over, Uncle Isham clapped on his hat, and hurried menacingly after the small boy, who had let the oxen wander along the roadside until one wheel of the cart was nearly in the ditch. Aunt Patsy now partook of a collation, consisting of a piece of hoe-cake dipped in pork fat, and a cup of coffee, which having finished, she declared herself ready to start. A chair was put into the cart, and secured by ropes to keep it from slipping; and then, with two women on one side and Uncle Isham on the other, while another woman stood in the cart to receive and adjust her, she was placed in position.

Once properly disposed she presented a figure which elicited the lively admiration of her friends, whose number was now increased by the arrival of a couple of negro boys on mules, who were going to the post-office, it being Saturday, and mail-day. Around Aunt Patsy's shoulders was a bright-blue worsted shawl, and upon her head a voluminous turban of vivid red and yellow. Since their emancipation, the negroes in that part of the country had discarded the positive and gaudy colors that were their delight when they were slaves, and had transferred their fancy to delicate pinks, pale blues, and similar shades. But Aunt Patsy's ideas about dress were those of bygone days, and she was too old now to change them, and her brightest handkerchief had been selected for her head on this important day. Above her she held a parasol, which had been graciously loaned by her descendant of the fourth generation. It was white, and lined with pink, and on the edges still lingered some fragments of cotton lace.

Uncle Isham now took his position by the side of his oxen, and started them; and slowly creaking, Aunt Patsy's vehicle moved off, followed by the two boys on mules, three colored women and two girls on foot, and by two little black urchins who were sometimes on foot, but invariably on the tail of the cart when they could manage to evade the backward turn of Uncle Isham's eye.

"Ef I should go to glory on de road, Uncle Isham," said Aunt Patsy, as the right wheel of the cart emerged from a rather awkward rut, "I don' want no fuss made 'bout me. You kin jes bury me in de clothes I got on, 'cep'n' de pararsol, ob course, which is 'Liza's. Jes wrop de quilt all roun' me, an' hab a extry-size coffin. You needn't do nuffin more'n dat."

"Oh, you's not gwine to glory dis time, Aun' Patsy," replied Uncle Isham, who did not want to encourage the idea of the old woman's departure from life while in his ox-cart. But after this remark of the old woman he was extraordinarily careful in regard to jolts and bumps.

When the procession reached the domain of Miss Harriet Corvey, there was gathered inside the yard quite a number of the usual attendants on mail-days awaiting the arrival of Wesley Green with his waddling horse and leather bag. But all interest in the coming of the mail was lost in the surprise and admiration excited by the astounding apparition of old

Aunt Patsy in the ox-cart, attended by her retinue. As the oxen, skilfully guided by Uncle Isham's long prod, turned into the yard, everybody came forward to find out the reason of this unlooked-for occurrence. Even old Madison Chalkley, his stout legs swaddled in home-made overalls, dismounted from his horse, and Colonel Iston raised his tall form from the porch step, where he had been sitting, and approached the cart.

"Upon my word," said a young fellow with high boots, slouched hat, and a riding-whip, "if here ain't old Aunt Patsy come after a letter! Where do you expect a letter from, Aunt Patsy?"

The old woman fixed her spectacles on him for an instant, and then said in a clear voice which could be heard by all the little crowd: "'Tain't from nobody dat I owes any money to, nohow, Mahs' Bill Trimble."

A general laugh followed this rejoinder, and Uncle Isham grinned with gratified pride in the enduring powers of his charge. The old woman now put down her parasol, and made as if she would descend from the cart.

"You needn't git out, Aun' Patsy," said several negro boys at once. "We'll fotch your letters to you."

"Git 'long wid you!" said the old woman, angrily. "I didn't come here fur no letters. Ef I wanted letters I'd sen' 'Liza fur 'em. Git out de way."

A chair was now brought, and placed near the cart; a woman mounted into the vehicle to assist her; Uncle Isham and another colored man stood ready to receive her, and Aunt Patsy began her descent. This, to her mind, was a much more difficult and dangerous proceeding than getting into the cart, and she was very slow and cautious about it. First, one of her great green-baize feet was put over the tail of the cart, and resting her weight upon the two men, Aunt Patsy allowed it to descend to the chair, where it was gradually followed by the other foot. Having safely accomplished this much, the old woman ejaculated: "Bress de Lor'!" When, in the same prudent manner, she had reached the ground, she heaved a sigh of relief, and fervently exclaimed: "De Lor' be bressed!"

Supported by Uncle Isham and the other man, Aunt Patsy now approached the steps. She was so old, so little, so bowed, and so apparently feeble, that several persons remonstrated with her for attempting to go into the house when anything she wanted would be gladly done for her. "Much 'bliged," said the old woman, "but I don' want no letters nor nuffin. I'se come to make a call on de white folks, an' I'se gwine in."

This announcement was received with a laugh, and she was allowed to proceed without further hindrance. She got up the porch steps without much difficulty, her supporters taking upon themselves most of the necessary exertion; but when she reached the top, she dispensed with their assistance. Shuffling to the front door, she there met Miss Harriet Corvey, who greeted the old woman with much surprise, but shook hands with her very cordially.

"Ebenin', Miss Har'et," said Aunt Patsy. And then, lowering her voice, she asked: "Is ole miss h'yar?"

Miss Harriet hesitated a moment, and then she answered: "Yes, she is; but I don't believe she'll come down to see you."

THE LATE MRS. NULL

"Oh, I'll go up-sta'rs," said Aunt Patsy. "Whar she?"

"She's in the spare chamber," said Miss Harriet; and Aunt Patsy, with a nod of the head signifying that she knew all about that room, crossed the hall, and began, slowly but steadily, to ascend the stairs. Miss Harriet gazed upon her with amazement, for Aunt Patsy had been considered chair-ridden when the post-mistress was a young woman. Arrived at the end of her toilsome ascent, Aunt Patsy knocked at the door of the spare chamber, and as the voice of her old mistress said, "Come in!" she went in.

CHAPTER VII

WHEN Lawrence Croft reached the Green Sulphur Springs, after his interview with Miss March, his soul was still bubbling and boiling with emotion, and it continued in that condition all night, at least during that great part of the night of which he was conscious. The sight of the lady he loved, under the new circumstances in which he found her, had determined him to throw prudence and precaution to the winds, and to ask her at once to be his wife.

But the next morning Lawrence arose very late. His coffee had evidently been warmed over, and his bacon had been cooked for a long, long time. The world did not appear to him in a favorable light, and he was obliged to smoke two cigars before he was at all satisfied with it. While he was smoking he did a good deal of thinking, and it was then that he came to the conclusion that he would not go over to Mid-branch and propose to Roberta March. Such precipitate action would be unjust to himself and unjust to her. In her eyes it would probably appear to be the act of a man who had been suddenly spurred to action by the sight of a rival, and this, if Roberta was the woman he believed her to be, would prejudice her against him. And yet he knew very well that these

76

reasons would avail nothing if he should see her as he intended. He had found that he was much more in love with her than he had supposed, and he felt positively certain that the next time he was alone with her he would declare his passion.

Another thing that he felt he should consider was that the presence of Keswick, if looked upon with a philosophic eye, was not a reason for immediate action. If the old engagement had positively been broken off, he was at the house merely as a family friend ; while, on the other hand, if the rupture had not been absolute, and if Roberta really loved this tall Southerner and wished to marry him, there was a feeling of honor about Lawrence which forbade him to interfere at this moment. When she came to New York he would find out how matters really stood, and then he would determine on his own action.

And yet he would have proposed to Roberta that moment if he had had the opportunity. Her personal presence would have banished philosophy, and even honor.

Lawrence was a long time in coming to these conclusions, and it was late in the afternoon when he despatched his note. Having now given up his North Carolina trip,—one object of which had been still another visit to Midbranch on his return,—he was obliged to wait until the next day for a train to the North ; and, consequently, he had another evening to devote to reflections. These, after a time, became unsatisfactory. He had told the exact truth in his note to Roberta, for he felt that it was necessary for him to leave that part of the country in order to make impossible an interview for which he believed the proper

77

time had not arrived. He was consulting his best interests, and also, no doubt, those of the lady. And yet, in spite of this reasoning, he was not satisfied with himself. He felt that his note was not entirely honest and true. There was subterfuge about it, and something of duplicity. This he believed was foreign to his nature, and he did not like it.

Lawrence had scarcely finished his breakfast the next morning when Mr. Junius Keswick arrived at the door of his cottage. This gentleman had walked over from Midbranch, and was a little dusty about his boots and the lower part of his trousers. Lawrence greeted him politely, but was unable to restrain a slight indication of surprise. It being more pleasant on the porch than in the house, Mr. Croft invited his visitor to take a seat there, and the latter very kindly accepted the cigar which was offered him, although he would have preferred the pipe he had in his pocket.

"I thought it possible," said Keswick, as soon as the two had fairly begun to smoke, "that you might not yet have left here, and so came over in the hope of seeing you."

"Very kind," said Lawrence.

Keswick smiled. "I must admit," said he, "that it was not solely for the pleasure of meeting you again that I came, although I am very glad to have an opportunity for renewing our acquaintance. I came because I am quite convinced that Miss March wished very much to see you at the time arranged between you, and that she was annoyed and discomposed by your failure to keep your engagement. Considering that you did not, and probably could not, know this,

I deemed I would do you a service by informing you of the fact."

"Did Miss March send you to tell me this?" exclaimed Lawrence.

"Miss March knows nothing whatever of my coming," was the answer.

"Then I must say, sir," exclaimed Lawrence, "that you have taken a great deal upon yourself."

Keswick leaned forward, and after knocking off the ashes of his cigar on the outside of the railing, he replied in a tone quite unmoved by the reproach of his companion : "It may appear so on the face of it, but, in fact, I am actuated only by a desire to serve Miss March, for whom I would do any service that I thought she desired. And, looking at it from your side, I am sure that I would be very much obliged to any one who would inform me, if I did not know it, that a lady greatly wished to see me."

"Why does she want to see me?" asked Croft. "What has she to say to me?"

"I do not know," said Keswick. "I only know that she was very much disappointed in not seeing you yesterday."

"If that is the case, she might have written to me," said Lawrence.

"I do not think you quite understand the situation," observed his companion. "Miss March is not a lady who would even intimate to a gentleman that she wished him to come to her when it was obvious that such was not his desire. But it seemed to me that if the gentleman should become aware of the lady's wishes through the medium of a third party, the matter would arrange itself without difficulty."

"By the gentleman going to her, I suppose," remarked Croft.

"Of course," said Keswick.

"There is no 'of course' about it," was Lawrence's rather quick reply.

At that moment some letters were brought to him from a little post-office near by, to which he had ordered his mail to be forwarded. As the address on one of these letters caught his eye, the somewhat stern expression on his face gave place to a smile, and begging his visitor to excuse him, he put his other letters into his pocket, and opened this one. It was very short, and was from Mr. Candy's cashier. It was written from Howlett's, Virginia, a place unknown to him, and stated that the writer expected in a very short time to give him some accurate information in regard to Mr. Keswick, and expressed the hope that he would allow the affair to remain entirely in her hands until she should write again. It was quite natural that, under the circumstances, Lawrence should smile broadly as he folded up this note. The man in question was sitting beside him, and, in a measure, was turning the tables upon him. Lawrence had been very anxious to find out what sort of a man was Keswick, and the latter now seemed in the way of making some discoveries in the same line in regard to Lawrence. One thing he must certainly do : he must write as soon as possible to his enterprising agent, and tell her that her services were no longer needed. She must have pushed the matter with a great deal of energy to have brought her down to Virginia, and he could not help hoping that her discretion was equal to her investigative capacity.

THE LATE MRS. NULL

When, after this little interruption, Lawrence again addressed Junius Keswick, his manner was so much more affable that the other could not fail but notice it.

"Mr. Keswick," he said, "as our conversation seems to be based upon personalities, perhaps you will excuse me if I ask you if I am mistaken in believing that you were once engaged to be married to Miss March?"

"You are entirely correct," said Junius. "I was engaged to her, and I hope to be engaged to her again."

"Indeed!" exclaimed Croft, turning in his chair with a start.

"Yes," continued Keswick; "our engagement was dissolved in consequence of a certain family complication, and, as I said before, I hope in time to be able to renew it."

Lawrence threw away his cigar, and sat for a few moments in thought. The engagement, then, did not exist. Roberta was free. Recollections came to him of his own intercourse with her during the past summer, and his heart gave a bound. "Mr. Keswick," said he, "upon consideration of the matter I think I will call upon Miss March this morning."

If Keswick had expressed himself entirely satisfied with this decision he would have done injustice to his feelings. The service he had taken upon himself to perform for Miss March he had considered a duty, but if his mission had failed he would have been better pleased than with its success. He made, however, a courteous reply to Croft's remark, and rose to depart. But this the other would not allow.

"You told me," said Croft, "that you walked over here; but it is much warmer now, and you must not

81

think of such a thing as walking back.   The man here has a horse and buggy.   I will get him to harness up, and I will drive you over to Midbranch."

As there was no good reason why he should decline this offer, Junius accepted it, and in half an hour the two were on their way.

CHAPTER VIII

OLD Mr. Brandon of Midbranch was not in a very happy frame of mind, and he had good reasons for dissatisfaction. He was an ardent supporter of a marriage between his niece and Junius Keswick; and when the engagement had been broken off he had considered that both these young people had acted in a manner very foolish and contrary to their best interests. There was no opposition to the match except from old Mrs. Keswick, who was the aunt of Junius, but who considered herself as occupying the position of a mother. Junius was the son of a sister who had also married into the Keswick family, and his parents having died while he was a boy, his aunt had taken him under her charge, and her house had then become his home; although of late years some of his absences had been long ones. Mrs. Keswick had no personal objections to Roberta, never having seen that lady, and knowing little of her; but an alliance between her Junius and any member of that branch of the Brandons "which," to use the old lady's own words, "had for four generations cheated, stripped, and scornfully used my people, scattering their atoms over the face of three counties," was monstrous. Nothing could make her consent to such an enormity, and she had informed Junius that if he married that March girl three of them should live together—himself, his wife, and her undying curse. In order that Miss March might not fail to hear of this post-connubial arrangement, she had been informed of it by letter. Of course this had broken off the engagement, for Roberta would not live under a curse, nor would she tear a man from the only near relative he had in the world. Keswick himself, like most men, would have been willing to have this tearing take place for the sake of uniting himself to such a charming creature as Roberta March. But the lady on one side was as inflexible as the lady on the other, and the engagement was definitely and absolutely ended.

Mr. Brandon considered all this as stuff and nonsense. He could not deny that his branch of the Brandons had certainly got a good deal out of Mrs. Keswick's family. But here was a chance to make everything all right again, and he would be delighted to see Junius, a relative, although a distant one, come into possession of Midbranch. As for the old lady's opposition, that should not be considered at all, he thought. It was his opinion that her mind had been twisted by her bad temper, and nothing she could say could hurt anybody.

Of late Mr. Brandon had been much encouraged by the fact that Junius had begun to resume his position as a friend of the family. This was all very well. If the young people, by occasional meetings, could keep alive their sentiments towards each other, the time would come when all opposition would cease, and the marriage would become an assured fact. He did not believe either of the young people would care enough for a post-mortem curse, if there should be one, to keep themselves separated from each other on its account for the rest of their lives.

But the recent quite unexpected return of Lawrence Croft to Midbranch, combined with the evident discomposure into which Roberta had been thrown by his failure to come the next day, had given the old gentleman some unpleasant ideas. His niece had mentioned that she expected Mr. Croft that day, and although she said nothing in regard to her subsequent disappointment and vexation, his mind was quite acute enough to perceive it. Exactly what it all meant he knew not, but it augured danger. For the first time he began to look upon Mr. Croft in the light of a suitor for Roberta. If a jealous feeling at finding another person on the ground was the cause of his not coming again, it showed that he was in earnest, and this, added to the evident disturbance of mind of both Roberta and Junius, was enough to give Mr. Brandon most serious fears that an obstacle to his cherished plan was arising. Roberta was fond of city life, of society, of travel, and if she had really made up her mind that her union with Junius was no longer to be thought of, the advent of a man like Croft, who had been making her acquaintance all summer, and who had now returned to Virginia no doubt for the sole purpose of seeing her again, was, to say the least, exceedingly ominous. One thing only could correct this deplorable state of affairs. The absurd bar to the union of Junius and Roberta should be removed, and they should be allowed to enter upon the happiness that was their right.

Above all, the estate of Midbranch should not be

suffered to go into the possession of an outsider, who might be good enough, but who was of no earthly moment or interest to the Brandons. He would go himself, and see the widow Keswick, and talk her out of her nonsense. It was a long time since he had met the old wildcat, as he termed her, and his recollection of the last interview was not pleasant; but he was not afraid of her, and he hoped that the common sense of what he would say would bring her to reason.

Mr. Brandon made up his mind during the night; and when he came down to breakfast he was very glad to find that Junius had already gone out for a walk. The distance to the widow Keswick's house was about fifteen miles, a pleasant day's ride for the old gentleman, and as he did not expect to return until the next day, he felt obliged to inform Roberta of his destination, although, of course, he said nothing about the object of his visit. He told his niece that he was obliged to see the widow Keswick on business, to which remark she listened without reply.

Soon after breakfast he mounted his good horse Albemarle, and early in the afternoon he arrived at the widow Keswick's gate. He had looked for a stormy reception, in which the thunder-bolts of rage should burst around him, and he was surprised, therefore, to be received with the frigidity of the North Pole.

"I never expected," she said, without any previous courtesy, "to see one of your people under my roof, and it is not very long ago since I would have gone away from it the moment any one of you came near it."

"I am happy, madam," said Mr. Brandon, in his most courteous manner, "that that day is past."

THE LATE MRS. NULL

" My staying won't do you any good," said the old lady, whose purple sunbonnet seemed to heave with the uprising of her hair, "except, perhaps, to get you a better meal than the servants would have given you. But I want a lawyer, and I can't afford to pay for one either, and when I saw you coming I just made up my mind to get something out of you, and if I do it, it'll be the first red mark for my side of the family."

Mr. Brandon assured her that nothing would give him more pleasure than to assist her in any way in his power.

" Very well, then," said Mrs. Keswick; "just sit down on that bench, and, when we have got through, your horse can be taken, and you can rest awhile, though it seems a very curious thing that you should want to stop here to rest."

" Well, madam," said Mr. Brandon, seating himself as comfortably as possible on a wooden bench, "I shall be happy to hear anything you have to say."

The old lady did not sit down, but stood up in front of him, leaning on her umbrella, with which faithful companion she had been about to set out on her walk. "When my son Junius came home awhile ago—" she began.

"Do you still call him your son?" interrupted Mr. Brandon.

"Indeed I do!" was the very prompt answer. "That's just what he is. And, as I was going to say, when he wrote me a short time ago that he was coming here, I believed, from his letter, that he had some scheme on hand in regard to your niece, and I made up my mind I wouldn't stay in the house to hear anything more said on that subject. I had told him that I never wanted him to say another word about it ; and it made my blood boil, sir, to think that he had come again to try to cozen me into the vile compact."

"Madam !" exclaimed Mr. Brandon.

"The next day," continued Mrs. Keswick, "a lady arrived; and as soon as I saw her drive into the gate I felt sure it was Roberta March, and that the two had hatched up a plot to come and work on my feelings, and so I wouldn't come near the house."

"Madam !" exclaimed Mr. Brandon, "how could you dream such a thing of my niece? You don't know her, madam."

"No," said the old lady, "I don't know her, but I knew she belonged to your family, and so I was not to be surprised at anything she did. But I found out I was mistaken. An old negro woman recognized this young person as the daughter of my younger sister— you know there were three of us. The child was born and raised here, but I have not seen and have scarcely heard of her since she was eight years old."

"That's very extraordinary, madam," said Mr. Brandon.

"No, it isn't, when you consider the stubbornness, the obstinacy, and the wickedness of some people. My sister sickened when the child was about six years old, and her husband, Harvey Peyton—"

"I have frequently heard of him, madam," said Mr. Brandon.

"And I wish I never had," said she. "Well, he was travelling most of the time, a thing my sister couldn't do; but he came here then, and stayed, off and on, till she died. And not long afterwards, just because I told him that I intended to consider the

child as my child, and that she should have the name
of Keswick instead of his name, and should know me
as her mother, and live with me always, he got angry
and flared up, and actually took the child away. I
gave it to him hot, I can tell you, before he left, and
I never saw him again. He was so eaten up with rage
because I wanted to take the little Annie for my own,
that he filled her mind with such prejudices against
me that when he died, a year or two ago, she actually
went to work to get her own living instead of applying
to me for help. But now she has come down here, and
I was really filled with joy to have her again and carry
out the plan on which my heart had long been set—
that is, to marry her to her cousin Junius, and let them
have this farm when I am gone—"

At this Mr. Brandon raised his eyebrows and lowered the corners of his mouth.

"But I suddenly discover," continued the old lady,
"that the little wretch is married—actually married."

At this Mr. Brandon lowered his eyebrows and raised
the corners of his mouth. "Did her husband come
with her?" he asked, pleasantly. And he gave a few
long, free breaths, as if he had just passed in safety a
very dangerous and unsuspected rock.

"No, he didn't," replied the old lady. "I don't
know where he is, and, from what I can make out, he
is an utterly good-for-nothing fellow, allowing his wife
to go where she pleases and take care of herself. Now
this abominable marriage stands square in the way of
the plan which again rose up in my mind the moment
I heard that the girl was in my house. If Junius and
she should marry, there would be no more dangers
for me to look out for."

"But the existence of a husband," said Mr. Brandon, blandly, "puts an end to all thoughts of such an alliance."

"No, it don't," said the old lady, bringing her umbrella down with force on the porch. "Not a bit of it. Such an outrageous marriage should not be suffered to exist. They should be divorced. He does nothing for her, and neglects and deserts her absolutely. There's every ground for a divorce, or enough grounds, at any rate. All that's necessary is for a lawyer to take it up. I don't know any lawyers, and when I saw you riding up from the road gate I said to myself: 'Here's the very man I want—and it's full time I should get something from people who have taken nearly everything from me.'"

Mr. Brandon bowed.

"And now," continued the old lady, "I am going to put the case into your hands. The man is evidently a good-for-nothing scoundrel, and has probably spent the little money that her miserable father left her. It's a clear case of desertion, and there should be no trouble at all in getting the divorce."

Mr. Brandon looked down upon the floor of the porch, and smiled. This was a pretty case, he thought, to put into his hands. Here was a marriage which was the strongest protection in the promotion of his own plan, and he was asked to annul it. "Very good," thought Mr. Brandon, "very good." And he smiled again. But he was an old-fashioned gentleman, and not used to refuse requests made to him by ladies. "I will look into it, madam," said he. "I will look into it, and see what can be done."

"Something must be done," said the old lady; "and

the right thing, too.   How long do you intend to stay here?"

"I thought of spending the night, madam, as my horse and myself are scarcely in condition to continue our journey to-day."

"Stay as long as you like," said Mrs. Keswick.   "I turn nobody from my doors, even if they belong to the Brandon family.   I want you to talk to my niece, and get all you can out of her about this thing, and then you can go to work and blot out this contemptible marriage as soon as possible."

"The first thing," said Mr. Brandon, "will be to talk to the lady."

This reply being satisfactory to Mrs. Keswick, Uncle Isham was called to take the horse and attend to him, while the master was invited into the house.

Mr. Brandon first met Mrs. Null at supper-time, and her appearance very much pleased him.   "It is not likely," he said to himself, "that the man lives who would willingly give up such a charming young creature as this."   They were obliged to introduce themselves to each other, as the lady of the house had not yet appeared.   After a while Letty, who was in attendance, advised them to sit down, as "de light bread an' de batterbread was gittin' cole."

"We could not think of such a thing as sitting at table before Mrs. Keswick arrives," said Mr. Brandon.

"Oh, dar's no knowin' when she'll come," said the blooming Letty.   "She may be h'yar by breakfus'-time, but dar ain't nobuddy in dis yere worl' kin tell. She's down at de bahn now, blowin' up Plez fur gwine to sleep when he was a-shellin' de cohn-fiel' peas.   An' when she's got froo wid him she's got a bone to pick wid Uncle Isham 'bout de gyardin. 'Tain't no use waitin' fur ole miss. She nebber do come when de bell rings. She come when she git ready, an' not afore."

Mr. Brandon now felt quite sure that it was the intention of his hostess not to break bread with one of his family, and so he seated himself, Mrs. Null taking the head of the table and pouring out the tea and coffee.

"It has been a long time, madam, since you were in this part of the country," said the old gentleman, as he drew the smoking batterbread towards him and began to cut it.

"Yes," said Mrs. Null; "not since I was a little girl. I suppose you have heard, sir, that Aunt Keswick and my father were on very bad terms, and would not have anything to do with each other?"

"Oh, yes," said Mr. Brandon; "I have heard that."

"But my father is not living now, and I am down here again."

"And your husband? He did not accompany you?" said Mr. Brandon.

"No," replied Mrs. Null, very quickly. "We were both very sorry that it was not possible for him to come with me."

Mr. Brandon's spirits began to rise. This did not look quite like desertion. "I have no doubt you have a very good husband. I am sure you deserve such a one," he said, with the air of a father and the purpose of a lawyer.

"Good!" exclaimed Mrs. Null, her eyes sparkling. "He couldn't be better if he tried! Will you have sweet milk or buttermilk?"

THE LATE MRS. NULL

"Buttermilk, if you please," said Mr. Brandon. "Of course your aunt was delighted to have you with her again."

"Oh," said Mrs. Null, with a laugh, "she was not at home when I arrived, but when she returned nothing could be too good for me. Why, she had been here scarcely half an hour, and hadn't taken off her sun-bonnet, before she told me I was to marry Junius and we two were to have this farm."

"A very pleasant plan, truly," said Mr. Brandon.

"But then, you see," continued the young girl, "Mr. Null stood dreadfully in the way of such an arrange-ment; and when Aunt Keswick heard about him you can't imagine what a change came over her."

"Oh, yes, I can; yes, I can," exclaimed Mr. Brandon, —"I can imagine it very well."

"But she didn't give up a bit," said Mrs. Null. "I don't think she ever does give up."

"You are right, there," said Mr. Brandon, "quite right. But what does she propose to do?"

"I don't know, I'm sure; but she said I had no right to marry without the consent of my surviving rela-tives, and that she was going to look into it. I can't think what she means by that."

Mr. Brandon made no immediate answer. He gave Mrs. Null some damson preserves, and he took some himself, and then he helped himself to a great hot roll from a plate that Letty had just brought in, and care-fully opening it he buttered it on the inside, and covered one half of it with the damson preserves. This he began slowly to eat, drinking at times from the foaming glass of buttermilk at the side of his plate, from which the coffee-cup had been removed. When he had finished the half-roll he again spoke: "I think, my dear young lady, that your aunt is desirous of having your marriage set aside."

"How can she do that?" exclaimed the girl, her face flushing. "Has she been talking to you about it?"

"I cannot deny that she has spoken to me on the subject," he answered, "I being a lawyer. But I will say to you, in strict confidence, please, that if you and your husband are sincerely attached to each other there is nothing on earth she can do to separate you."

"Attached!" exclaimed Mrs. Null. "It would be impossible for us to be more attached than we are. We never have had the slightest difference, even of opinion, since our wedding-day. Why, I believe that we are more like one person than any married couple in the world."

"I am very glad to hear it," said Mr. Brandon, finishing his buttermilk,—"very glad indeed. And, feeling as you do, I am certain that nothing your aunt can say will make any impression on you in regard to seeking a divorce."

"I should think not!" said Mrs. Null, sitting up very straight. "Divorce, indeed!"

"I fully uphold you in the stand you have taken," said Mr. Brandon. "But I beg you will not mention this conversation to your aunt. It would only annoy her. Is your cousin expected here shortly?"

"I believe so," she said. "To be sure, my aunt left the house the last time he came, but she has his address, and has written for him. I think she wants us to get acquainted as soon as possible, so that no time will be lost in marrying us after poor Mr. Null is disposed of."

THE LATE MRS. NULL

"Very good, very good," said Mr. Brandon, with a laugh. "And now, my dear young friend, I want to give you a piece of advice. Stay here as long as you can. Your aunt will soon perceive the absurdity of her ideas in regard to your husband, and will cease to annoy you. Make a friend of your cousin Junius, whom I know and respect highly; and he certainly will be of advantage to you. Above all things, endeavor to thoroughly reconcile him and Mrs. Keswick, so that she will cease to oppose his wishes, and to interfere with his future fortune. If you can bring back good feeling between these two, you will be the angel of the family."

"Thank you," said Mrs. Null, as they rose from the table.

The next morning, after Mr. Brandon and Mrs. Null had breakfasted together, the mistress of the house, having apparently finished the performance of the duties which had kept her from the breakfast-table, had some conversation with her visitor. In this he repeated very little of what he had said to the younger lady the night before, but he assured Mrs. Keswick that he had discovered that it would be a very delicate thing to propose to her niece a divorce from her husband, a thing to which she was not at all inclined, as he had found.

"Of course not! of course not!" exclaimed Mrs. Keswick. "She can't be expected to see what a wretched plight she has got herself into by marrying this straggler from nobody knows where."

"But, madam," said Mr. Brandon, "if you worry her about it, she will leave you, and then all will be at an end. Now, let me advise you as your lawyer.

THE LATE MRS. NULL

Keep her here as long as you can. Do everything possible to foster friendship and good feeling between her and Junius; and to do this you must forget as far as possible all that has gone by, and be friendly with both of them yourself."

"Humph!" said the widow Keswick. "I didn't ask you for advice of that sort."

"It is all a part of the successful working of the case, madam," said Mr. Brandon. "A thorough good feeling must be established before anything else can be done."

"I suppose so," said the old lady. "She must learn to like us before she begins to hate him. And how about your niece? Are you going to send her down here to help on in the good feeling?"

"I have not brought my niece into this affair," replied Mr. Brandon, with dignity.

"Well, then, see that you don't," was the widow Keswick's reply. And the interview terminated.

When Mr. Brandon rode away on his good horse Albemarle, he looked at the post of the road gate, from which he was lifting the latch by means of the long wooden handle arranged for the convenience of riders, and said to himself: "John Keswick was a good man, but I don't wonder he came out here and shot himself. It is a great pity, though, that it wasn't his wife who did it, instead of him. That would have been a blessing to all of us. But," he added contemplatively, as he closed the gate, "the people in this world who ought to blow out their brains never do."

Soon after he had gone, Mrs. Null went up Pine Top Hill, and sat down on the rock to have a "think." "Now, then, Freddy," she said, "everything depends

96

on you. If you don't stand by me I am lost—that is to say, I must go away from here before Junius comes; and you know I don't want to do that. I want to see him on my account, and on his account too; but I don't want him crammed down my throat for a husband the moment he arrives, and that is just what will happen if you don't do your duty, Mr. Null. Even if it wasn't for you, I don't want to look at him from the husband point of view, because, of course, he is a very different person from what he used to be, and is a total stranger to me.

" It is actually more than twelve years since I have seen him, and besides that, he is just as good as engaged to that niece of Mr. Brandon's, who is a horrible mixture of a she-wolf and a female mule, if I am to believe Aunt Keswick, but I expect she is, truly, a very nice girl. Though, to be sure, she can't have much spirit if she consented to break off her marriage just on account of the back-handed benediction which Aunt Keswick told me she offered her as a wedding-gift. If I had wanted to marry a man I would have let the old lady curse the heels off her boots before I would have paid any attention to her. Cursing don't hurt anybody but the curser.

" What I want of Junius is to make a friend of him, if he turns out to be the right kind of a person, and to tell him about this Mr. Croft who is so anxious to find him. The only person I have met yet who seems like an ordinary Christian is old Mr. Brandon, and he's a sly one, I'm afraid. Aunt Keswick thinks he stopped here on his way somewhere, but I don't believe a word of it. I believe he came for reasons of his own, and went right straight back again. You are almost as much to him, Freddy, as you are to me. It would have made you laugh if you could have seen how his face lighted up when he heard we were happy together, and that I would not listen to a divorce. And yet I am sure he has promised Aunt Keswick to see what he can do about getting one. He wants me to stay here and make friends of Aunt Keswick and Junius, but he wouldn't like that if it were not for you, Mr. Null. You make everything safe for him.

"And now, Freddy, I tell you again that all depends upon you. If I'm to stay here—and I want to do that, for a time anyway, for although Aunt Keswick is so awfully queer, she's my own aunt, and that's more than I can say for anybody else in the world—you must stiffen up and stand by me. It won't do to give way for a minute. If necessary you must take tonics, and have a steel rod down your back, if you can't keep yourself erect without it. You must have your legs padded, and your chest thrown out; and you must stand up very strong and sturdy, Freddy, and not let them push you an inch this way or that. And now that we have made up our minds on this subject, we'll go down, for it's getting a little cool on the top of this hill."

CHAPTER IX

ON the morning of her uncle's departure from Mid-branch, Roberta came out on the porch, and took her seat in a large wooden arm-chair, putting down her key-basket on the floor beside her. The day was bright and sunny, and the shadows of two or three turkey-buzzards, who were circling in the air, moved over the field in front of the house. In this field also moved, not so fast, nor so gracefully as the shadows, two ploughs, one near by, and the other at quite a distance. The woods which shut out a great part of the horizon showed many a bit of color, but the scene, although bright enough in some of its tones, was not a cheering one to Roberta; and she needed cheering.

Had it not been for the delay of her father in mak-ing his winter visit to New York, she would now be in that city; but if things had gone on as she expected they would, she would have been perfectly satisfied to remain several weeks longer at Midbranch. Junius Keswick, who had not visited the house for a long time, had come to them again; and, now that the sub-ject of love and marriage had been set aside, it was charming to have him there as a friend. They not only walked in the woods, but they took long rides over the country, Mr. Brandon having waived his ob--

99

jections in regard to his niece riding about with gentlemen. She had even been pleased with the unexpected return of Lawrence Croft, for, for reasons of her own, she wished very much to have a talk with him. But he had not fulfilled his promise to her, and had gone away in a very unsatisfactory manner.

This morning she felt a little lonely, too, for Junius had left the place before breakfast, and she did not know where he had gone; and her uncle had actually ridden away to see that horrible widow Keswick, merely stating that his errand was a business one, and that he would be back the next day. Roberta knew that there had been a great deal of business, particularly that of an unpleasant kind, between the two families, but she did not believe that there was any ordinary affair concerning dollars and cents which would require the presence of her uncle at the house of his old enemy. She was very much afraid that he had gone there to try to smooth up matters in regard to Junius and herself. The thought of this made her indignant. She did not know what her uncle would say, and she did not want him to say anything. He could not make the horrible old creature change her mind in regard to the marriage, and if this was not done, there was no use discussing the matter at all; and she did not wish people to think she was anxious for the match.

It was plain, however, that her uncle's desire for it had experienced a strong revival; and the unexpected return of Lawrence Croft had probably had a great effect on him. He had not objected to the visits of that gentleman during the summer, but he had never shown any strong liking for him, and Roberta said to herself that she could not see, for her part, why this should be; Mr. Croft was a thorough gentleman, an exceedingly well educated and agreeable man.

As to Junius, she was afraid that he had not the spirit which she used to think he possessed. There was something about him she could not understand. In former days, when Junius was in New York, she compared him with the young men there, very much to his advantage, but now Mr. Croft seemed to throw him somewhat in the background. When Croft wanted to do anything he did it; even his failure to come to her when he said he would do so showed strength of will. If Junius had promised to come he would have come, even if he had not wanted to do so, and there would have been something weak about that.

While she thus sat thinking, and gazing over the landscape, she saw afar off, on a portion of the road which ran alongside the woods, a vehicle slowly making its way to the house. Roberta had large and beautiful eyes, but they were not of the kind which would enable her to discover at so great a distance what sort of vehicle this was, and who was in it. As the road led nowhere but to Midbranch, she was naturally desirous to know who was coming. She stepped into the hall, and, taking a small bell, rang it vigorously, and in a moment her youthful handmaiden Peggy appeared upon the scene. Peggy's habit of projecting her eyes into the far-away could often be turned to practical account, for her vision was, in a measure, telescopic.

"What is that coming here along the road?" asked Miss Roberta, stepping upon the porch, and pointing out the distant vehicle.

Peggy stood up straight, let her arms hang close to

her sides, and looked steadfastly forth. "Wot's comin', Miss Rob," said she, "is de buggy 'longin' ter Mister Michaels, at de Springs, an' his ole mud-colored hoss is haulin' it. Dem dat's in it is Mahs' Junius an' Mister Crof'."

"Are you sure of that?" exclaimed Miss Roberta, in astonishment. "Look again."

"Yaas'm," replied Peggy. "I'se sartin shuh. But dey jes gwine behin' de trees now."

The road was not again visible for some distance, but when the buggy reappeared Peggy gave a start, and exclaimed: "Dar's on'y one pusson in it now, Miss Rob."

"Which is it?" exclaimed her mistress quickly, shading her eyes and endeavoring to see for herself.

"It's Mister Crof'," said Peggy. "Mahs' Junius mus' done gone back."

"It is too bad!" exclaimed Miss Roberta. "I will not see him. Peggy," she said, snatching up the key-basket and stepping towards the hall door, "when that gentleman, Mr. Croft, comes, you must tell him that I am up-stairs lying down, that I am not well and cannot see him, and that your Master Robert is not at home."

"Ef Mahs' Junius come, does you want me ter tell him de same thing?"

"But you said he was not in the buggy," said her mistress.

"No'm," answered Peggy; "but p'r'aps he done cut acrost de plough fiel' an' git h'yar fus'."

"If he comes first," said Miss Roberta, a shade of severity pervading her handsome features, "I want to see him." And with this she went up-stairs.

THE LATE MRS. NULL

Peggy with her shoes on possessed the stolid steadiness of a wooden grenadier, for the heaviness of the massive boots seemed to permeate her whole being, and communicated what might be considered a slow and heavy footfall to her intellect. Peggy without shoes was a panther on two legs, and her mind, like her body, was capable of enormous leaps. Slipping off her heavy brogans, she made a single bound and stood upon the railing of the porch, and, throwing her arm around a post, gazed forth from this point of vantage.

"Bress my eberlastin' soul!" she exclaimed, "if Mister Crof' ain't got ter de road gate, and is a-waitin' dar fur somebody ter come open it! Does he think anybody gwine ter see him all de way from de house, and come open de gate? Reckon he don' know dat ole mud-color hoss. He mought git out and let down de whole fence, an' dat ole hoss 'u'd nebber move. Bress my soul mo' p'intedly! ef Mahs' Junius ain't comin' 'long ter open de gate!"

For a few moments Peggy stood and stared, her mind not capable of grasping this astounding situation. "No, he ain't, nudder!" she presently exclaimed, with an air of relief. "Mahs' Junius done tole him dat ef he want dat gate open he better git down and open it hese'f. Dat's right, Mahs' Junius! Stick up ter dat! Dar go Mahs' Junius into de woods, an' Mister Crof' he git out an' go after him. Dey's gwine ter fight, sartin shuh! Lordy! wot fur dey 'low dem bushes ter grow 'long de fence ter keep folks from seein' wot's gwine on!"

There was nothing now to be seen from the railing, and Peggy jumped down on the porch. Her activity seemed to pervade her being. She ran down the front steps, crossed the lawn, and mounted the stile. Here she could catch sight of the two men, who seemed to be disputing. This was too much for Peggy. If there was to be a fight she wanted to see it; and, apart from her curiosity, she had a loyal interest in the event. Down the steps and along the road she went at the top of her speed, and soon reached the gate. Her arrival was not noticed by any one except the mud-colored horse, who gazed at her inquiringly; and looking through the bars without opening the gate, Peggy had a good view of the gentlemen.

The situation was a more simple one than Peggy had imagined. The road for the last half-mile had been an uphill one, and Keswick, as much to stretch his own legs as to save those of the horse, had alighted to walk, while Lawrence, as in duty bound, had waited for him at the gate. Here a little argument had arisen. Keswick, who did not wish to be at the house, or indeed about the place, while Roberta was having her conference with Mr. Croft, had said that he had concluded not to go up to the house at present, but would take a walk through the woods instead. Lawrence, who thought he divined his reason, felt an honorable indisposition to accept this advantage at the hands of a man who was, most indisputably, his rival. If they went together it would not appear as if he had waited for Keswick's absence to return; and there would still be no reason why he should not have his private walk and talk with Miss March.

At all events, it seemed to him unfair to leave Keswick at the gate while he went up to the house by himself, and the notion of it did not please him at all.

THE LATE MRS. NULL

Keswick, however, was very resolute in his opposition. He objected even to seeing Roberta and Croft together. He thought, besides, if he and Croft came to the house at the same time it would appear very much as if he, Junius, had brought the other, and this was an appearance he wished very much to avoid. He had walked away, and Lawrence had jumped from the buggy to continue the friendly argument, which was not finished when Peggy arrived. Almost immediately after this event Keswick positively insisted that he would go for a walk, and Lawrence reluctantly turned towards the vehicle.

Peggy's mind was filled with horror. Master Junius had been frightened away, and the other man was coming up to the house! She could not stand there and allow such a catastrophe. Jerking open the gate, she rushed into the road and confronted Keswick.

"Mahs' Junius," she exclaimed, "Miss Rob's orful sick wid her back an' her j'ints, an' she say she can't see no kump'ny folks, an' Mahs' Robert he done gone away ter see ole Miss Keswick. I jes run down h'yar ter tell you ter hurry up."

Keswick started. "Where did you say your Master Robert had gone?"

"Ter ole Miss Keswick's. He went dis mawnin'."

Junius turned slightly pale, and, addressing Mr. Croft, said: "Something very strange must have happened here! Miss March is ill, and Mr. Brandon has gone to a place to which I think nothing but a matter of the utmost importance could take him."

"In that case," said Mr. Croft, "it will be highly improper for me to go to the house just now. I am very glad that I heard the news before I got there. I

105

will return to the Springs, and will call to-morrow and inquire after Miss March's health. Do not let me detain you, as your presence is evidently much needed at the house."

"Thank you," said Keswick, hurriedly shaking hands with him. "I am afraid something very unexpected has happened, and so beg you will excuse me. Good morning." And passing through the gateway, he rapidly strode towards the house, while Lawrence prepared to turn his horse's head towards the Springs.

But, although Junius Keswick walked rapidly, Peggy, who had started first for the house, kept well in advance of him. Away she went, skipping, running, dancing. Once she stopped and turned, and saw that the buggy with the mud-colored horse was being driven away, and that Master Junius was coming along the road to the house; then she started off, and ran steadily, the rapid show of the light-colored soles of her feet behind her suggestive of a steamer's wake. Up the broad stile she went, two steps at a time, and down the other side in a couple of jumps; a dozen skips took her across the lawn; and she bounded up to the porch as if each wooden step had been a spring-board. She rushed up-stairs, and stood at the open door of Miss Roberta's room, where that lady reclined upon a lounge.

"Hi, Miss Rob!" she exclaimed, involuntarily snapping her fingers as she spoke. "Mahs' Junius comin' all by hese'f, an' I done sent de oder gemman clean off, kitin' !"

CHAPTER X

JUNIUS KESWICK was received by Miss Roberta in the parlor. Her face was colder and sterner than he had ever seen it before, and his countenance was very much troubled. Each wished to speak first, and ask questions, but the lady went immediately to the front.

"How did it happen that you and Mr. Croft were coming here together? Where had you been?"

"We came from the Green Sulphur Springs, where I called on him this morning."

"I thought he was obliged to return immediately to the North. What made him change his mind?"

"Perhaps it will be better not to discuss that now," said Junius.

"I wish to discuss it," was the reply. "What induced him not to go?"

"I did," answered Junius, looking steadfastly at her. "Did you not wish to see him?"

For a moment Miss Roberta did not answer, but her face grew pale, and she threw herself back in the chair in which she was sitting. "Never in my life," she said, "have I been subjected to such mortification! Of course I wished him to come, but to come of his own accord, and not at my bidding. How do you suppose I would have felt if he had presented himself, and

107

asked me what I wished to say to him? It is an insult you have offered me."

"It is not an insult," said Keswick, quietly. "It was a service of—of affection. I saw that you were annoyed and troubled by Mr. Croft's failure to keep his engagement, and what I did was simply—"

"Stop!" said Roberta, peremptorily. "I do not wish to talk of it any more."

Junius stood before her a moment in silence, and then he said: "Will you tell me if my Aunt Keswick is ill or dead, and why did Mr. Brandon go there?"

"She is neither," answered Roberta; "and he went there on business." And with this she arose and left the room.

Peggy, who had been in the hall, now made a bolt down the back stairs into the basement regions, where was situated the kitchen. In this spacious apartment she found Aunt Judy, the cook, sitting before a large wood fire, and holding in her hand a long iron ladle. There was nothing near her which she could dip or stir with a ladle, and it was probably retained during her period of leisure as a symbol of her position and authority.

Peggy squatted on her heels, close to Aunt Judy's side, and thus addressed her: "Aun' Judy, ef I tell you sumfin, soul an' honor, hope o' glory, you'll nebber tell?"

"Hope o' glory, nebber!" said Aunt Judy, turning a look of interest on the girl.

"Well, den, look h'yar. You know Miss Rob she got two beaux; one is Mahs' Junius, an' de oder is de gemman wid de speckle trousers from de Norf."

"Yes, I know dat," said Aunt Judy. "Has dey fit?"

THE LATE MRS. NULL

"Not yit, but dey wos gwine ter," said Peggy, "but I seed 'em, an' I tore down de road ter de gate whar dey wos gittin' ready ter fight, an' I jes let dat dar Mister Crof' know wot low-down white trash Miss Rob think he wos, an' den he said ef dat war so 'twa'n't no use fur ter come in, an' he turn roun' de buggy an' cl'ar'd out. Den Mahs' Junius he come ter de house, an' dar Miss Rob in de parlor waitin' fur him. I stood jes outside de do', so's ter be out de way, but Mahs' Junius he kinder back ag'in' de do' an' shet it. But I clap'd my year ter de crack, an' I hear eberything dey said."

"Wot dey say?" asked Aunt Judy, her mouth open, her eyes dilated, and the long ladle trembling in her hand.

"Mahs' Junius he say ter Miss Rob dat he lub her better'n his own skin, or de clouds in de sky, or de flowers in de fiel' wot perish, an' dat de oder man he done cut an' run, an' would she be Miss Junius all de res' ob der libes forebber an' ebber, amen?"

"Dat wos pow'ful movin'!" ejaculated Aunt Judy. "An' wot did Miss Rob say?"

"Miss Rob she say, 'I 'cept yo' kind offer, sah, wid pleasure.' An' den I hearn 'em comin', an' I cut down h'yar."

"Glory! Hallelujah!" exclaimed Aunt Judy, bringing her ladle down upon the brick hearth. "Now is I ready ter die when my time comes, fur Mahs' Junius'll have dis farm, an' de house, an' de cabins, an' dey won't go ter no strahnger from de Norf."

"Amen," said Peggy. "An' Aun' Judy, dat ar piece ob pie ain't no 'count to nobuddy."

"You kin hab it, chile," said Aunt Judy, rising and

taking from a shelf a large piece of cold apple-pie, " an' bressed be de foots ob dem wot fotch good tidin's."

Junius Keswick did not see Miss Roberta again that day, and early in the morning he borrowed one of the Midbranch horses, and rode away. He did not wish to be at the house when Mr. Croft should come; and, besides, he was very anxious and disturbed in regard to matters at the Keswick farm. Of all places in the world, why should Mr. Brandon go there?

It was not a very pleasant ride that Junius Keswick took that morning. He had anxieties in regard to what he would meet with at his aunt's house, and he had even greater anxieties as to what he was leaving behind him at Midbranch. It was quite evident that Roberta was angry with him, and this was enough to sadden the soul of a man who loved her as he loved her, who would have married her at any moment, in spite of all opposition, all threats, all curses. He was not in the habit of looking at himself after the manner of Lawrence Croft, but on this occasion he could not help a little self-survey. Was it a purely disinterested motive, he asked himself, that took him over to the Springs to bring back Lawrence Croft? Did he not believe in his soul that Roberta would never have spoken so freely to him in regard to what the gentleman from the North would probably say to her if she had not intended to decline that gentleman's offer? And was there not a wish in his heart that this matter might be definitely and satisfactorily settled before Roberta and Mr. Croft went to New York for the winter? He could not deny that this issue to the affair had been in his mind; and yet he felt that he could conscientiously assure himself that if he had thought things would turn out otherwise, he still would have endeavored to make the man perform the duty expected of him by Roberta, in whose service Junius always felt himself to be. But, apparently, he had not benefited himself or anybody else, except, perhaps, Croft, by this service which he had performed.

It was late in the forenoon when Junius met Mr. Brandon returning to Midbranch. In answer to his expressions of surprise, Mr. Brandon, who appeared in an exceptionally good humor, informed Junius of his reasons for the visit to the widow Keswick, and what he had found when he arrived there.

"Your little cousin," said he, "is a most charming young creature, and on interested motives I should oppose your going to your aunt's house, were it not for the fact that she is married, and, therefore, of no danger to you. I was very glad to find her there. Her influence over your aunt will, I think, be highly advantageous, and the first-fruit of it is that the old lady will now welcome you with open arms. Would you believe it! she has already announced that she wishes to make a match between you and this little cousin; and in order to do so, has actually engaged me to endeavor to bring about a divorce between the young lady and her absent husband. The widow Keswick has as many cranks and crotchets in her head as there are seeds in a tobacco-pod; but this is the queerest and the wildest of them all. The couple seem very much attached to each other, and nothing can be said against the husband except that he did not accompany his wife on her visit to her relatives; and if he knew anything about the old lady I don't blame him a bit. Now your course, my dear boy, is perfectly plain. Let

111

your aunt talk as much as she pleases about this divorce and your union with the little Annie. It won't hurt anybody, and she must talk herself out in time. In the meantime take advantage of the present circumstances to mollify and tone down, so to speak, the good old lady. Make her understand that we are all her friends, and that there is no one in the connection who would wish to do her the slightest harm. This would be our Christian duty at any time, but it is more particularly our duty now. I would like you to bring your cousin over to see us before Roberta goes away. I invited her to come, and told her that my niece would first call upon her were it not for the peculiar circumstances. But if the families can be in a measure brought together,—and I shall make it a point to ride over there occasionally,—if your aunt can be made to understand the kindly feelings we really have towards her, and can be induced to set aside, even in a slight degree, the violent prejudice she now holds against us, all may yet turn out well. Now go, my boy, and may the best of success go with you. Don't trouble yourself about sending back the horse. Keep him as long as you want him."

Mr. Brandon rode on, leaving Junius to pursue his way. "It is very pleasant," thought the young man, who had said scarcely a word during the interview, "to hear Mr. Brandon talk about all turning out well, but when he gets home he may discover that there is something to be done at Midbranch as well as on the Keswick place."

Mr. Brandon's reflections were very different from those of Junius. It appeared to him that a reconciliation between the two families, even though it should

THE LATE MRS. NULL

be a partial one, was reasonably to be expected. That newly arrived cousin was an angel. She was bound to do good. A marriage between his niece and Junius Keswick was the great object of the old gentleman's heart, and he longed to see the former engagement between them reëstablished before Roberta went to New York, where her beauty and attractiveness would expose his cherished plan to many dangers.

The road he was on led directly north, and it was joined about a quarter of a mile above by the road which ran through the woods to the Green Sulphur Springs. On this road, at a point nearly opposite to him, he could see, through the foliage, a horseman riding towards the point of junction. Something about this person attracted his attention, and Mr. Brandon took out a pair of eye-glasses and put them on. As soon as he had obtained another good view of the horseman he recognized him as Mr. Croft. The old gentleman took off his glasses and returned them to his vest pocket, and his face began to flush. In his early acquaintance with Mr. Croft he had not objected to him, because he wished his niece to have company, and he had a firm belief in the enduring quality of her affection for Junius. But latterly his ideas in regard to the New York gentleman had changed. He had thought him somewhat too assiduous, and when he had unexpectedly returned from the North, Mr. Brandon had not been at all pleased, although he had been careful not to show his displeasure. This condition of things made him feel uneasy, and had prompted his visit to the widow Keswick. And now that everything looked so fair and promising, here was that man, whom

113

he had supposed to have left this part of the country, riding towards his house.

Mr. Brandon was an easy-going man, but he had a backbone which could be greatly stiffened on occasion. He sat up very straight on his horse, and urged the animal to a better pace, so that he arrived first at the point where the roads met. Here he awaited Mr. Croft, who soon rode up. The old gentleman's greeting was very courteous.

"You are on the way to my house, I presume," he said.

Mr. Croft assured him that he was, and hoped that Miss March was quite well.

"I have been from home for a little while," said Mr. Brandon, "but I believe my niece enjoys her usual health. I have had a long ride this morning," he continued, "and feel a little tired. Would it inconvenience you, sir, if we should dismount and sit for a time on yonder log by the roadside? It would rest me, and I would like to have a little talk with you."

Lawrence wondered very much that the old gentleman should want to rest when he was not a mile from his own house, but of course he consented to the proposed plan, and imitated Mr. Brandon by riding under a large tree, and fastening his bridle to a low-hanging bough. The two gentlemen seated themselves on the log, and Mr. Brandon, without preface, began his remarks.

"May I be pardoned for supposing, sir," he said, "that your present visit to my house is intended for my niece?"

Lawrence looked at him a little earnestly, and replied that it was so intended.

THE LATE MRS. NULL

"Then, sir, I think I have the right to ask, as my niece's present guardian, and almost indeed as her father, whether or not your visit is connected in any way with matrimonial overtures towards that lady?"

Not wishing to foolishly and dishonorably deny that such was his purpose in going to Midbranch, and feeling that it would be as unwise to decline answering the question as it would be unmanly to resort to subterfuge about it, Lawrence replied that his object in visiting Miss March that day was to make matrimonial overtures to her.

"I think," said Mr. Brandon, "that you will be obliged to me if I make you acquainted with the present condition of affairs between Miss March and Mr. Junius Keswick."

"Has not their engagement been broken off?" interrupted Lawrence.

"Only conditionally," answered the old gentleman. "They love each other. They wish to be married. With one exception, all their relatives desire that they should marry. It would be a union, not only congenial in the highest degree to the parties concerned, but of the greatest advantage to our family and our family fortunes. There is but a single obstacle to this most desirable union, and that is the unwarrantable opposition of one person. But I am happy to say that this opposition is on the point of being removed. I consider it to be but a matter of days when my niece and Mr. Keswick, with the full approbation of the relatives on either side, will renew in the eyes of the world that engagement which I consider still exists in fact."

"If this is so," said Lawrence, grinding his heel

very deeply into the ground, "why was I not told of it?"

"My dear sir!" exclaimed Mr. Brandon, "have you ever intimated to me or to any of my family that your intentions in visiting Midbranch were other than those of an ordinary friend or acquaintance?"

Lawrence admitted that he had never made any such intimation.

"Then, sir," said Mr. Brandon, "what reason could we have for mentioning this subject to you—a subject that would not have been referred to now, had it not been for your admission of your intended object in visiting my house?"

Lawrence had no answer to make to this, but it was not easy to turn him from his purpose. "Excuse me, sir," he said, "but I think a matter of this sort should be left to the lady. If she is not inclined to receive my addresses she will say so, and there is an end of it."

The face of Mr. Brandon slightly reddened, but his voice remained as quiet and courteous as before. "You do not comprehend, sir, the state of affairs, or you would see that a procedure of that kind would be extremely ill-judged at this time. Were it known that at this critical moment Miss March was addressed by another suitor, it would seriously jeopardize the success of plans which we all have very much at heart."

Lawrence did not immediately reply to this crafty speech. His teeth were very firmly set, and he looked steadfastly before him. "I do not understand all this," he said presently, "nor do I see that there is any need for my understanding it. In fact, I have nothing to do with it. I wish to propose marriage to Miss March. If she declines my offer there is an end of the matter. If she accepts me, then it is quite proper that all your plans should fall to the ground. She is the principal in the affair, and it is due to her and due to me that she should make the decision in this case."

Mr. Brandon had not quite so many teeth as his younger companion, but the very fair number which remained with him were set together quite as firmly as those of Lawrence had been. He remarked, speaking very distinctly but without any show of emotion: "I see, sir, that it is quite impossible for us to think alike on this subject, and there is, therefore, nothing left for me to do but to ask you—and I assure you, sir, that the request is as destitute of any intention of discourtesy as if it were based upon the presence of sickness or family affliction—that you will not visit my house at present."

Lawrence rose to his feet with a good deal of color in his face. "That settles the matter for the present," he said. "Of course I shall not go to a house which is forbidden to me. I wish you good morning, sir." And he stalked to his horse, and endeavored to pull down the limb to which its bridle was attached.

Mr. Brandon followed him. "You must mount before you can unfasten your bridle," he said. "And allow me to assure you, sir, that as soon as this little affair is settled I shall be very happy indeed to see you again at my house."

Lawrence, having succeeded in loosening his bridle from the tree, made answer with a bow, and galloped away to the Green Sulphur Springs.

Mr. Brandon now mounted and rode home. This

was the first time in his life that he had ever forbidden any one to visit Midbranch, and yet he did not feel that he had been either discourteous or inhospitable. "There are times," he said to himself, "when a man must stand up for his own interest; and this is one of the times."

CHAPTER XI

In the little dining-room of the cottage at the Green
Sulphur Springs sat that evening Lawrence Croft, a
perturbed and angry but a resolute man. He had
been quite a long time coming to the conclusion to
propose to Roberta March, and now that he had made
up his mind to do so, even in spite of certain convic-
tions, it naturally aroused his indignation to find himself suddenly stopped short by such an insignificant
person as Mr. Brandon, a gentleman to whom, in this
affair, he had given no consideration whatever. The
fact that the lady wished to see him added much to
his annoyance and discomfiture. He had no idea what
reason she had for desiring an interview with him, but
whatever she should say to him he intended to follow
by a declaration of his sentiments. He had not the
slightest notion in the world of giving up the prosecution of his suit ; but having been requested not to come
to Midbranch, what was he to do ? He might write to
Miss March, but that would not suit him. In a matter
like this he would wish to adapt his words and his
manner to the moods and disposition of the lady, and
he could not do this in a letter. When he wooed a
woman, he must see her and speak to her. To any
clandestine approach, any whispered conversation

119

beneath her window, he would give no thought. Having been asked by the master of the house not to go there, he would not go. But he would see her, and tell his love; and, more than that, he would win her.

That morning, while waiting for the time to approach when it would be proper for him to go to Mid-branch, he had been reading in a bound volume of an old English magazine, which was one of the five books the cottage possessed, an account of a battle which had interested him very much. The commander of one army had massed his forces along and below the crest of a line of low hills, the extreme right of his line being occupied by a strong force of cavalry. The army opposed to him was much stronger than his own, and it was not long before the battle began to go very much against him. His positions on the left were carried by the combined charge of the larger portion of the enemy's forces, and, in spite of a vigorous resistance, his lines were forced back, down the hill, and into the valley. It was quite evident he could make no stand, and was badly beaten. Thereupon he sent orders to his generals on the left to retreat, in as good order as possible, across a small river in their rear. While this movement was in progress, and the enemy was making the greatest efforts to prevent it, the commander put himself at the head of his cavalry and led them swiftly from the scene of battle. He took them diagonally over the crest of the hill, down the other side, and then, charging with this fresh body of horse upon the rear and camp of the enemy, he swiftly captured the general-in-chief, his staff, and the minister of war, who had come down to see how things were going on. With these important prisoners he dashed away, leaving the acephalous enemy to capture his broken columns if he could.

This was the kind of thing Lawrence Croft would like to do. For an hour or more he puzzled his brains as to how he should make such a cavalry charge, and at last he came to a determination: he would ask Junius Keswick to assist him. There was something odd about this plan which pleased Croft. Keswick was his rival, with the powerful backing of Mr. Brandon and a whole tribe of relatives, and it might naturally be supposed that he was the last man in the world of whom he would ask assistance. But, looking at it from his point of view, Lawrence thought that not only would he be taking no undue advantage of the other in asking him to help him in this matter, but that Keswick ought not and would not object to it. If Miss March really preferred Croft, Keswick should feel himself bound in honor to do everything he could to let the two settle the affair between themselves. This was drawing the point very fine, but Lawrence persuaded himself that if the case were reversed he would not marry a girl who had not chosen another man simply because she had had no opportunity of doing so. He had a strong belief that Keswick was of his way of thinking, and before he went to bed he wrote his rival a note, asking him to call upon him the following day.

Early the next morning the note was carried over to Midbranch by a messenger, who returned, saying that Mr. Keswick had gone away, and that his present address was Howlett's in the same county. This piece of information caused Lawrence Croft to open his eyes very wide. A few days before he had received a letter

from Mrs. Null, written at Howlett's, and now Keswick
had gone there. He had been very much surprised
when he found that the cashier had so successfully
carried on the search for Keswick as to come into the
very county in Virginia where he was; and he intended to write to her that he had no further occasion
for her services; but he had not done so, and here
were the pursuer and the pursued in the same town,
or village, or whatever Howlett's was. He gave Mrs.
Null credit for being one of the best detectives he had
ever heard of; for, apparently, she had not only been
able to successfully track the man she was in search of,
but to find out where he was going, and had reached
the place in question before he did. But he also be-
rated her soundly in his mind for her over-officious-
ness. He had not wished her to swoop down upon the
man, but only to inform him of his whereabouts. The
next thing that would probably happen would be the
appearance of Mrs. Null at the Green Sulphur Springs,
holding Keswick by the collar. He deeply regretted
that he had ever intrusted this young woman with the
investigation, not because he had since met Keswick
himself, but for the reason that she was entirely too
energetic and imprudent. If Keswick should find out
from her that she had been in search of him, and why,
it might bring about a very unpleasant state of affairs.

Croft saw now, quite plainly, what he must do. He
must go to Howlett's as quickly as possible. Perhaps
Keswick and the cashier had not yet met, and, in that
case, all he would have to do would be to remunerate
the young woman and her husband—for she had informed him that she intended to combine this business
with a wedding-tour—and send them off immediately.

He could then have his conference with Keswick there as well as at the Springs. If any mischief had already been done, he did not know what course he might have to pursue, but it was highly necessary for him to be on the spot as soon as possible. He greatly disliked to leave the neighborhood of Roberta March, but his absence would only be temporary.

After an early dinner, he mounted the horse which he had hired from his host of the Springs, and, with a valise strapped behind him, set out for Howlett's. He had made careful inquiries in regard to the road, and after a ride somewhat tiresome to a man not used to such protracted horseback exercise, arrived at his destination about sundown. When he reached the scattered houses which formed, as he supposed, the outskirts of the village, for such he had been told it was, he rode on, but soon found that he had left Howlett's behind him, and that those supposed outskirts was the place itself. Howlett's was nothing, in fact, but a collection of eight or ten houses quite widely separated from one another, and the only one of them which exhibited any public character whatever was the store, a large frame building standing a little back from the road. Turning his horse, Lawrence rode up to the store and inquired if there was any house in the neighborhood where he could get lodging for the night.

The storekeeper, who came out to him, was a very little man, whose appearance recalled to Croft the fact that he had noticed, in this part of the State, a great many men who were extremely tall, and a great many who were extremely small, which peculiarity, he thought, might assist a physiologist in discovering the different effects of hot bread upon different organizations. He was quite as cordial, however, as the biggest, burliest, and jolliest host who ever welcomed a guest to his inn, as he informed Mr. Croft that there was no house in the village which made a business of entertaining strangers, but if he chose to stop with him he would keep him and his horse for the night, and do what he could to make him comfortable.

Lawrence ate supper that night with the storekeeper, his wife, and five of his children; but as he was very hungry, and the meal was a plentiful one, he enjoyed the experience.

"I suppose you're goin' on to Westerville in the mornin'?" said the little host.

"No," replied Croft; "I am not going any farther than this place. Do you know if a gentleman named Keswick arrived here recently?"

"Why, yaas," said the man, "if you mean Junius Keswick."

"Certainly he did," said Mrs. Storekeeper. "He rode through here yesterday, and he stopped at the store to see if we had any of that Lynchburg tobacco he used to smoke when he lived here. He's gone on to his aunt's."

"Where is that?" asked Croft.

"It's about two miles out on the Westerville road," said the little man. "If I'd knowed you wanted to see him, I'd 'a' told you to keep right on, and you could 'a' stopped with Mrs. Keswick overnight."

Lawrence wished to ask some questions about Mrs. Null, but he was afraid to do so lest he might excite suspicions by connecting her with Keswick. If the latter had gone two miles out of town, perhaps she had not yet seen him.

THE LATE MRS. NULL

The room in which Lawrence slept that night was to him a very odd one. It was a long apartment, at one end of which was a clean, comfortable bed, a couple of chairs, and a table on which was a basin and pitcher. At the other end were piles of new-looking boxes, containing groceries of various kinds, rolls of cotton cloth and other dry-goods, and, what attracted his attention more than anything else, a vast number of bright tin cans, bearing on their sides brilliant pictures of tomatoes, peaches, green corn, and other preservable eatables. These were evidently the reserved stores of the establishment, and they were so different from the bedroom decorations to which he was accustomed that it quite pleased Lawrence to think that with all his experience in life he was now lodged in a manner entirely novel to him. As he lay awake looking at the moonlight glittering on the sides of the multitude of cans, the thought came into his mind that this had probably been the room of the Nulls when they were here.

" As this is the only house in the place where travellers are entertained," he said to himself, "of course they must have come to it. And as they are not here now, it is quite plain that they must have gone away. I am very glad of it, especially if they left before Keswick arrived, for their departure probably prevented an awkward situation. But I shall ask the storekeeper no questions about these people. There is no better way of giving inquisitive folk the entrée to your affairs than by asking questions. Of course there was no reason why they should stay here after they had successfully traced Keswick to this part of the country, and every reason, if they wanted to enjoy themselves, why they should go away. But I can't help being sorry that I did not meet the young woman, and have an opportunity of paying her for her trouble, and giving her a few words of advice in regard to her action, or rather non-action, in this matter. She has a fine head for business, but I should like to feel certain that she understands that her business with me is over." And he turned his eyes from the glittering cans, and slept.

The next morning Lawrence Croft rode on to Mrs. Keswick's house, and when he reached the second or inner gate, he saw, on the other side of it, an elderly female, wearing a purple sunbonnet and carrying a purple umbrella. There was something very eccentric about the garb of this elderly personage, and many an inexperienced city man would have taken her for a retired nurse, or some other domestic retainer of the family; but there was a steadfastness in her gaze, and a fire in her eye, which indicated to Lawrence that she was one much more accustomed to give orders than to take them. He raised his hat very politely, and asked if Mr. Keswick was to be found there.

If the commander of the army about whom Mr. Croft had recently been reading had beheld in the earlier stages of the battle a strong, friendly force advancing to his aid, he would not have been more delighted than Lawrence would have been had he known what a powerful ally to his cause stood beneath that purple sunbonnet.

"Do you mean Junius Keswick?" said the old lady.

"Yes, madam," answered Croft.

"He is here, and you will find him at the house."

THE LATE MRS. NULL

The gate was partly open, and Lawrence rode in. The old lady stepped aside to let him pass.

"Do you want to see him on business?" she said.

"How did you know he was here?"

"I inquired at Howlett's, madam."

Mrs. Keswick would have liked to ask some further questions, but there was something about Lawrence's appearance that deterred her.

"You can tie your horse under that tree over there," she said, pointing to a spot more trampled by hoofs than the old lady wished any other portion of her house-yard to be.

When Lawrence had tied his bridle to a hook suspended by a strap from one of the lower branches of the indicated tree, he advanced to the house; and a very much astonished man was he, to see sitting side by side on the porch, Junius Keswick and Mr. Candy's cashier. They were seated in the shade of a mass of honeysuckle vines, and were so busily engaged in conversation that they had not perceived his approach. Even now Lawrence had time to look at them for a few moments before they turned their eyes upon him.

Equally astonished were the two people on the porch, who now rose to their feet. Junius Keswick naturally wondered very much why Mr. Croft should come to see him here; and as for the young lady, she was almost as much terrified as surprised. Had this man come down from New York to swoop upon her cousin? Had it been possible that she could have given him any idea of the whereabouts of Junius? In her last note to him she had been very careful to promise information, but not to give any, hoping thus to gain time to get an insight into the matter, and to keep her

127

cousin out of danger, if, indeed, any danger threatened. But here the pursuer had found Junius in less than a day after she had first met him herself. But when she saw Junius advance and shake hands in a very friendly way with Mr. Croft, her terror began to decrease, although her surprise continued at the same high-water mark; and Keswick found himself in a flood of the same emotion when Croft very politely saluted his cousin by name, which salutation was returned in a manner which indicated that the parties were acquainted.

At first Croft had been prompted to ignore all knowledge of the cashier, and meet her as a stranger, but his better sense prevented this, for how could he know what she had been saying about him?

"I was about to introduce you to my cousin," said Keswick, "but I see that you already know each other."

"I have had the pleasure of meeting Mrs. Null in New York," said Lawrence, to whom the word cousin gave what might be called a more important surprise than anything with which this three-sided interview had yet furnished its participants. He gave a quick glance at the lady, and discovered her very steadfastly gazing at him. "I hope," he said, "that you and your husband have had a very pleasant trip."

"Mr. Null did not come with me," she quietly replied.

Lawrence Croft was a man to whom it gave pleasure to deal with problematic situations, unexpected developments, and the like; but this was too much of a conundrum for him. That the man whose address he had employed this girl to find out should prove to be

"I was about to introduce you to my cousin."

her cousin, and that she should start on her bridal trip without her husband, were points on which his reason had no power to work. One thing, however, he quickly determined upon : he would have an interview with Madam Cashier, and have her explain these mysteries. She was, virtually, his agent, and had no right to conceal from him what she had been doing, and why she had done it.

It was necessary, however, that he should waste no time in thoughts of this kind, but should immediately state to Mr. Keswick the reason of his visit; for it could not be supposed he had called in a merely social way. "I wish to speak to you," he said, "on a little matter of business."

At these words Mrs. Null excused herself, and went into the house. Her mind was troubled as she wondered what the business was which had made this New York gentleman so extraordinarily desirous to find her cousin. Was it anything that would injure Junius? She looked back as she entered the door, but the object of her solicitude was sitting with a face so calm and composed that it showed very plainly he did not expect any communication which would be harmful to him.

"It is a satisfaction," thought Mr. Croft, "a very great satisfaction, that I can enter upon the object of my visit knowing that my affairs and my actions have not been discussed by this gentleman and Mrs. Null."

CHAPTER XII

OLD Mrs. Keswick would willingly have followed the strange gentleman to the house in order to know the object of his visit, but as he had come to see Junius she refrained, for she knew her nephew would not like any appearance of curiosity on her part. Her reception of Junius had been very different indeed from that she had previously accorded him when she declined to be found under the same roof with him. Now he was here under very different auspices, and for him the very plumpest poultry was slain, and everything was done to make him comfortable and willing to stay and become acquainted with his cousin, Mrs. Null. A match between these two young people was the present object of the old lady's existence, and she set about making it with as much determination and confidence as if there had been no such person as Mr. Null. Of this individual she had the most contemptible opinion. She had never asked many questions about him, because, in her intercourse with her niece, she wished, as far as possible, to ignore him. Having mentally pictured him in various mean conditions of life, she had finally settled it in her mind that he was an agent for some patent fertilizer—a man of this kind being a very obnoxious person to her. This avocation, however, constituted in the old lady's mind no excusable reason for his protracted absence; and if ever a wife was deserted, she believed that her niece Annie was such a wife.

"If he should stay away much longer," she said to herself, "we shall have no more trouble in getting a divorce than to have his funeral sermon preached. And if there is any talk of his coming here, or of her going to him, I'll put my foot down on that sort of thing, if I've a foot left to do it with."

When she had first perceived the approach of Mr. Croft, a fear had seized her that this might be the recreant husband, but the gentlemanly appearance of the stranger soon dispelled this idea from her prejudiced mind. Apart from the fact that she had no business at the house with her nephew's visitor, she had positive business in the garden with old Uncle Isham, and there she repaired. There was some work to be done in regard to a flower-pit, in which some of her choicest plants were to be domiciled during the winter, and this she wished personally to oversee. Although the autumn was well advanced, the day was somewhat warm; and as the pair whom Mr. Croft had seen on the porch had been glad to shelter themselves in the shade of the honeysuckle vines, so Mrs. Keswick seated herself on a little bench behind a large arbor, still covered by heavy vines, which stood on the boundary line between the garden and the front yard, and opened on the latter. This bench, which was always shady in the morning, she had had placed there that she might comfortably direct the labors of old Isham, the boy Plez, or whoever, for the time being, happened to be her gardener.

Mr. Croft did not immediately begin the statement

of the business which had brought him to see Junius Keswick. Several windows of the house opened on the porch, and he did not wish what he had to say to be heard by any one except the person he was addressing. "I desire to talk to you on some private matters," he said. "Could we not walk a little away from the house?"

"Certainly," said Junius, rising. "We will step over to that arbor by the garden. We shall be quite comfortable and secluded there. This is the place," said Junius, as they seated themselves in the arbor, "where, when a boy, I used to come to smoke. My aunt did not allow this diversion, but I managed to do a good deal of puffing before I was found out."

"Then you used to live here?" asked Croft.

"Oh, yes," said Keswick; "my parents died when I was quite a little fellow, and my aunt had charge of me until I had grown up."

"Was that your aunt whom I met at the gate? There was something about her bearing and general appearance which greatly interested me."

"She is a most estimable lady," returned Junius. And not wishing further to discuss his relative, he added: "And now, what is it, sir, that I can have the pleasure of doing for you?"

"The matter regards Miss March," said Croft.

"I presumed so," remarked the other.

"I will state it as briefly as possible," continued Croft. "In consequence of your visit to me at the Springs, I set out, the day before yesterday, to make another attempt to call on Miss March, the first one having been frustrated, as you may remember, by the information we received at the gate in regard to Miss

March's indisposition, which, as I have heard nothing more of it, I hope was of no importance."

"Of none whatever," said Junius.

"When I was within a mile or so of Midbranch," continued Croft, "I met Mr. Brandon, who requested me not to come to his house, and, in fact, to cease my visits altogether."

"What!" cried Keswick, very much surprised. "That is not at all like Mr. Brandon. What reason could he have for treating you in such a manner?"

"The very best in the world," said Croft. "Having, as the guardian of his niece, asked me the object of my visit to Miss March, and having been informed by me that it was my intention to propose matrimony to the lady, he requested that I would not visit at his house."

"On what ground did he base his objection to your visit?" asked Keswick.

"He made no objection to me; he simply stated that he did not desire me to come, because he wished his niece to marry you."

"Quite plainly spoken," remarked Keswick.

"Nothing could be more so," replied Croft. "I could not expect any one to be franker with me than he was. He went on to inform me that a match between the lady and yourself was greatly desired by the whole family connection, with a single exception, which, however, he did not name, and while he gave me to understand that he had no reason to fear, that, so far as the lady was concerned, my proposal would interfere with your prospects, still, were it known that there was another aspirant in the field, a very undesirable state of things might ensue. What this state of affairs was he did not state, but I presume it had something to do with the exceptional opposition to which he referred."

"And what did you say to all that?" asked Junius.

"I said very little. When a man asks me not to come to his house, I don't go. But, nevertheless, I have fully made up my mind to propose to Miss March as soon as I can get an opportunity. I have nothing to do with family arrangements or family opposition. You have told me that you are not engaged to her, and I am going to try to be engaged to her. She is the one to decide this matter. And now I have called upon you, Mr. Keswick, to see if there is any way in which you can assist me in obtaining an interview with Miss March."

"Don't you think," said Junius, "that it is rather cool in you to ask me to assist you in this matter?"

"Not at all," replied the other. "If it had not been for you I should now be in New York, with no thought of present proposals of marriage. But you came to me, and insisted that I should see the lady."

"That was simply because she had expressed a strong desire to see you."

"Very good," said Lawrence. "I tried to go to her, as you know, and was prevented. Now all I ask of you is to help me to do what you so strongly urged me to do. There is nothing particularly cool in that, I think."

Keswick did not immediately reply. "I am not sure," he said, "that Miss March still wishes to see you."

"That may be," replied Croft, speaking a little warmly. "None of us exactly know what she thinks or wishes. But I want to find out what she thinks about me by distinctly asking her. And I should suppose you would consider it to your advantage, as well as mine, that I should do so."

"I have my own opinion on that point," said Keswick, "which it is not necessary to discuss at present. If I were to assist you to an interview with Miss March it would be on the lady's account, not on yours or mine. But apart from the fact that I do not know if she now desires an interview, I would not do anything that would offend or annoy Mr. Brandon."

"I don't ask that of you," said Croft, "but couldn't you use your influence with him to give me a fair chance with the lady? That is all I ask, and, whether she accepts me or rejects me, I am sure everybody ought to be satisfied."

Keswick smiled. "You don't leave any margin for sentiment," he said, "but I suppose it is just as well to deal with this matter in a practical way. I do not think, however, that any influence I can exert on Mr. Brandon would induce him to allow you to address his niece if he is opposed to it, and I am sure he would have a very strange opinion of me if I attempted such a thing. At present I do not see that I can help you at all, but I will think over the matter, and we will talk of it again."

"Thank you," said Croft, rising. "And when shall I call upon you to hear your decision?"

It was rather difficult for Junius Keswick to answer a question like this on the spur of the moment. He arose and walked with Croft out of the arbor. His first impulse, as a Virginia gentleman, was to invite his visitor to stay at the house until the matter should be settled, but he did not know what extraordinary freak on the part of his aunt might be caused by such an invitation. But before he had decided what to say, they were met by Mrs. Keswick coming from the garden. Junius thereupon presented Mr. Croft, who was welcomed by the old lady with extended hand and exceeding cordiality.

"I am very glad," she said, "to meet a friend of my nephew. But where are you going, sir? Certainly not towards your horse! You must stay and dine with us."

Lawrence hesitated. He had no claims on the hospitality of these people, but he wished very much to have an opportunity to speak to Mrs. Null. "Thank you," he said, "but I am staying down here at the village, and it is but a short ride."

"Staying at Howlett's!" exclaimed Mrs. Keswick. "At which hotel, may I ask?"

Lawrence laughed. "I am stopping with the storekeeper," he said.

"That settles it!" said the old lady, giving her umbrella a jab into the ground. "Tom Peckett's accommodations may be good enough for pedlers and travelling agents, but they are not fit for gentlemen, especially one of my nephew's friends. You must stay with us, sir, as long as you are in this neighborhood. I insist upon it."

Junius was very much astonished at his aunt's speech and manner. The old lady was not at all inhospitable; so far was it otherwise the case that, rather than deprive an objectionable visitor of the shelter of her roof, she would go from under it herself; but he had never known her to "gush" in this manner upon a stranger.

THE LATE MRS. NULL

He now felt at liberty, however, to obey his own impulses, and urged Mr. Croft to stay with them.

"You are very kind indeed," said Lawrence, "and I shall be glad to defer for the present my return to my 'hotel.' This will give me t'.e additional pleasure of renewing my acquaintance with Mrs. Null."

"What!" exclaimed Mrs. Keswick, "do you know her, too? And to think of your stopping at Peckett's! Your home, sir, while you stay in these parts, is here."

Before the three reached the house, Mrs. Keswick had inquired how long Mr. Croft had known her niece; and had discovered, much to her disappointment, that he had never met Mr. Null.

Shortly after the arrival at the house of the gentleman on horseback, little Plez ran into the kitchen, where Letty was engaged in preparing vegetables for dinner.

"Who d'ye think is done come?" he exclaimed. "Miss Annie's husband! Jes rid up to de house."

"Dat so?" cried Letty, dropping into her lap the knife and the potato she was peeling. "Well, truly, when things does happen in dis worl' dey comes all in a lump. None ob de fam'ly been nigh de house fur ebber so long; an' den, 'long comes Mahs' Junius hisse'f, an' Miss Annie, dat's been away sence she was a chile, an' ole Mr. Brandon, wot Uncle Isham say ain't been h'yar fur years an' years; an' now Miss Annie's husband comes kitin' up! An' dar's ole Aun' Patsy wot says dat if dat gemman ebber come h'yar she want to know it fus' thing. She was dreffle p'inted about dat. An' now, look h'yar, you Plez, jes you cut round to your Aun' Patsy's, an' tell her Miss Annie's husband's done come."

"Whar ole miss?" inquired Plez.   "She 'sleep?"

"No, she mighty wide awake," said Letty.   "But you take dem knives an' dat board an' brick, an' run down to de branch to clean 'em.   An' when you gits dar, you jes slip along 'hind de bushes till you's got ter de cohn-fiel', an' den you cut 'cross dar to Aun' Patsy's.   An' don' you stop no time dar, fur if ole miss finds you's done gone, she'll chop you up wid dem knives."

Plez was quite ready for a reckless dash of this kind, and in less than twenty minutes old Patsy was informed that Mr. Null had arrived.   The old woman was much affected by the information.   She was uneasy and restless, and talked a good deal to herself, occasionally throwing out a moan or a lament in the direction of her "son Tom's yaller boy Bob's chile." The crazy-quilt, which was not yet finished, though several pieces had been added since we last saw it, was laid aside ; and by the help of the above-mentioned great-granddaughter the old hair trunk was hauled out and opened.   Over this hoard of treasures Aunt Patsy spent nearly two hours, slowly taking up the various articles it contained, turning them over, mumbling over them, and mentally referring many of them to periods which had become historic.   At length she pulled out from one of the corners of the trunk a pair of very little blue morocco shoes tied together by their strings.   These she took into her lap, and, shortly afterwards, had the trunk locked and pushed back into its place.   The shoes, having been thoroughly examined through her great iron-bound spectacles, were thrust under the mattress of her bed.

That evening Uncle Isham stepped in to see the

old woman, who was counteracting the effects of the cool evening air by sitting as close as possible to the remains of the fire which had cooked the supper. She was very glad to see him. She wanted somebody to whom she could unburden her mind.

"Wot you got to say 'bout Miss Annie's husband," she asked, "wot done come to-day ?"

"Was dat him ?" exclaimed the old man. "Nobody tole me dat."

This was true, for the good-natured Letty, having discovered the mistake that had been made, had concluded to say nothing about it, and to keep away from Aunt Patsy's for a few days, until the matter should be forgotten.

"Well, I 'spec' Miss Annie's mighty glad to git him back ag'in," continued the old man, after a moment's reflection. "He's right much of a nice-lookin' gemman. I seed him dis ebenin' a-ridin' wid Mahs' Junius."

"P'r'aps Miss Annie is glad," said the old woman, "cos she don' know. But I ain't."

"Wot's de reason fur dat ?" inquired Isham.

"It's a pow'ful dreffle thing dat Miss Annie's husband's done come down h'yar. He don' know ole miss."

"Wot's de matter wid ole miss ?" asked Isham, in a quick tone.

"She done talk to me 'bout him," said the old woman. "She done tole me jes wot she think ob him. She hate him from he heel up. I dunno wot she'll do to him now she got him. Mighty great pity fur pore Miss Annie dat he efer come h'yar."

"Ole miss ain't gwine to do nuffin to him," said Isham, in a gruff and troubled tone.

THE LATE MRS. NULL

"Don' you b'lieve dat," said Aunt Patsy. "When ole miss don' like a pusson, dat pusson had better look out. But I ain't gwine to be sottin' h'yar an' see mis'ry comin' to Miss Annie."

"Wot you gwine to do?" asked Isham.

"I'se gwine to speak my min' to ole miss. I'se gwine to tell her not to do no kunjerin' to Miss Annie's husban'. She gwine to hurt dat little gal more'n she hurt anybody else."

Old Isham sat looking into the fire with a very worried and anxious expression on his face. He was intensely loyal to his mistress, aware as he was of her shortcomings, or rather her long-goings. Although he felt a good deal of fear that there might be some truth in Aunt Patsy's words, he was very sure that if she took it upon herself to give warning or reproof to old Mrs. Keswick, a storm would ensue; and where the lightning would strike he did not know. "You better look out, Aun' Patsy," he said. "You an' ole miss been mighty good fr'en's fur a pow'ful long time, an' now don' you go gittin' yourse'f in no fraction wid her, jes as you 'bout to die."

"Ain't gwine to die," said the old woman, "till I done tole her wot's on my min'."

"Aun' Patsy," said Uncle Isham, after gazing silently in the fire for a minute or two, "dar was a brudder wot come up from 'Melia County to de las' big preachin', an' he tole in his sarment a par'ble wot I b'lieve will 'ply fus'-rate to dis 'casion. I'se gwine to tell you dat."

"Go 'long wid it," said Aunt Patsy.

"Well, den," said Isham, "dar was once a cullud angel wot went up to de gate ob heaben to git in. He

140

didn't know nuffin 'bout de ways ob de place, bein' a strahnger, an' when he see all de white angels a-crowdin' in at de gate where Sent Peter was a-settin', he sorter looked round to see if dar warn't no gate wot he might go in at. Den ole Sent Peter he sings out : 'Look h'yar, uncle, whar you gwine? Dar ain't no cullud gal'ry in dis 'stablishment. You's got to come in dis same gate wid de oder folks.' So de cullud angel he come up to de gate, but he kin'er hung back till de oders had got in. Jes den' long comes a white angel on hossback, wot was in a dreffle hurry to git in to de gate. De cullud angel he mighty p'lite, an' he went up an' tuk de hoss, an' when de white angel had got down an' gone in, he went roun' lookin' fur a tree to hitch him to. But when he went back ag'in to de gate, Sent Peter had jes shet it, and was lockin' it up wid a big padlock. He jes looks ober de gate at de cullud angel an' he says : 'No 'mittance ahfter six o'clock.' An' den he go in to his supper."

"An' wot dat cullud angel do den?" asked Eliza, who had been listening breathlessly to this narrative.

"Dunno," said Isham, "but I reckon de debbil come 'long in de night an' tuk him off. Dar's a lesson in dis h'yar par'ble wot 'u'd do you good to clap to your heart, Aun' Patsy. Don' you be gwine roun' tryin' to help oder people jes as you is all ready to go inter de gate ob heaben. Ef you try any ob dat dar foolishness, de fus' thing you know you'll find dat gate shet."

"Is dat your 'Melia County par'ble?" asked the old woman.

"Dat's it," answered Isham.

"Reckon dat country's better fur 'bacca dan fur par'bles," grunted Aunt Patsy.

141

CHAPTER XIII

LAWRENCE CROFT had no idea of leaving the neighborhood of Howlett's until Keswick had made up his mind what he was going to do, and until he had had a private talk with Mrs. Null; and, as it was quite evident that the family would be offended if a visitor to them should lodge at Peckett's store, he accepted the invitation to spend the night at the Keswick house; and in the afternoon Junius rode with him to Howlett's, where he got his valise and paid his account.

But no opportunity occurred that day for a tête-à-tête with Mrs. Null. Keswick was with him nearly all the afternoon; and in the evening the family sat together in the parlor, where the conversation was a general one, occasionally very much brightened by some of the caustic remarks of the old lady in regard to particular men and women, as well as society at large. Of course he had many opportunities of judging, to the best of his capacity, of certain phases of character appertaining to Mr. Candy's cashier; and, among other things, he came to the conclusion that probably she was a young woman who would get up early in the morning, and he, therefore, determined to do that thing himself, and see if he could not have

142

a talk with her before the rest of the family were astir.

Early rising was not one of Croft's accustomed habits, but the next morning he arose a good hour before breakfast-time. He found the lower part of the house quite deserted, and when he went out on the porch he was glad to button up his coat, for the morning air was very cool. While walking up and down with his hands in his pockets, and looking in at the front door every time he passed it, in hopes that he might see Mrs. Null coming down the stairs, he was greeted with a cheery "Good morning" by a voice in the front yard. Turning hastily, he beheld Mrs. Keswick, wearing her purple sunbonnet, but without her umbrella.

"Glad you like to be up betimes, sir," said she. "That's my way, and I find it pays. Nobody works as well, and I don't believe the plants and stock grow as well, while we are asleep."

Lawrence replied that in the city he did not get up so early, but that the morning air in the country was very fine.

"And pretty sharp, too," said Mrs. Keswick. "Come down here in the sunshine, and you will find it pleasanter. Step back a little this way, sir," she said, when Lawrence had joined her, "and give me your opinion of that locust-tree by the corner of the porch. I am thinking of having it cut down. Locusts are very apt to get diseased inside, and break off, and I am afraid that one will blow over some day and fall on the house."

Lawrence said he thought it looked like a very good tree, and it would be a pity to lose the shade it made.

"I might plant one of another sort," said the old

143

lady, "but trees grow too slow for old people, though plenty fast enough for young ones. I reckon I'll let it stand awhile yet. You were talking last night of Midbranch, sir. There used to be fine trees there, though it's many years since I've seen them. Have you been long acquainted with the family there?"

Lawrence replied that he had known Miss March a good while, having met her in New York.

"She is said to be a right smart young lady," said Mrs. Keswick, "well educated, and has travelled in Europe. I am told that she is not only a regular town lady, but that she makes a first-rate housekeeper when she is down here in the country."

Lawrence replied that he had no doubt that all this was very true.

"I have never seen her," continued the old lady, "for there has not been much communication between the two families of late years, although they used to be intimate enough. But my nephew and niece have been away a great deal, and old people can't be expected to do much in the way of visiting. But I have a notion," she said, after gazing a few moments in a reflective way at the corner of the house, "that it would be well now to be a little more sociable again. My niece has no company here of her own sex, except me, and I think it would do her good to know a young lady like Miss March. Mr. Brandon has asked me to let Annie come there, but I think it would be a great deal better for his niece to visit us. Mrs. Null is the latest comer."

Lawrence, speaking much more earnestly than when discussing the locust-tree, replied that he thought this would be quite proper.

THE LATE MRS. NULL

"I think I may invite her to come here next week," said Mrs. Keswick, still meditatively and without apparent regard to the presence of Croft, "probably on Friday, and ask her to spend a week. And, by the way, sir," she said, turning to her companion, "if you are still in this part of the country I would be glad to have you ride over and stay a day or two while Miss March is here. I will have a little party of young folks in honor of Mrs. Null. I have done nothing of the kind for her, so far."

Lawrence said he had no doubt that he would stay at the Green Sulphur a week or two longer, and that he would be most happy to accept Mrs. Keswick's kind invitation.

They then moved towards the house, but, suddenly stopping, as if she had just thought of something, Mrs. Keswick remarked : "I shall be obliged to you, sir, if you will not say anything about this little plan of mine just now. I have not spoken of it to any one, having scarcely made up my mind to it, and I suppose I should not have mentioned it to you if we had not been talking about Midbranch. There is nothing I hate so much as to have people hear I am going to give them an invitation, or that I am going to do anything, in fact, before I have fully made up my mind about it."

Lawrence assured her that he would say nothing on the subject, and she promised to send him a note to the Green Sulphur, in case she finally determined on having the little company at her house.

"Now," triumphantly thought Croft, "it matters not what Keswick decides to do, for I don't need his assistance. An elderly angel in a purple sunbonnet has come to my aid. She is about to do ever so much

145

more for me than I could expect of him, and I prefer her assistance to that of my rival. Altogether it is the most unexpected piece of good luck."

After breakfast there came to Lawrence the opportunity of a private conference with Mrs. Null. He was standing alone on the porch when she came out of the door with her hat on and a basket in her hand, and said she was going to see a very old colored woman who lived in the neighborhood, who was considered a very interesting personage ; and perhaps he would like to go there with her. Nothing could suit Croft better than this, and off they started.

As soon as they were outside the yard gate the lady remarked : " I have been trying hard to give you a chance to talk to me when the others were not by. I knew you must be perfectly wild to ask me what all this meant—why I never told you that Mr. Keswick was my cousin, and the rest of it."

" I can't say," said Lawrence, " that I am absolutely untamed and ferocious in regard to the matter, but I do really wish very much that you would give me some explanation of your very odd doings. In fact, that is the only thing that now keeps me here."

" I thought so," said Mrs. Null. " As I supposed you had got through with your business with Junius, I did not wish to detain you here any longer than was necessary."

" Thank you," said Lawrence.

" You are welcome," she said. " And when I saw you standing on the porch by yourself, the idea of being generous to old Aunt Patsy came into my mind. And here we are. Now, what do you want to know first ? "

" Well," said Mr. Croft, " I would like very much to

know how a young lady like you came to be Mr. Candy's cashier."

"I supposed you would want to know that," she said. "It's a dreadfully long story, and as it is a strictly family matter I had almost made up my mind last night that I ought not to tell it to you at all; but as I don't know how much you are mixed up with the family, I afterwards thought it best, for my own sake, to explain the matter to you. So I will give you the principal points. My mother was a sister of Mrs. Keswick, and Junius's mother was another sister. Both his parents died when he was a boy, and Aunt Keswick brought him up. My mother died here when I was quite small, and I stayed until I was eight years old. Aunt Keswick and my father were not very good friends, and when she came to look upon me as entirely her own child, and wished to deprive him of all rights and privileges as a parent, he resented it very much, and at last took me away. I don't remember exactly how this was done, but I know there was a tremendous quarrel, and my father and aunt never met again.

"He took me to New York; and there we lived very happily until about two years ago, when my father died. He was a lawyer by profession, but at that time held a salaried position in a railroad company, and when he died, of course our income ceased. The money that was left did not last very long, and then I had to decide what I was to do. It would have been natural for me to go to my only relatives, Aunt Keswick and Junius. But my father had been so opposed to my aunt having anything to do with me that I could not bear to go to her. He had really

been so much afraid that she would try to win me
away from him, or in some way gain possession of me,
that he would not even let her know our address, and
never answered the few letters from her which reached
him, and which, he told me, were nothing but demands
that her sister's child should be given back to her.
Junius had written to me, how many times I do not
know, but two letters had come to me that were very
good and affectionate, quite different from my aunt's;
but even these my father would not let me answer; it
would be all the same thing, he said, as if I opened
communication with my Aunt Keswick.

"Therefore, out of respect to my father, and also in
accordance with my own wishes, I gave up all idea of
coming down here, and went to work to support myself. I tried several things, and at last, through a
friend of my father, who was a regular customer of
Mr. Candy, I got the position of cashier in the Information Shop. It was an awfully queer place, but the
work was very easy, and I soon got used to it. Then
you came making inquiries for an address. At first I
did not know that the person you wanted was Junius
Keswick, and my cousin, but after I began to look into
the matter I found that it must be he who you were
after. Then I became very much troubled, for I liked
Junius, who was the only one of my blood whom I had
any reason to care for; and when one sees a person
setting a detective—for it is all the same thing—upon
the track of another person, one is very apt to think
that some harm is intended to the person that is being
looked up. I did not know what business Junius was
in, nor what his condition was, but even if he had been
doing wrong, I did not wish you to find him until I

had first seen him, and then, if I found you could do him any harm, I would warn him to keep out of your way."

"Do you think that was fair treatment of me?" asked Croft.

"You were nothing to me, and Junius was a great deal," she answered. "And yet I think I was fair enough. The only money you paid was what Mr. Candy charged; and when I spoke of receiving money for my services when the affair was finished I only did it that it might all be more businesslike, and that you should not drop me and set somebody else looking after Junius. That was the great thing I was afraid of, so I did all I could to make you satisfied with me."

"I don't see how your conscience could allow you to do all this," said Croft.

"My conscience was very much pleased with me," was the answer. "What I did was a stratagem, and perfectly fair, too. If I had found that it was right for you to see Junius, I would have done everything I could to help you communicate with him. But when I did at last see him, down you swooped upon us before I had an opportunity of saying a word about you."

"Your marriage was a very fortunate thing for you," said Mr. Croft, "for if it had not been for that I should never have allowed you to go about the country looking up a gentleman in my behalf. But how did you get over your repugnance to your aunt?"

"I didn't get over it," she said; "I conquered it, for I found that this was the most likely place to meet Junius. And Aunt Keswick has certainly treated me in the kindest manner, although she is very angry about Mr. Null. But when I first came, and she did not know who I was, she behaved in the most extraordinary manner."

"What did she do?" asked Croft.

"Never you mind," she answered, with a little laugh. "You can't expect to know all the family affairs."

They had now arrived at Aunt Patsy's cabin, and Mrs. Null entered, followed at a little distance by Croft. The old woman had seen them as they were walking along the road, and her little black eyes sparkled with peculiar animation behind her great spectacles. Her granddaughter happened not to be at home, but Aunt Patsy got up, and with her apron rubbed off the bottoms of two chairs, which she placed in convenient positions for her expected visitors. When they came in they found her in a very perturbed condition. She answered Mrs. Null's questions with a very few words and a great many grunts, and kept her eyes fixed nearly all the time upon Mr. Croft, endeavoring to find out, perhaps, if he had yet been subjected to any kind of conjuring.

When all the questions which young people generally put to old servants had been asked by Mrs. Null, and Croft had made as many remarks as might have been expected of him in regard to the age and recollections of this interesting old negress, Aunt Patsy began to be much more disturbed, fearing that the interview was about to come to an end. She actually got up and went to the back door to look for Eliza.

"Do you want her?" anxiously inquired Mrs. Null, going to the old woman's side.

"Yaas, I wants her," said Aunt Patsy. "I 'spec' she at Aggy's house,—dat cabin ober dar,—but I can't holler loud 'nuf to make her h'yere me."

THE LATE MRS. NULL

"I'll run over there and tell her you want her," said Mrs. Null, stepping out of the door.

"Dat's a good chile," said Aunt Patsy, with more warmth than she had yet exhibited. "Dat's your own mudder's good chile!" And then she turned quickly into the room.

Croft had risen as if he were about to follow Mrs. Null, or, at least, to see where she had gone. But Aunt Patsy stopped him. "Jes you stay h'yar one little minute," she said hurriedly. "I got one word to say to you, sah." And she stood up before him as erect as she could, fixing her great spectacles directly upon him. "You look out, sah, fur ole miss," she said, in a voice naturally shrill, but now heavily handicapped by age and emotion; "ole Miss Keswick, I means. She boun' to do you harm, sah. She tole me so wid her own mouf."

"Mrs. Keswick!" exclaimed Croft. "Why, you must be mistaken, good aunty. She can have no ill feelings towards me."

"Don' you b'lieve dat!" said the old woman. "Don' you b'lieve one word ob dat! She hate you, sah, she hate you! She not gwine to tell you dat. She make you think she like you fus'-rate, an' den de nex' thing you knows, she kunjer you, an' shribble up de siners ob your legs, an' gib you mis'ry in your back, wot you nebber git rid ob no mo'. Can't tell you nuffin else now, for h'yar comes Miss Annie," she added hurriedly, and, stepping to the bedside, she drew from under the mattress a pair of little blue shoes, tied together by their strings. "Jes you take dese h'yar shoes," she said, "an' ef ebber you think ole miss gwine to kunjer you, jes you hol' up dem shoes right afore her face. Dar, now, stuff 'em in your pocket. Don' you tell Miss Annie wot I done say to you. 'Member dat, sah. It 'u'd kill her, shuh."

At this moment Mrs. Null entered, just as the shoes had been slipped into the side-pocket of Mr. Croft's coat by the old woman. And as she did so she whispered, in a tone that could not but have its effect upon him, "Now, nebber tell her, honey."

"Here is Eliza," said Mrs. Null, as she came in, followed by the great-granddaughter. "And I think," she said to Mr. Croft, "it is time for us to go. Goodby, Aunt Patsy. You can send back the basket by Eliza."

When the two left the cabin, Croft walked thoughtfully for a few moments, wondering what in the world the old woman could have meant by her strange words and gift to him. Concluding, however, that they could have been nothing but the drivellings of weak-minded old age, he dismissed them from his mind and turned his attention to his companion. "We were speaking," he said, "of Mr. Null. Do you expect him shortly?"

"Well, no," said the lady. "I can't say that I do."

"That is odd," said Lawrence. "I thought this was your wedding-journey."

"So it is, in a measure," said she, "but there is no necessity of his coming here. Didn't I tell you that my aunt was opposed to the marriage?"

"But she might as well make up her mind to it now," he said.

"She is not in the habit of making up her mind to things she doesn't like. Do you know," she added, looking around with a half-smile, as if she took pleasure in astonishing him, "that Aunt Keswick is going to try to have us divorced?"

"What!" exclaimed Croft. "Divorced! Is there any ground for it?"

"She has other matrimonial plans for me, that's all."

"What an extraordinary individual she must be!" he exclaimed. "But she can never carry out such a ridiculous scheme as that."

"I don't know," she said. "She has already consulted Mr. Brandon on the subject."

"What nonsense!" cried Croft. "If you and Mr. Null are satisfied, nobody else has anything to do with it."

"Mr. Null and I are of one mind," said she, "and agree perfectly. But don't you think it is a terrible thing to know you must always face an irritated aunt?"

"Oh," said Croft, looking around at her very coldly and sternly, "I begin to see. I suppose a separation would improve your prospects in life. But it can't be done if your husband is opposed to it."

"Mr. Croft," said the lady, her face flushing a good deal, "you have no right to speak to me in that way, and attribute such motives to me. No matter whom I had married, I would never give him up for the sake of money, or a farm, or anything you think my aunt could give me."

"I beg your pardon," said Croft, "if I made a mistake, but I don't see what else I could infer from your remarks."

"My remarks," said she, "were—well, they have a different meaning from what you supposed." She walked on in silence for a few moments, and then, looking up to her companion, she said: "I have a great mind to tell you something, if you will promise, at least for the present, not to breathe it to a living soul."

Instantly the lookout on the bow of Lawrence Croft's life action called out: "Breakers ahead!" and almost instantly its engine was stopped, and every faculty of its commander was on the alert. "I do not know," he said, "that I am entitled to your confidence. Would it be of any advantage to you to tell me what you propose?"

"It would be of advantage, and you are entitled," she added quickly. "It is about Mr. Null, and you ought to know it, for you instigated my wedded life."

"I instigated!" exclaimed Mr. Croft. And then he stopped short, both in his speech and walk.

"Yes," said the lady, stopping also, and turning to face him, "you did, and you ought to remember it. You said if I had a husband to travel about with me you would like very much to employ me in the search for Mr. Keswick, and it was solely on that account that I went and got married."

Observing the look of blank and utter amazement on his face, she smiled, and said: "Please don't look so horribly astonished. Mr. Null is void."

As she made this remark the lady looked up at her companion with a smile and an expression of curiosity as to how he would take the announcement. Lawrence gazed blankly at her for a moment, and then he broke into a laugh. "You don't mean to say," he exclaimed, "that Mr. Null is an imaginary being?"

"Entirely so," she replied. "My dear Freddy is nothing but a fanciful idea, with no attribute whatever except the name."

THE LATE MRS. NULL

"You are a most extraordinary young person," said Lawrence,—"almost as extraordinary as your aunt. What in the world made you think of doing such a thing? and why do you wish to keep up the delusion among your relatives, even so far as to drive your aunt to the point of getting you divorced from your airy husband?" And he laughed again.

"I told you how I came to think of it," she said, as they walked on again. "It was very plain that if I wanted to travel about as your agent I must be married, and I have found a husband quite a protection and an advantage, even when he doesn't go about with me; and as to keeping up the delusion, as you call it, in my own family, I have found that to be absolutely necessary, at least for the present. My aunt, even when I was a little girl, determined to take my marriage into her own hands; and since I have returned to her, this desire has come up again in the most astonishing way. It is her principal subject of conversation with me. Were it not for the protection which my dear Freddy Null gives me I should be thrown bodily into the arms of the person whom my aunt has selected, and he would be obliged to take me, whether he wanted to or not, or be cast forth forever. So you see how important it is that my aunt should think I am married; and I do hope you will not tell anybody about Mr. Null."

"Of course I will keep your secret," said Croft; "you may rely upon that. But don't you think—do you believe that this sort of thing is altogether right?"

She did not answer for a few moments, and then she said: "I suppose you must consider me a very deceptive sort of person, but you should remember that these things were not done for my own good, and, as far as I can see, they were the only things that could be done. Do you suppose I was going to let you pounce down on my cousin and do him some injury? For, as you kept your object such a secret, I did not suppose it could be anything but an injury you intended him."

" A fine opinion of me ! " said Croft.

" And then, do you suppose," she continued, " that I would allow my aunt to quarrel with Junius and disinherit him, as she says she will should he decline to marry me? I expected to drop my married name when I came here, but I had not been with my aunt fifteen minutes before I saw that it would never do for me to be a single woman while I stayed with her ; and so I kept my Freddy by me. I did not intend, at all, to tell you all these things about my cousin, and I only did it because I did not wish you to think that I was a sly, mean creature, deceiving others for my own good."

" Well," said Croft, " although I can't say you are right in making your relatives believe you are married when you are not, still, I see you had very fair reasons for what you did, and you certainly showed a great deal of ingenuity and pluck in carrying out your remarkable schemes. By the way," he continued, somewhat hesitatingly, " I am in your debt for your services to me."

" Not a bit of it ! " she exclaimed quickly. " I never did a thing for you. It was all for myself, or, rather, for my cousin. The only money due was that which you paid to Mr. Candy before I took charge of the matter."

THE LATE MRS NULL

Lawrence felt that this was rather a sore subject with his companion, and he dropped it. "Do you still hold the position of cashier in the Information Shop?"

"No," she said. "When I started out on my lonely wedding-tour I gave up that, and if I should go back to New York, I do not think I should want to take it again."

"Do you propose soon to return to New York?" he asked.

"No; at least, I have made no plans in regard to it. I think it would grieve my aunt very much if I were to go away from her now, and as long as I have Mr. Null to protect me from her matrimonial schemes, I am glad to stay with her. She is very kind to me."

"I think you are entirely right in deciding to stay here," he said, looking around at her, and contrasting in his mind the bright-faced and somewhat plump young person walking beside him with the thin-faced girl in black whom he had seen behind the cashier's desk.

"Now," said she, with a vivacious little laugh, "I have poured out my whole soul before you, and, in return, I want you to gratify a curiosity which is fairly eating me up. Why were you so anxious to find my cousin Junius? And how did you happen to come here the very day after he arrived? And, more than that, how was it that you had seen him at Midbranch so recently? You were talking about it last night. It couldn't have been my letter from Howlett's that brought you down here?"

"No," said Lawrence; "my meeting with Mr. Keswick at Midbranch was entirely accidental. When I arrived there, a few days ago, I had no reason to

157

suppose that I should meet him. But I must ask you to excuse me from giving my reasons for wishing to find your cousin, and for coming to see him here. The matter between us has now become one of no importance, and will be dropped."

The lady's face flushed. "Oh, indeed!" she said. And during the short remainder of their walk to the house she made no further remark.

CHAPTER XIV

WHEN Lawrence and his companion reached the house, they found on the porch Mrs. Keswick and her nephew; and after a little general conversation, the latter remarked to Mr. Croft that he had found it would not be in his power to attend to that matter he had spoken of; to which Croft replied that he was very much obliged to him for thinking of it, and that it was of no consequence at all, as he would probably make other arrangements. He then stated that he would be obliged to return to the Green Sulphur Springs that day, and that, as it was a long ride, he would like to start as soon as his horse could be brought to him. But this procedure was condemned utterly by the old lady, who insisted that Mr. Croft should not leave until after dinner, which meal should be served earlier than usual in order to give him plenty of time to get to the Springs before dark; and as Lawrence had nothing to oppose to her very urgent protest, he consented to stay. Before dinner was ready he found out why the protest was made. The old lady took him aside and made inquiries of him in regard to Mr. Null. He had already informed her that he was not acquainted with that gentleman; but she thought, as Mr. Croft seemed to be going about the country a good deal, he might possibly meet with her niece's husband, and, if he should do so, she would be very glad to have him become acquainted with him.

To this Lawrence replied with much gravity that he would be happy to do so.

"Mr. Null has not yet come to my house," said Mrs. Keswick, "and it is very natural that one should desire to know the husband of her only niece, who is, or should be, the same as a daughter to her."

"A very natural wish, indeed," said Lawrence.

"I am not quite sure in what business Mr. Null is engaged," she continued, "and although I asked my niece about it, she answered in a very evasive way, which makes me think his occupation is one she is not proud of. I have reason to suppose, however, that he is an agent for the sale of some fertilizing compound."

At this Lawrence could not help smiling very broadly.

"It may appear very odd and ridiculous to you," she said, "that a person connected with my family should be engaged in a business like that, for those fertilizers, as you ought to know, are all humbugs of the vilest kind. The only time I bought any it took my whole wheat crop to pay for it, and as for the clover I got afterwards, a grasshopper could have eaten the whole of it. I am afraid he didn't tell her his business before he married her, and I'm glad she's ashamed of it. As far as I can find out, it does not seem as if Mr. Null has any intention of coming here for some time ; and, as I said before, I do very much want to know something about him—that is, from a disinterested outsider. One cannot expect a recently married young woman to give a correct account of her husband."

"I do not believe," said Mr. Croft, "that there is any probability that I shall ever meet the gentleman —our walks in life being so different."

"I should hope so, indeed!" interrupted Mrs. Keswick. "But people of all sorts do run across each other."

"But if I do meet with him," he continued, "I shall take great pleasure in giving you my impressions by letter, or in person, of your nephew-in-law."

"Don't call him that!" exclaimed the old lady, with much asperity. "I don't acknowledge the title. But I won't say any more about him," with a grim smile, "or you may think I don't like him."

"Some of these days," he said, "you may come to be of the opinion that he is exactly the husband you would wish your niece to have."

"Never!" she cried. "If he were an angel in broadcloth. But I mustn't talk about these things. I mentioned Mr. Null to you because you are the only person of my acquaintance who, I suppose, is likely to meet with him. In regard to that little company I spoke of to you, I have not quite made up my mind about it, and therefore haven't mentioned it; but if I carry out the plan I will write to you at the Springs, and shall certainly expect you to be one of us."

"That would give me great pleasure," said Lawrence, in a tone which indicated to the quick brain of the old lady that he would like to make a condition, but was too polite to do so.

"If Miss March should agree to come," she said, "it might be pleasant for you to make one of her party and ride over at the same time. However, I'll let you know if she is coming, and then you can join her or not, as suits your convenience."

"Thank you very much," said Lawrence, in a tone which betrayed no reserves.

As he rode away that afternoon, Lawrence Croft, as his habit was on such occasions, revolved in his mind what he had heard and said and done during this little visit to the Keswick family. "Nothing could have turned out better," he thought. "To be sure, the young man could not or would not be of any assistance to me, which is probably what I ought to have expected; but the strong-tempered old lady, his aunt, promises to be of tenfold more service than he could possibly be. As to that very odd young lady, Mrs. Keswick's niece, I imagine that she does not regard me very favorably, for she was quite cool after I refused to let her into the secret of my desire to find her cousin; but as I did not ask for her confidences, she had no right to expect a return for them. And, by the way, it's odd how many confidences have been reposed in me since I've been down here. Keswick begins it; then old Brandon takes up the strain; after that Mr. Candy's ex-cashier tells me the story of her life, and intrusts me with the secret of her marriage with a man of wind—that most useful Mr. Null; after that, her aunt makes me understand how much she hates Mr. Null, and how she would like me to find out something disreputable about him; and then—by George! I forgot the old negro woman in the cabin!" At this he put his hand in the side-pocket of his coat and drew out the pair of little blue shoes. "Why in the name of common sense did the old hag give me these? And why should she suppose that Mrs. Keswick intended me a harm? The old lady never saw or heard of me until yesterday, and her manner certainly indicated no dislike of me. But, of course, Aunt Patsy's brain is cracked, and she didn't know what she was talking about. I shall keep the shoes, however, and if ever the venerable purple sunbonnet runs afoul of me, I shall hold them up before it and see what happens."

And so, very well satisfied with the result of his visit to Howlett's, he rode on to the Green Sulphur Springs.

On the afternoon of the next day Miss March received an invitation from Mrs. Keswick to spend a few days with her, and make the acquaintance of her niece who had recently returned to the home of her childhood. The letter, for it was much more than a note of invitation, was cordial, and in parts pathetic. It dwelt upon the sundered pleasant relations of the two families, and expressed the hope that Mr. Brandon's visit to her might be the beginning of a renewal of the old intimacy. Mrs. Keswick took occasion to incidentally mention that the house would be particularly dull for her niece just now, as Junius was on the point of starting for Washington, where he would be detained some weeks on business; and she hoped most earnestly that Miss Roberta would accept this invitation to make her acquaintance and that of her niece; and she designated Thursday of the following week as the day on which she would like her to come.

As may reasonably be supposed, this letter greatly astonished Miss March, who carried it to her uncle, and asked him to explain, if he could, what it meant.

THE LATE MRS. NULL

The old gentleman was a good deal surprised when he read it; but it delighted him in a far greater degree. He perceived in it the first-fruits of his diplomacy. Mrs. Keswick saw that it would be to her interest, for a time at least, to make friends with him; and this was the way she took to do it. She would not come to Midbranch herself, and bring the niece, but she would have Roberta come to her. In the pathos and cordiality Mr. Brandon believed not at all. What the old hypocrite probably wanted was to enlist his grateful sympathy in that ridiculous divorce case. But, whatever her motives might be, he would be very glad to have his niece go to her; for if anything could make an impression upon that time-hardened and seasoned old chopping-block of a woman, it was Roberta's personal influence. If Mrs. Keswick should come to know Roberta, that knowledge would do more than anything else in the world to remove her objections to the marriage he so greatly desired.

He said nothing of all this to his niece; but he most earnestly counselled her to accept the invitation and make a visit to the two ladies. Of course Roberta did not care to go, but as her uncle appeared to take the matter so much to heart, she consented to gratify him, and wrote an acceptance. She found, also, when she had thought more on the matter, that she had a good deal of curiosity to see this Mrs. Keswick, of whom she had heard so much, and who had had such an important influence on her life.

CHAPTER XV

On the afternoon of the day on which Mrs. Keswick's letter arrived at Midbranch, Peggy had great news to communicate to Aunt Judy, the cook: "Miss Rob's gwine to Mahs' Junius's house in de kerridge, an' I'se gwine 'long wid her to set in front wid Sam."

"Mahs' Junius ain't got no house," said Aunt Judy, turning around very suddenly. "Does you mean she gwine to old Miss Keswick's?"

"Yaas," answered Peggy.

"Well, den, why don' you say so? Dat ain't Mahs' Junius's house nohow, though he lib dar as much as he lib anywhar. Wot she gwine dar fur?"

"Gwine to git married, I reckon," said Peggy.

"Git out!" ejaculated Aunt Judy. "Wid you fur bride'maid?"

"Dunno," answered Peggy. "She done tole me she didn't think she'd have much use fur me, but Mahs' Robert he said it were too far fur her to go widout a maid; but ef she want me fur bride'maid I'll do dat too."

"You bawn fool!" shouted Aunt Judy. "You ain't got sense 'nuf to hook de frocks ob de bride'maids. An' dat's all fool talk about Miss Rob gwine dar to be married. When she an' Mahs' Junius hab de weddin', dey'll hab it h'yar, ob course. She gwine to see ole Miss Keswick, cos dat's de way de fus' fam'lies allus does afore dey hab der weddin'. I'se pow'ful glad she's gwine dar, instid ob ole Miss Keswick comin' h'yar. I don' wan' her kunjerin' me, an' she'd do dat as quick as winkin' ef de batterbread's a leetle burned, or dar's too much salt in de soup. You's got to keep yo'se'f mighty straight, you Peggy, when you gits whar ole Miss Keswick is. Don' you come none ob your fool tricks, or she kunjer you, an' one ob your legs curl up like a pig's tail, an' nebber uncurl no mo'. How you like dat?"

To this Peggy made no reply, but with her eyes steadfastly fixed on Aunt Judy, and her lower jaw very much dropped, she mentally resolved to keep herself as straight as possible during her stay at the Keswicks'.

"Dar's ole Aun' Patsy," continued the speaker. "It's a mighty long time sence I've seen Aun' Patsy. Dat was when I went ober dar wid Miss Rob's mudder when de two fam'lies was fr'en's. I was her maid, an' went wid her jes as Mahs' Robert wants you to go 'long wid Miss Rob. He ain't gwine to furgit how dey did in de ole times when de ladies went visitin' in der kerridges fur to stay free, four days. Aun' Patsy were pow'ful ole den, but she didn't die soon 'nuf, an' ole Miss Keswick she kunjer her, an' now she can't die at all."

"Nebber die!" ejaculated Peggy.

"Nebber die, nohow!" answered Aunt Judy. "Mighty offen she thought she gwine to die, but 'twarn't no use. She can't do it. An' de las' time I hear ob her, she alibe yit, jes de same as ebber. An'

THE LATE MRS. NULL

dar was Mahs' John Keswick. She kunjer him cos he rode de gray colt to de coht-house when she done tole him to let dat gray colt alone, cos 'twarn't hisn but hern, an' he go shoot hese'f dead by de gate-pos'. You's got to go fru by dat pos' when you go inter de gate."

"Dat same pos'!" cried Peggy.

"Yaas," said Aunt Judy, "dat same one. An' dey tells me dat on third Chewsdays, which is coht-day, de same as when he took de gray colt, as soon as it git dark he ghos' climb up to de top ob dat pos', an' set dar all night."

With a conjuring old woman in the house, and a monthly ghost on the gate-post outside, the Keswick residence did not appear as attractive to Peggy as it had done before, but she mentally determined that while she was there she would be very careful to look out sharp for herself—a performance for which she was very well adapted.

It was on a pleasant autumn morning that Mr. Brandon very carefully ensconced his niece in the family carriage, with Peggy and a trusty negro man, Sam, on the outside front seat. "I would gladly go with you, my dear," he said, "even without the formality of an invitation, but it is far better for you to go by yourself. My very presence would provoke an antagonism in the old lady, while with you personally it is impossible that any such feeling should exist. I hope your visit may do away with all ill feeling between our families."

"I want you to understand, uncle," said Miss Roberta, "that I am making this visit almost entirely to please you, and I shall do everything in my power to

167

THE LATE MRS. NULL

make Mrs. Keswick feel that you and I are perfectly well disposed towards her; but you can't expect me to exhibit any great warmth of friendship towards a person who once used such remarkable and violent expressions in regard to me."

"But those feelings, my dear," said Mr. Brandon, "if we are to believe Mrs. Keswick's letter, have entirely disappeared."

"It is quite natural that they should do so," said Roberta, "as there is no longer any reason for them. And there is another thing I want to impress on your mind, Uncle Robert: you must expect no result from this visit except a renewal of amity between yourself and Mrs. Keswick."

"I understand it perfectly," said the old gentleman, feeling quite confident that if his family and Mrs. Keswick should once again become friendly, the main object of his desires would not be difficult of accomplishment. "And now, my dear, I will not detain you any longer. I hope you may have a very pleasant visit, and I advise you to cultivate that young Mrs. Null, whom I take to be a very sensible and charming person." Then he kissed her good-by and shut the carriage door.

It was about the middle of the afternoon when Sam drove through the outer Keswick gate, and Peggy, who had jumped down to open said gate, had made herself positively sure that, at present, there was no ghost sitting upon the post. Before she reached the house, Roberta began to wonder a good deal if she should find Mrs. Keswick the woman she had pictured in her mind. But when the carriage drew up in front of the porch there came out to meet her, not the mistress of the estate, but a much younger lady, who tripped down the steps and reached Roberta as she descended from the carriage.

"We are very glad to see you, Miss March," she said. "My aunt is not here just now, but will be back directly."

"This is Mrs. Null, isn't it?" said Roberta; and as the other smiled and answered with a slight flush that it was, Roberta stooped just the little that was necessary, and kissed her. Mrs. Keswick's niece had not expected so warm a greeting from this lady, to whom she was almost a stranger, and instantly she said to herself: "In that kiss Freddy dies to you." For some days she had been turning over and over in her mind the question whether or not she should tell Roberta March that she was not Mrs. Null. She greatly disliked keeping up the deception where it was not necessary, and with Roberta, if she would keep the secret, there was no need of this aërial matrimony. Besides her natural desire to confide in a person of her own sex and age, she did not wish Mr. Croft to be the only one who shared her secret; and so she had determined that her decision would depend on what sort of girl Roberta proved to be. "If I like her I'll tell her; if I don't I won't," was the final decision. And when Roberta March looked down upon her with her beautiful eyes and kissed her, Freddy Null departed this life so far as those two were concerned.

Mrs. Keswick had, apparently, made a very great miscalculation in regard to the probable time of arrival of her guest, for Miss March and Peggy, and even Sam and the horses, had been properly received and cared for, and Miss March had been sitting in the parlor for some time, and still the old lady did not come into the house. Her niece had grown very anxious about this absence, and had begun to fear that her aunt had treated Miss March as she had treated her on her arrival, and had gone away to stay. But Plez, whom she had sent to tell his mistress that her visitor was in the house, returned with the information that "ole miss" was in one of the lower fields directing some men who were digging a ditch, and that she would return to the house in a very short time. Thus assured that no permanent absence was intended, she went into the parlor to entertain Miss March, and to explain, as well as she could, the state of affairs ; when, as she entered the door, she saw that lady suddenly arise and look steadfastly out of the window.

"Can that be Mr. Croft?" Miss March exclaimed.

The younger girl made a dash forward and also looked out of the window. Yes, there was Mr. Croft, riding across the yard towards the tree where horses were commonly tied.

"Did you expect him?" asked Roberta, quickly.

"No more than I expected the man in the moon," was the impulsive and honest answer of her companion.

"I am very glad to see you, Mrs. Null," said Lawrence, when that lady met him on the porch. And when he was shown into the parlor, he greeted Miss March with much cordiality, but no surprise. But when he inquired after other members of the family, he was much surprised to find that Mr. Keswick had gone to Washington. "Was not this very unexpected, Mrs. Null?" he asked.

"Why, no," she answered. "Junius told us, almost

as soon as he came here, that he would have to be in Washington by the first of this week."

Mr. Croft did not pursue this subject further, but presently remarked : " Are you and I the first comers, Miss March ? "

Roberta looked from one of her companions to the other, and remarked : " I do not understand you."

Lawrence now perceived that he was treading a very uncertain and, perhaps, dangerous path of conversation, and the sooner he got out of it the better ; but before he could decide what answer to make, a silent and stealthy figure appeared at the door, beckoning and nodding in a very mysterious way. This proved to be the plump black maid Letty, who, having attracted the attention of the company, whispered loudly, " Miss Annie ! " whereupon that young lady immediately left the room.

" What other comers did you expect ? " then asked Roberta of Mr. Croft.

" I certainly supposed there would be a small company here," he said, " probably neighborhood people ; but if I was mistaken, of course I don't wish to say anything more about it to the family."

" Were you invited yourself ? " asked Roberta.

Croft wished very much that he could say that he had accidentally dropped in. But this he could not do, and he answered that Mrs. Keswick asked him to come about this time. He did not consider it necessary to add that she had written to him at the Springs, renewing her invitation very earnestly, and mentioning that Miss March had consented to make one of the party.

This was as far as Roberta saw fit to continue the

subject on the present occasion, and she began to talk about the charming weather, and the pretty way in which the foliage was reddening on the side of a hill opposite the window. Mr. Croft was delighted to enter into this new channel of speech, and discussed with considerable fervor the attractiveness of autumn in Virginia.

Miss Annie found Letty in a very disturbed state of mind. The dinner had been postponed until the arrival of Miss March, and now it had been still further delayed by the non-arrival of the mistress of the house, and everything was becoming dried up and unfit to eat.

"This will never do!" exclaimed Miss Annie. "I will go myself and look for aunt. She must have forgotten the time of day, and everything else."

Putting on her hat, she ran out of the back door; but she did not have to go very far, for she found the old lady in the garden, earnestly regarding a bed of turnips. "Where have you been, my dear aunt?" cried the girl. "Miss March has been here ever so long, and Mr. Croft has come, and dinner has been waiting until it has all dried up. I was afraid that you had forgotten that company was coming to-day."

"Forgotten!" said the old lady, glaring at the turnips. "It isn't an easy thing to forget. I invited the girl, and I expected her to come. But I tell you, Annie, when I saw that carriage coming along the road, all the old feeling came back to me. I remembered what its owners had done to me and mine, and what they are still trying to do, and I felt I could not go into the house and give her my hand. It would be like taking hold of a snake."

THE LATE MRS. NULL

"A snake!" cried her niece, with much warmth. "She is a lovely woman! And her coming shows what kindly feelings she has for you. But, no matter what you think about it, aunt, you have asked her here, and you must come in and see her. Dinner is waiting, and I don't know what more to say about your absence."

"Go in and have dinner," said Mrs. Keswick. "Don't wait for me. I'll come in and see her after a while; but I haven't yet got to the point of sitting down to the table and eating with her."

"Oh, aunt!" exclaimed Annie, "you ought never to have asked her if you are going to treat her in this way! And what am I to say to her? What excuse am I to make? Are you not sick? Isn't something the matter with you?"

"You can tell them I'm flustrated," said the old lady, "and that is all that's the matter with me. But I'm not coming in to dinner, and there is no use of saying anything more about it."

Annie looked at her, the tears of mortification still standing in her eyes. "I suppose I must go and do the best I can," she said; "but, aunt, please tell me one thing. Did you invite any other people here? Mr. Croft spoke as if he expected to see other visitors, and if they ask anything more about it, I don't know what to say."

"The only other people I invited," said the old lady, with a grim grin, "were the King of Norway and the Prime Minister of Spain, and neither of them could come."

Annie said no more, but hurrying back to the house, she ordered dinner to be served immediately. At first the meal was not a very lively one. The young hostess *pro tempore* explained the absence of the mistress of the house by stating that she had had a nervous attack,—which was quite true,—and that she begged them to excuse her until after dinner. The two guests expressed their regret at this unfortunate indisposition, but each felt a degree of embarrassment at the absence of Mrs. Keswick. Roberta, who had heard many stories of the old woman, guessed at the true reason, and if the distance had not been so great she would have gone home that afternoon. Lawrence Croft, of course, could imagine no reason for the old lady's absence except the one that had been given them, but he suspected that there must be some other. He did his best, however, to make pleasant conversation ; and Roberta, who began to have a tender feeling for the little lady at the head of the table, who, she could easily see, had been placed in an unpleasant position, seconded his efforts with such effect that when the little party had concluded their dinner with a course of hot pound-cake and cream-sauce, they were chatting together quite sociably.

In about ten minutes after they had all gone into the parlor, Miss Annie excused herself, and presently returned with a message to Miss March that Mrs. Keswick would be very glad to see her in another room. This was a very natural message from an elderly lady who was not well, but Roberta arose and walked out of the parlor with a feeling as if she were about to enter the cage of an erratic tigress. But she met with no such creature. She saw in the back room into which she was ushered a small old woman, dressed very plainly, who came forward to meet her, extending both hands, into one of which Roberta placed one of her own.

"I may as well say at once, Roberta March," said Mrs. Keswick, "that the reason I didn't come to meet you when you first arrived was that I couldn't get over, all of a sudden, the feelings I have had against your family for so many years."

"Why, then, Mrs. Keswick," said Roberta, very coldly, "did you ask me to come?"

"Because I wanted you to come," said Mrs. Keswick, "and because I thought I was stronger than I turned out to be ; but you must make allowances for the stiffness which gets into old people's dispositions as well as their backs. I want you to understand, however, that I meant all I said in that letter, and I am very glad to see you. If anything in my conduct has seemed to you out of the way, you must set it down to the fact that I was making a very sudden turn, and starting out on a new track, in which I hope we shall all keep for the rest of our lives."

Roberta could not help thinking that the sudden turn in the new track began with the visit of her uncle to this house, and that the old lady need not have inflicted upon her the disagreeable necessity of witnessing a hostess taking a very repulsive cold plunge ; but all she said was that she hoped the families would now live together in friendly relations, and that she was sure that if this were to be it would give her uncle a great deal of pleasure. She very much wanted to ask Mrs. Keswick how Mr. Croft happened to be here at this time, but she felt that her very brief acquaintance with the lady would not warrant the discussion of a subject like that.

THE LATE MRS. NULL

"She is very much the kind of woman I thought she was," said Roberta to herself, when, after some further hospitable remarks from Mrs. Keswick, the two went to the parlor together to find Mr. Croft. But that gentleman, having been deserted by all the ladies, was walking up and down the greensward in front of the house, smoking a cigar. Mrs. Keswick went out to him, and greeted him very cordially, begging him to excuse her for not being able to see him as soon as he came.

Lawrence set all this aside in his politest manner, but declared himself very much disappointed in not seeing Mr. Keswick, and also remarked that from what she had said to him on his last visit he had expected to find quite a little party here.

"I am sorry," said the old lady, "that Junius is away, for he would be very glad to see you, and it never came into my mind to mention to you that he was obliged to be in Washington at this time. And as for the party, I thought afterwards that it would be a great deal cosier just to have a few persons here."

"Oh, yes," said Lawrence ; "most certainly, a great deal cosier."

Mrs. Keswick ate supper with her guests, and behaved very well. During the evening she sustained the main part of the conversation, giving the company a great many anecdotes and reminiscences of old times and old families, relating them in an odd and peculiar way that was very interesting, especially to Croft, to whom the subject-matter was quite new. But although her three companions listened to the old lady with deferential attention, interspersed with appropriate observations, each one made her the object

176

of severe mental scrutiny, and endeavored to discover the present object of her scheming old mind. Roberta was quite sure that her invitation and that of Mr. Croft was a piece of artful management on the part of the old lady, and imagined, though she was not quite sure about it, that it was intended as a bit of matchmaking. To get her married to somebody else would be, of course, the best possible method of preventing her marrying Junius; and this, she had reason to believe, was the prime object of old Mrs. Keswick's existence. But why should Mr. Croft be chosen as the man with whom she was to be thrown. She had learned that the old lady had seen him before, but was quite certain that her acquaintance with him was slight. Could Junius have told his aunt about the friendship between herself and Mr. Croft? It was not like him, but a great many unlikely things take place.

As for Lawrence, he knew very well there was a trick beneath his invitation, but he could not at all make out why it had been played. He had been given an admirable opportunity of offering himself to Miss March, but there was no reason apparent to him why this should have been done.

Miss Annie, watching her aunt very carefully, and speaking but seldom, quite promptly made up her mind in regard to the matter. She knew very well the bitter opposition of the old woman to a marriage between Junius and Miss March; and saw, as plainly as she saw the lamp on the table, that Roberta had been brought here on purpose to be sacrificed to Mr. Croft. Everything had been made ready, the altar cleared, and, as well as the old lady's grindstone would act, the knife sharpened. "But," said Miss Annie to herself, "she needn't suppose that I am going to sit quiet and see all this going on, with Junius away off there in Washington, knowing nothing about any of it."

Miss Roberta retired quite early to her room, being fatigued by her long drive, and she was just about to put out her light when she heard a little knock at the door. Opening it slightly, she saw there Junius Keswick's cousin, who also appeared quite ready for bed.

"May I come in for a minute?" said Annie.

"Certainly," replied Miss March, admitting her, and closing the door after her.

"I have something to tell you," said the younger lady, admiring, as she spoke, the length of her companion's braided hair. "I intended to keep it until to-morrow; but since I came up-stairs I felt I could not let you sleep a night under the same roof with me without knowing it. I am not Mrs. Null."

"What!" exclaimed Roberta, in a tone which made Annie lift up her hands and implore her not to speak so loud, for fear that her aunt should hear her.

"I know she hasn't come up-stairs yet, for she sits up dreadfully late; but she can hear things almost anywhere. No, I am not Mrs. Null. There is no such person as Mr. Null, or, at least, he is a mere gaseous myth, whom I married for the sake of the protection his name gave me."

"This is the most extraordinary thing I ever heard," said Roberta. "You must tell me all about it."

"I don't want to keep you up," said Annie; "you must be tired."

"I am not tired," said Roberta, "for every particle

178

of fatigue has flown away." And with this she made
Annie sit down beside her on the lounge. "Now you
must tell me what this means," she said. "Can it be
that your aunt does not know about it?"

"Indeed, she does not," said Annie. "I married
Freddy Null in New York, for reasons which we need
not talk of now, for that matter is all past and gone;
but when I came here, I found, almost immediately,
that he would be more necessary to me in this house
than anywhere else."

"I cannot imagine," said Roberta, "why a gaseous
husband should be necessary to you here."

"It is not a very easy thing to explain," said the
other; "that is, it is easy enough, but—"

"Oh," said Roberta, catching the reason of her companion's hesitation, "I don't think you ought to object
to telling me your reason. Does it relate to your cousin
Junius?"

"Well," said Annie, "not altogether, and not so
much to him as to my aunt."

"I think I see," said Roberta. "A marriage
between you two would suit her very well. Are you
afraid that she would try to force him on you?"

"Oh, no," said Annie; "that would be bad enough,
but it would not be so embarrassing, and so dreadfully unpleasant, as forcing me on him, and that is
what aunt wants to do. And you can easily see that,
in that case, I could not stay in this house at all. I
scarcely know my cousin as a man, my strongest recollection of him being that of a big and very nice boy,
who used to climb up in the apple-trees to get me
apples, and then come down to the very lowest branch,
where he could drop the ripest ones right into my

apron, and not bruise them. But even if I had been acquainted with him all these years, and liked him ever so much, I couldn't stay here and have aunt make him take me, whether he wanted to or not. And unless you knew my aunt very well, you could not conceive how unscrupulously straightforward she is in carrying out her plans."

"And so," said Roberta, "you have quite baffled her by this little ruse of a marriage."

"Not altogether," said Annie, with a smile, "for she vows she is going to get me divorced from Mr. Null."

"That is funnier than the rest of it," said Roberta, laughing. And they both laughed together, but in a subdued way, so as not to attract the attention of the old lady below stairs.

"And now you see," said Annie, "why I must be Mrs. Null while I stay here. And you will promise me that you will never tell any one?"

"You may be sure I shall keep your queer secret. But have you not told it to any one but me?"

"Yes," said Annie; "but I have only told it to one other—Mr. Croft. But please don't speak of it to him."

"Mr. Croft!" exclaimed Roberta. "How in the world did you come to tell him? Do you know him so well as that?"

"Well," said Annie, "it does seem out of the way, I admit, that I should tell him; but I can't give you the whole story of how I came to do it. It wouldn't interest you—at least, it would, but I oughtn't to tell it. It is a twisty sort of thing."

"Twisty?" said Roberta, drawing herself up and a little away from her companion.

THE LATE MRS. NULL

Annie looked up, and caught the glance by which this word was accompanied, and the tone in which it was spoken went straight to her soul. "Now," said she, "if you are going to look at me and speak in that way, I'll tell you every bit of it." And she did tell the whole story, from her first meeting with Mr. Croft in the Information Shop, down to the present moment.

"What is your name, anyway?" said Roberta. when the story had been told.

"My name," said the other, "is Annie Peyton."

"And now, do you know, Annie Peyton," said Roberta, passing her fingers gently among the short, light-brown curls on her companion's forehead, "that I think you must have a very, very kindly recollection of the boy who used to come down to the lowest branches of the tree to drop apples into your apron."

CHAPTER XVI

SHORTLY after Peggy arrived with her mistress at the Keswick residence, her mind began to be a good deal disturbed. She had been surprised, when the carriage drew up to the door, that "Mahs' Junius" had not rushed down to meet his intended bride, and when she found he was not in the house, and had, indeed, gone away from home, she did not at all know what to make of it. If Miss Rob took the trouble to travel all the way to the home of the man that the Midbranch people had decided she should marry, it was a very wonderful thing indeed that he should not be there to meet her. And while these thoughts were turning themselves over in the mind of this meditative girl of color, and the outgoing look in her eyes was extending itself farther and farther, as if in search of some solution of the mystery, up rode Mr. Croft.

"Dar *he!*" exclaimed Peggy, as she stood at the corner of the house where she had been pursuing her meditations. "He!" she continued, in a voice that would have been quite audible to any one standing near. "Upon my libin' soul, wot brung him h'yar? Miss Rob don' wan' him roun', nohow. I done druv him off wunst. Upon my libin' soul, he's done brung

182

his bag behin' him on de saddle, an' I reckon he's gwine to stay."

As Mr. Croft dismounted and went into the house, Peggy glowered at him, sundry expressions, sounding very much like odds and ends of imprecations which she had picked up in the course of a short but investigative existence, gurgling from her lips.

"I wish dat ole Miss Keswick kunjer him. Ef she knew how Miss Rob hate him, she curl he legs up, an' gib him mis'ry spranglin' down he back."

The hope of seeing this intruder well "kunjered" by the old lady was the only thing that gave a promise of peace to the mind of Peggy; and though her nature was by no means a social one, she determined to make the acquaintance of some one or other in the house, hoping to find out how Mrs. Keswick conducted her conjurations, at what time of day or night they were generally put into operation, and how persons could be brought under their influence.

The breakfast-hour in the Keswick house was a variable one. Sometimes the mistress of the establishment rose early and wanted her morning meal before she went out of doors; at other times she would go off to some distant point on the farm to see about something that was doing, or ought to be done, and breakfast would be kept waiting for her. The delays, however, were not all due to the old lady's irregular habits. Very often Letty would come up-stairs with the information that the "bread ain't riz"; and as a Virginia breakfast without hot bread would be an impossibility, the meal would be postponed until the bread did conclude to rise, or until some substitute, such as "beaten biscuit," had been provided.

THE LATE MRS. NULL

On the morning after his arrival, Lawrence Croft came down-stairs about eight o'clock, and found the lower part of the house deserted; and glancing into the dining-room as he passed its open door, he saw no signs of breakfast. The house was cool, but the sun appeared to be shining warmly outside, and he stepped out of the open back door into a small flower-garden with a series of broad boards down the walk which lay along the middle of it. Up and down this broad walk Lawrence strode, breathing the fresh air, and thinking over matters. He was not at all satisfied at being here during Keswick's absence, feeling that he was enjoying an advantage which, although it was quite honorable, did not appear so. What he had to do was to get an interview with Miss March as soon as possible, and have that matter over. When he had been definitely accepted or rejected, he would go away. And, whatever the result might be, he would write to his rival as soon as he returned to the Springs, and inform him of it, and would also explain how he had happened to be here with Miss March. While he was engaged in planning these honorable intentions, there came from the house Mrs. Keswick's niece, with a basket in one hand, and a pair of scissors in the other, and she immediately applied herself to cutting some geraniums and chrysanthemums, which were about the last flowers left blooming at that season in the garden.

"Good morning," said Croft, from the other end of the walk. "I am glad to see you out so early."

"Good morning," she replied, with a look which indicated that she was not at all glad to see him, "but I don't think it is early."

Croft had noticed on the preceding day that her

184

THE LATE MRS. NULL

coolness towards him still continued, but it did not
suit him to let her know that he perceived it. He
went up to her, and in a very friendly way remarked:
"There is something I wish very much you would tell
me. What is your name? It is very odd that during
all the time I have been acquainted with you I have
never known your name."

"You must have taken an immense interest in it,"
she said, as she snipped some dried leaves off a twig of
geranium she had cut.

"It was not that I did not take any interest," said
Croft, "but at first your name never came forward,
and I soon began to know you by the title which your
remarkable condition of wedlock gave you."

"And that is the name," said the lady, very decidedly,
"by which I am to be known in this house. I am very
proud of my maiden name, but I am not going to tell
it to you for fear that some time you will use it."

"Oh!" ejaculated Mr. Croft. "Then I suppose I
am to continue even to think of you as Mrs. Null."

"You needn't think of me at all," said she, "but
when you speak to me I most certainly expect you
to use that name. It was only by a sort of accident
that you came to know it was not my name."

"I don't consider it an accident at all," said Croft.
"I look upon it as a piece of very kindly confidence."

Miss Annie gave a little twist to her mouth, which
seemed to indicate that if she spoke she should express
her contempt of such an opinion, and Croft continued:

"I am very sorry that upon that occasion I should
have felt myself obliged to refuse your request that I
should make you acquainted with my reasons for desiring to know Mr. Keswick's whereabouts. But I am

185

sure, if you understood the matter, you would not be in the least degree—"

"Oh, you need not trouble yourself about that," she interrupted. "I don't want you to tell me anything at all. It is quite easy now to see why you wished to know where my cousin was."

"It is impossible that you should know!" exclaimed Croft.

"We will say no more about it," replied Annie. "I am quite satisfied."

"I would give a good deal," said Lawrence, after looking steadily at her for a few moments, "to know what you really do think."

Annie had cut all the flowers she wanted, or, rather, all she could get; and she now stood up and looked her companion full in the face. "Mr. Croft," she said, "it has been necessary, and it is necessary now, for me to have some concealments, and I am sorry for it; but it isn't at all necessary for me to conceal my opinion of your reasons for wanting to know about Junius. You were really in pursuit of Miss March, and, knowing that he was in love with her, you wanted to make sure that when you went to her he wouldn't be there. It is my firm opinion that is all there is about it; and the fact of your turning up here just after my cousin left proves it."

"Miss Annie," exclaimed Croft,—"I have heard you called by that name, and I vow I won't call you Mrs. Null when there is no need for it,—you were never more mistaken in your life, and I am very sorry that you should have such a low opinion of me as to think I would wish to take advantage of your cousin during his absence."

THE LATE MRS. NULL

"Then why do you do it?" asked Miss Annie, with a little upward pitch of her chin.

At this moment the breakfast-bell rang, and Mrs. Keswick appeared in the back door, evidently somewhat surprised to see these two conversing in the garden.

"I am very much vexed," said Lawrence, as he followed his companion, who had suddenly turned towards the house, "that you should think of me in this way."

But to this remark Miss Annie had no opportunity to reply.

After breakfast, Mrs. Keswick proved the truth of what her niece had said about her unscrupulous straightforwardness when carrying out her projects. She had invited Mr. Croft and Miss March to her house in order that the former might have the opportunity, which she had discovered he wanted and could not get, of offering himself in marriage to the lady; and she now made it her business to see that Mr. Croft's opportunity should stand up very clear and definite before him, and that all interfering circumstances should be carefully removed. She informed her niece that she wished her to go with her to a thicket on the other side of the wheat-field (which that young lady had advised should be ploughed for pickles) to look for a turkey-hen which she had reason to believe had been ridiculous enough to hatch out a brood of young at this improper season. Annie demurred, for she did not want to go to look for turkeys, nor did she want to give Mr. Croft any opportunities; but the old lady insisted, and carried her off. Croft felt that there was something very bare and rawboned about the position in which he was left with Miss March ; and he thought that lady might readily suppose that Mrs. Keswick's object was to leave them together. He imagined that himself, though why she should be so kind to him he could not feel quite certain. However, his path lay straight before him, and if the old lady had whitewashed it to make it more distinct, he did not intend to refuse to walk in it.

"I have been looking at that hill over yonder," said he, "with a cluster of pine-trees on the brow of it. I should think there would be a fine view from that hill. Would you not like to walk up there?"

Lawrence felt that this proposition was quite in keeping with the bareness of the previous proceedings, but he did not wish to stay in the house and be subject to the unexpected return of the old lady and her niece.

"Certainly," said Miss March, "nothing would please me better." And so they walked up Pine Top Hill.

When they reached this elevated position, they sat down on the rock on which Mrs. Null had once conversed with Freddy, and admired the view, which was, indeed, a very fine one. After about five minutes of this, which Lawrence thought was quite enough, he turned to his companion and said :

"Miss March, I do not wish you to suppose that I brought you up here for the purpose of viewing those rolling hills and distant forests."

"You didn't?" exclaimed Roberta, in a tone of surprise.

"No," said he, "I brought you here because it is a

place where I could speak freely to you, and tell you I love you."

"That was not at all necessary," said Miss March. "We had the lower floor of the house entirely to ourselves, and I am sure that Mrs. Keswick would not have returned until you had waved a handkerchief, or given some signal from the back of the house that it was all over."

Croft looked at her with a troubled expression. "Miss March," said he, "do you not think I am in earnest? Do you not believe what I have said?"

"I have not the slightest doubt you are in earnest," she answered. "The magnitude of the preparation proves it."

"I am glad you said that, for it gives me the opportunity for making an explanation," said Lawrence. "Our meeting at this place may be a carefully contrived stratagem, but it was not contrived by me. I am very well aware that Mr. Keswick also wishes to marry you—"

"Did you see that in the Richmond "Despatch," or in one of the New York papers?" interrupted Miss March.

"That is a point," said Lawrence, overlooking the ridicule, "which we need not discuss. I am perfectly aware that Mr. Keswick is my rival, but I wish you to understand that I am not voluntarily taking any undue advantage of his absence. I believe him to be a very fair and generous man, and I would wish to be as open and generous as he is. When I came, I expected to find him here, and, standing on equal ground with him, I intended to ask you to accept my love."

"Well, then," said Roberta, "would it not be more fair and generous for you to go away now, and postpone this proposal until some time when you would each have an equal chance?"

"No, it would not," said Lawrence, vehemently. "I have now an opportunity of telling you that I love you ardently, passionately; and nothing shall cause me to postpone it. Will you not consider what I say? Will you make no answer to this declaration of most true and honest love?"

"I am considering what you have said," she answered, "and I am very glad to hear that you did not know of this cunning little trap that Mrs. Keswick has laid for me. It is all very plain to me, but I do not know why she should have selected you as one of the actors in the plot. Have you ever told her that you are a suitor for my hand?"

"Never!" exclaimed Lawrence. "She may have imagined it, for she heard I was a frequent visitor to Midbranch. But let us set all that aside. I am on fire with love for you. Will you tell me that you can return that love, or that I must give up all hope? This is the most important question of my whole life. I beg you, from the bottom of my heart, to decide it."

"Mr. Croft," said she, "when you used to come, nearly every day, to see me at Midbranch, and we took those long walks in the woods, you never talked in this way. I considered you as a gentleman whose prudence and good sense would not allow him to step outside of the path of perfectly conventional social intercourse. This is not conventional and not pru-dent."

190

THE LATE MRS. NULL

"I loved you then, and I love you now!" exclaimed
Lawrence. "You must have known that I loved
you, for my declaration does not in the least surprise
you."

"Once—it was the last time you visited Midbranch
—I suspected, just a little, that your mind might be
affected somewhat in the way you speak of, but I
supposed that attack of weakness had passed away."

"I know what you mean," said Lawrence, "but I
can't endure to talk of such trifles. I love you,
Roberta—"

"Miss March," she interrupted.

"And I want you to tell me if you love me in
return."

Miss March rose from the rock where she had been
sitting, and her companion rose with her. After a
moment's silence, during which he watched her with
intense eagerness, she said: "Mr. Croft, I am going
to give you your choice. Would you prefer being
refused under a cherry-tree or under a sycamore?"

There was a little smile on her lips as she said this,
which Lawrence could not interpret.

"I decline being refused under any tree," he said
with vehemence.

"I prefer the cherry-tree," said she; "there is a
very pretty one over there on the ridge of this hill,
and its leaves are nearly all gone, which would make
it quite appropriate. But what is the meaning of
this? There comes Peggy. It isn't possible that she
thinks it's time for me to give out something to Aunt
Judy."

Croft turned, and there was the wooden Peggy,
marching steadily up the hill, and almost upon them.

191

"What do you want, Peggy?" asked Miss Roberta.

"Dar's a man down to de house dat wants him," pointing to Mr. Croft.

Lawrence was very much surprised. "A man who wants me!" he exclaimed. "You must be mistaken."

"No, sah," replied Peggy; "you's de one."

For a moment Lawrence hesitated. His disposition was to let any man in the world, be he president or king, wait until he had settled this matter with Miss March. But with Peggy present it was impossible to go on with the love-making. He might, indeed, send her back with a message; but the thought came to him that it would be well to postpone for a little the pressing of his suit, for the lady was certainly in a very untowards humor, and he was not altogether sorry to have an excuse for breaking off the interview at this point. He had not yet been discarded, and he would like to think over the matter, and see if he could discover any reason for the very disrespectful manner, to say the least of it, with which Miss March had received his amatory advances. "I suppose I must go and see the man," he said, "though I can't imagine who it can possibly be. Will you return to the house?"

"No," said Miss Roberta, "I will stay here a little longer, and enjoy the view."

CHAPTER XVII

As Lawrence Croft walked down Pine Top Hill his mind was in a good deal of a hubbub. The mind of almost any lover would be stirred up if he came fresh from an interview in which his lady had pinned him, to use a cruel figure, in various places on the wall to see how he would spin and buzz in different lights. But the disdainful pin had not yet gone through a vital part of Lawrence's hopes, and they had strength to spin and buzz a good deal yet. As soon as he should have an opportunity he would rack his brains to find out what it was that had put Roberta March into such a strange humor. No one who simply desired to decline the addresses of a gentleman would treat her lover as Miss March had treated him. It was quite evident that she wished to punish him. But what had been his crime?

But the immediate business on his hands was to go and see what man it was who wished to see him. Ordinarily the fact that a man had called upon him would not be considered by Lawrence a matter for cogitation, but as he walked towards the house it seemed to him very odd that any one should call upon him in such an out-of-the-way place as this, where so few people knew him to be. He was not a business man, but a large portion of his funds was invested in a business concern, and it might be that something had gone wrong, and that a message had been sent him. His address at the Green Sulphur Springs was known, and the man in charge there knew that he was visiting Mrs. Keswick.

These considerations made him a little anxious, and helped to keep his mind in the hubbub which has been mentioned.

When he reached the front of the house, Lawrence saw a lean gray horse tied to a tree, and a man sitting upon the porch; and as soon as he made his appearance the latter came down the steps to meet him.

"I didn't go into the house, sir," he said, "because I thought you'd just as lief have a talk outside."

"What is your business?" asked Croft.

The man moved a few steps farther from the house, and Lawrence followed him.

"Is it anything secret you have to tell me?" he asked.

"Well, yes, sir; I should think it was," replied the other—a tall man with sandy hair and beard, and dressed in a checkered business suit which had lost a good deal of the freshness of its early youth. "I may as well tell you at once who I am. I am an anti-detective. Never heard of that sort of person, I suppose?"

"Never," said Lawrence, curtly.

"Well, sir, the organization which I belong to is one which is filling a long-felt want. You know very well, sir, that this country is full of detective officers, not only those who belong to a regular police force, but lots of private ones, who, if anybody will pay them for it, will go to Jericho to hunt a man up. Now, sir, our object is to protect society against these people. When we get information that a man is going to be hounded down by any of these detectives—and we have private ways of knowing these things—we just go to that man, and if he is willing to become one of our clients we take him into our charge; and our business, after that, is to keep him informed of just what is being done against him. He can stay at home in comfort with his wife, settle up his accounts, and do what he likes, and the day before he is to be swooped down on he gets notice from us, and comfortably goes to Chicago, or Jacksonville, where he can take his ease until we post him of the next move of the enemy. If he wants to take extra precautions, and writes a letter to anybody in the place where he lives, dated from London or Hong-Kong, and sends that letter under cover to us, we'll see that it is mailed from the place it is dated from, and that it gets into the hands of the detectives. There have been cases where a gentleman has had six months or a year of perfect comfort by the detectives being thrown off by a letter like this. That is only one of the ways in which we help and protect persons in difficulties, who, if it wasn't for us, would be dragged off, handcuffed, from the bosom of their families, and who, even if they never got convicted, would have to pay a lot of money to get out of the scrape. Now, I have put myself a good deal out of the way, sir, to come to you and offer you our assistance."

"Me!" exclaimed Croft. "What are you talking about?"

The man smiled. "Of course it's all right to know

nothing about it, and it's just what we would advise; but I assure you we are thoroughly posted in your affair, and to let you know that we are, I'll just mention that the case is that of Croft after Keswick, through Candy."

"Stuff and nonsense!" exclaimed Lawrence, getting red in the face. "There is no such case!"

He was about to say more, when a few words from the anti-detective stopped him suddenly.

"Look here, Mr. Keswick," said the man, levelling a long forefinger at him, and speaking very earnestly, "don't you go and flatter yourself that this thing has been dropped because you haven't heard of it for a month or two; and if you'll take my advice, you'll make up your mind on the spot, either to let things go on and be nabbed, or to put yourself under our protection, and live in entire safety until this thing has blown over, without any trouble except a little travelling."

At the mention of Keswick's name Lawrence had seen through the whole affair at a single mental glance. The man was after Junius Keswick, and his business was to Lawrence more startling and repugnant than it could possibly be to any one else. It was necessary to be very careful. If he immediately avowed who he was, the man might yet find Keswick before warning and explanation could be got to him, and not only put that gentleman in a very unpleasant state of mind, but do a lot of mischief besides. He did not believe that Mr. Candy had recommenced his investigations without consultation with him, but this person evidently knew that such an investigation had been set on foot, and that would be sufficient for his purposes.

196

THE LATE MRS. NULL

Lawrence decided to be very wary, and he said to the man, "Did you ask for me here by name?"

"No, *sir*," said the other; "I had information that you were here, and that you were the only gentleman who lived here; and although you are in your own home, I did not know but this was one of those cases in which names were dropped and servants changed to suit an emergency. I asked the little darky I saw at the front of the house if she lived here, and she told me she had only just come. That put me on my guard, and so I merely asked if the gentleman was in, and she went and got you. We're very careful about calling names, and you needn't be afraid that any of our people will ever give you away on that line."

Lawrence reflected for a moment, and then he said: "What are your terms and arrangements for carrying on an affair of this kind?"

"They are very simple and moderate," said the man, taking a wallet from his pocket. "There is one of our printed slips, which we show but don't give away. To become a client all you have to do is to send fifteen dollars to the office, or to pay it to me if you think no time should be lost. That will entitle you to protection for a year. After that we make the nominal charge of five dollars for each letter sent you giving you information of what is going on against you. For extra services, such as mailing letters from distant points, of course there will be extra charges."

Lawrence glanced over the printed slip, which contained information very similar to that the man had given him, and as he did so he came to the conclusion that there would be nothing dishonest in allowing the fellow to continue in his mistake, and to endeavor to find out what mischief was about to be done in his, Lawrence's, name, and under his apparent authority.

"I will become a subscriber," said he, taking out his pocket-book, "and request that you give me all the information you possess, here and immediately."

"That is the best thing to do," said the man, taking the money, "for, in my opinion, no time is to be lost. I'll give you a receipt for this."

"Don't trouble yourself about that," said Lawrence; "let me have your information."

"You're very right," said the man. "It's a great deal better not to have your name on anything. And now for the points. Candy, who has charge of Croft's job, is going more into the detective business than he used to be, and we have information that he has lately taken up your affair in good, solid earnest. He found out that Croft had put somebody else on your track without regularly taking the business out of his hands, and this made him mad; and I don't wonder at it, for Croft, as I understand, has plenty of money, and if he concluded to throw Candy over, he ought to have done it fair and square, and paid him something handsome in consideration for having taken the job away. But he didn't do anything of the kind, and Candy considers himself still in his employment, and vows he's going to get hold of you before the other party does; so, you see, you have got two sets of detectives after you, and they'll be mighty sharp, for the first one that gets you will make the money."

"Where are Candy's detectives now?" asked Lawrence.

"That I can't tell you positively, as I am so far from our New York office, to which all information comes.

THE LATE MRS. NULL

But now that you are a subscriber I'll communicate with headquarters and the necessary points will be immediately sent to you, by telegraph if necessary. All that you have to do is to stay here until you hear from us."

"From the way you spoke just now," said Lawrence, "I supposed the detective would be here to-day or to-morrow."

"Oh, no," said the other, "Candy has not the facilities for finding people that we have. But it takes some time for me to communicate with headquarters and for you to hear from there, and so, as I said before, there isn't an hour to be lost. But you're all right now."

"I expected you to give me more definite information than this," said Lawrence; "but now, I suppose, I must wait until I hear from New York, at five dollars a message."

"My business is to enlist subscribers," said the other. "You couldn't expect me to tell you anything definite when I am in an out-of-the-way place like this."

"Did you come down to Virginia on purpose to find me?" asked Lawrence.

"No," said the man, "I am on my way to Mobile, and I only lose one train by stopping here to attend to your business."

"How did you know I was here?"

"Ah," said the anti-detective, with a smile, "as I told you, we have facilities. I knew you were at this house, and I came here, straight as a die."

"It is truly wonderful," said Lawrence, "how accurate your information is. And now I will tell you something you can have gratis. You have made one of the most stupid blunders that I ever heard of. Mr.

Keswick went away from here nearly a week ago, and I am the Mr. Croft whom you supposed to be in pursuit of him."

The man started, and gave vent to an unpleasant ejaculation.

"To prove it," said Lawrence, "there is my card, and," putting his hand into his pocket, "here are several letters addressed to me. And I want to let you know that I am not in pursuit of Mr. Keswick; that he and I are very good friends, and that I have frequently seen him of late; and so you can just drop this business at once. And as for Candy, he has no right to take a single step for which I have not authorized him. I merely employed him to get Mr. Keswick's address, which I wished for a very friendly motive. I shall write to Candy at once."

The man's face was not an agreeable study. He looked angry; he looked baffled; and yet he looked incredulous. "Now, come," said he; "if you are not Keswick, what did you pay me that money for?"

"I paid it to you," said Lawrence, "because I wanted to find out what dirty business you were doing in my name. I have had the worth of my money, and you can now go."

The man did not go, but stood gazing at Lawrence in a very peculiar way. "If Mr. Keswick isn't here," he said, "I believe you are here waiting for him, and I am going to stay and warn him. People don't set private detectives on other men's tracks just for friendly motives."

Lawrence's face flushed and he made a step forward, but suddenly checking himself, he looked at the man for a moment and then said: "I suppose you want

me to understand that if I become one of your subscribers in my own name, you will be willing to with-
hold the information you intended to give Mr.
Keswick."

"Well," said the man, relapsing into his former con-
fidential tones, "business is business. If I could see
Mr. Keswick, I don't know whether he would employ
me or not. I have no reason to work for one person
more than another, and, of course, if one man comes
to me and another doesn't, I'm bound to work for the
man who comes. That's business!"

"You have said quite enough," said Lawrence.
"Now leave this place instantly!"

"No, I won't!" said the man, shutting his mouth
very tightly, as he drew himself up and folded his arms
on his chest.

Lawrence was young, well made, and strong, but the
other man was taller, heavier, and perhaps stronger.
To engage in a personal contest to compel a fellow like
this to depart would be a very unpleasant thing for
Lawrence to do, even if he succeeded. He was a
visitor here; the ladies would probably be witnesses
of the conflict; and although the natural impulse of
his heart, predominant over everything else at that
moment, prompted him to spring upon the impudent
fellow and endeavor to thrash him, still his instincts
as a gentleman forbade him to enter into such a contest, which would probably have no good effect, no
matter how it resulted. Never before did he feel the
weakness of the moral power of a just cause when
opposed to brutal obstinacy. Still he did not retreat
from his position. "Did you hear what I said?" he
cried. "Leave this place!"

THE LATE MRS. NULL

"You are not master here," said the other, still preserving his defiant attitude, "and you have no right to order me away. I am not going."

Despite his inferiority in size, despite his gentlemanly instincts, and despite his prudent desire not to make an exhibition of himself before Miss March and the household, it is probable that Lawrence's anger would have assumed some form of physical manifestation, had not Mrs. Keswick appeared suddenly on the porch. It was quite evident to her, from the aspect of the two men, that something was wrong, and she called out: "Who's that?"

"That, madam," said Lawrence, stepping a little back, "is a very impertinent man who has no business here, and whom I've ordered off the place, and as he has refused to go, I propose—"

"Stop!" cried the old lady; and turning, she rushed into the house. Before either of the men could recover from their surprise at her sudden action, she reappeared upon the porch, carrying a double-barrelled gun. Taking her position on the top of the flight of steps, with a quick movement of her thumb she cocked both barrels. Then, drawing herself up and resting firmly on her right leg, with the left advanced, she raised the gun, her right elbow well against her side, and with her extended left arm as steady as one of the beams of the roof above her. She hooked her forefinger around one of the triggers, her eagle eye glanced along the barrels straight at the head of the anti-detective, and in a clarion voice she sang out: "Go!"

The man stared at her. He saw the open muzzles of the gun-barrels; beyond them, he saw the bright tops of the two percussion-caps; and still beyond them, he saw the bright and determined eye that was taking sight along the barrels. All this he took in at a glance, and, without word or comment, he made a quick dodge of his head, jumped to one side, made a dash for his horse, and, untying the bridle with a jerk, he mounted and galloped out of the open gate, turning as he did so to find himself still covered by the muzzles of that gun. When he had nearly reached the outer gate, and felt himself out of range, he turned in his saddle, and looking back at Lawrence, who was still standing where he had left him, he violently shook his fist in the air.

"Which means," said Lawrence to himself, "that he intends to make trouble with Keswick."

"That settled him," said the old lady, with a grim smile, as she lowered the barrels of the gun and gently let down the hammers.

"Madam," said Lawrence, advancing towards her, "may I ask if that gun is loaded?"

"I should say so," replied the old lady. "In each barrel are two thimblefuls of powder, and half a box of Windfall's Teaberry Tonic Pills, each one of them as big and as hard as a buckshot. They were brought here by a travelling agent, who sold some of them to my people; and I tell you, sir, that those pills made them so sick that one man wasn't able to work for two days, and another for three. I vowed if that agent ever came back, I'd shoot his abominable pills into him, and I've kept the gun loaded for the purpose. Was this a pill man? I scarcely think he was a fertilizer, because it is rather late in the season for those bandits."

"He is a man," said Lawrence, coming up the steps, "who belongs to a class much worse than those you have mentioned. He is what is called a blackmailer."

"Is that so?" cried the old lady, her eyes flashing as she brought the butt of the gun heavily upon the porch floor. "I'm very glad I did not know it—very glad, indeed; for I might have been tempted to give him what belonged to another, without waiting for him to disobey my order to go. I am very much troubled, sir, that this annoyance should have happened to you in my house. Pray do not allow it to interfere with the enjoyment of your visit here, which I hope may continue as long as you can make it convenient."

The words and manner convinced Lawrence that they did not merely indicate a conventional hospitality. The old lady meant what she said. She wanted him to stay.

That morning he had become convinced that he had been invited there because Mrs. Keswick wished him to marry Miss March; and she had done this, not out of any kind feeling towards him, because that would be impossible considering the shortness of their acquaintance, but because she was opposed to her nephew's marriage with Miss March, and because he, Lawrence, was the only available person who could be brought forward to supplant him. "But whatever her motive is," thought Lawrence, "her invitation comes in admirably for me, and I hope I shall get the proper advantage from it."

Shortly after this, Lawrence sat in the parlor, by himself, writing a letter. It was to Junius Keswick, and in it he related the facts of his search for him in New York, and the reason why he desired to make his acquaintance. He concealed nothing but the fact that Keswick's cousin had had anything to do with the affair. "If she wants him to know that," he thought, "she can tell him herself. It is not my business to make any revelations in that quarter." He concluded the letter by informing Mr. Keswick of the visit of the anti-detective, and warning him against any attempts which that individual might make upon his pocket, assuring him that the man could tell him nothing in regard to the affair that he now did not know.

After dinner, during which meal Miss March appeared in a very good humor, and talked rather more than she had yet done in the bosom of that family, Lawrence had his horse saddled, and rode to the railroad-station, about six miles distant, where he posted his letter, and also sent a telegram to Mr. Junius Keswick, warning him to pay no attention to any man who might call upon him on business connected with Croft and Keswick, and stating that an explanatory letter had been sent.

The anti-detective had left on a train an hour before, but Lawrence felt certain that the telegram would reach Keswick before the man could possibly get to him, especially as the latter had probably not yet found out his intended victim's address.

CHAPTER XVIII

As Lawrence Croft rode back to Mrs. Keswick's house, after having posted to his rival the facts in the case of Croft after Keswick, he did not feel in a very happy or triumphant mood. The visit of the anti-detective had compelled him to write to Keswick at a time when it was not at all desirable that he should make any disclosures whatever in regard to his love-affair with Miss March, except that very important disclosure which he had made to the lady herself that morning. Of course there was no great danger that any intimation would reach Miss March of Mr. Croft's rather eccentric search for his predecessor in the position which he wished to occupy in her affections. But the matter was particularly unpleasant just now, and Lawrence wished to occupy his time here in business very different from that of sending explanations to rivals and warding off unfriendly entanglements threatened by a blackmailer.

It was absolutely necessary for him to find out what he had done to offend Miss March. Offended that lady certainly was, and he even felt that she was glad of the opportunity his declaration gave her to inflict punishment upon him. But still he did not despair. When she had made him pay the penalty she thought proper for whatever error he had committed, she might be willing to listen to him. He had not said anything to her in regard to his failure to make her the promised visit at Midbranch, for, during the only time he had been alone with her here, the subject of an immediate statement of his feelings towards her had wholly occupied his mind. But it now occurred to him that she had reason to feel aggrieved at his failure to keep his promise to her, and she must have shown that feeling, for, otherwise, her most devoted friend, Mr. Junius Keswick, would never have made that rather remarkable visit to him at the Green Sulphur Springs. Of course he would not allude to that visit, nor to her wish to see him, for she had sent him no message, nor did he know what object she had in desiring an interview. But it was quite possible that she might have taken umbrage at his failure to come to her when expected, and that this was the reason for her present treatment of him. To this treatment Lawrence might have taken exception, but now he did not wish to judge her in any way. His only desire in regard to her was to possess her, and therefore, instead of condemning her for her unjust method of showing her resentment, he merely considered how he should set himself right with her. Cruel or kind, just or unjust, he wanted her.

And then, as he slowly trotted along the lonely and uneven road, it suddenly flashed upon him—as if, in mounting a hill, a far-reaching landscape, hitherto unseen, had in a moment spread itself out before him —that perhaps Miss March had divined the reason of his extremely discreet behavior towards her. Was it possible that she had seen his motives, and knew the truth, and that she resented the prudence and caution he had shown in his intercourse with her?

If she had read the truth, he felt that she had good reason for her resentment, and Lawrence did not trouble himself to consider if she had shown too much of it or not. He remembered the story of the defeated general, and, feeling that so far he had been thoroughly defeated, he determined to admit the fact, and to sound a retreat from all the positions he had held, but, at the same time, to make a bold dash into the enemy's camp, and, if possible, capture the commander-in-chief and the minister of war.

He would go to Roberta, tell her all that he had thought, and explain all that he had done. There should be no bit of truth which she could have reasoned out, which he would not plainly avow and set before her. Then he would declare to her that his love for her had become so great that, rushing over every barrier, whether of prudence, doubt, or indecision, it had carried him with it and laid him at her feet. When he had come to this bold conclusion, he cheered up his horse with a thump of his heel, and cantered rapidly over the rest of the road.

Peggy, having nothing else to do, was standing by the yard gate when he came in sight, and she watched his approach with feelings of surprise and disgust. She had seen him ride away, and not considering the fact that he did not carry his valise with him, she supposed he had taken his final departure. She had conceived a violent dislike to Mr. Croft, looking upon him in the light of an interloper and a robber, who had come to break up that expected marriage between Master Junius and Miss Rob, which the servants at

THE LATE MRS. NULL

Midbranch looked forward to as necessary for the prosperity of the family, and the preliminary stages of which she had taken upon herself the responsibility of describing with so much minuteness of detail. With the politeness natural to the Southern negro, she opened the gate for the gentleman, but as she closed it behind him, she cast after him a look of earnest malevolence. "Ef dat ole Miss Keswick don' kunjer you, sah," she said in an undertone, "I'se gwine to do it myse'f. So dar!" And she gave her foot a stamp on the ground.

Lawrence, ignorant of the malignant feeling he had excited in this, to him, very unimportant and uninteresting black girl, tied his horse and went into the house. As he passed the open door of the parlor he saw a lady reading by a window in the farthest corner. Hanging up his hat, he entered, hoping that the reader, whose form was partially concealed by the back of the large rocking-chair in which she was sitting, was Miss March. But it was not; it was Mrs. Keswick's niece, deeply engrossed in a large-paged novel. She turned her head as he entered, and said: "Good evening."

"Good evening, Miss Annie," said Lawrence, seating himself in a chair opposite her on the other side of the window.

"Mr. Croft," said she, laying her book on her lap, and inclining herself slightly towards him, "you have no right to call me Miss Annie, and I wish you would not do it. The servants in the South call ladies by their first names, whether they are married or not, but people would think it very strange if you should imitate them. My name in this house is Mrs. Null, and I wish you would not forget it."

"The trouble with me is," said Lawrence, with a smile, "that I cannot forget it is not Mrs. Null, but, of course, if you desire it, I will give you that name."

"I told you before how much I desired it," said she, "and why. When my aunt finds out the exact state of this affair, I shall wish to stay no longer in this house, and I don't want my stay to come to an end at present. I am very happy here with the only relatives I have in the world, who are ever so much nicer people than I supposed they were, and you have no right to come here and drive me away."

"My dear young lady," said Croft, "I wouldn't do such a thing for the world. I admit that I am very sorry that it is necessary, or appears to you to be so, that you should be here under false colors, but—"

"*Appears* to be," said she, with much emphasis on the first word. "Why, can't you see that it would be impossible for me, as a young unmarried woman, to come to the house of a man whose proprietor, as Aunt Keswick considers herself to be, has been trying to marry to me, even before I was grown up?—for the letters that used to make my father most angry were about this. I hate to talk of these family affairs, and I only do it so that you can be made to understand things."

"Mrs. Null," said Lawrence, "do not think I wish to blame you. You have had a hard time of it, and I can see the peculiarities of your residence here. Don't be afraid of me ; I will not betray your secret. While I am here I will address you, and will try to think of you, as a very grave young matron. But I wish very much that you were not quite so grave and severe when you address me. When I was here last week your manner was very different. We were quite friendly then."

"I see no particular reason," said Annie, "why we should be friendly."

"Mrs. Null," said Lawrence, after a little pause, during which he looked at her attentively, "I don't believe you approve of me."

"No," said she, "I don't."

He could not help smiling at the earnest directness of her answer, though he did not like it. "I am sorry," he said, "that you should have so poor an opinion of me. And now, let me tell you what I was going to say this morning: that my only object in finding your cousin was to know the man who had been engaged to Miss March."

"So that you could find out what she probably objected to in him, and could then try and not let her see anything of that sort in you."

"Mrs. Null," said Lawrence, "you are unjust. There is no reason why you should speak to me in this way."

"I would like to know," she said, "what cause there could possibly be for your wanting to become acquainted with a man who had been engaged to the lady you wished to marry, if you didn't intend to study him up, and try to do better yourself."

"My motive in desiring to become acquainted with Mr. Keswick," said Lawrence, "is one you could scarcely understand, and all I can say about it is that I believed that if I knew the gentleman who had formerly been the accepted lover of a lady, I should better know the lady."

"You must be awfully suspicious," said she.

"No, I am not," he answered, "and I knew you would not understand me. My only desire in speaking to you upon this subject is that you may not unreasonably judge me."

"But I am not unreasonable," said Annie. "You are trying to get Miss March away from my cousin; and I don't think it is fair, and I don't want you to do it. When you were here before, I thought you two were good friends, but now I don't believe it."

How friendly might be the relations between himself and Keswick when the latter should read his letter about the Candy affair, and should know that he was in this house with Miss March, Lawrence could not say; but he did not allude to this point in his companion's remarks. "I do not think," he said, "that you have any reason to object to my endeavoring to win Miss March. Even if she accepts me, it will be to the advantage of your cousin, because if he still hopes to obtain her, the sooner he knows he cannot do so, the better it will be for him. My course is perfectly fair. I am aware that the lady is not at present engaged to any one, and I am endeavoring to induce her to engage herself to me. If I fail, then I step aside."

"Entirely aside, and out of the way?" asked Mrs. Null.

"Entirely," answered Lawrence.

"Well," said Annie, leaning back in her chair, in which before she had been sitting very upright, "you have at last given me a good deal of your confidence— almost as much as I gave you. Some of the things you say I believe, others I don't."

Lawrence was annoyed, but he would not allow himself to get angry. "I am not accustomed to being disbelieved," he said gravely. "It is a very unusual experience, I assure you. Which of my statements do you doubt?"

"I don't believe," said Annie, "that you will give her up if she rejects you while you are here. You are too wilful. You will follow her, and try again."

"Mrs. Null," said Lawrence, "I do not feel justified in speaking to a third person of these things, but this is a peculiar case, and therefore I assure you, and request you to believe me, that if Miss March shall now positively refuse me, I shall feel convinced that her affections are already occupied, and that I have no right to press my suit any longer."

"Would you like to begin now?" said Annie. "She is coming down-stairs."

"You are entirely too matter-of-fact," said Lawrence, smiling in spite of himself, and in a moment Roberta entered the room.

If the young lady in the high-backed rocking-chair had any idea of giving Mr. Croft and Miss March an opportunity of expressing their sentiments towards each other, she took no immediate steps to do so: for she gently rocked herself; she talked about the novel she had been reading; she blamed Miss March for staying so long in her room on such a beautiful afternoon; and she was the primary cause of a conversation among the three upon the differences between New York weather and that of Virginia; and this continued until old Mrs. Keswick joined the party, and changed the conversation to the consideration of the fact that a fertilizer agent, a pill man, or a blackmailer would find out a person's whereabouts, even if he were attending the funeral of his grandmother on a desert island.

The next morning, about an hour after breakfast, Lawrence was walking up and down on the grass in front of the house, smoking a cigar, and troubling his mind. He had had no opportunity on the previous evening to be alone with Miss March, for the little party sat together in the parlor until they separated for bed ; and so, of course, nothing was yet settled. He was overstaying the time he had expected to spend here, and he felt nervous about it. He had hoped to see Miss March after breakfast, but she seemed to have withdrawn herself entirely from observation. Perhaps she considered that she had sufficiently rejected him on the previous morning, and that she now intended, except when she was sure of the company of the others, to remain in her room until he should go away. But he had no such opinion in regard to their interview on Pine Top Hill. He believed that he had been punished, not rejected, and that when he should be able to explain everything to her, he would be forgiven. That, at least, was his earnest hope, and hope makes us believe almost anything.

But although there were so many difficulties in his way, Lawrence had a friend in that household who still remained true to him. Mrs. Keswick, with sunbonnet and umbrella, came out upon the porch, and said cheerily : " I should think a gentleman like you would prefer to be with the ladies than to be walking about here by yourself. They have gone to take a walk in the woods. I should have said that Miss March has gone on ahead, with her little maid Peggy. My niece was going with her, but I called her back to attend to some housekeeping matters for me, and I think she will be kept longer than she expected, for I have just sent Letty to her to be shown how to cut out a frock. But you needn't wait; you can go right through the flower-garden, and take the path over the fields into the woods." And having concluded this bit of conscienceless and transparent management, the old lady remarked that she herself was going for a walk, and left him.

Lawrence lost no time in following her suggestions. Throwing away his cigar, he hurried through the house and the little flower-garden, a gate at the back of which opened into a wide pasture-field. This field sloped down gently to a branch, or little stream, which ran through the middle of it, and then the ground ascended until it reached the edge of the woods. Following the well-defined path, he looked across the little valley before him, and could see, just inside the edge of the woods,—the trees and bushes being much more thinly attired than in the summer-time,—the form of a lady in a light-colored dress with a red scarf upon her shoulders, sometimes moving slowly, sometimes stopping. This was Roberta; and those woods were a far better place than the exposed summit of Pine Top Hill in which to plight his troth, if it should be so that he should be able to do it, and there were doubtless paths in those woods through which they might afterwards wander, if things should turn out propitiously. At all events, in those woods would he settle this affair.

His intention was still strong to make a very clean breast of it to Roberta. If she had blamed him for his prudent reserve, she should have full opportunity to

forgive him.   All that he had been she should know ;
but, far more important than that, he would try to
make her know, better than he had done before, what
he was now.   Abandoning all his previous positions,
and mounted on these strong resolutions, thus would
he dash into her camp, and hope to capture her.

Reaching the little ravine, at the bottom of which
flowed the branch, now but two or three feet wide, he
ran down the rather steep slope, and stepped upon the
stout plank which bridged the stream.   The instant he
did so, the plank turned beneath him as if it had been
hung on pivots, and he fell into the stony bed of the
branch.   It was an awkward fall, for the leg which
was undermost came down at an angle, and his foot,
striking a slippery stone, turned under him.   In a
moment he was on his feet, and scrambled up the side
of the ravine down which he had just come.   When
he reached the top he sat down and put both his hands
on his right ankle, in which he felt considerable pain.
In a few minutes he arose and began to walk towards
the house ; but he had not taken a dozen steps before
he sat down again.   The pain in his ankle was very
severe, and he felt quite sure that he had sprained it.
He knew enough about such things to understand that
if he walked upon this injured joint, he would not only
make the pain worse, but the consequences might be
serious.   He was very much annoyed, not only that
this thing had happened to him, but that it had happened at such an inauspicious moment.   Of course he
could not now go on to the woods, and he must get somebody to help him to the house.   Looking about, he saw,
at a distance, Uncle Isham, and he called loudly to him.

As soon as Lawrence was well away from the edge

of the ravine, there emerged from some thick bushes on the other side of it, and at a short distance from the crossing-place, a negro girl, who slipped noiselessly down to the branch, moved with quick steps and crouching body to the plank, removed the two round stones on which it had been skilfully poised, and replaced it in its usual firm position. This done, she slipped back into the bushes, and by the time Isham had heard the call of Mr. Croft, she was slowly walking down the opposite hill, as if she were coming from the woods to see why the gentleman was shouting.

Miss March also heard the call, and came out of the woods, and when she saw Lawrence sitting on the grass on the other side of the branch, with one hand upon his ankle, she knew that something had happened, and came down towards him. Lawrence saw her approaching, and before she was even near enough to hear him, he began to shout to her to be careful about crossing the branch, as the board was unsafe. Peggy joined her, and walked on in front of her; and when Miss March understood what Lawrence was saying, she called back that she would be careful. When they reached the ravine, Peggy ran down, stepped upon the plank, jumped on the middle of it, walked over it and then back again, and assured her mistress that it was just as good as ever it was, and that she reckoned the city gentleman didn't know how to walk on planks, and that "he jes done fall off."

Miss March crossed, stepping a little cautiously, and reached Lawrence just as Uncle Isham, with strong arms and many words of sympathy, had assisted him to his feet. "What has happened to you, Mr. Croft?" she exclaimed.

"I was coming to you," he said, "and in crossing the stream the plank turned under me, and I am afraid I have sprained my ankle. I can't walk on it."

"I am very sorry," she said.

"Because I was coming to you," he said grimly, "or because I hurt myself?"

"You ought to be ashamed to speak in that way," she answered; "but I won't find fault with you, now that you are in such pain. Is there anything I can do for you?"

"No, thank you," said Lawrence. "I will lean on this good man, and I think I can hop to the house."

"Peggy," said Miss Roberta, "walk on the other side of the gentleman, and let him lean upon your shoulder. I will go on and have something prepared to put on his ankle."

With one side supported by the stout Isham, and his other hand resting on the shoulder of the good little Peggy, who bore up as strongly under it as if she had been a big walking-stick, Lawrence slowly made his way to the house. Miss March got there some time before he did, and was very glad to find that Mrs. Keswick had not yet gone out on the walk for which she was prepared. That circumspect old lady had found this and that to occupy her, while she so managed her household matters that one thing should follow another to detain her niece. But when she heard what had happened, all other impulses gave way to those which belonged to a head nurse and a mistress of emergencies. She set down her umbrella; shouted an order to Letty to put a kettle of water on the fire; brought from her own room some flannel and two bottles of embrocation; and then, stopping a mo-

ment to reflect, ordered that the office should be prepared for Mr. Croft, for it would be a shame to make
a gentleman with a sprained ankle clamber up-stairs.

The office was a small building in the wide front
yard, not very far from the house, and opposite to the
arbor which has been before mentioned. It was one
story high, and contained one large and comfortable
room. Such buildings are quite common on Virginia
farms, and, although called offices, are seldom used in
an official way, being generally appropriated to the
bachelors of the family or their gentleman visitors.
This one was occupied by Junius Keswick when he
was at home, and a good many of his belongings were
now in it; but as it was at present unoccupied, nothing could be more proper than that Mr. Croft should
have it.

CHAPTER XIX

ABOUT noon of the day of Mr. Croft's accident, Uncle Isham had occasion to go to the cabin of the venerable Aunt Patsy, and of course he told her what had happened to the gentleman whom he and Aunt Patsy still supposed to be Miss Annie's husband. The news produced a very marked effect upon the old woman. She put down the crazy-quilt, upon the unfinished corner of which she was making a few feeble stitches, and looked at Uncle Isham with a troubled frown. She was certain that this was the work of old Mrs. Keswick, who had succeeded, at last, in conjuring the young husband ; and the charm she had given him, and upon which she had relied to avert the ill will of " ole miss," had proved unavailing. The conjuring had been accomplished so craftily and slyly, the bewitched plank in one place and Mrs. Keswick far off in another, that there had been no chance to use the counteracting charm. And yet Aunt Patsy had thought it a good charm—a very good one indeed.

Early in her married life Mrs. Keswick had been the mother of a little girl. It had died when it was very small, and it was the only child she ever had. Of this infant she preserved, as a memento, a complete suit of its clothes, which she regarded with a feeling almost religious. Years ago, however, Aunt Patsy, in order to protect herself against the conjuring powers of the mistress of the house, in which she then served as a sort of supervising cook, had possessed herself of the shoes belonging to the cherished suit of clothes. She knew the sacred light in which they were regarded by their owner, and she felt quite sure that if "ole miss" ever attempted, in one of her fits of anger, to exercise her power of limb-twisting or back-contortion upon her, that the sight of those little blue shoes would create a revulsion of feeling, and, as she put it to herself, "stop her mighty short." The shoes had never been missed, for the box containing the suit was only opened on one day of the year, and then all the old lady could endure was a peep at the little white frock which covered the rest of the contents; and Aunt Patsy well knew that the sight of those little blue shoes would be to her mistress like two little feet coming back from the grave.

Patsy had been much too old to act as nurse to the infant Annie Peyton, then regarded as the daughter of the house, but she had always felt for the child the deepest affection; and now that she herself was so near the end of her career that she had little fear of being bewitched, she was willing to give up the safeguards she had so long possessed, in order that they might protect the man whom Miss Annie had loved and married. But they had failed, or rather it had been impossible to use them, and Miss Annie's husband had been stricken down.

"It's pow'ful hard to git roun' ole miss," she groaned. "She too much fur ole folks like I is."

At this remark Uncle Isham fired up. Although

the conduct of his mistress troubled him at times very much, he was intensely loyal to her, and he instantly caught the meaning of this aspersion against her. "Now, look h'yar, Aun' Patsy!" he exclaimed, "wot you talkin' 'bout? Wot ole miss got to do wid Mister Crof' sprainin' he ankle? Ole miss warn't dar; an' when I done fotch him up to de house, she cut roun' an' do more fur him dan anybody else. She got de hot water, an' she dipped de flannels in it, an' she wrop up de ankle all herse'f; an' when she got him all fixed comf'able in de office, she says to me, says she: 'Now, Isham, you wait on Mister Crof', an' you gib him eberything he want; an' when de cool ob de ebenin' comes on you make a fire in dat fireplace, an' stay whar he kin call you whenebber he wants you to wait on him.' I didn't eben come down h'yar till I axed him would he want me fur half an hour."

"Well," said Aunt Patsy, her eyes softening a little, "p'r'aps she didn't do it dis time. It mought 'a' been his own orkardness. I hopes to mussiful goodness dat dat was so. But wot fur you call him Mister Crof'? Is dat he fus' name?"

"I reckon so," said Isham. "He one ob de fam'ly now, an' I reckon dey calls him by he fus' name. An' now, look h'yar, Aun' Patsy, I wants you not to dis-remember dis h'yar. Don' you go imaginin', ebery time anything happens to folks, dat ole miss done been kunjerin' 'em. Dat ain't pious, an' 'tain't suitable fur a ole pusson like you, Aun' Patsy, wots jes settin' on de poach steps ob heaben, a-waitin' till somebody finds out you's dar an' lets you in."

Aunt Patsy turned her great spectacles full upon him, and then she said: "You Isham, ef ebber you gits

a call to preach to folks, you jes sing out: 'Oh, Lor',
I ain't fit!' And den you go crack your head wid a
millstone, fur fear you git called ag'in, fru mistake."

Uncle Isham made no answer to this piece of advice,
but taking up some clothes which Aunt Patsy's great-
granddaughter had washed and ironed for him, he left
the cabin. He was a man much given to attending to
his own business, and paying very little attention to
those affairs of his mistress's household with which he
had no personal concern. When Mr. Croft first came
to the house, he, as well as Aunt Patsy, had been told
that it was Mr. Null, the husband of Miss Annie, and
although not thinking much about it, he had always
supposed this to be the case. But now it struck him
as a very strange thing that Miss Annie did not attend
to her husband, but allowed his mistress and himself
to do everything that was done for him. It was a
question which his mind was totally incapable of
solving; but when he reached the house, he spoke
to Letty on the subject.

"Bress your soul!" exclaimed that well-nourished
person, "dat's not Mister Null, wot married Miss
Annie. Dat's Mister Crof', an' he ain't married to
nobody. Mister Null he ain't come yet, but I reckon
he'll be along soon."

"Well, den," exclaimed Isham, much surprised,
"how come Aun' Patsy to take he fur Miss Annie's
husband?"

"Oh, git out!" contemptuously exclaimed Letty.
"Don' you go put no 'count on dem fool notions wot
Aun' Patsy got in she ole head. Nobody knows how
dey come dar, no more'n how dey ebber manage to git
out. 'Tain't no use 'splainin' nothin' to Aun' Patsy,

THE LATE MRS. NULL

an' if she b'lieves dat's Miss Annie's husband, you can't make her b'lieve it's anybody else. Jes you lef her alone. Nuffin she b'lieves ain't gwine to hurt her."

And Isham, remembering his frequent ill success in endeavoring to make Aunt Patsy think as she ought to think, concluded that this was good advice.

At the time of the conversation just mentioned, Lawrence was sitting in a large easy-chair in front of the open door of the room of which he had been put in possession. His injured foot was resting upon a cushioned stool; a small table stood by him, on which were his cigar- and match-cases, a pitcher of iced water and a glass, and a late copy of a semi-weekly paper. Through the doorway, which was but two steps higher than the grass sward before it, his eyes fell upon a very pleasing scene. To the right was the house, with its vine-covered porch and several great oak-trees overhanging it, which still retained their heavy foliage, although it was beginning to lose something of its summer green. In front of him, at the opposite end of the grassy yard, was the pretty little arbor in which he had told Mr. Junius Keswick of the difficulties in the way of his speaking his mind to Miss March. Beyond the large garden, at the back of this arbor, stretched a wide field with a fringe of woods at its distant edge, gay with the colors of autumn. The sky was bright and blue, and fair white clouds moved slowly over its surface; the air was sunny and warm, with bumblebees humming about some late-flowering shrubs; and high in the air floated two great turkey-buzzards, with a beauty of motion surpassed by no other flying thing, with never a movement of their wide-spread wings, except to give them the necessary inclination as they rose with the wind, and then turned and descended in a long sweep, only to rise again and complete the circle—sailing thus for hours, around and around, their shadows moving over the fields below them.

Fearing that he had sustained some injury more than a mere sprain, Lawrence had had the Howlett's doctor summoned, and that general practitioner had come and gone, after having assured Mr. Croft that no bones had been broken, that Mrs. Keswick's treatment was exactly what it should be, and that all that was necessary for him was to remain quiet for a few days, and be very careful not to use the injured ankle. Thus he had the prospect of but a short confinement; he felt no present pain; and there was nothing of the sick-room atmosphere in his surroundings, for his position close to the door almost gave him the advantage of sitting in the open air of this bright autumnal day.

But Lawrence's mind dwelt not at all on these ameliorating circumstances; it dwelt only upon the fact that he was in one house and Miss March was in another. It was impossible for him to go to her, and he had no reason to believe that she would come to him. Under ordinary circumstances it would be natural enough for her to look in upon him and inquire into his condition, but now the case was very different. She knew that he desired to see her, that he had been coming to her when he met with his accident, and she knew, too, exactly what he wanted to say; and it was not to be supposed that a lady would come to a man to be wooed, especially this lady, who had been in such an unfavorable humor when he had wooed her the day before.

But it was quite impossible for Lawrence, at this most important crisis of his life, to sit without action for three or four days, during which time it was not unlikely that Miss March might go home. But what was he to do? It would be ridiculous to think of sending for her, she knowing for what purpose she was wanted; and as for writing a letter, that did not suit him at all. There was too much to be explained, too much to be urged, too much to be avowed, and probably too many contingencies to be met, for him to even consider the subject of writing a letter. A proposal on paper would most certainly bring a rejection on paper. He could think of no plan; he must trust to chance. If his lucky star—and it had shone a good deal in his life—should give him an opportunity of speaking to her, he would lose not an instant in broaching the important subject. He was happy to think he had a friend in the old lady. Perhaps she might bring about the desired interview. But although this thought was encouraging, he could not but tremble when he remembered the very plain and unvarnished way she had of doing such things.

While these thoughts were passing through his mind, a lady came out upon the porch and descended the steps. At the first sight of her through the vines, Lawrence had thought it might be Miss March, and his heart had given a jump. But it was not; it was Mrs. Null; and she came over the grass towards him, and stopped in front of his door. "How are you feeling now?" she asked. "Does your foot still hurt you?"

"Oh, no," said Lawrence, "I am in no pain. The only thing that troubles me is that I have to stay just here."

"It might have been better on some accounts," said she, "if you had been taken into the house; but it would have hurt you dreadfully to go up-stairs, unless Uncle Isham carried you on his back, which I don't believe he could do."

"Of course it's a great deal better out here," said Lawrence. "In fact, this is a perfectly charming place to be laid up in. But I want to get about. I want to see people."

"Many people?" asked she, with a significant little smile.

Lawrence smiled in return. "You must know, Mrs. Null, from what I have told you," he said, "that there is one person I want to see very much, and that is why I am so annoyed at being kept here in this chair."

"You must be of an uncommonly impatient turn of mind," she said, "for you haven't been here three hours altogether, and hundreds of persons sit still that long just because they want to."

"I don't want to sit still a minute," said Lawrence. "I very much wish to speak to Miss March. Couldn't you contrive an opportunity for me to do so?"

"It is possible that I might," she said, "but I won't. Haven't I told you that I don't approve of this affair of yours? My cousin is in love with Miss March, and all I should do for you would be directly against him. Aunt so managed things this morning that I was actually obliged to give you an opportunity to be with her; but I had intended going with Roberta to the woods, as she had asked me to do."

"You are very cruel," said Lawrence.

"No, I am not," said she; "I am only just."

"I explained to you yesterday," said he, "that your course of thinking and acting is not just, and is of no possible advantage to anybody. How can it injure your cousin if Miss March refuses me and I go away and never see her again? And if she accepts me, then you should be glad that I had put an end to your cousin's pursuit of a woman who does not love him."

"That is nonsense," said she. "I shouldn't be glad at all to see him disappointed. I should feel like a traitor if I helped you. But I did not come to talk about these things. I came to ask you what you would have for dinner."

"I had an idea," said Lawrence, not regarding this remark, "that you were a young lady of a kindly disposition."

"And you don't think so now?" she said.

"No," answered Lawrence, "I cannot. I cannot think a woman kind who will refuse to assist a man situated as I am to settle the most important question of his life, especially as I have told you before that it is really to the interest of the one you are acting for that it should be settled."

Miss Annie, still standing in front of the door, now regarded Lawrence with a certain degree of thoughtfulness on her countenance, which presently changed to a half-smile. "If I were perfectly sure," she said, "that she would reject you, I would try to get her here, and have the matter settled; but I don't know her very well yet, and can't feel at all certain as to what she might do."

"I like your frankness," said Lawrence, "but, as I said before, you are very cruel."

"Not at all," said she; "I am very kind, only—"

"You don't show it," interrupted Lawrence.

At this Miss Annie laughed. "Kindness isn't of much use if it is shut up, is it?" she said. "I suppose you think it is one of those virtues that we ought to act out, as well as feel, if we want any credit. And now, isn't there something I can do for you besides bringing another man's sweetheart to you?"

Lawrence smiled. "I don't believe she is his sweetheart," he said, "and I want to find out if I am right."

"It is my opinion," said Miss Annie, "that you ought to think more about your sprained ankle and your general health than about having your mind settled by Miss March. I should think that keeping your blood boiling, in this way, would inflame your joints."

"The doctor didn't tell me what to think about," said Lawrence. "He only said I must not walk."

"I haven't heard yet," said Miss Annie, "what you would like to have to eat."

"I don't wish to give the slightest trouble," answered Lawrence. "What do you generally give people in such scrapes as this? Tea and toast?"

Annie laughed. "Nonsense," said she. "What you want is the best meal you can get. Aunt said if there was anything you particularly liked she would have it made for you."

"Do not think of such a thing," said Lawrence. "Give me just what the family has."

"Would you like Miss March to bring it out to you?" she asked.

"The word cruel cannot express your disposition," said Lawrence. "I pity Mr. Null."

"Poor man," said she; "but it would be a good thing for you if you could keep your mind as quiet as his is." And with that she went into the house.

After dinner, Miss March did come out to inquire into Mr. Croft's condition, but she was accompanied by Mrs. Keswick. Lawrence invited the ladies to come in and be seated; but Roberta stood on the grass in front of the door, as Miss Annie had done, while Mrs. Keswick entered the room, looked into the ice-water pitcher, and examined things generally, to see if Uncle Isham had been guilty of any sins of omission.

"Do you feel quite at ease now?" said Miss March.

"My ankle doesn't trouble me," said Lawrence, "but I never felt so uncomfortable and dissatisfied in my life." And with these latter words he gave the lady a look which was intended to be, and which probably was, full of meaning to her.

"Wouldn't you like some books?" said Mrs. Keswick, now appearing from the back of the room. "You haven't anything to read. There are plenty of books in the house, but they are all old."

"I think those are the most delightful of books," said Miss March. "I have been looking over the volumes on your shelves, Mrs. Keswick. I am sure there are a good many of them Mr. Croft would like to read, even if he has read them before. There are lots of queer old-time histories and biographies, and sets of bound magazines, some of them over a hundred years old. Would you like me to select some for you, Mr. Croft? Or shall I write some of the titles on a slip of paper, and let you select for yourself?"

"I shall be delighted," said Lawrence, "to have you make a choice for me; and I think the list would be the better plan, because books would be so heavy to carry about."

"I will do it immediately," said Miss March, and she walked rapidly to the house.

"Now, then," said Mrs. Keswick, "I'll put a chair out here on the grass, close to the door. It's shady there, and I should think it would be pleasant for both of you if she would sit there and read to you out of those books. She is a fine woman, that Miss March—a much finer woman than I thought she could be, before I knew her."

"She is, indeed," said Lawrence.

"I suppose you think she is the finest woman in the world?" said the old lady, with a genial grin.

"What makes you suppose so?" asked Lawrence.

"Haven't I eyes?" said Mrs. Keswick. "But you needn't make any excuses. You have made an excellent choice, and I hope you may succeed in getting her. Perhaps you have succeeded?" she added, giving Lawrence an earnest look, with a question in it.

Lawrence did not immediately reply. It was not in his nature to confide his affairs to other people, and yet he had done so much of it, of late, that he did not see why he should make an exception against Mrs. Keswick, who was, indeed, the only person who seemed inclined to be friendly to his suit. He might as well let her know how matters stood. "No," he said, "I have not yet succeeded, and I am very sorry that this accident has interfered with my efforts to do so."

"Don't let it interfere," said the old lady, her eyes sparkling, while her purple sunbonnet was suddenly and severely bobbed. "You have just as good a chance now as you ever had, and all you have to do is to make the most of it. When she comes out here to read to you, you can talk to her just as well as if you were in the woods or on top of a hill. Nobody'll come here to disturb you; I'll take care of that."

"You are very kind," said Lawrence, somewhat wondering at her enthusiasm.

"I intended to go away and leave her here with you," continued Mrs. Keswick, "if I could find a good opportunity to do so, but she hit on the best plan herself. And now I'll be off and leave the coast clear. I will come again before dark and put some more of that stuff on your ankle. If you want anything, ring this bell, and if Isham doesn't hear you, somebody will call him. He has orders to keep about the house."

"You are putting me under very great obligations to you, madam," said Lawrence.

But the old lady did not stop to hear any thanks, and hastened to clear the coast.

Lawrence had to wait a long time for his list of books, but at last it came; and, much to his surprise and chagrin, Mrs. Null brought it. "Miss March asked me to give you this," she said, "so that you can pick out just what books you want."

Lawrence took the paper, but did not look at it. He was deeply disappointed and hurt. His whole appearance showed it.

"You don't seem glad to get it," said Miss Annie.

THE LATE MRS. NULL

Lawrence looked at her, his face darkening. "Did you persuade Miss March," he said, "to stay in the house and let you bring this?"

"Now, Mr. Croft," said the young lady, a very decided flush coming into her face, "that is going too far. You have no right to accuse me of such a thing. I am not going to help in your love-affairs, but I don't intend to be mean about it, either. Miss March asked me to bring that list, and at first I wouldn't do it, for I knew, just as well as I know anything, that you expected her to come to you with it, and I was very sure you wanted to see her more than the paper. I refused two or three times, but she said, at last, that if I didn't take it she'd send it by some one in the house; so I just picked it up and brought it right along. I don't like her as much as I did."

"Why not?" asked Lawrence.

"You needn't accept a man if you don't want him," said Miss Annie, "but there is no need of being cruel to him, especially when he is laid up. If she didn't intend to come out to you again, she ought not to have made you believe so. You did expect her to come, didn't you?"

"Most certainly," said Lawrence, in rather a doleful tone.

"Yes, and there is the chair she was to sit in," said Miss Annie, "while you said seven words about the books and ten thousand about the way your heart was throbbing. I see Aunt Keswick's hand in that, as plain as can be. I don't say I'd put her in that chair if I could do it, but I certainly am sorry she disappointed you so. Would you like to have any of those books? If you would, I'll get them for you."

THE LATE MRS. NULL

"I am much obliged, Mrs. Null," said Lawrence, "but I don't think I care for any books. And let me say that I am very sorry for the way I spoke to you just now."

"Oh, don't mention that," said she. "If I'd been in your place I should have been mad enough to say anything. But it's no use to sit here and be grumpy. You'd better let me go and get you a book. The 'Critical Magazine' for 1767 and 1768 is on that list, and I know there are lots of queer, interesting things in it, but it takes a good while to hunt them out from the other things for which you would not care at all. And then, there are all the 'Spectators' and 'Ramblers,' and 'The World Displayed' in eight volumes, which, from what I saw when I looked through it, seems to be a different kind of world from the one I live in; and there are others that you will see on your list. But there is one book which I have been reading lately, which I think you will find odder and funnier than any of the rest. It is the 'Geographical Grammar,' by Mr. Salmon. Suppose I bring you that. It is a description of the whole world, written more than a hundred years ago by an Irish gentleman who, I think, never went anywhere."

"Thank you," said Lawrence; "I shall be obliged to you if you will be kind enough to bring me that one." He was glad for her to go away, even for a little time, that he might think. The smart of the disappointment caused by the non-appearance of Miss March was beginning to subside a little. Looking at it more quietly and reasonably, he could see that, in her position, it would be actually unmaidenly for her to come to him by herself. It was altogether another thing for this other girl, and therefore perhaps it was quite proper to send her. But, in spite of whatever reasonableness there might have been in it, he chafed under this propriety. It would have been far better, he thought, if she had come and told him that she could not possibly accept him, and that nothing more must be said about it. But then, he did not believe, if she had given him time to say the words he wished to say, that she would have come to such a decision; and as he called up her lovely face and figure as it stood framed in the open doorway, with a background of the sunlit arbor and fields, the gorgeous distant foliage, with the blue sky and its white clouds and circling birds, he thought of the rapture and ecstasy which would have come to him if she had listened to his words and had given him but a smile of encouragement.

But here came Mrs. Null, with a fat brown book in her hand. "One of the funniest things," she said, as she came to the door, "is Mr. Salmon's chapter on paradoxes. He thinks it would be quite improper to issue a book of this kind without alluding to geographical paradoxes. Listen to this one." And then she read to him the elucidation of the apparent paradox that there is a certain place in this world where the wind always blows from the south; and another explaining the statement that in certain cannibal islands the people eat themselves. "There is something he says about Virginia," said she, turning over the pages, "which I want you to be sure to read."

"Won't you sit down," said Lawrence, "and read to me some of those extracts? You know just where to find them."

THE LATE MRS. NULL

"That chair wasn't put there for me," said Miss Annie, with a smile.

"Nonsense," said Lawrence. "Won't you please sit down? I ought to have asked you before. Perhaps it is too cool for you out there."

"Oh, not at all," said she. "The air is still quite warm." And she took her seat on the chair, which was placed close to the door-step, and she read to him some of the surprising and interesting facts which Mr. Salmon had heard, in a Dublin coffee-house, about Virginia and the other colonies, and also some of those relating to the kindly way in which slave-holders in South America, when they killed a slave to feed their hounds, would send a quarter to a neighbor, expecting some day to receive a similar favor in return. When they had laughed over these, she read some very odd and surprising statements about southern Europe, and the people of far-away lands; and so she went on from one thing to another, talking a good deal about what she had read, and always on the point of stopping and giving the book to Lawrence, until the short autumnal afternoon began to draw to its close, and he told her that it was growing too chilly for her to sit out on the grass any longer.

"Very well," said she, closing the book and handing it to him; "you can read the rest of it yourself; and if you want any other books on the list, just let me know by Uncle Isham, and I will send them to you. He is coming now to see after you. I wonder," she said, stopping for a moment as she turned to leave, "if Miss March had been sitting in that chair, if you would have had the heart to tell her to go away, or if you would have let her sit still and take cold?"

236

Lawrence smiled, but very slightly. "That subject," said he, "is one on which I don't joke."

"Goodness!" exclaimed Miss Annie, clasping her hands and gazing with an air of comical commiseration at Mr. Croft's serious face. "I should think not!" And away she went.

Just before supper-time, when Lawrence's door had been closed and his lamp lighted, there came a knock, and Mrs. Keswick appeared. "That plan of mine didn't work," she said; "but I will bring Miss March out here, and manage it so that she'll have to stay till I come back. I have an idea about that. All that you have to do is to be ready when you get your chance."

Lawrence thanked her, and assured her he would be very glad to have a chance, although he hoped— without much ground for it—that Roberta would not see through the old lady's schemes.

Mrs. Keswick lotioned and rebandaged the sprained ankle, and then she said: "I think it would be pleasant if we were all to come out here after supper and have a game of whist. I used to play whist, and shouldn't mind taking a hand. You could have the table drawn up to your chair, and—let me see—yes, there are three more chairs. It won't be like having her alone with you," she said, with the cordial grin in which she sometimes indulged, "but you will have her opposite to you for an hour, and that will be something."

Lawrence approved heartily of the whist-party, and assured Mrs. Keswick that she was his guardian angel.

"Not much of that," she said; "but I have been

told often enough that I'm a regular old match-maker, and I expect I am."

"If you make this match," said Lawrence, "you will have my eternal gratitude."

The supper sent out to Lawrence was a very good one, and the anticipation of what was to follow made him enjoy it still more ; for his passion had now reached such a point that even to look at his love, although he could only speak to her of trumps and of tricks, would be a refreshing solace which would go down deep into his thirsty soul.

But bedtime and old Isham came, and the whist-players came not. It needed no one to tell Lawrence whose disinclination it was that had prevented their coming.

"I reckon," said Uncle Isham, as he looked in at Letty's cabin on his way to his own, " dat dat ar Mister Crof' ain't much use' to gittin' hisse'f hurt. All de time I was helpin' him go to bed he was a-growlin' like de bery debbil."

CHAPTER XX

ALTHOUGH October in southern Virginia can generally be counted upon as a very charming month, it must not be expected that her face will wear one continuous smile. On the day after Lawrence Croft's misadventure the sky was gray with low-hanging clouds, there was a disagreeable wind from the northeast, and the air was filled with the slight drizzle of rain. The morning was so cool that Lawrence was obliged to keep his door shut, and Uncle Isham had made him a small wood fire on the hearth. As he sat before this fire, after breakfast, his foot still upon a stool, and vigorously puffed at a cigar, he said to himself that it mattered very little to him whether the sun shone, or all the rains of heaven descended, so long as Roberta March would not come out to him ; and that she did not intend to come, rain or shine, was just as plain as the marks on the sides of the fireplace, probably made by the heels of Mr. Junius Keswick during many a long, reflective smoke.

On second thoughts, however, Lawrence concluded that a rainy day was worse for his prospects than a bright one. If the sun shone and everything was fair, Miss March might come across the grassy yard, and might possibly stop before his open door to bid him good morning, and to tell him that she was sorry that a headache had prevented her from coming to play whist the evening before. But this last, he presently admitted, was rather too much to expect, for he did not think she was subject to headaches, or to making excuses. At any rate, he might have caught sight of her ; and if he had, he certainly would have called to her, and would have had his say with her, even had she persisted in standing six feet from the door-step. But now this dreary day had shut his door and put an interdict upon strolls across the grass. Therefore it was that he must resign any opportunity, for that day at least, of soothing the harrowing perturbations of his passion by either the comforting warmth of hope, or by the deadening frigidity of a consummated despair. This last, in truth, he did not expect ; but still, if it came, it would be better than perturbations. They must be soothed at any cost. But how to incur this cost was a difficult question altogether. So, puffing, gazing into the fire, and knitting his brows, he sat and thought.

As a good-looking young man, as a well-dressed young man, as an educated and cultured man, as a man of the clubs and of society, and, when occasion required, as a very sensible man of business, Mr. Croft might be looked upon as essentially a commonplace personage, and in our walks abroad we meet a great many like him. But there dwelt within him a certain disposition which, at times, removed him to quite a distance from the arena in which commonplace people go through their prescribed performances. He would come to a determination, generally quite suddenly, to attain a desired end in his own way, without any reference to traditionary or conventional methods; and the more original and startling these plans, the better he liked it.

This disposition it was which made Lawrence read with so much interest the account of the defeated general who made the cavalry charge into the camp of his victorious enemy. Defeat had been his all through his short campaign, and it now seemed that the time had come to make another bold effort to get the better of his bad luck. As he could not woo Miss March himself, he must get some one else to do it for him, or, if not actually to woo the lady, to get her at last into such a frame of mind that she would allow him to woo her, even in spite of his present disadvantages. This would be a very bold stroke, but Lawrence put a good deal of faith in it.

If Miss March were properly talked to by one of her own sex, she might see, as perhaps she did not now see, how cruel was her line of conduct towards him, and might be persuaded to relent, at least enough to allow his voice to reach her; and that was all he asked for. He had not the slightest doubt that the widow Keswick would gladly consent to carry any message he chose to send to Miss March, and, more than that, to throw all the force of her peculiar style of persuasion into the support of his cause. But this, he knew very well, would finish the affair, and not at all in the way he desired. The person he wanted to act as his envoy was Mrs. Null. To be sure, she had refused to act for him; but he thought he could persuade her. She was quiet, she was sensible, and could talk very gently and confidingly when she chose; she would say just what he told her to say, and if a contingency demanded that she should add anything, she would probably do it very prudently. But then, it would be almost as difficult to communicate with her as with Miss March.

While he was thus thinking, in came the old lady, very cross. "You didn't get any rubber of whist last night, did you?" said she, without salutatory preface. "But, I can tell you, it wasn't my fault. I did all that I could, and more than I ought, to make her come; but she just put her foot down and wouldn't stir an inch, and at last I got mad and went to bed. I don't know whether she saw it or not, but I was as mad a hops; and I am that way yet. I had a plan that would have given you a chance to talk to her, but that ain't any good, now that it is raining. Let me look at your ankle; I hope that is getting along all right, anyway."

While the old lady was engaged in ministering o his needs, he told her of his plan. He said he wished to send a message to Miss March by some one, and if he could get the message properly delivered, it would help him very much.

"I'll take it," said she, looking up suddenly from the piece of soft old linen she was folding; "I'll go o her this very minute, and tell her just what you wat me to."

"Mrs. Keswick," said Lawrence, "you are as kid as you can possibly be, but I do not think it would e right for you to go on an errand like this. Miss Mah might not receive you well, and that would annoy e very much. And besides, to speak frankly, you he taken up my cause so warmly, and have been sucla good friend to me, that I am afraid your earnest esire to assist me might perhaps carry you a little too far. Please do not misunderstand me. I don't mean that you would say anything imprudent, but as you are kind enough to say that you really desire this match, it will be very natural for you to show your interest in it to a degree that would arouse Miss March's opposition."

"Yes, I see," said the old lady, reflectively; "she'd suspect what was at the bottom of my interest. She's a sharp one; I've found that out. I reckon it will be better for me not to meddle with her. I came very near quarrelling with her last night, and that wouldn't do at all."

"You see, madam," said Lawrence, well satisfied that he had succeeded in warding off the old lady's offer without offending her, "that I do not want any one to go to Miss March and make a proposal for me. I could do that in a letter. But I very much object to a letter. In fact, it wouldn't do at all. All I wish is that some one, by the exercise of a little female diplomacy, should induce her to let me speak to her. Now, I think that Mrs. Null might do this very well."

"That is so," said the old lady, who, having now finished her bandaging, was seated on a chair by the fireplace. "My niece is smart and quick, and could do this thing for you just as well as not. But she has her quips and her cranks, like the rest of us. I called her out of the room last night to know why she didn't back me up better about the whist-party, and she said she couldn't see why a gentleman who hadn't been confined to the house for quite a whole day should be so desperately lonely that people must go to his room to play whist with him. It seemed to me exactly as if she thought that Mr. Null wouldn't like it. Mr. Null, indeed! As if his wishes and desires were to be considered in my house! I never mention that man now, and Annie does not speak of him either. What I want is that he shall stay away just as long as he will; and if he will only stay away long enough to make his absence what the law calls desertion, I'll have those two divorced before they know it. Can you tell me, sir, how long a man must stay away from his wife before he can be legally charged with desertion?"

"No, madam, I cannot," said Lawrence. "The laws, I believe, differ in the various States."

"Well, I'm going to make it my business to find out all about it," said Mrs. Keswick. "Mr. Brandon has promised to attend to this matter for me, and I must write to him to know what he has been doing. Well, Mrs. Null and Miss March seem to be very good friends, and I dare say my niece could manage things so as to give you the chance you want. I'll go to the house now, and send her over to you, so that you can tell her what you want her to say or do."

"Do you think she will come, madam?" asked Lawrence.

The old lady rose to her feet, and knitted her brows until something like a perpendicular mouth appeared on her forehead. "No," said she, "now I come to think of it, I don't believe she will. In fact, I know she won't. Bother take it all, sir! What these young women want is a good whipping. Nothing else will ever bring them to their senses. What possible difference could it make to Mr. Null whether she came to you and took a message for you, or whether she didn't come—especially in a case like this, when you can't walk or go to anybody?"

"I don't think it ought to make any difference whatever," said Lawrence. "In fact, I don't believe it would."

"It's no use talking about it, Mr. Croft," said the old lady, moving towards the door. "I can go to my niece and talk to her, but the first thing I'd know I'd blaze out at her, and then, as like as not, she'd blaze back again, and then the next thing would be that she'd pack up her things and go off to hunt up her fertilizer agent. And that mustn't be. I don't want to get myself in any snarls just now. There is nothing for you to do, Mr. Croft, but to wait till it clears off, so that dainty young woman can come out of doors ; and then I think I can manage it so that you can get a chance to speak to her."

"I am very much obliged to you," said Lawrence. "I suppose I must wait."

"I'll see that Isham brings you a lot of dry hickory, so that you can have a cheerful fire, even if you can't have cheerful company," said Mrs. Keswick, as she closed the door after her.

Lawrence looked through the window at the sky, which gave no promise of clearing. And then he gazed into the fire, and considered his case. He had spent a large portion of his life in considering his case, and therefore the operation was a familiar one to him. This time the case was not a satisfactory one. Everything in this love-affair with Miss March had gone on in a manner in which he had not intended, and of which he greatly disapproved. No one in the world could have planned the affair more prudently than he had planned it. He had been so careful not to do anything rash that he had, at first, concealed, even from the lady herself, the fact that he was in love with her, and nothing could be farther from his thoughts and desires than that any one else should know of it. And yet, how had it all turned out? He had taken into his confidence Mr. Junius Keswick, Mr. Brandon, old Mrs. Keswick, Mrs. Null, as she wished to be called, and, almost lastly, the lady herself. "If I should lay bare my heart to the colored man Isham," he said to himself, "and the old centenarian in the cabin down there, I believe there would be no one else to tell. Oh, yes; there is Candy and the anti-detective. By rights, they ought to know." He did not include the good little Peggy in this category, because he was not aware that there was such a person.

After about an hour of these doleful cogitations, he again turned to look out of his front window, which commanded a view of the larger house, when he saw, coming down the steps of the porch, a not very tall figure, wrapped in a waterproof cloak, with the hood drawn over its head. He did not see the face of the figure, but he thought from the light way in which it moved that it was Mrs. Null; and when it stepped upon the grass and turned its head, he saw that he was right.

"Can her aunt have induced her to come to me?" was Lawrence's first thought. But his second was very different, for she began to walk towards the large gate which led out of the yard. Instantly Lawrence rose, and hopped on one foot to the window, where he tapped loudly on the glass. The lady turned, and then he threw up the sash.

"Won't you step here, please?" he called out.

Without answering, she immediately came over the wet grass to the window.

"I have something to say to you," he said, "and I don't want to keep you standing in the rain. Won't you come inside for a few minutes?"

"No, thank you," said she. "I don't mind a slight rain like this. I have lived so long in the city that I can't imagine how country people can bear to shut themselves in when it happens to be a little wet. I can't stand it, and I am going out for a walk."

"It is a very sensible thing to do," said Lawrence, "and I wish I could go with you and have a good long talk."

"What about?" said she.

"About Miss March."

"Well, I am rather tired of that subject," she said, "and so I reckon it is just as well that you should stay here by your fire,—I see you have one there,—and that I should take my walk by myself."

"Mrs. Null," said Lawrence, "I want to implore you to do a favor for me. I don't see how it can be disagreeable to you, and I am sure it will confer the greatest possible obligation upon me."

"What is it?" she asked.

"I want you to go to Miss March, and endeavor, in some way,—you will know how better than I can tell you,—to induce her to let me have a few words with her. If it is only here at this open window it will do."

Mrs. Null laughed. "Imagine," she said, "a woman

247

putting on a waterproof and overshoes, and coming out in the rain, to stand with an umbrella over her head, to be proposed to! That would be the funniest proceeding I ever heard of!"

Lawrence could not help smiling, though he was not in the mood for it. "It may seem amusing to you," he said, "but I am very much in earnest. I am in constant fear that she will go away while I am confined to this house. Do you know how long she intends to stay?"

"She has not told me," was the answer.

"If you will carry it," he said, "I will give you a message for her."

"Why don't you write it?" said Miss Annie.

"I don't want to write anything," he said. "I should not know how it had been received, nor would it be likely to get me any satisfaction. I want a live, sympathetic medium, such as you are. Won't you do this favor for me?"

"No, I won't," said Miss Annie, her very decided tone appearing to give a shade of paleness to her features. "How often must I tell you that I will not help you in this thing?"

"I would not ask you," said Lawrence, "if I could help myself."

"It is not right that you should ask me any more," she said. "I am not in favor of your coming here to court Miss March while my cousin is away, and I should feel like a traitor if I helped you at all, especially if I were to carry messages to her. Of course I am very sorry for you, shut up here, and I will do anything I can to make you more comfortable and contented; but what you ask is too hard for me."

And as she said this a little air of trouble came into the large eyes with which she was steadfastly regarding him. "I don't want to seem unkind to you, and I wish you would ask me something that I can do for you. I'll walk down to Howlett's and get you anything you may like to have. I'll bring you a lot of novels which I found in the house, and which I expect, anyway, you will like better than those old-time books. And I'll cook you anything that is in the cook-book. But I really cannot go wooing for you, and if you ask me to do that, every time I come near you, I really must—"

"My dear Mrs. Null," interrupted Lawrence, "I promise not to say any more to you on this subject. I see it is distasteful to you, and I beg your pardon for having mentioned it so often. You have been very kind to me indeed, and I should be exceedingly sorry to do anything to offend you. It would be very bad for me to lose one of my friends, now that I am shut up in this box and feel so very dependent."

"Oh, indeed!" said Miss Annie. "But I suppose if you were able to step around as you used to do, it wouldn't matter whether you offended me or not."

"Mrs. Null," said Lawrence, "you know I did not mean anything like that. Do you intend to be angry with me, no matter what I say?"

"Not a bit of it," she answered, with a little smile that brought back to her face that warm brightness which had grown upon it since she had come down here. "I haven't the least wish in the world to be angry with you, and I promise you I won't be, provided you'll stop everlastingly asking me to go about helping you to make love to people."

Lawrence laughed. "Very good," said he. "I have promised to ask nothing more of that sort. Let us shake hands on it."

He stretched his hand from the window, and Miss Annie withdrew from the folds of her waterproof a very soft and white little hand, and put it into his. "And now I must be off," she said. "Are you certain you don't want anything from the store at Howlett's?"

"Surely you are not going as far as that," he said.

"Not if you don't want anything," she answered. "Have you tobacco enough to last through your imprisonment? They keep it."

"Now, miss," said Lawrence, "do you want to make me angry by supposing I would smoke any tobacco that they sell in that country store?"

"It ought to be better than any other," said Miss Annie. "They grow it in the fields all about here, and the storekeepers can get it perfectly fresh and pure, and a great deal better for you, no doubt, than the stuff they manufacture in the cities."

"When you learn to smoke," said Lawrence, "your opinion concerning tobacco will be more valuable."

"Thank you," she said; "and I will wait till then before I give you any more of it. Good morning." And away she went.

Lawrence shut down the window, and hopped back to the fire. "There is my last chance gone," said he to himself. "I suppose I may as well take old Mrs. Keswick's advice, and wait for fair weather. But, even then, who can say what sort of sky Roberta March will show?" And not being able to answer this question, he put two fresh sticks on the fire, and then sedately sat and watched their gradual annihilation.

As for Miss Annie, she took her walk, and stepped along the road as lightly and blithely as if the skies had been blue and the sun shining ; and almost before she knew it, she had reached the store at Howlett's. Ascending the high steps to the porch, quite deserted on this damp, unpleasant morning, she entered the store, the proprietor of which immediately jumped up from the mackerel-kit at the extreme end of the room, where he had been sitting in converse with some of his neighbors, and hurried behind the counter.

"Have you any tea," said Miss Annie, "better than the kind which you usually sell to Mrs. Keswick?"

"No, ma'am," said he. "We send her the very best tea we have."

"I am not finding fault with it," she said, "but I thought you might have some extra kind, more expensive than people usually buy for common use."

"No, ma'am," said he ; "there is fancy teas of that kind, but you'd have to send to Philadelphia or New York for them."

"How long would that take?" she asked.

"I reckon it would be four or five days before you'd get it, ma'am," said the storekeeper.

"I am afraid," said Miss Annie, looking reflectively along the counter, "that that would be too long." And then she turned to go, but suddenly stopped. "Have you any guava jelly?" she asked.

The man smiled. "We don't have no call for anything as fancy as that, ma'am," he said. "Is there anything else?"

"Not to-day," answered Miss Annie, after throwing

a despairing glance upon the rolls of calicoes, the coils of clothes-lines, the battered tin boxes of tea and sugar, the dusty and chimneyless kerosene lamps, and the long rows of canned goods with their gaudy labels; and then she departed.

When she had gone, the storekeeper returned to his seat on the mackerel-kit, and was accosted by a pensive neighbor in high boots, who sat upon the upturned end of a case of brogans. "You didn't make no sale that time, Peckett," said he.

"No," said the storekeeper, "her idees is a little too fancy for our stock of goods."

"Whar's her husband, anyway?" asked a stout, elderly man in linen trousers and faded alpaca coat, who was seated on two boxes of pearl starch, one on top of the other. "I've heard that he was a member of the legislatur'. Is that so?"

"He's not that, you can take my word for it," said Tom Peckett. "Old Miss Keswick give me to understand that he was in the fertilizing business."

"That ought to be a good thing for the old lady," said the man on the starch-boxes. "She'll git a discount off her gwarner."

"I never did see," said the pensive neighbor on the brogan-case, "how such things do git twisted. It was only yesterday that I met a man at Tyson's Mill, who'd just come over from the Valley, and he said he'd seen this Mr. Noles over thar. He's a hoss-doctor, and he's going up through all the farms along thar."

"I reckon when he gits up as fur as he wants to go," said the man on the starch-boxes, "he'll come here and settle fur a while."

THE LATE MRS. NULL

"That won't be so much help to the old lady," said
the storekeeper, "for it wouldn't pay to keep a neffy-
in-law just to doctor one sorrel horse and a pa'r o'
oxen."

"I reckon his wife must be 'spectin' him," said the
man on the brogan-case, "from her comin' after fancy
vittles."

"If he do come," said the stout, elderly neighbor,
"I wish you'd let me know, Tom Peckett, fur my
black mar' has got a hitch in her shoulder I can't
understand, and I'd like him to look at her."

The storekeeper smiled at the pensive man, and
the pensive man smiled back at the storekeeper.
"You needn't trouble yourself about that young
woman's husband," said Mr. Peckett. "There'll be
a horse-doctor coming along afore you know it, and
he'll attend to that old mar' of yourn without chargin'
you a cent."

CHAPTER XXI

THE second afternoon of Lawrence Croft's confinement in the little building in Mrs. Keswick's yard passed drearily enough. The sky retained its sombre covering of clouds, and the rain came down in a melancholy, capricious way, as if it were tears shed by a child who was crying because it was bad. The monotony of the slowly moving hours was broken only by a very brief visit from the old lady, who was going somewhere in the covered spring-wagon, and who looked in, before she started, to see if her patient wanted anything, and by the arrival of a bundle of old novels sent by Mrs. Null. These books Lawrence looked over with indifferent interest, hoping to find one among them that was not a love-story; but he was disappointed. They were all based upon, and most of them permeated with the tender passion, and Lawrence was not in the mood for reading about that sort of thing. A person afflicted with a disease is not apt to find agreeable occupation in reading hospital reports upon his particular ailment.

The novels were put aside, and although Lawrence felt that he had smoked almost too much during that day, he was about to light another cigar, when he

254

heard a carriage drive into the yard. Turning to the window, he saw a barouche, evidently a hired one, drawn by a pair of horses, very lean and bony, but with their heads reined up so high that they had an appearance of considerable spirit, and driven by a colored man, sitting upon a very elevated seat, with a jaunty air and a well-worn whip. The carriage drove over the grass to the front of the house,—there was no roadway in the yard, the short, crisp, tough grass having long resisted the occasional action of wheels and hoofs,—and there stopping, a gentleman with a valise got out. He paid the driver, who immediately turned the vehicle about and drove away. The gentleman put his foot upon the bottom step as if he were about to ascend, and then, apparently changing his mind, he picked up his valise and came directly towards the office, drawing a key from his pocket as he walked. It was Junius Keswick, and in a few minutes his key was heard in the lock. As it was not locked, the key merely rattled, and Lawrence called out: "Come in."

The door opened, and Junius looked in, evidently surprised. "I beg your pardon," said he, "I didn't know you were in here."

"Please walk in," said Lawrence. "I know I am occupying your room, and it is I who should ask your pardon. But you see the reason why it was thought well that I should not have stairs to ascend." And he pointed to his bandaged foot.

"Have you hurt yourself?" asked Junius, with an air of concern.

And then Lawrence gave an account of his accident, expressing at the same time his regret that he found himself occupying the room which belonged to the other.

"Oh, don't mention that," said Junius, who had taken a seat near the window. "There are rooms enough in the house, and I shall be perfectly comfortable. It was quite right in my aunt to have you brought in here, and I should have insisted upon it myself if I had been at home. I expected to be away for a week or more, but I have now come back on account of your letter."

"Does that need explanation?" asked Lawrence.

"Not at all," said Junius. "I had no difficulty in understanding it, although I must say that it surprised me. But I came because I am not satisfied with the condition of things here, and I wish to be on the spot. I do not understand why you and Miss March should be invited here during my absence."

"That I do not understand either," said Lawrence, quickly, "and I wish to impress it on your mind, Mr. Keswick, that when I came here I not only expected to find you, but a party of invited guests. I will say, however, that I came with the express intention of meeting Miss March and having that interview with her which I could not have in her uncle's house."

"I was not entirely correct," said Junius, "when I said that I did not know why these rather peculiar arrangements had been made. My aunt is a very managing person, and I think I perceive her purpose in this piece of management."

"She is opposed to a marriage between you and Miss March?"

"Most decidedly," said Junius. "Has she told you so?"

THE LATE MRS. NULL

"No," said Lawrence, "but it has gradually dawned upon me that such is the case. I believe she would be glad to have Miss March married and out of your way."

Junius made no answer to this remark, but sat silent for a few moments. Then he said: "Well, have you settled it with Miss March?"

"No, I have not," said Lawrence. "If the matter had been decided, one way or the other, I should not be here. I have no right to trespass on your aunt's hospitality, and I should have departed as soon as I had discovered Miss March's sentiments in regard to me. But I have not been able to settle the matter at all. I had one opportunity of seeing the lady, and that was not a satisfactory interview. Yesterday morning I made another attempt, but before I could get to her I sprained my ankle. And here I am. I cannot go to her and of course she will not come to me. You cannot imagine how I chafe under this harassing restraint."

"I can imagine it very easily," said Junius.

"The only thing I have to hope for," said Lawrence, "is that to-morrow may be a fine day, and that the lady may come outside and give me the chance of speaking to her at this open door."

Junius smiled grimly. "It appears to me," he said, "as if it were likely to rain for several days. But now I must go into the house and see the family. I hope you believe me, sir, when I say I am sorry to find you in your present predicament."

"Yes," said Lawrence, smiling, although he did not feel at all gay, "for otherwise I might have been finally rejected and far away."

"If you had been rejected," said Junius, "I should have been very glad indeed to have you stay with us."

"Thank you," said Lawrence.

"I will look in upon you again," said Junius, as he left the room.

Lawrence's mind, which had been in a very unpleasant state of troubled restiveness for some days, was now thrown into a sad turmoil by this arrival of Junius Keswick. As he saw that tall and good-looking young man going up the steps of the house porch with his valise in his hand, he clinched both his fists as they rested on the arm of his chair, and objurgated the anti-detective.

"If it had not been for that rascal," he said to himself, "I should not have written to Keswick, and he would not have thought of coming back at this untimely moment. The only advantage I had was a clear coast, and now that is gone. Of course Keswick was frightened when he found I was staying in the same house with Roberta March, and hurried back to attend to his own interests. The first thing he will do now will be to propose to her himself; and, as they have been engaged once, it is as like as not she will take him again. If I could use this foot, I would go into the house this minute, and have the first word with her." At this he rose to his feet and made a step with his sprained ankle; but the sudden pain occasioned by this action caused him to sit down again with a groan. Lawrence Croft was not a man to do himself a physical injury which might be permanent, if such doing could possibly be avoided, and he gave up the idea of trying to go into the house.

THE LATE MRS. NULL

"I tell you what it is, Letty," said Uncle Isham, when he returned to the kitchen after having carried Lawrence's supper to him, " dat ar Mister Croft in de office is a-gittin' wus an' wus in he min' ebery day. I nebber seed a man more pow'ful glowerin' dan he is dis ebenin'."

"I reckon he j'ints is healin' up," said Letty. "Dey tells me dat de healin' pains mos' gen'rally runs into de min'."

About nine o'clock in the evening Junius Keswick paid Lawrence a visit, and, taking a seat by one side of the fireplace, accepted the offer of a cigar.

"How are things going on in the house?" asked Lawrence.

"Well," said Keswick, speaking slowly, "as you know so much of our family affairs, I might as well tell you that they are in a somewhat upset condition. When I went in, I saw, at first, no one but my cousin, and she seemed so extraordinarily glad to see me that I thought something must be wrong, somewhere ; and when my aunt returned—she was not at home when I arrived—she was thrown into such a state of mind on seeing me that I didn't know whether she was going to order me out of the house or go herself. But she restrained herself wonderfully, considering her provocation ; for, of course, I have entirely disordered her plans by appearing here, when she had arranged everything for you to have Miss March to yourself. But, so far, the peace has been kept between us, although she scarcely speaks to me."

"And Miss March?" said Lawrence. "You have seen her?"

"Yes," said Junius; "I saw her at supper and for

THE LATE MRS. NULL

a short time afterwards, but she soon retired to her room."

"Do you think she was disturbed by your return?" asked Lawrence.

"I won't say that," said Junius, "but she was certainly not herself. Mrs. Null tells me that she expects to go home to-morrow morning, having written to her uncle to send for her."

"That is bad, bad, very bad," said Lawrence.

After that there was a pause in the conversation, during which Mr. Croft, with brows very much knit, gazed steadfastly into the fire. "Mr. Keswick," he said presently, "what you tell me fills me with consternation. It is quite plain that I shall have no chance to see Miss March; and as there is no one else in the world who will do it for me, I am going to ask you to go to her to-morrow morning, and speak to her in my behalf."

When this had been said, Junius Keswick dropped his cigar upon the floor, and sat up very straight in his chair, gazing fixedly at Lawrence. "Upon my word!" he said. "I knew you were a cool man, but that request freezes my imagination. I cannot conceive how any man can ask another to try to win for him a lady whom he knows the other man desires to win for himself. You have made some requests before that were rather astounding, but this one overshadows them all."

"I admit," said Lawrence, "that what I ask is somewhat out of the way, but you must consider the circumstances. Suppose I had met you in mortal combat, and I had dropped my sword where you could reach it and I could not; would you pick it up and give it to me, or would you run me through?"

"I don't think that comparison is altogether a good one," said Junius.

"Yes, it is," said Lawrence, "and covers the case entirely. I am here, disabled, and if you pick up my sword, as I have just asked you to do, it is not to be assumed that your action gives me the victory. It merely gives me an equal chance with yourself."

"Do you mean," said Junius, "that you want me to go to Miss March and deliberately ask her if she will marry you?"

"No," said Lawrence, "I have done that myself. But there are certain points in regard to which I want to be set right with Miss March. And now I wish you to understand me, Mr. Keswick. I speak to you, not only as a generous and honorable man, which I have found you to be, but as a rival. I cannot believe that you would be willing to profit by my present disadvantages, and, as I have said two or three times before, it would certainly be for your interest, as a suitor for the lady, to have this matter settled."

"Wouldn't it be better, then," said Junius, "if I were to go immediately and speak to her for myself?"

"No," said Lawrence; "I don't think that would settle the affair at all. From what I understand of your relations with Miss March, she knows you are her lover, and yet she neither accepts nor declines you. If you were to go to her now, it is not likely she would give you any definite answer. But in regard to me, it would be different. She would say yes or no. And if she made the latter answer I think you could walk over the course. I am not vain enough to say that I have been an obstacle to your success, but I assure you that I have tried very hard to make myself such an obstacle."

"It seems to me," said Junius, imitating his companion in the matter of knitting his brows and gazing into the fire, "that this affair could be managed very simply. Miss March is not going at the break of day. Why don't you contrive to see her before she starts, and say for yourself what you have to say?"

"Nothing would please me better than that," said Croft; "but I don't believe she would give me any chance to speak with her. Since my accident, she has persistently and pointedly refused to grant me even the shortest interview."

"That ought to prove to you," said Keswick, "that she does not desire your attentions. You should consider it as a positive answer."

"Not at all," said Lawrence, "not at all. And I don't think you would consider it a positive answer if you were in my place. I think she has taken some offence which is entirely groundless, and if you will consent to act for me it will enable me to set straight this misunderstanding."

"Confound it!" exclaimed Keswick. "Can't you write to her, or get some one else to take your love-messages?"

"No," said Lawrence, "I cannot write to her, for I am not sure that under the circumstances she would answer my letter. And I have already asked Mrs. Null, the only other person I could ask, to speak for me, but she has declined."

THE LATE MRS. NULL

"By the Lord Harry!" exclaimed Junius, "you are the rarest wooer I ever heard of."

"I assure you," said Lawrence, his face flushing somewhat, "that it is not my desire to carry on my wooing in this fashion. My whole soul is opposed to it, but circumstances will have it so. And as I don't intend, if I can help it, to have my life determined by circumstances, I must go ahead in despite of them, although I admit that it makes the road very rough."

"I should think it would," said Junius. And then there was a pause in the conversation.

"Well, Mr. Keswick," said Lawrence, presently, "will you do this thing for me?"

"Am I to understand," said Junius, "that if I don't do it, it won't be done?"

"Yes," said Lawrence; "you are positively my last chance. I have racked my brains to think of some other way of presenting my case to Miss March, but there is no other way. I might stand at my door and call to her as she entered the carriage; but that would be the height of absurdity. I might hop on one foot into the house; but, even if I wished to present myself in that way, I don't believe I could get up that long flight of steps. It would be worse than useless to write, for I should not know what was thought of my letter, or even if it had been read. Mrs. Keswick cannot carry my message; Mrs. Null will not; and I have only you to call upon. I know it is a great deal to ask, but it means so much to me —to both of us, in fact—that I ask it."

"You were kind enough to say, a little while ago," said Junius, "that you considered me an honorable man. I try to be such, and therefore will frankly state to you that I can think of but three motives, satisfactory to myself, for undertaking this business for you, and not one of them is a generous one. In the first place, I might care to do it in order to have this matter settled; for you are such an extraordinary suitor that I don't know in what form you may turn up the next time. Secondly, from what you tell me of Miss March's repugnance to meet you, I don't believe my mission will have an issue favorable to you; and the more unfavorable it is, the better I shall like it. My third reason for acting for you is that the whole affair is such an original one that it will rather interest me to be engaged in it. This last reason would not hold, however, if I had the least expectation of being successful."

"You consent, then?" said Lawrence, quickly, turning towards the other. "You'll go to Miss March for me?"

"Yes, I think I will," said Junius, "if you will accept the services of a man who is decidedly opposed to your interests."

"Of course I never expected you to favor them," said Lawrence, "nor is it necessary that you should. All I ask is that you carry a message to Miss March, and, if she needs any explanation of it, that you will explain in the way that I shall indicate; that you shall tell me how she received my message; and that you shall bring me back her answer. There is no need of your making any proposition to her; that has already been done; what I want is that she should not go away from here with a misunderstanding between us, and that she shall give me at least the promise of a hearing."

THE LATE MRS. NULL

"Very good," said Junius; "now, what is it that you want me to say?"

This was not an easy question for Lawrence to answer. He knew very well what he wanted to say, if he had a chance of saying it himself. He wanted to pour his whole heart out to Roberta March, and, showing her its present passion, to ask her to forgive those days in which his mind only had appeared to be engaged. He believed he could say things that would force from her the pardon of his previous shortcomings, if she considered them as such. She had been very gracious to him in time past, and he did not see why she should not be still more gracious now, if he could remove the feelings of resentment which he believed were occasioned by her womanly insight into the motives of his conduct towards her during those delightful summer days at Midbranch.

But to get another person to say all this was a very different thing. He was sure, however, that if it were not said now, it would never be said. It would be death to all his hopes if Miss March went away, feeling towards him as she now felt; therefore he stiffened his purpose, which was quite used to being stiffened, hardened his sensibilities, and took his plunge. Gazing steadfastly at the back of the fireplace while he spoke, he endeavored to make Junius Keswick understand the nature and the probable force of the objections to his line of action as a suitor, which had grown up in the mind of Miss March; and he also endeavored to show how completely and absolutely he had been changed by the vigor and ardor of his present affection; and how he was entitled to be considered by Miss March as a lover who had but one thought and

265

purpose, and that was to win her; and, as such, he asked her to give him an opportunity to renew his proposal to her. "Now, then," said Lawrence, "I have placed the case before you, and I beg you will present it as nearly as possible in the form in which I have given it to you."

"Mr. Croft," said Junius, "this case of yours is worse than I thought it was. What woman of spirit would accept a man who admitted that during the whole of his acquaintance with her he had had his doubts in regard to suitability, etc., but who, when a crisis arrived, and another man turned up, had determined to overlook all his objections and take her, anyway."

"That is a very cold-blooded way of putting it," said Lawrence, "and I don't believe at all that she will look upon it in that light. If you will set the matter before her as I have put it to you, I believe she will see it as I wish her to see it."

"Very well," said Junius, rising and taking out his watch; "I will make your statement as accurately as I can, and without any interpretations of my own. And now I must bid you good night. I had no idea it was after twelve o'clock."

"And you will observe her moods?" asked Lawrence.

"Yes," said Junius, as he opened the door, "I will carefully observe her moods."

When Junius had gone, Lawrence turned his face again towards the fireplace, where the last smouldering stick had just broken apart in the middle, and the two ends had wearily fallen over the andirons as if they wished it understood that they could do no more burning that night. Taking this as a hint, Lawrence prepared to retire. "Old Isham must have gone to bed long ago," he said; "but as I have asked for so much assistance to-day, I think it is well that I should try to do some things for myself."

It was, indeed, very late; but behind the partially closed shutters of a lower room of the house sat old Mrs. Keswick, gazing at the light that was streaming from the window of the office, and wondering what those two men were saying to each other that was keeping them sitting up together until after midnight.

Annie Peyton, too, had not gone to bed, and looking through her chamber window, at the office, she hoped that Cousin Junius would come away before he lost his temper. Of course she thought he must have been very angry when he came home and found Mr. Croft here at the only time that Roberta March had ever visited the house, and it was quite natural that he should go to his rival and tell him what he thought about it. But he had been there a long, long time, and she did hope they would not get very angry with each other, and that nothing would happen. One thought comforted her very much: Mr. Croft was disabled, and Junius would scorn to take advantage of a man in that condition.

At an upper window, at the other end of the house, sat Roberta March, ready for bed, but with no intention of going there until Junius Keswick had come out of the office. Knowing the two men as she did, she had no fear that any harm would come to either of them during this long conference, whatever its subject might be. That she herself was that subject she had not the slightest doubt, and although it was of no earthly use for her to sit there and gaze upon that light streaming into the darkness of the yard, but revealing to her no more of what was going on inside the room than if it had been the light of a distant star, still she sat and speculated. At last the office door opened, and Junius came out, turning to speak to the occupant of the room as he did so. The brief vision of him which the watchers caught, as he stood for a moment in the lighted doorway before stepping out into the darkness, showed that his demeanor was as quiet and composed as usual; and one of the three women went to bed very much relieved.

CHAPTER XXII

FROM breakfast-time, the next morning, until ten o'clock in the forenoon, at which hour the Midbranch carriage arrived, Junius Keswick had been vainly endeavoring to get an opportunity to speak with Miss March. That lady had remained in her own room nearly all the morning, where his cousin had been with her; and his aunt, who had her own peculiar ways of speeding the parting guest, had retired to some distant spot on the estate, either to plan out some farming operation for the ensuing season, or to prevent her pent-up passion from boiling over in her own house.

Thus Junius had the lower floor to himself, and he strode about in much disquietude, debating whether he ought to send a message to Roberta, or whether he should wait till she had finished her packing, or whatever it was, that was keeping her up-stairs. His last private interview with her had not been a pleasant one, and if he had intended to speak to her for himself, he would not have felt much encouraged by her manner of the preceding evening; but he was now engaged on the affairs of another, and he believed that a failure to attend to them would be regarded as a breach of faith.

269

THE LATE MRS. NULL

When Mr. Brandon's carriage drove into the yard he began to despair; but now Roberta came running down-stairs to speak to Sam, the driver, and ask him how long it would be necessary to rest his horses. Sam thought an hour would be long enough, as they would have a good rest when they got home; and this matter having been settled, Junius came forward, and requested Roberta to step in the parlor, as he had something to say to her. Without reply, she followed him into the room, and he closed the door. They sat down, one on one side of the round centre-table, and one on the other, and Junius began his statement.

He was by profession a lawyer, and he had given a great deal of attention to the art of putting things plainly, and with a view to a just effect. He had carefully prepared in his mind what he should say to Roberta. He wished to present this man's message without the slightest exhibition of desire for its success, and yet without any tendency to that cold-blooded way of stating it to which Croft had objected. He had, indeed, picked up his adversary's sword, and while he did not wish, in handing it to him, to prick him with it, or do him some such underhand injury, he did not think it at all necessary to sharpen the weapon before giving it back.

What Junius had to say occupied a good deal of time. He expressed himself carefully and deliberately; and as nearly as a skilfully stuffed and prepared animal in a museum resembles its wild original of the forest, so did his remarks resemble those that Lawrence would have made had he been there.

Roberta listened to him in silence until he had finished, and then she rose to her feet, and her man-

THE LATE MRS. NULL

ner was such that Junius rose also. "Junius Keswick," she said, "you have deliberately come to me
and offered me the hand of another man in marriage."

"Not that," said Junius. "I merely came to explain—"

"Do not split hairs," she interrupted. "You did
exactly that. You came to me because he could not
come himself, and offered him to me. Now go to him
from me, and tell him that I accept him." And with
that she swept out of the room, and came down-stairs
no more until, bonneted, and accompanied by Miss
Annie, she hurried to the front door, and entered the
carriage which was there waiting for her, with Peggy
by the driver. With some quick good-bys and
kisses to Annie, but never a word to Junius or anybody else, she drove away.

If Junius Keswick had been nervous and anxious
that morning, as he strode about the house waiting
for an opportunity to speak to Miss March, it may
well be supposed that Lawrence Croft, shut up in his
little room at the end of the yard, would be more so.
He had sat at his window, waiting and waiting. He
had occasionally seen Mr. Keswick come out on the
porch and with long strides pace backward and forward, and he knew by that sign that he had yet no
message to bring him. He had seen the Midbranch
carriage drive into the yard; he had seen Miss March
come out on the porch and speak to the driver, and
then go in again; he had seen the carriage driven
under a large tree, where the horses were taken out
and led away to be refreshed; in an hour or more, he
saw them brought back and harnessed to the vehicle,
which was turned and driven up again to the door,

when some baggage was brought down and strapped on a little platform behind. Shortly afterwards Peggy came round the end of the house, with a hat on, and a little bundle under her arm, and approached the carriage, making, however, a wide turn towards the office, at which, and a mile or two beyond, her far-off gaze was steadily directed.

Lawrence threw up the sash and called to her, and his guardian imp approached the window. "Are you Miss March's maid? I think I have seen you at Midbranch."

"Yaas, sah; you's done seen me offen," said Peggy.

"Does Miss March intend to start immediately?" he asked.

"Yaas, sah," said the good Peggy; "she'll be out in a minute, soon as she done kissin' Mahs' Junius good-by in de parlor." And then, noticing a look of astonishment on the gentleman's face, she added: "Dey's gwine to be mar'ed Chris'mus."

"What!" exclaimed Lawrence.

"Good-by, Mister Crof'," said Peggy; "I'se got to hurry up."

Lawrence made no answer, but mechanically tossed her a coin, which picking up, she gave him a fare-well grin, and hastened to take her seat by the driver.

Very soon afterwards Lawrence saw Roberta come out, accompanied only by Mrs. Null, and hurry down the steps. Forgetting his injured ankle, he sprang to his feet, and stepping quickly to the door, opened it, and stood on the threshold. But Miss March did not even look his way. He gazed at her with wide-open eyes as she hastily kissed Mrs. Null and sprang into

THE LATE MRS. NULL

the carriage, which was immediately driven off. As Mrs. Null turned to go into the house, she looked towards the office and nodded to him. He believed that she would have come to him if he had called her, but he did not call. His mind was in such a condition that he would not have been capable of framing a question, had she come. He felt that he could speak to no one until he had seen Keswick. Closing the door, he went back to his chair; and as he did so his ankle pained him sadly, but of this he scarcely thought.

He did not have to wait long for Junius Keswick, for in about ten minutes that individual entered. Lawrence turned as his visitor opened the door, and he saw a countenance which had undergone a very noticeable change. It was not dark or lowering; it was not pale; but it was gray and hard, and the eyes looked larger than Lawrence had remembered them.

Without preface or greeting, Junius approached him and said: "I have taken your message to Miss March, and have brought you one in return. You are accepted."

Lawrence pushed back his chair, and stared blankly at the other. "What do you mean?" he presently asked.

"I mean what I say," said Keswick. "Miss March has accepted you."

A crowd of emotions rushed through the brain of Lawrence Croft; joy was among them, but it was a joy that was jostled and shaken and pushed this way and that. "I do not understand," he said. "I did not expect such a decisive message. I supposed she might send me some encouragement, some—why didn't she see me before she left?"

"I am not here to explain her actions, if I could," said Junius, who had not sat down. "She said: 'Tell him I accept him.' That is all. Good morning."

"But stop!" cried Lawrence, on his feet again. "You must tell me more than that. Did you say to her only what I said to you? How did it affect her?"

"Oh," said Junius, turning suddenly at the door, "I forgot that you asked me to observe her mood. Well, she was very angry."

"With me?" cried Lawrence.

"With me," said Junius. And closing the door behind him, he strode away.

The accepted lover sat down. He had never spoken more truly than when he said he did not understand it. "Is she really mine?" he exclaimed. And with his eyes fixed on the blank wall over the mantelpiece, he repeated over and over again: "Is she mine? Is she really mine?" He had well-developed mental powers, but the work of setting this matter straight and plain was too difficult for him.

If she had sent him some such message as this, "I am very angry with you, but some day you can come and explain yourself to me," his heart would have leaped for joy. He would have believed that his peace had been made, and that he had only to go to her to call her his own. Now his heart desired to leap with joy, but it did not seem to know how to do it. The situation was such an anomalous one. After such a message as this, why had she not let him see her? Why had she been angry with Keswick? Was

THE LATE MRS. NULL

that pique? And then a dark thought crossed his mind. Had he been accepted to punish the other? No, he could not believe that; no woman such as Roberta March would give herself away from such a motive. Had Keswick been joking with him? No, he could not believe that; no man could joke with such a face.

Even the fact that Mrs. Keswick had not bidden Miss March farewell troubled the mind of Lawrence. It was true that she might not yet know that the match which she had so much encouraged had been finally made, but something must be very wrong, or she would not have been absent at the moment of her guest's departure. And what did that beastly little negro mean by telling him that Keswick and Miss March were to be married at Christmas, and that the two were kissing each other good-by in the parlor? Why, the man had not even come out to put her in the carriage, and the omission of this courtesy was very remarkable. These questions were entirely too difficult for him to resolve by himself. It was absolutely necessary that more should be told to him and explained to him. Seeing the negro boy Plez crossing the yard, he called him and asked him to tell Mr. Keswick that Mr. Croft wished to see him immediately.

"Mahs' Junius," said the boy, "he done gone to de railroad to take de kyars. He done took he knapsack on he back, an' walk 'cross de fiel's."

When, about an hour or two afterwards, Uncle Isham brought Mr. Croft his dinner, the old negro appeared to have lost that air of attentive geniality which he usually put on while waiting on the gentle-

275

man. Lawrence, however, took no notice of this, but before the man reached the table on which he was to place the tray he carried, he asked: "Is it true that Mr. Keswick has gone away by train?"

"Yaas, sah," answered Isham.

"And where is Mrs. Keswick?" asked Lawrence. "Isn't she in the house?"

"No, sah; done gwine vis'tin', I 'spec'."

"When will she return?"

"Dunno," said Isham. "She nebber comes to me an' tells me whar she gwine an' when she comin' back."

And then, after satisfying himself that nothing more was needed of him for the present, Isham left the room; and when he reached the kitchen, he addressed himself to its plump mistress. "Letty," said he, "when dat ar Mister Crof' has got fru wid his dinner, you go an' fotch back de plates an' dishes. He axes too many questions to suit me dis day."

"You is po'ly to-day, Uncle Isham," said Letty.

"Yaas," said the old man; "I'se right much on de careen."

Uncle Isham, perhaps, was not more loyal to the widow Keswick than many old servants were and are to their former mistresses, but his loyalty was peculiar in that it related principally to his regard for her character. This regard he wished to be very high, and it always troubled and unsettled his mind when the old lady herself or anybody else interfered with his efforts to keep it high. For years he had been hoping that the time would come when she would cease to "r'ar and chawge," but she had continued, at intervals, to indulge in that most unsuitable exercise;

and now that it appeared that she had reared and charged again, her old servant was much depressed. She had gone away from the house, and, for all he knew, she might stay away for days or weeks, as she had done before; and Uncle Isham was never so much "on the careen" as when he found himself forced to believe that his old mistress was still a woman who could do a thing like that.

Letty had no objections to answering questions, but, much to her disappointment, Lawrence asked her none. He had had enough of catechising negroes. But he requested her to ask Mrs. Null if she would be kind enough to step out, for a few minutes, and speak to him. When, very shortly thereafter, that lady appeared, Lawrence was seated at his open door, ready to receive her.

"How are you?" she said. "And how is your ankle to-day? You have had nobody to attend to it."

"It has hurt me a good deal," he answered. "I think I must have given it a wrench this morning; but I put on it some of the lotion Mrs. Keswick left with me, and it feels better."

"It is too bad," said Mrs. Null, "that you have to attend to it yourself."

"Not at all," said Lawrence. "Now that I know how, I can do it perfectly well; and I don't care a snap about my ankle, except that it interferes with more important affairs. Why do you suppose Miss March went away without speaking to me, or taking leave of me in any way?"

"I thought that would trouble you," said she, "and, to speak honestly, I don't think it was right. But Roberta was in a very agitated condition when she left here, and I don't believe she ever thought of taking leave of you, or any one, except me. She and I are very good friends, but she doesn't confide much in me. But one thing I am pretty sure of, and that is that she is dreadfully angry with my cousin Junius, and I am very sorry for that."

"How did he anger her?" asked Lawrence, wishing to find out how much this young woman knew.

"I haven't the least idea," said Miss Annie. "All I know is, she had quite a long talk with him in the parlor, and after that she came flying up-stairs, just as indignant as she could be. She didn't say much, but I could see how her soul raged within her." And now the young lady stopped speaking, and looked straight into Lawrence's face. "It isn't possible," she said, "that you have been sending my cousin to propose to her for you?"

This was not a pleasant question to answer, and, besides, Lawrence had made up his mind that the period had passed for making confidants of other persons in regard to his love-affairs. "Do you suppose I would do that?" he said.

"No, I don't," Miss Annie answered. "Cousin Junius would never have undertaken such a thing, and I don't believe you would be cruel enough to ask him."

"Thank you for your good opinion," said Lawrence. "And now can you tell me when Mr. Keswick is expected to return?"

"He has gone back to Washington, and he told me he should stay there some time."

"And why has not Mrs. Keswick been out to see me?" asked Lawrence.

THE LATE MRS. NULL

"You are dreadfully inquisitive," said Miss Annie; "but, to tell you the simple truth, Mr. Croft, I don't believe Aunt Keswick takes any further interest in you, now that Roberta has gone. She had set her heart on making a match between you two, and doing it here without delay; and I think that everything going wrong about this has put her into the state of mind she is in now."

"Has she really gone away?" asked Lawrence.

"Oh, that doesn't amount to anything," said Miss Annie. "She went over the fields to Howlett's, to see the postmistress, who is an old friend, to whom she often goes for comfort when things are not right at home. But I am going after her this afternoon in the spring-wagon. I'll take Plez along with me to open the gates. I am sure I shall bring her back."

"I must admit, Mrs. Null," said Lawrence, "that I am very inquisitive, but you can easily understand how much I am troubled and perplexed."

"I expect Miss March's going away troubled you more than anything else," said she.

"That is true," he answered; "but then, there are other things which give me a great deal of anxiety. I came here to be, for a day or two, the guest of a lady on whom I have no manner of claim for prolonged hospitality. And now here I am, compelled to stay in this room and depend on her kindness or forbearance for everything I have. I would go away immediately, but I know it would injure me to travel. The few steps I took yesterday have probably set me back for several days."

"Oh, it would never do for you to travel," said she, "with such a sprained ankle as you have. It would certainly injure you very much to be driven all the way to the Green Sulphur Springs. I am told the road is very rough between here and there; but perhaps you didn't notice it, having come over on horseback."

"Yes, I did notice it, and I could not stand that drive. And even if I could be got to the train to go North, I should have to walk a good deal at the stations."

"You simply must not think of it," said Miss Annie. "And now let me give you a piece of advice. I am a practical person, as you may know, and I like to do things in a practical way. The very best thing that you can do is to arrange with Aunt Keswick to stay here as a boarder until your ankle is well. She has taken boarders, and in this case I don't think she would refuse. As I told you before, you must not expect her to take the same interest in you that she did when you first came; but she is really a kind woman, though she has such dreadfully funny ways, and she wouldn't have neglected you to-day if it hadn't been that her mind is entirely wrapped up in other things. If you like, I'll propose such an arrangement to her this afternoon."

"You are very kind indeed," said Lawrence; "but is there not danger of offending her by such a proposition?"

"Yes, I think there is," answered Miss Annie, "and I have no doubt she will fly out into a passion when she hears that the gentleman whom she invited here as a guest proposes to stay as a boarder; but I think I can pacify her, and make her look at the matter in the proper way."

THE LATE MRS. NULL

"But why mention it at all, and put yourself to all that trouble about it?" said Lawrence.

"Why, of course, because I think you will be so much better satisfied, and content to keep quiet and get well, if you feel that you have a right to stay here. If Aunt Keswick wasn't so very different from other people, I wouldn't have mentioned this matter, for, really, there is no necessity for it; but I know very well that if you were to drop out of her mind for two or three days, and shouldn't see anything of her, that you would become dreadfully nervous about staying here."

"You are certainly very practical, Mrs. Null, and very sensible, and very, very kind; and nothing could suit me better, under the circumstances, than the plan you propose. But I am extremely anxious not to give offence to your aunt. She has treated me with the utmost kindness and hospitality."

"Oh, don't trouble yourself about that," said Miss Annie, with a little laugh. "I am getting to know her so well that I think I can manage an affair like this very easily. And now I must be off, or it will be too late for me to go to Howlett's this afternoon, and I am a very slow driver. Are you sure there is nothing you want? I shall go directly past the store, and can stop as well as not."

"Thank you very much," said Lawrence, "but I do not believe that Howlett's possesses an article that I need. One thing I will ask you to do for me before you go. I want to write a letter, and I find that I am out of paper; therefore I shall be very much obliged to you if you will let me have some, and some envelopes."

"Why, certainly," said Miss Annie, and she went into the house.

She looked over the stock of paper which her aunt kept in a desk in the dining-room, but she did not like it. "I don't believe he will want to write on such ordinary paper as this," she said to herself. Whereupon she went up-stairs and got some of her own paper and envelopes, which were much finer in material and more correct in style. "I don't like it a bit," she thought, "to give this to him to write that letter on; but I suppose it's bound to be written, anyway, so he might as well have the satisfaction of good paper."

"You must excuse these little sheets," she said, when she took it to him, "but you couldn't expect anything else in an Amazonian household like ours. Cousin Junius has manly stationery, of course, but I suppose it is all locked up in that secretary in your room."

"Oh, this will do very well indeed," said Lawrence; "and I wish I could come out and help you into your vehicle," regarding the spring-wagon, which now stood at the door, with Plez at the head of the solemn sorrel.

"Thank you," said Miss Annie; "that is not at all necessary." And she tripped over to the spring-wagon, and mounting into its altitudes without the least trouble in the world, she took up the reins. With these firmly grasped in her little hands, which were stretched very far out and held very wide apart, she gave the horse a great jerk and told him to "get up!" As she moved off, Lawrence from his open door called out, "*Bon voyage*"; and in a full, clear voice she thanked him, but did not dare to look around, so intent was she upon her charioteering.

Slowly turning the horse towards the yard gate, which Plez stood holding open, her whole soul was absorbed in the act of guiding the equipage through the gateway. Quickly glancing from side to side, and then at the horse's back, which ought to occupy a medium position between the two gate-posts, she safely steered the front wheels through the dangerous pass, although a grin of delight covered the face of Plez as he noticed that the hub of one of the hind wheels almost grazed a post. Then the observant boy ran on to open the other gate, and with many jerks and clucks, Miss Annie induced the sorrel to break into a gentle trot.

As Lawrence looked after her, a little pang made itself noticeable in his conscience. This girl was certainly very kind to him, and most remarkably considerate of him in the plan she had proposed. And yet, he felt that he had prevaricated to her, and, in fact, deceived her, in the answer he had made when she asked him if he had sent her cousin to speak for him to Miss March. Would she have such friendly feelings towards him, and be so willing to oblige him, if she knew that he had in effect done the thing which she considered so wrong and so cruel? But it could not be helped. The time had passed for confidences. He must now work out this affair for himself, without regard to persons who really had nothing whatever to do with it.

Closing his door, he hopped back to his table, and, seating himself at it, he opened his travelling-inkstand and prepared to write to Miss March. It was abso-

lutely necessary that he should write this letter immediately, for, after the message he had received from the
lady of his love, no time should be lost in putting himself in communication with her. But before beginning
to write he must decide upon the spirit of his letter.

Under the very peculiar circumstances of his acceptance, he did not feel that he ought to indulge in
those rapturous expressions of ecstasy in which he
most certainly would have indulged if the lady had
personally delivered her decision to him. He did
not doubt her, for what woman would play a joke like
that on a man—upon two men, in fact? Even if
there were no other reason, she would not dare to do
it. Nor did he doubt Keswick. It would have been
impossible for him to come with such a message if it
had not been delivered to him. And yet, Lawrence
could not bring himself to be rapturous. If he had
been accepted in cold blood, and a hand, and not a
heart, had been given to him, he would gladly take
that hand and trust to himself to so warm the heart
that it, also, would soon be his. But he did not know
what Roberta March had given him.

On the other hand, he knew very well if, in his first
letter as an accepted lover, he should exhibit any of
that caution and prudence which, in the course of his
courtship, had proved to be shoals on which he had
very nearly run aground, that Roberta's resentment,
which had shown itself very marked in this regard,
would probably be roused to such an extent that the
affair would be brought to a very speedy and abrupt
termination. If she had been obliged to forgive him
once for this line of conduct, he could not expect her
to do it again. To write a letter which should err in

neither of these respects was a very difficult thing to do, and required so much preparatory thought that when, towards the close of the afternoon, Miss Annie drove in at the yard gate, with Mrs. Keswick on the seat beside her, not a line had been written.

Mrs. Keswick descended from the spring-wagon and went into the house; but Miss Annie remained at the bottom of the steps, for the apparent purpose of speaking to Plez—perhaps to give him some instructions in regard to the leading of a horse to its stable, or to instil into his mind some moral principle or other; but the moment the vehicle moved away, she ran over to the office and tapped at the window, which was quickly opened by Lawrence.

"I have spoken to her about it," she said; "and although she blazed up at first, so that I thought I should be burned alive, I made her understand just how matters really are, and she has agreed to let you stay here as a boarder."

"You are extremely good," said Lawrence, "and must be a most admirable manager. This arrangement makes me feel much better satisfied than I could have been otherwise." Then, leaning a little farther out of the window, he asked: "But what am I to do for company while I am shut up here?"

"Oh, you will have Uncle Isham, and Aunt Keswick, and sometimes me. But I hope that you will soon be able to come into the house and take your meals and spend your evenings with us."

"You have nothing but good wishes for me," he said, "and I believe, if you could manage it, you would have me cured by magic, and sent off, well and whole, to-morrow."

285

"Of course," said Miss Annie, very promptly. "Good night."

Just before supper, Mrs. Keswick came in to see Lawrence. She was very grave, almost severe, and her conversation was confined to inquiries as to the state of his ankle, and his general comfort. But Lawrence took no offence at her manner, and was very gracious, saying some exceedingly neat things about the way he had been treated; and after a little her manner slightly mollified, and she remarked: "And so you let Miss March go away without settling anything."

Now, Lawrence considered this a very incorrect statement, but he had no wish to set the old lady right. He knew it would joy her heart, and make her more his friend than ever, if he should tell her that Miss March had accepted him, but this would be a very dangerous piece of information to put in her hands. He did not know what use she would make of it, or what damage she might unwittingly do to his prospects. And so he merely answered: "I had no idea she would leave so soon."

"Well," said the old lady, "I suppose, after all, that you needn't give it up yet. I understand that she is not going to New York before the end of the month, and you may be well enough before that to ride over to Midbranch."

"I hope so, most assuredly," said he.

Lawrence devoted that evening to his letter. It was a long one, and was written with a most earnest desire to embrace all the merits of each of the two kinds of letters which have before been alluded to, and to avoid all their faults. When it was finished, he read it, tore it up, and threw it in the fire.

CHAPTER XXIII

THE next day opened bright and clear, and before ten o'clock the thermometer had risen to seventy degrees. Instead of sitting in front of the fireplace, Lawrence had his chair and table brought close to his open doorway, where he could look out on the same beautiful scene which had greeted his eyes a few days before. "But what is the good," he thought, "of this green grass, this sunny air, that blue sky, those white clouds, and the distant tinted foliage, without that figure which a few days ago stood in the foreground of the picture?" But as the woman to whom, in his soul's sight, the whole world was but a background, was not there, he turned his eyes from the warm autumnal scene, and prepared again to write to her. He had scarcely taken up his pen, however, when he was interrupted by the arrival of Miss Annie, who came to bring him a book she had just finished reading, a late English novel which she thought might be more interesting than those she had sent him. The book was one which Lawrence had not seen and wanted to see; but in talking about it to the young lady, he discovered that she had not read all of it.

"Don't let me deprive you of the book," said Law-

287

rence. "If you have begun it, you ought to go on with it."

"Oh, don't trouble your mind about that," she said, with a laugh. "I have finished it, but I have not read a word of the beginning. I only looked at the end of it to see how the story turned out. I always do that before I read a novel."

This remark much amused Lawrence. "Do you know," said he, "that I would rather not read novels at all than to read them in that way. I must begin at the beginning, and go regularly through, as the author wishes his readers to do."

"And perhaps, when you get to the end," said Miss Annie, "you'll find that the wrong man got her, and then you'll wish you had not read the story."

"As you appear to be satisfied with this novel," said Lawrence, "I wish you would read it to me, and then I would feel that I was not taking an uncourteous precedence of you."

"I'll read it to you," said she, "or, at least, as much as you want me to, for I feel quite sure that after you get interested in it you will want to take it yourself, and read straight on till it is finished, instead of waiting for some one to come and give you a chapter or two at a time. That would be the way with me, I know."

"I shall be delighted to have you read to me," said Lawrence. "When can you begin?"

"Now," she said, "if you choose. But perhaps you wish to write."

"Not at this moment," said Lawrence, turning from the table. "Unfortunately, I have plenty of leisure. Where will you sit?" And he reached out his hand for a chair.

THE LATE MRS. NULL

"Oh, I don't want a chair," said Annie, taking her seat on the broad door-step. "This is exactly what I like. I am devoted to sitting on steps. Don't you think there is something dreadfully stiff about always being perched up in a chair?"

"Yes," said Lawrence, "on some occasions."

And forthwith she began upon the first chapter; and having read five lines of this, she went back and read the title-page, suddenly remembering that Mr. Croft liked to begin a book at the very beginning. Miss Annie had been accustomed to read to her father, and she read aloud very well, and liked it. As she sat there, shaded by a great locust-tree, which had dropped so many yellow leaves upon the grass that, now and then, it could not help letting a little fleck of sunshine come down upon her, sometimes gilding for a moment her light-brown hair, sometimes touching the end of a crimson ribbon she wore, and again resting for a brief space on the toe of a very small boot just visible at the edge of her dress, Lawrence looked at her, and said to himself: "Is it possible that this is the rather pale young girl in black who gave me change from behind the desk of Mr. Candy's Information Shop? I don't believe it. That young person sprang up temporarily, and is defunct. This is some one else."

She read three chapters before she considered it time to go into the house to see if it were necessary for her to do anything about dinner. When she left him, Lawrence turned again to his writing.

That afternoon he sent Mrs. Null a little note on the back of a card, asking her if she could let him have a few more sheets of paper. Lawrence found this request necessary, as he had used up that day all the paper she had sent him, and the small torn pieces of it now littered the fireplace.

"He must be writing a diary letter," said Miss Annie to herself, when she received this message, "such as we girls used to write when we were at school." And bringing down a little the corners of her mouth, she took from her stationery-box what she thought would be quite paper enough to send to a man for such a purpose.

But although the means were thus made abundant, the letter to Miss March was not then written. Lawrence finally determined that it was simply impossible for him to write to the lady until he knew more. What Keswick had told him had been absurdly little, and he had hurried away before there had been time to ask further questions. Instead of sending a letter to Miss March, he would write to Keswick, and would put to him a series of interrogations, the answers to which would make him understand better the position in which he stood. Then he would write to Miss March.

The next day Miss Annie could not read to him in the morning, because, as she came and told him, she was going to Howlett's, on an errand for her aunt. But there would be time to give him a chapter or two before dinner, when she came back.

"Would it be any trouble," said Lawrence, "for you to mail a letter for me?"

"Oh, no," said Miss Annie, but not precisely in the same tone in which she would have told him that it would be no trouble to read to him two or three chapters of a novel. And yet she would pass directly by the residence of Miss Harriet Corvey, the post-mistress.

"Is it possible that this is the rather pale young girl in black
who gave me change?"

THE LATE MRS. NULL

As Miss Annie walked along the narrow path which ran by the roadside to Howlett's, with the blue sky above her and the pleasant October sunshine all about her, and followed at a little distance by the boy Plez, carrying a basket, she did not seem to be taking that enjoyment in her walk which was her wont. Her brows were slightly contracted, and she looked straight in front of her without seeing anything in particular, after the manner of persons whose attention is entirely occupied in looking into their own minds at something they do not like. "It is too much!" she said, almost aloud, her brows contracting a little more as she spoke. "It was bad enough to have to furnish the paper; but for me to have to carry the letter is entirely too much!" And at this she involuntarily glanced at the thick and double-stamped missive, which, having no pocket, she carried in her hand. She had not looked at it before, and as her eyes fell upon the address, she stopped so suddenly that Plez, who was dozing as he walked, nearly ran into her.

"What!" she exclaimed, "'Junius Keswick, 5 Q Street, Washington, District of Columbia!' Is it possible that Mr. Croft has been writing to him all this time?" She now walked on; and although she still seemed to notice not the material objects around her, the frown disappeared from her brow, and her mental vision seemed to be fixed upon something more pleasant than that which had occupied it before. As it will be remembered, she had refused positively to have anything to do with Lawrence's suit to Miss March, and it was a relief to her to know that the letter she was carrying was not for that lady. "But why," thought she, "should he be writing for two whole evenings to Junius? I expected that he would write to her to find out why she went off and left him in that way, but I did not suppose he would want to write to Junius. It seems to me they had time enough, that night they were together, to talk over everything they had to say."

And then she began to wonder what they had to say, and gradually the conviction grew upon her that Mr. Croft was a very, very honorable man. Of course it was wrong that he should have come here to try to win a lady who, if one looked at it in the proper light, really belonged to another. But it now came into her mind that Mr. Croft must, by degrees, have seen this for himself, and that it was the subject of his long conference with Junius, and also, most probably, of this letter. The conference certainly ended amicably, and, in that case, it was scarcely possible that Junius had given up his claim. He was not that kind of a man.

If Mr. Croft had become convinced that he ought to retire from this contest, and had done so, and Roberta had been informed of it, that would explain everything that had happened. Roberta's state of mind after she had had the talk in the parlor with Junius, and her hurried departure without taking the slightest notice of either of the gentlemen, was quite natural. What woman would like to know that she had been bargained about, and that her two lovers had agreed which of them should have her? It was quite to be expected that she would be very angry at first, though there was no doubt she would get over it, so far as Junius was concerned.

Having thus decided, entirely to her own satisfaction, that this was the state of affairs, she thought it was a grand thing that there were two such young men in the world as her cousin and Mr. Croft, who could arrange such an affair in so kindly and honorable a manner, without feeling that they were obliged to fight—that horribly stupid way in which such things used to be settled.

This vision of masculine high-mindedness which Miss Annie had called up seemed very pleasant to her, and her mental satisfaction was denoted by a pretty little glow which came into her face, and by a certain increase of sprightliness in her walk. "Now, then," she said to herself; and although she did not finish the sentence, even in her own mind, the sky increased the intensity of its beautiful blue; the sun began to shine with a more golden radiance; the little birds who had not yet gone south chirped to each other as merrily as if it had been early summer; the yellow and purple wild flowers of autumn threw into their blossoms a richer coloring; and even the blades of grass seemed to stretch themselves upward, green, tender, and promising; and when the young lady skipped up the step of the post-office, she dropped the letter into Miss Harriet Corvey's little box with the air of a mother-bird feeding a young one with the first ripe cherry of the year.

A day or two after this, Lawrence found himself able, by the aid of a cane and a rude crutch, which Uncle Isham had made for him and the top of which Mrs. Keswick had carefully padded, to make his way from the office to the house; and after that he took his meals and passed the greater part of his time in the larger edifice. Sometimes he ransacked the old library; sometimes Miss Annie read to him, and sometimes he read to her. In the evening there were games of cards, in which the old lady would occasionally take a hand, although more frequently Miss Annie and Mr. Croft were obliged to content themselves with some game at which two could play. But the pleasantest hours, perhaps, were those which were spent in talking; for Lawrence had travelled a good deal, and had seen so many of the things in foreign lands which Miss Annie had always wished that she could see.

Lawrence was waiting until he should hear from Mr. Keswick, so that, with some confidence in his position, he could write to Miss March. His trunk had been sent over from the Green Sulphur Springs, and he was much better satisfied to wait here than at that deserted watering-place. It was, indeed, a very agreeable spot in which to wait, and quite near enough to Midbranch for him to carry on his desired operations, when the time should arrive. He was a little annoyed that Keswick's answer should be so long in coming, but he resolved not to worry himself about it. The answer was probably a difficult letter to write, and one which Keswick would not be likely to dash off in a hurry. He remembered, too, that the mail was sent and received only twice a week at Howlett's.

Old Mrs. Keswick was kind to him, but grave and rather silent. Once she passed the open door of the parlor, by the window of which sat Miss Annie and Lawrence, deeply engaged, their heads together, in studying out something on a map; and as she went up-stairs she grimly grinned and said to herself: "If that Null could look in and see them now, I reckon our young man would wish he had the use of all his arms and legs."

But if Mr. Null should disapprove of his wife and that gentleman from New York spending so much of their time together, old Mrs. Keswick had not the least objection in the world. She was well satisfied that Mr. Croft should find it interesting enough to stay here until the time came when he should be able to go to Midbranch. When that period arrived she would not be slow to urge him to his duty, in spite of any obstacles Mr. Brandon might put in his way. So, for the present, she possessed her soul in as much peace as the soul of a headstrong and very wilful old lady is capable of being possessed.

CHAPTER XXIV

THE letter which Lawrence Croft had written to Junius Keswick was not answered for more than a week; and when the answer arrived, it did not come through the Howlett's post-office, but was brought from a mail-station on the railway by a special messenger. In this epistle Mr. Keswick stated that he would have written much sooner but for the fact that he had been away from Washington, and having just returned, had found Mr. Croft's letter waiting for him. The answer was written in a tone which Lawrence did not at all expect. It breathed the spirit of a man who was determined and almost defiant. It told Mr. Croft that the writer did not now believe that Miss March's acceptance of the said Mr. Croft should be considered of any value whatever. It was the result of a very peculiar condition of things, in which he regretted having taken a part, and it was given in a moment of pique and indignation, which gave Miss March a right to reconsider her hasty decision, if she chose to do so. It would not be fair for either of them to accept, as conclusive, words said under the extraordinary circumstances which surrounded Miss March when she said those words.

"You asked me to do you a favor," wrote Junius

Keswick, "and, very much against my inclination, and against what is now my judgment, I did it. I now ask you to do me a favor, and I do not think you should refuse it. I ask you not to communicate with Miss March until I have seen her, and have obtained from her an explanation of the acceptance in question. I have a right to this explanation, and I feel confident that it will be given to me. You ask me what I truly believe Miss March meant by her message to you. I answer that I do not know, but I intend to find out what she meant, and as soon as I do so, I will write to you. I think, therefore, considering what you have asked me to do, and what you have written to me about what I have done, that you cannot refuse to abstain from any further action in the matter until I am enabled to answer you. I cannot leave Washington immediately, but I shall go to Midbranch in a very few days."

This letter was very far from being a categorical answer to Lawrence's questions, and it disappointed and somewhat annoyed that gentleman; but after he had read it for the second time, and carefully considered it, he put it in his pocket and said to himself: "This ends all discussion of this subject. Mr. Keswick may be right in the position he takes, or he may be wrong. He may go to Midbranch, he may get his explanation, and he may send it to me. But, without any regard to what he does, or says, or writes, I shall go to Miss March as soon as I am able to use my ankle; and whether she be at her uncle's house, or whether she has gone to New York or to any other place, I shall see her and myself obtain from her an explanation of this acceptance. This is due to me as well as to Mr. Keswick, and if he thinks he ought to get it for himself, I also think I ought to get it for myself."

The good results of Lawrence's great care in regard to his injured ankle soon began to show themselves. The joint had slowly but steadily regained its strength and usual healthy condition, and Lawrence now found that he could walk about without the assistance of his rude crutch. He was still prudent, however, and took but very short walks, and in these he leaned upon his trusty cane. The charming autumn days which often come to Virginia in late October and early November were now at their best. Day after day the sun shone brightly ; but there was in the air an invigorating coolness which made its radiance something to be sought for and not avoided.

It was just after dinner, and it was Saturday afternoon, when Miss Annie announced that she was going to see old Aunt Patsy, whom she had somewhat neglected of late.

"May I go with you?" said Lawrence.

Miss Annie shook her head doubtfully. "I should be very glad to have your company," she said, "but I am afraid it will be entirely too much of a walk for you. The days are so short that the sun will be low before we could get back, and if you should be tired, it would not do for you to sit down and rest, at that time of day."

"I believe," said Lawrence, "that my ankle is quite strong enough for me to walk to Aunt Patsy's and back without sitting down to rest. I would be very glad to go with you, and I would like, too, to see that venerable colored woman again."

298

THE LATE MRS. NULL

"Well," said Miss Annie, "if you really think you can walk so far, it will be very nice indeed to have you go; but you ought to feel very sure that it will not hurt you."

"Come along," said Lawrence, taking up his hat and cane.

After a man has been shut up as Lawrence had been, a pleasant ramble like this is a most delightful change, and he did not hesitate to manifest his pleasure. This touched the very sensitive soul of his companion, and with such a sparkle of talk did she evince her gratification that almost any one would have been able to see that she was a young lady who had an earnest sympathy with those who had undergone afflictions, but were now freed from them.

Aunt Patsy was glad to see her visitors, particularly glad, it seemed, to see Mr. Croft. She was quite loquacious, considering the great length of her days and the proverbial shortness of her tongue.

"Why, Aunt Patsy," said Miss Annie, "you seem to have grown younger since I last saw you! I do believe you are getting old backward! What are you going to do with that dress-body?"

"I'se lookin' at dis h'yar," said Aunt Patsy, turning over the well-worn body of a black woollen dress which lay in her lap instead of the crazy-quilt on which she was usually occupied, "to see if it's done gib way in any ob de seams or de elbers. 'Twas a right smart good frock once, an' I'se gwine to wear it ter-morrer."

"To-morrow!" exclaimed Annie. "You don't mean to say you are going to church!"

"Dat's jes wot I'se gwine to do, Miss Annie. I'se

299

gwine to chu'ch to-morrer mawnin'. Dar's gwine to be a big preachin'. Brudder Enick Hines is to be dar, an' dey tell me dey allus has pow'ful wakenin's when Brudder Enick preaches. I ain't ever heared Brudder Enick yit, cos he was a little boy when I use to go to chu'ch."

"Will it be in the old church, in the woods just beyond Howlett's?" asked Annie.

"Right dar," replied Aunt Patsy, with an approving glance towards the young lady. "You 'members dem ar places fus'-rate, Miss Annie. Why you didn't tole me, when you fus' come h'yar, dat you was dat little Miss Annie dat I use to tote roun' afore I gin up walkin'?"

"Oh, that's too long a story," said Miss Annie, with a laugh. "You know, I hadn't seen Aunt Keswick then. I couldn't go about introducing myself to other people before I had seen her."

Aunt Patsy gave a sagacious nod of her head. "I reckon you thought she'd be right much disgruntled when she heared you was mar'ed, an' you wanted to tell her yo'se'f. But I'se pow'ful glad dat it's all right now. You-all don' know how pow'ful glad I is." And she looked at Mr. Croft and Miss Annie with a glance as benignant as her time-set countenance was capable of.

"But, Aunt Patsy," said Annie, quite willing to change the conversation, although she did not know the import of the old woman's last remark, "I thought you were not able to go out."

The old woman gave a little chuckle. "Dat's wot eberybody thought; an', to tell you de truf, Miss Annie, I thought so too. But ef I was strong 'nuf to go to de pos'-office,—an' I did dat, Miss Annie, an' not long ago, nuther,—I reckon I'se strong 'nuf to go to chu'ch ; an' Uncle Isham is a-comin' wid de ox-cart to take me to-morrer mawnin'. Dar'll be pow'ful wakenin's, an' I ain't seen de Jerus'lum Jump in a mighty long time."

"Are they going to have the Jerusalem Jump?" asked Miss Annie.

"Oh, yaas, Miss Annie," said the old woman ; "dey's sartin shuh to hab dat when dey gits wakened."

"I should so like to see the Jerusalem Jump again," said Miss Annie. "I saw it once, when I was a little girl. Did you ever see it?" she said, turning to Mr. Croft.

"I have not," he answered. "I never even heard of it."

"Suppose we go to-morrow and hear Brother Enoch," she said.

"I should like it very much," answered Lawrence.

"Aunt Patsy," said Miss Annie, "would there be any objection to our going to your church to-morrow?"

The old woman gave her head a little shake. "Dunno," she said. "As a gin'ral rule we don't like white folks at our preachin's. Dey's got dere chu'ches an' dere ways, an' we's got our chu'ches an' our ways. But den, it's dif'rent wid you-all. An' you-all's not like white folks in gin'ral, an' specially strawngers. You-all isn't strawngers now. I don't reckon dar'll be no 'jections to your comin', ef you set solemn ; an' I know you'll do dat, Miss Annie, cos you did it when you was a little gal. An' I reckon it'll be de same wid him?" looking at Mr. Croft.

THE LATE MRS. NULL

Miss Annie assured her that she and her companion would be certain to "set solemn," and that they would not think of such a thing as going to church and behaving indecorously.

"Dere is white folks," said Aunt Patsy, "wot comes to a cullud chu'ch fur nothin' else but to larf. De debbil gits dem folks; but dat don' do us no good, Miss Annie, an' we'd rudder dey stay away. But you-all's not dat kin'. I knows dat, sartin shuh."

When the two had taken leave of the old woman, and Miss Annie had gone out of the door, Aunt Patsy leaned very far forward, and stretching out her long arm, seized Mr. Croft by the skirt of his coat. He stepped back, quite surprised, and then she said to him, in a low but very earnest voice: "I reckon dat dat ar sprain ankle was nuffin but a acciden'; but you look out, sah, you look out! Hab you got dem little shoes handy?"

"Oh, yes," said Lawrence, "I have them in my trunk."

"Keep 'em whar you kin put your han' on 'em," said Aunt Patsy, impressively. "You may want 'em yit. You min' my wuhds."

"I shall be sure to remember," said Lawrence, as he hastened out to rejoin Annie.

"What in the world had Aunt Patsy to say to you?" asked that somewhat surprised young lady.

Then Lawrence told her how some time before Aunt Patsy had given him a pair of blue shoes, which she said would act as a preventive charm in case Mrs. Keswick should ever wish to do him harm, and that she had now called him back to remind him not to neglect this means of personal protection. "I

302

can't imagine," said Lawrence, "that your aunt would ever think of such a thing as doing me a harm, or how those little shoes would prevent her, if she wanted to ; but I suppose Aunt Patsy is crack-brained on some subjects, and so I thought it best to humor her, and took the shoes."

"Do you know," said Miss Annie, after walking a little distance in silence, "that I am afraid Aunt Patsy has done a dreadful thing, and one I never should have suspected her of. Aunt Keswick had a little baby once, and it died very young. She keeps its clothes in a box, and I remember when I was a little girl that she once showed them to me, and told me I was to take the place of that little girl, and that frightened me dreadfully, because I thought that I would have to die, and have my clothes put in a box. I recollect perfectly that there was a pair of little blue shoes among these clothes, and Aunt Patsy must have stolen them."

"That surprises me," said Lawrence. "I supposed, from what I had heard of the old woman, that she was perfectly honest."

"So she is," said Annie. "She has been a trusted servant in our family nearly all her life. But some negroes have very queer ideas about taking certain things, and I suppose Aunt Patsy had some particular reason for taking those shoes, for of course they could be of no value to her."

"I am very sorry," said Lawrence, "that such sacred relics should have come into my possession, but I must admit that I would not like to give them back to your aunt."

"Oh, no," said Annie, "that would never do ; and

303

I wouldn't dare to try to find her box and put them in it. It would seem like a desecration for any hand but her own to touch those things."

"That is true," said Lawrence, "and you might get yourself into a lot of trouble by endeavoring to repair the mischief. Before I leave here, we may think of some plan of disposing of the little trotters. It might be well to give them back to Aunt Patsy and tell her to restore them."

"I don't know," said Miss Annie, with a slowness of reply and an irrelevance of demeanor which indicated she was not thinking of the words she was speaking.

The sun was now very near the horizon, and that evening coolness which, in the autumn, comes on so quickly after the sunshine fades out of the air, made Lawrence give a little shrug with his shoulders. He proposed that they should quicken their pace, and as his companion made no objection, they soon reached the house.

The next day being Sunday, breakfast was rather later than usual, and as Lawrence looked out on the bright morning, with the mists just disengaging themselves from the many-hued foliage which crowned the tops of the surrounding hills, and on the recently risen sun, hanging in an atmosphere of gray and lilac, with the smile of Indian summer on its face, he thought he would like to take a stroll before that meal; but either the length of his walk on the previous day, or the rapidity of the latter portion ot it, had been rather too much for the newly recovered strength of his ankle, which now felt somewhat stiff and sore. When he mentioned this at the breakfast-table, he received a good deal of condolence from the two ladies, especially Mrs. Keswick ; and at first it was thought that it might be well for him to give up his proposed attendance at the negro church. But to this Lawrence strongly objected, for he very much desired to see some of the peculiar religious services of the negroes. He had been talking on the subject the evening before with Mrs. Keswick, who had told him that in this part of the country, which lay in the "black belt" of Virginia, where the negro population had always been thickest, these ceremonies were more characteristic of the religious disposition of the African than in those sections of the State where the white race exerted a greater influence upon the manners and customs of the colored people.

"But it will not be necessary to walk much," said Miss Annie. "We can take the spring-wagon, and you can go with us, aunt."

The old lady permitted herself a little grin. "When I go to church," she said, "I go to a white folks' church, and try to see what I can of white folks' Christianity, though I must say that Christianity of the other color is often just as good, as far as works go. But it is natural that a stranger should want to see what kind of services the colored people have, so you two might as well get into the spring-wagon and go along."

"But shall we not deprive you of the vehicle?" said Lawrence.

"I never go to church in the spring-wagon," said the old lady, "so long as I am able to walk. And, besides, this is not our Sunday for preaching."

It seemed to Lawrence that an elderly person who

went about in a purple calico sunbonnet, and with an umbrella of the same material, might go to church in a wheelbarrow, so far as appearances were concerned; but he had long ceased to wonder at Mrs. Keswick's idiosyncrasies.

"I remember very well," said Miss Annie, after the old lady had left the table, which she always did as soon as she had finished a meal, "when Aunt Keswick used to go to church in a big family carriage, which is now sleeping itself to pieces out there in the barn. But then she had a pair of big gray horses, one of them named Doctor and the other Colonel. But now she has only one horse, and I am going to tell Uncle Isham to harness that one up before he goes to church himself. You know, he is to take Aunt Patsy in the ox-cart, so he will have to go early."

They went to the negro church in the spring-wagon, Lawrence driving the jogging sorrel, and Miss Annie on the seat beside him. When they reached the old frame edifice in the woods beyond Howlett's, they found gathered there quite a large assemblage, for this was one of those very attractive occasions called a "big preaching." Horses and mules, and wagons of various kinds, many of the latter containing baskets of refreshments, were standing about under the trees; and Mrs. Keswick's cart and oxen, tethered to a little pine-tree, gave proof that Aunt Patsy had arrived. The inside of the church was nearly full, and outside, around the door, stood a large number of men and boys. The white visitors were looked upon with some surprise, but way was made for them to approach the door, and as soon as they entered the building two of the officers of the church came forward to show them to one of the uppermost seats. But this honor Miss Annie strenuously declined. She preferred a seat near the open door, and therefore she and Mr. Croft were given a bench in that vicinity, of which they had sole possession.

To Lawrence, who had never seen anything of the sort, the services which now began were exceedingly interesting; and as Annie had not been to a negro church since she was a little girl, and very seldom then, she gave very earnest and animated attention to what was going on. The singing, as it always is among the negroes, was powerful and melodious, and the long prayer of Brother Enoch Hines was one of those spirited and emotional statements of personal condition, and wild and ardent supplication, which generally pave the way for a most powerful awakening in an assemblage of this kind. Another hymn, sung in more vigorous tones than the first one, warmed up the congregation to such a degree that when Brother Hines opened the Bible, and made preparations for his discourse, he looked out upon an audience as anxious to be moved and stirred as he was to move and stir it. The sermon was intended to be a long one, for, had it been otherwise, Brother Hines had lost his reputation; and therefore the preacher, after a few prefatory statements, delivered in a grave and solemn manner, plunged boldly into the midst of his exhortations, knowing that he could go either backward or forward, presenting, with equal acceptance, fresh subject-matter or that already used, so long as his strength held out.

He had not preached half an hour before his hearers were so stirred and moved that a majority of them found it utterly impossible to merely sit still and listen. In different ways their awakening was manifested: some began to sing in a low voice; others gently rocked their bodies; while fervent ejaculations of various kinds were heard from all parts of the church. From this beginning arose gradually a scene of religious activity such as Lawrence had never imagined. Each individual allowed his or her fervor to express itself according to the method which best pleased the worshipper. Some kept to their seats and listened to the words of the preacher, interrupting him occasionally by fervent ejaculations; others sang and shouted, sometimes standing up, clapping their hands, and stamping their feet; while a large proportion of the able-bodied members left their seats and pushed their way forward to the wide, open space which surrounded the preacher's desk, and prepared to engage in the exhilarating ceremony of the "Jerusalem Jump."

Two concentric rings were formed around the preacher, the inner one composed of women, the outer one of men, the faces of those forming the inner ring being turned towards those in the outer. As soon as all were in place, each brother reached forth his hand and took the hand of the sister opposite to him, and then each couple began to jump up and down violently, shaking hands and singing at the top of their voices. After about a minute of this, the two circles moved, one one way and one another, so that each brother found himself opposite a different sister. Hands were again immediately seized, and the jumping, hand-shaking, and singing went on.

THE LATE MRS. NULL

Minute by minute the excitement increased; faster the worshippers jumped, and louder they sang. Through it all Brother Enoch Hines kept on with his sermon. It was very difficult now to make himself heard, and the time for explanation or elucidation had long since passed; all he could do was to shout forth certain important and moving facts, and this he did over and over again, holding his hand at the side of his mouth, as if he were hailing a vessel in the wind. Much of what he said was lost in the din of the jumpers, but ever and anon could be heard ringing through the church the announcement: "De wheel ob time is a-turnin' roun'!"

In a group by themselves, in an upper corner of the congregation, were four or five very old women, who were able to manifest their pious enthusiasm in no other way than by rocking their bodies backward and forward, and singing with their cracked voices a grewsome and monotonous chant. This rude song had something of a wild and uncivilized nature, as if it had come down to these old people from the savage rites of their African ancestors. They did not sing in unison, but each squeaked or piped out her "Yi, wiho, yi, hoo!" according to the strength of her lungs and the degree of her exaltation. Prominent among these was old Aunt Patsy; her little black eyes sparkling through her great iron-bound spectacles; her head and body moving in unison with the wild air of the unintelligible chant she sang; her long, skinny hands clapping up and down upon her knees; while her feet, incased in their great green-baize slippers, unceasingly beat time upon the floor.

So many persons being absent from their seats, the

group of old women was clearly visible to Annie and Lawrence, and Aunt Patsy also could easily see them. Whenever her head, in its ceaseless moving from side to side, allowed her eyes to fall upon the two white visitors, her ardor and fervency increased, and she seemed to be expressing a pious gratitude that Miss Annie and he whom she supposed to be her husband were still together in peace and safety.

Annie was much affected by all she saw and heard. Her face was slightly pale, and occasionally she was moved by a little nervous tremor. Mr. Croft, too, was very attentive. His soul was not moved to enthusiasm, and he did not feel, as his companion did now and then, that he would like to jump up and join in the dancing and the shouting; but the scene made a very strong impression upon him.

Around and around went the two rings of men and women, jumping, singing, and hand-shaking. Out from the centre of them came the stentorian shout: "De wheel ob time is a-turnin' roun'!" From all parts of the church rose snatches of hymns, exultant shouts, groans, and prayers; and, in the corner, the shrill chants of the old women were fitfully heard through the storm of discordant worship.

In the midst of all the wild din and hubbub, the soul of Aunt Patsy looked out from the habitation where it had dwelt so long, and, without giving the slightest notice to any one, or attracting the least attention by its movements, it silently slipped away.

The old habitation of the soul still sat in its chair, but no one noticed that it no longer sang, or beat time with its hands and feet.

THE LATE MRS. NULL

Not long after this, Lawrence looked round at his companion, and noticed that she was slightly trembling. "Don't you think we have had enough of this?" he whispered.

"Yes," she answered, and they rose and went out. They thought they were the first who had left.

CHAPTER XXV

WHEN Mr. Croft and Miss Annie got into the spring-wagon, and the head of the sorrel was turned away from the church, Lawrence looked at his watch, and remarked that, as it was still quite early, there might be time for a little drive before going back to the house for dinner. The face of the young lady beside him was still slightly pale, and the thought came to him that it would be very well for her if her mind could be diverted from the abnormally inspiriting scene she had just witnessed.

"Dinner will be late to-day," she said, "for I saw Letty doing her best among the Jerusalem Jumpers."

"Very well," said he, "we will drive. And now, where shall we go?"

"If we take the cross-road at the store," said Miss Annie, "and go on for about half a mile, we can turn into the woods, and then there is a beautiful road through the trees which will bring us out on the other side of Aunt Keswick's house. Junius took me that way not long ago."

So they turned at the store, much to the disgust of the plodding sorrel, who thought he was going directly home, and they soon reached the road that led through the woods. This was hard and sandy, as are many of the roads through the forests in that part of the coun-

312

THE LATE MRS. NULL

try, and it would have been a very good driving road,
had it not been for the occasional protrusion of tree-
roots, which gave the wheels a little bump, and for the
branches which, now and then, hung down somewhat
too low for the comfort of a lady and gentleman riding in a rather high spring-wagon without a cover.
But Lawrence drove slowly, and so the root bumps
were not noticed; and when the low-hanging boughs
were on his side, he lifted them so that his companion's
head could pass under, and when they happened to
be on her side, Annie ducked her head, and her hat
was never brushed off.   But at times they drove
quite a distance without overhanging boughs, and the
pine-trees, surrounded by their smooth carpet of
brown spines, gave forth a spicy fragrance in the
warm but sparkling air; the oak-trees stood up still
dark and green, while the chestnuts were all dressed
in rich yellow, with the chinquapin bushes by the
roadside imitating them in color, as they tried to do
in fruit.   Sometimes a spray of purple flowers could
be seen among the trees, and great patches of sunlight,
which here and there came through the thinning
foliage, fell, now upon the brilliantly scarlet leaves of
a sweet-gum, and now upon the polished and brown-
red dress of a neighboring black-gum.

The woods were very quiet.   There was no sound
of bird or insect, and the occasional hare, or "Molly
Cottontail," as Annie delightedly called it, who
hopped across the road, made no noise at all.   A
gentle wind among the tops of the taller trees made
a sound as of a distant sea; but, besides this, little was
heard but the low, crunching noise of the wheels, and
the voices of Lawrence and Miss Annie.

313

THE LATE MRS. NULL

Reaching a place where the road branched, Lawrence stopped the horse, and looked up each leafy lane. They were completely deserted. White people seldom walked abroad at this hour on Sunday, and the negroes of the neighborhood were at church. "Is not this a frightfully lonely place?" he said. "One might imagine himself in a desert."

"I like it," replied Annie. "It is so different from the wild, exciting tumult of that church. I am glad you took me away. At first I would not have missed it for the world, but there seemed to come into the stormy scene something oppressive and almost terrifying."

"I am glad I took you away," said Lawrence, "but it seems to me that your impression was not altogether natural. I thought that, amid all that mad enthusiasm, you were over-excited, not depressed. A solemn solitude like this would, to my thinking, be much more likely to lower your spirits. I don't like solitude myself, and therefore I suppose it is that I thought an impressible nature like yours would find something sad in the loneliness of these silent woods."

Annie turned and fixed on him her large gray eyes. "But I am not alone," she said.

As Lawrence looked into her eyes he saw that they were as clear as the purest crystal, and that he could look through them straight into her soul, and there he saw that this woman loved him. The vision was as sudden as if it had been a night scene lighted up by a flash of lightning, but it was as clear and plain as if it had been that same scene under the noonday sun.

There are times in the life of a man when the goddess of Reasonable Impulse raises her arms above her head and allows herself a little yawn. Then she takes off her crown and hangs it on the back of her throne; after which she rests her sceptre on the floor, and, rising, stretches herself to her full height, and goes forth to take a long, refreshing walk by the waters of Unreflection. Then her minister, Prudence, stretches himself upon a bench, and, with his handkerchief over his eyes, composes himself for a nap. Discretion, Worldly Wisdom, and other trusted officers of her court, and even, sometimes, that agile page called Memory, no sooner see their royal mistress depart, than, by various doors, they leave the palace and wander far away. Then, silently, with sparkling eyes and parted lips, comes that fair being, Unthinking Love. She puts one foot upon the lower step of the throne; she looks about her; and, with a quick bound, she seats herself. Upon her tumbled curls she hastily puts the crown; with her small white hand she grasps the sceptre; and then, rising, waves it, and issues her commands. The crowd of emotions which serve as her satellites seize the great seal from the sleeping Prudence, and the new Queen reigns!

All this now happened to Lawrence. Never before had he looked into the eyes of a woman who loved him; and leaning over towards this one, he put his arm around her and drew her towards him. "And never shall you be alone," he said.

She looked up at him with tears starting to her eyes, and then she put her head against his breast. She was too happy to say anything, and she did not try.

It was about a minute after this that the sober

315

sorrel, who took no interest in what had occurred behind him, and a great deal of interest in his stable at home, started in an uncertain and hesitating way, and, finding that he was not checked, began to move onward. Lawrence looked up from the little head upon his breast, and called out, "Whoa!" To this, however, the sorrel paid no attention. Lawrence then put forth his right hand to grasp the reins; but having lately forgotten all about them, they had fallen out of the spring-wagon, and were now dragging upon the ground. It was impossible for him to reach them, and so, seizing the whip, he endeavored with its aid to hook them up. Failing in this, he was about to jump out and run to the horse's head; but perceiving his intention, Annie seized his arm. "Don't you do it!" she exclaimed. "You'll ruin your ankle!"

Lawrence could not but admit to himself that he was not in condition to execute any feats of agility, and he also felt that Annie had a very charming way of holding fast to his arm as if she had a right to keep him out of danger. And now the sorrel broke into the jog-trot which was his usual pace. "It is very provoking," said Lawrence. "I don't think I ever allowed myself to drop the reins before."

"It doesn't make the slightest difference," said Annie, comfortingly. "This old horse knows the road perfectly well, and he doesn't need a bit of driving. He will take us home just as safely as if you held the reins; and now, don't you try to get them, for you will only hurt yourself."

"Very well," said Lawrence, putting his arm around her again; "I am resigned. But I think you are very

brave to sit so quiet and composed, under the circumstances."

She looked at him with a smile. "Such a little
circumstance don't count just now," she said. "You
must stop that," she added presently, "when we get
to the edge of the woods."

Before long they came out into the open country,
and found themselves in a lane which led by a wide
circuit to the road passing Mrs. Keswick's house. The
old sorrel certainly behaved admirably : he held back
when he descended a declivity ; he walked over the
rough places ; he trotted steadily where the road was
smooth.

"It seems like our fate," said Annie, who now sat
up without an arm around her, the protecting woods
having been left behind ; "he just takes us along without our having anything to do with it."

"He is not much of a horse," said Lawrence, clasping, in an unobservable way, the little hand which
lay by his side, "but the fate is charming."

Fortunately, there was no one upon the road to
notice the reinless plight in which these two young
people found themselves, and they were quite as well
satisfied as if they had been doing their own driving.
After a little period of thought, Annie turned an
earnest face to Lawrence, and she said : "Do you
know that I never believed that you were really in
love with Roberta March."

Lawrence squeezed her hand, but did not reply.
He knew very well that he had loved Roberta March,
and he was not going to lie about it.

"I thought so," she continued, "because I did not
believe that any one who was truly in love would

317

want to send other people about to propose for him, as you did."

"That is not exactly the state of the case," he said, "but we must not talk of those things now; that is all past and gone."

"But if there ever was any love," she persisted, "are you sure that it is all gone?"

"Gone," he answered earnestly, "as utterly and completely as the days of last summer."

And now the sorrel, of his own accord, stopped at Mrs. Keswick's outer gate; and Lawrence, getting down, opened the gate, took up the reins, and drove to the house in quite a proper way.

When Mr. Croft helped Annie to descend from the spring-wagon, he did not squeeze her hand, nor exchange with her any tender glances, for old Mrs. Keswick was standing at the top of the steps. "Have you seen Letty?" she asked.

"Letty?" said Miss Annie. "Oh, yes," she added, as if she suddenly remembered that such a person existed; "Letty was at church, and she was very active."

"Well," said the old lady, "she must have taken more interest in the exercises than you did, for it is long past the time when I told her she must be home."

"I do not believe, madam," said Lawrence, "that any one could have taken more interest in the exercises of this morning than we have."

At this, Annie could not help giving him a little look which would have provoked reflection in the mind of the old lady, had she not been very earnestly engaged in gazing out into the road, in the hope of seeing Letty.

When Lawrence had gone into the office, and had

closed the door behind him, he stood in a meditative mood before the empty fireplace. He was making inquiries of himself in regard to what he had just done. He was not accusing himself, nor indulging in regrets; he was simply investigating the matter. Here he stood, a man accepted by two women. If he had ever heard of any other man in a like condition, he would have called that man a scoundrel; and yet he did not deem himself a scoundrel.

The facts in the case were easy enough to understand. For the first time in his life he had looked into the eyes of a woman who loved him, and he had discovered, to his utter surprise, that he loved her. There had been no plan—no prudent outlook into her nature and feelings, no cautious insight into his own. He had taken part in a most unpremeditated act of pure and simple love; and that it was real and pure love on each side he no more doubted than he doubted that he lived. And yet, had he been an impostor when, on that hill over there, he told Roberta March he loved her? No, he had been honest; he had loved her; and since the time that he had been roused to action by the discovery of Junius Keswick's intentions to renew his suit, it had been a love full of a rare and alluring beauty. But its charm, its fascination, its very existence, had disappeared in the first flash of his knowledge that Annie Peyton loved him. Had his love for Roberta been a perfect one, had he been sure that she returned it, then it could not have been overthrown; but it had gone, and a love complete and perfect stood in its place. He had seen that he was loved, and he loved. That was all; but it would stand forever.

THE LATE MRS. NULL

This was the state of the case; and now Lawrence set himself to discover if, in all ways, he had acted truly and honestly. He had been accepted by Miss March, but what sort of acceptance was it? Should he, as a man true to himself, accept such an acceptance? What was he to think of a woman who, very angry, as he had been informed, had sent him a message which meant everything in the world to him, if it meant anything, and had then dashed away without allowing him a chance to speak to her, or even giving him a nod of farewell? The last thing she had really said to him in this connection were those cruel words on Pine Top Hill with which she had asked him to choose a spot in which to be rejected. Could he consider himself engaged? Would a woman who cared for him act towards him in such a manner? After all, was that acceptance anything more than the result of pique? And could he not, quite as justly, accept the rejection which she had professed herself anxious to give him?

A short time before, Lawrence had done his best to explain to his advantage these peculiarities of his status in regard to Miss March. He had said to himself that she had threatened to reject him because she wished to punish him, and he had intended to implore her pardon, and expected to receive it. Over and over again had he argued with himself in this strain; and yet, in spite of it all, he had not been able to bring himself into a state of mind in which he could sit down and write to her a letter which, in his estimation, would be certain to seal and complete the engagement. "How very glad I am," he now said to himself, "that I never wrote that letter!" And this was the only decision at which he had arrived when he heard Mrs. Keswick calling to him from the yard.

He immediately went to the door, when the old lady informed him that, as Letty had not come back, and did not appear to be intending to come back, and that as none of the other servants on the place had made their appearance, he might as well come into the house and try to satisfy his hunger on what cold food she and Mrs. Null had managed to collect.

The most biting and spicy condiments of the little meal to which the three sat down were supplied by Mrs. Keswick, who reviled without stint those utterly thoughtless and heedless colored people who, once in the midst of their crazy religious exercises, totally forgot that they owed any duty whatever to those who employed them. Lawrence and Annie did not say much, but there was something peculiarly piquant in the way in which Annie brought and poured out the tea she had made, and which, with the exception of the old lady's remarks, was the only warm part of the repast; and there was an element of buoyancy in the manner of Mr. Croft as he took his cup to drink the tea. Although he said little at this meal, he thought a great deal, listening not at all to Mrs. Keswick's tirades. "What a charmingly inconsiderate affair this has been!" he said to himself. "Nothing planned, nothing provided for or against; all spontaneous and from our very hearts. I never thought to tell her that she must say nothing to her aunt until we had agreed how everything should be explained, and I don't believe the idea that it is necessary to say anything to anybody has entered her mind. But I must keep my eyes away from her, if I don't want to bring on a premature explosion."

Whatever might be the result of the reasoning which this young man had to do with himself, it was quite plain that he was abundantly satisfied with things as they were.

It was beginning to be dark when Letty and Uncle Isham returned and explained why they had been so late in returning.

Old Aunt Patsy had died in church.

CHAPTER XXVI

"LAWRENCE," said Annie, on the forenoon of the next day, as they were sitting together in the parlor with the house to themselves, Mrs. Keswick having gone to Aunt Patsy's cabin to supervise proceedings there, "Lawrence, don't you feel glad that we did not have a chance to speak to dear old Aunt Patsy about those little shoes? Perhaps she had forgotten that she had stolen them, and so went to heaven without that sin on her soul."

"That is a very comfortable way of looking at it," said Lawrence, "but wouldn't it be better to assume that she did not steal them?"

"I am very sorry," said Annie, "but that is not easy to do. But don't let us think anything more about that. And don't you feel very glad that the poor old creature, who looked so happy as she sat singing and clapping her hands on her knees, didn't die until after we had left the church? If it had happened while we were there, I don't believe—"

"Don't believe what?" asked Lawrence.

"Well, that you now would be sitting with your arm on the back of my chair."

Lawrence was quite sure, from what had been told him, that Aunt Patsy's demise had taken place before they left the church. But he did not say so to Annie. He merely took his arm from the back of her chair and placed it around her.

"And do you know," said she, "that Letty told me something, this morning, that is so funny, and yet in a certain way so pathetic, that it made me laugh and cry both. She said that Aunt Patsy always thought that you were Mr. Null."

At this Lawrence burst out laughing; but Annie checked him and went on: "And she told Letty in church, when she saw us two come in, that she believed she could die happy now, since she had seen Miss Annie married to such a pert gentleman, and that it looked as if old miss had got over her grudge against him."

"And didn't Letty undeceive her?" asked Lawrence.

"No; she said it would be a pity to upset the mind of such an old woman, and she didn't do it."

"Then the good Aunt Patsy died," said Lawrence, "thinking I was that wretched tramp of a bone-dust pedler which the fancy of your aunt has conjured up. That explains the interest the venerable colored woman took in me. It is now quite easy to understand; for if your aunt abused your mythical husband to everybody as she did to me, I don't wonder Aunt Patsy thought I was in danger."

"Poor old woman!" said Annie, looking down at the floor; "I am so glad that we helped her to die happy."

"As she was obliged to anticipate the truth," said Lawrence, "in order to derive any comfort from it, I am glad she did it. But although I am delighted, more than my words can tell you, to take the place of your Mr. Null, you must not expect me to have any of his attributes."

"Now just listen to me, sir," said Annie. "I don't want you to say one word against Mr. Null. If it had not been for that good Freddy, things would have been very different from what they are now. If you care for me at all, you owe me entirely to Freddy Null."

"Entirely?" asked Lawrence.

"Of course I mean in regard to opportunities of finding out things and saying them. If Aunt Keswick had supposed I was only Annie Peyton, she would not have allowed Mr. Croft to interfere with her plans for Junius and me. I expected Mr. Null to be of service to me, but no one could have imagined that he would have brought about anything like this."

"Blessed be Null!" exclaimed Lawrence.

Annie asked him to please be more careful, for how did he know that one of the servants might not be sweeping the front porch, and of course she would look in at the windows.

"But, my dear child," said Lawrence, pushing back his chair to a prudent distance, "we must seriously consider this Null business. We shall have to inform your aunt of the present state of affairs, and before we do that we must explain what sort of person Frederick Null, Esquire, really was—I am not willing to admit that he exists, even as a myth."

"Oh, dear! oh, dear!" exclaimed Annie. "We shall have a dreadful time! When Aunt Keswick knows that there never was any Mr. Null, and then hears that you and I are engaged, it will throw her into the most dreadful state of mind that she has ever been in, in her life; and father has told me of some of the awful family earthquakes that Aunt Keswick has brought about when things went wrong with her."

"We must be very cautious," said Lawrence, "and neither of us must say a word, or do anything that may arouse her suspicions, until we have settled upon the best possible method of making the facts known to her. The case is indeed a complicated one."

"And what makes it more so," said Annie, "is Aunt Keswick's belief that you are in love with Miss March, and that you want to get a chance to propose to her. She does think that, doesn't she?"

"Yes," said Lawrence, "I must admit that she does."

"And she must be made to understand that that is entirely at an end," continued Annie. "All this will be a very difficult task, Lawrence, and I don't see how it is to be done."

"But we shall do it," he answered; "and we must not forget to be very prudent until it is fully settled how we shall do it."

When Lawrence retired to his room, and sat down to hold that peculiar court in which he was judge, jury, lawyers, and witnesses, as well as the prisoner at the bar, he had to do with a case a great deal more complicated and difficult than that which perplexed the mind of Miss Annie Peyton. He began by the very unjudicial act of pledging himself, to himself, that nothing should interfere with this new, this true love. In spite of all that might be said, done, or thought, Annie Peyton should be his wife. There was no indecision whatever in regard to the new love; the only question was, "What is to be done about the old one?"

Lawrence could not admit, for a moment, that he could have spoken to Roberta March as he had spoken if he had not loved her; but he could now perceive that that love had been in no small degree impaired and weakened by the manner of its acceptance. The action of Miss March on her last day here had much more chilled his ardor than her words on Pine Top Hill. He had not before examined thoroughly into the condition of that ardor after the departure of the lady, but it was plain enough now.

There was, therefore, no doubt whatever in regard to his love for Miss March; he was quite ready and able to lay that aside. But what about her acceptance of it? How could he lay that aside?

This was the real case before the court. The witnesses could give no available testimony; the lawyers argued feebly; the jury disagreed; and Lawrence, in his capacity of judge, dismissed the case.

In his efforts to conduct his mind through the channels of law and equity, Lawrence had not satisfied himself, and his thoughts began to be moved by what might be termed his military impulses. "I made a charge into the camp," he said, with a little downward drawing of the corners of his mouth, "and I did not capture the commander-in-chief. And now I intend to charge out again."

He sat down to his table and wrote the following note :

"MY DEAR MISS MARCH: I have been waiting for a good many days, hoping to receive, either from you or Mr. Keswick, an explanation of the message you sent to me by him. I now believe that it will be impossible to give a satisfactory explanation of that message. I therefore recur to our last private interview, and wish to say to you that I am ready, at any time, to meet you under either a sycamore or a cherry-tree."

And then he signed it, and addressed it to Miss March at Midbranch. This being done, he put on his hat and stepped out to see if a messenger could be found to carry the letter to its destination, for he did not wish to wait for the semi-weekly mail. Near the house he met Annie.

"What have you been doing all this time?" she asked.

"I have been writing a letter," he said, "and am now looking for some colored boy who will carry it for me."

"Whom is it to?" she asked.

"Miss March," was his answer.

"Let me see it," said Annie.

At this Lawrence looked at her with wide-open eyes, and then he laughed. Never, since he had been a child, had there been any one who would have thought of such a thing as asking to see a private letter which he had written to some one else; and that this young girl should stand up before him with her straightforward, expectant gaze, and make such a request of him, in the first instance amused him.

"You don't mean to say," she added, "that you would write anything to Miss March which you would not let me see?"

"This letter," said Lawrence, "was written for Miss March, and no one else. It is simply the winding up of that old affair."

THE LATE MRS. NULL

"Give it to me," said Annie, "and let me see how you wound it up."

Lawrence smiled, looked at her in silence for a moment, and then handed her the letter.

"I don't want you to think," she said, as she took it, "that I am going to ask you to show me all the letters you write. But when you write one to a lady like Miss March, I want to know what you say to her." And then she read the letter. When she had finished, she turned to Lawrence and, with her countenance full of amazement, exclaimed: "I haven't the least idea in the world what all this means! What message did she send you? And why should you meet her under a tree?"

These questions went so straight to the core of the affair, and were so peculiarly difficult to answer, that Lawrence, for the moment, found himself in the very unusual position of not knowing what to say; but he presently remarked: "Do you think it is of any advantage to either of us to talk over this affair, which is now past and gone?"

"I don't want to talk over any of it," said Annie, very promptly, "except the part of it which is referred to in this letter; but I want to know about that."

"That covers the most important part of it," said Lawrence.

"Very good," she answered, "and so you can tell it to me. And, now that I think of it, you can tell me, at the same time, exactly why you wanted to find my cousin Junius. I think I ought to know that, too."

"Very well, then," replied Lawrence; "if you have the least feeling about it, I will relate the whole affair, from beginning to end."

"That, perhaps, will be the best thing to do, after all," said Annie. "And suppose we take a walk over the fields, and then you can tell it without being interrupted."

But Lawrence did not feel that his ankle would allow him to accept this invitation, for it had hurt him a good deal since his walk to Aunt Patsy's cabin. He said so to Annie, and excited in her the deepest feelings of commiseration.

"You must take no more walks of any length," she exclaimed, "until you are quite, quite well! It was my fault that you took that tramp to Aunt Patsy's. I ought to have known better. But then," she said, looking up at him, "you were not under my charge. I shall take very good care of you now."

"For my part," he said, "I am glad I have this little relapse, for now I can stay here longer."

"I am very, very sorry for the relapse," said she, "but awfully glad for the stay. And you mustn't stand another minute. Let us go and sit in the arbor. The sun is shining straight into it, and that will make it all the more comfortable while you are telling me about those things."

They sat down in the arbor, and Lawrence told Annie the whole history of his affair with Miss March, from the beginning to the end; that is, if the end had been reached; although he intimated no doubt to her upon this point. This avowal he had never expected to make. In fact, he had never contemplated its possibility. But now he felt a certain satisfaction in telling it. Every item, as it was related, seemed thrown aside forever. "And now, then, my dear Annie," he said, when he had finished, "what do you think of all that?"

THE LATE MRS. NULL

"Well," she said, "in the first place, I am still more of the opinion than I was before that you never were really in love with her. You did entirely too much planning and investigating and calculating; and when, at last, you did come to the conclusion to propose to her, you did not do it so much of your own accord as because you found that another man would be likely to get her if you did not make a pretty quick move yourself. And as to that acceptance, I don't think anything of it at all. I believe she was very angry at Junius because he consented to bring your messages, when he ought to have been his own messenger, and that she gave him that answer just to rack his soul with agony. I don't believe she ever dreamed that he would take it to you. And, to tell the simple truth, I believe, from what I saw of her that morning, that she was thinking very little of you, and a great deal of him. To be sure, she was fiery angry with him, but it is better to be that way with a lover than to pay no attention to him at all."

This was a view of the case which had never struck Lawrence before, and although it was not very flattering to him, it was very comforting. He felt that it was extremely likely that this young woman had been able to truthfully divine, in a case in which he had failed, the motives of another young woman. Here was a further reason for congratulating himself that he had not written to Miss March.

"And as to the last part of the letter," said Annie, "you are not going under any cherry-tree, or sycamore either, to be refused by her. What she said to you was quite enough for a final answer, without any signing or sealing under trees or anywhere else. I

331

think the best thing that can be done with this precious epistle is to tear it up."

Lawrence was amused by the piquant earnestness of this decision. "But what am I to do?" he asked. "I can't let the matter rest in this unfinished and unsatisfactory condition."

"You might write to her," said Annie, "and tell her that you have accepted what she said to you on Pine Top Hill as a conclusive answer, and that you now take back everything you ever said on the subject you talked of that day. And do you think it would be well to put in anything about your being otherwise engaged?"

At this Lawrence laughed. "I think that expression would hardly answer," he said, "but I will write another note, and we shall see how you like it."

"That will be very well," said the happy Annie, "and if I were you I'd make it as gentle as I could. It's of no use to hurt her feelings."

"Oh, I don't want to do that," said Lawrence; "and now that we have the opportunity, let us consider the question of informing your aunt of our engagement."

"Oh, dear, dear, dear!" said Annie, "that is a great deal worse than informing Miss March that you don't want to be engaged to her."

"That is true," said Lawrence. "It is not by any means an easy piece of business. But we might as well look it square in the face, and determine what is to be done about it."

"It is simple enough, just as we look at it," said Annie. "All we have to do is to say that, knowing that Aunt Keswick had written to my father that she was determined to make a match between Cousin

THE LATE MRS. NULL

Junius and me, I was afraid to come down here without putting up some insurmountable obstacle between me and a man that I had not seen since I was a little girl. Of course I would say very decidedly that I wouldn't have married him if I hadn't wanted to; but then, considering Aunt Keswick's very open way of carrying out her plans, it would have been very unpleasant, and indeed impossible, for me to be in the house with him unless she saw that there was no hope of a marriage between us; and for this reason I took the name of Mrs. Null, or Mrs. Nothing, and came down here secure under the protection of a husband who never existed. And then, we could say that you and I were a good deal together, and that, although you had supposed, when you came here, that you were in love with Miss March, you had discovered that this was a mistake, and that afterwards we fell in love with each other, and are now engaged. That would be a straightforward statement of everything, just as it happened; but the great trouble is, how are we going to tell it to Aunt Keswick?"

"You are right," said Lawrence. "How are we going to tell it?"

"It need not be told!" thundered a strong voice close to their ears. And then there was a noise of breaking latticework and cracking vines, and through the back part of the arbor came an old woman wearing a purple sunbonnet, and beating down all obstacles before her with a great purple umbrella. "You needn't tell it!" cried Mrs. Keswick, standing in the middle of the arbor, her eyes glistening, her form trembling, and her umbrella quivering in the air. "You needn't tell it! It's told!"

333

THE LATE MRS. NULL

Graphic and vivid descriptions have been written of those furious storms of devastating wind and deluging rain which suddenly sweep away the beauty of some fair tropical scene; and we have read, too, of dreadful cyclones and tornadoes, which rush, in mad rage, over land and sea, burying great ships in a vast tumult of frenzied waves, or crushing to the earth forests, buildings, everything that may lie in their awful paths: but no description could be written which could give an adequate idea of the storm which now burst upon Lawrence and Annie. The old lady had seen these two standing together in the yard, conversing most earnestly; she had then seen Annie read a letter that Lawrence gave her; and then she had perceived the two, in close converse, enter the arbor and sit down together, without the slightest regard for the rights of Mr. Null.

Mrs. Keswick looked upon all this as somewhat more out-of-the-way than the usual proceedings of these young people, and there came into her mind a curiosity to know what they were saying to each other. So she immediately repaired to the large garden, and quietly made her way to the back of the arbor, in which advantageous position she heard the whole of Lawrence's story of his love-affair with Miss March, Annie's remarks upon the same, and the facts of this young lady's proposed confession in regard to her marriage with Mr. Null and her engagement to Mr. Croft.

Then she burst in upon them. The tornado and the cyclone raged; the thunder rolled and crashed; and the white lightning of her wrath flashed upon the two as if it would scathe and annihilate them as they stood

334

before her. Neither of them had ever known or
imagined anything like this. It had been long since
Mrs. Keswick had had an opportunity of exercising
that power of vituperative torment which had driven
a husband to the refuge of a reverted pistol, which
had banished for life relatives and friends, and
which, in the shape of a promissory curse, had held
apart those who would have been husband and wife;
and now, like the long-stored-up venom of a serpent,
it burst out with the direful force given by concentra-
tion and retention.

At the first outburst Annie had turned pale and
shrunk back, but now she clung to the side of Lawrence, who, although his face was somewhat blanched
and his form trembled a little with excitement, still
stood up bravely, and endeavored, but ineffectually,
to force upon the old lady's attention a denial of her
bitter accusations. With face almost as purple as the
bonnet she wore or the umbrella she shook in the
air, the old lady first addressed her niece. With
scorn and condemnation she spoke of the deceit which
the young girl had practised upon her. But this part
of the exercises was soon over. She seemed to think
that, although nothing could be viler than Annie's
conduct towards her, still, the fact that Mr. Null no
longer existed put Annie again within her grasp and
control, and made it unnecessary to say much to her
on this occasion. It was upon Lawrence that the
main cataract of her fury poured. It would be wrong
to say that she could not find words to express her ire
towards him. She found plenty of them, and used
them all. He had deceived her most abominably; he
had come there the expressed and avowed lover of

Miss March; he had connived with her niece in her deceit; he had taken advantage of all the opportunities she gave him to attain the legitimate object of his visit, to inveigle into his snares this silly and absurd young woman; and he had dared to interfere with the plans which, by day and by night, she had been maturing for years. In vain did Lawrence endeavor to answer or explain. She stopped not, nor listened to one word.

"And you need not imagine," she screamed at him, "that you are going to turn round, when you like, and marry anybody you please. You are engaged, body and soul, to Roberta March, and have no right, by laws of man or Heaven, to marry anybody else. If you breathe a word of love to any other woman, it makes you a vile criminal in the eyes of the law, and renders you liable to prosecution, sir! Your affianced bride knows nothing of what her double-faced snake of a lover is doing here, but she shall know speedily. That is a matter which I take into my own hands. Out of my way, both of you!"

And with these words she charged by them, and rushed out of the arbor and into the house.

CHAPTER XXVII

THEY were not a happy pair, Lawrence Croft and
Annie Peyton, as they stood together in the arbor
after old Mrs. Keswick had left them. They were
both a good deal shaken by the storm they had passed
through.

"Lawrence," said Annie, looking up to him with
her large eyes full of earnestness, "there surely is no
truth in what she said about your being legally bound
to Miss March?"

"None in the least," said Lawrence. "No man,
under the circumstances, would consider himself engaged to a woman. At any rate, there is one thing
which I wish you to understand, and that is that I
am not engaged to Miss March, and that I am engaged
to you. No matter what is said or done, you and I
belong to each other."

Annie made no answer, but she pressed his hand
tightly as she looked up into his face. He kissed her
as she stood, notwithstanding his belief that old Mrs.
Keswick was fully capable of bounding down on him,
umbrella in hand, from an upper window.

"What do you think she is going to do?" Annie
asked presently.

"My dear Annie," said he, "I do not believe that

there is a person on earth who could divine what your Aunt Keswick is going to do. As to that, we must simply wait and see. But, for my part, I know what I must do. I must write a letter to Miss March, and inform her, plainly and definitely, that I have ceased to be a suitor for her hand. I think, also, that it will be well to let her know that we are engaged?"

"Yes," said Annie, "for she will be sure to hear it now. But she will think it is a very prompt proceeding."

"That's exactly what it was," said Lawrence, smiling,—"prompt and determined. There was no doubt or indecision about any part of our affair, was there, little one?"

"Not a bit of it," said Annie, proudly.

At dinner, that day, Annie took her place at one end of the table, and Lawrence his at the other, but the old lady did not make her appearance. She was so erratic in her goings and comings, and had so often told them they must never wait for her, that Annie cut the ham and Lawrence carved the fowl, and the meal proceeded without her. But while they were eating Mrs. Keswick was heard coming down-stairs from her room, the front door was opened and slammed violently, and from the dining-room windows they saw her go down the steps, across the yard, and out of the gate.

"I do hope," ejaculated Annie, "that she has not gone away to stay!"

If Annie had remembered that the boy Plez, in a clean jacket and long white apron, officiated as waiter, she would not have said this, but then she would have lost some information. "Ole miss not gone to stay," he said, with the license of an untrained retainer.

338

"She gone to Howlettses, an' she done tole Aun' Letty she'll be back ag'in dis ebenin'."

"If Aunt Keswick don't come back," said Annie, when the two were in the parlor after dinner, "I shall go after her. I don't intend to drive her out of the house."

"Don't you trouble yourself about that, my dear," said Lawrence. "She is too angry not to come back."

"There is one thing," said Annie, after a while, "that we really ought to do. To-morrow Aunt Patsy is to be buried, and before she is put into the ground those little shoes should be returned to Aunt Keswick. It seems to me that justice to poor Aunt Patsy requires that this should be done. Perhaps now she knows how wicked it was to steal them."

"Yes," said Lawrence, "I think it would be well to put them back where they belong; but how can you manage it?"

"If you will give them to me," said Annie, "I will go up to aunt's room, now that she is away, and if she keeps the box in the same place where it used to be, I'll slip them into it. I hate dreadfully to do it, but I really feel that it is a duty."

When Lawrence, with some little difficulty, walked across the yard to get the shoes from his trunk, Annie ran after him, and waited at the office door. "You must not take a step more than necessary," she said, "and so I won't make you come back to the house."

When Lawrence gave her the shoes, and her hand a little squeeze at the same time, he told her that he should sit down immediately and write his letter.

"And I," said Annie, "will go and see what I can do with these."

THE LATE MRS. NULL

With the shoes in her pocket, she went up-stairs into her aunt's room; and after looking around hastily, as if to see that the old lady had not left the ghost of herself in charge, she approached the closet in which the sacred pasteboard box had always been kept. But the closet was locked. Turning away, she looked about the room. There was no other place in which there was any probability that the box would be kept. Then she became nervous; she fancied she heard the click of the yard gate. She would not for anything have her aunt catch her in that room; nor would she take the shoes away with her. Hastily placing them upon a table, she slipped out, and hurried into her own room.

It was about an hour after this that Mrs. Keswick came rapidly up the steps of the front porch. She had been to Howlett's to carry a letter which she had written to Miss March, and had there made arrangements to have that letter taken to Midbranch very early the next morning. She had wished to find some one who would start immediately; but as there was no moon, and as the messenger would arrive after the family were all in bed, she had been obliged to abandon this more energetic line of action. But the letter would get there soon enough; and if it did not bring down retribution on the head of the man who lodged in her office, and who, she said to herself, had worked himself into her plans like the rot in a field of potatoes, she would ever after admit that she did not know how to write a letter. All the way home she had conned over her method of action until Mr. Brandon, or a letter, should come from Midbranch.

She had already attacked, together, the unprincipled

pair who found shelter in her house, and she now determined to come upon them separately, and torment each soul by itself. Annie, of course, would come in for the lesser share of the punishment, for the fact that the wretched and depraved Null was no more, had, in a great measure, mitigated her offence. She was safe, and her aunt intended to hold her fast, and do with her as she would when the time and Junius came. But upon Lawrence she would have no mercy. When she had delivered him into the hands of Mr. Brandon, or those of Roberta's father, or the clutches of the law, she would have nothing more to do with him; but until that time she would make him bewail the day when he deceived and imposed upon her by causing her to believe that he was in love with another when he was, in reality, trying to get possession of her niece. There were a great many things which she had not thought to say to him in the arbor, but she would pour the whole hot mass upon his head that evening.

Stamping up the stairs, and thumping her umbrella upon every step as she went, hot vengeance breathing from between her parted lips, and her eyes flashing with the delight of prospective fury, she entered her room. The light of the afternoon had but just begun to wane, and she had not made three steps into the apartment before her eyes fell upon a pair of faded, light-blue shoes, which stood side by side upon a table. She stopped suddenly, and stood, pale and rigid. Her grasp upon her umbrella loosened, and, unnoticed, it fell upon the floor. Then, her eyes still fixed upon the shoes, she moved slowly sidewise towards the closet. She tried the door, and found it still locked;

then she put her hand in her pocket, drew out the key, looked at it, and dropped it. With faltering steps she drew near the table, and stood supporting herself by the back of a chair. Any one else would have seen upon that table merely a pair of baby's shoes; but she saw more. She saw the tops of the little socks which she had folded away for the last time so many years before. She saw the first short dress her child had ever worn; it was tied up with pink ribbons at the shoulders, from which hung two white, plump little arms. There was a little neck, around which was a double string of coral fastened by a small gold clasp. Above this was a face, a baby face with soft, pale eyes, and its head covered with curls of the lightest yellow, not arranged in artistic negligence, but smooth, even, and regular, as she so often had turned, twisted, and set them. It was indeed her baby girl who had come to her, as clear and vivid in every feature, limb, and garment as were the real shoes upon the table. For many minutes she stood, her eyes fixed upon the little apparition; then, slowly, she sank upon her knees by the chair; her sunbonnet, which she had not removed, was bowed, so the pale eyes of the little one could not see her face, and from her own eyes came the first tears that that old woman had shed since her baby's clothes had been put away in the box.

Lawrence's letter to Miss March was a definitely expressed document, intended to cover all the ground necessary, and no more; but it could not be said that it was entirely satisfactory to himself. His case, to say the least of it, was a difficult one to defend. He was aware that his course might be looked upon by others as dishonorable, although he assured himself that he had acted justly. It might have been better to wait for a positive declaration from Miss March, that she had not truly accepted him, before engaging himself to another lady. But then, he said to himself, true love never waits for anything. At all events, he could write no better letter than the one he had produced, and he hoped he should have an opportunity to show it to Annie before he sent it.

He need not have troubled himself in this regard, for he and Annie were not disturbed during the rest of that day by the appearance of Mrs. Keswick. But after the letter had been duly considered and approved, he found it difficult to obtain a messenger. There was no one on the place who would undertake to walk to Midbranch, and he could not take the liberty of using Mrs. Keswick's horse for the trip, so it was found necessary to wait until the morrow, when the letter could be taken to Howlett's, where, if no one could be found to carry it immediately, it would have to be intrusted to the mail, which went out the next day. Lawrence, of course, knew nothing of Mrs. Keswick's message to Midbranch, or he would have been still more desirous that his letter should be promptly despatched.

The evening was not a very pleasant one. The lovers did not know at what moment the old lady might descend upon them, and the element of unpleasant expectancy which pervaded the atmosphere of the house was somewhat depressing. They talked a good deal of the probabilities of Mrs. Keswick's action. Lawrence expected that she would order him away,

although Annie had stoutly maintained that her aunt
would have no right to do this, as he was not in a
condition to travel. This argument, however, made
little impression upon Lawrence, who was not the
man to stay in any house where he was not wanted;
besides, he knew very well that for any one to stay in
Mrs. Keswick's house when she did not want him
would be an impossibility. But he did not intend to
slip away in any cowardly manner, and leave Annie
to bear alone the brunt of the second storm. He felt
sure that such a storm was impending, and he was also
quite certain that its greatest violence would break
upon him. He would stay, therefore, and meet the
old lady when she next descended upon them; and
before he went away he would endeavor to utter some
words in defence of himself and Annie.

They separated early, and a good deal of thinking
was done by them before they went to sleep.

The next morning they had only each other for
company at breakfast; but they had just risen from
that meal when they were startled by the entrance
of Mrs. Keswick. Having expected her appearance
during the whole of the time they were eating, they
had no reason to be startled by her coming now, but
for their subsequent amazement at her appearance and
demeanor they had every reason in the world. Her
face was pale and grave, with an air of rigidity about
it which was not common to her, for, in general,
she possessed a very mobile countenance. Without
speaking a word, she advanced towards Lawrence,
and extended her hand to him. He was so much surprised that, while he took her hand in his, he could
only murmur some unintelligible form of morning

THE LATE MRS. NULL

salutation. Then Mrs. Keswick turned to Annie, and shook hands with her. The young girl grew pale, but said not a word; but some tears came into her eyes, although why this happened she could not have explained to herself. Having finished this little performance, the old lady walked to the back window and looked out into the flower-garden, although there was really nothing there to see. Now Annie found voice to ask her aunt if she would not have some breakfast.

"No," said Mrs. Keswick; "my breakfast was brought up-stairs to me." And with that she turned and went out of the room. She closed the door behind her, but scarcely had she done so when she opened it again and looked in. It was quite plain to the two silent and astonished observers of her actions that she was engaged in the occupation, very unusual with her, of controlling an excited condition of mind. She looked first at one and then at the other, and then she said, in a voice which seemed to meet with occasional obstructions in its course: "I have nothing more to say about anything. Do just what you please, only don't talk to me about it." And she closed the door.

"What is the meaning of all this?" said Lawrence, advancing towards Annie. "What has come over her?"

"I am sure I don't know," said Annie; and with this she burst into tears, and cried as she would have scorned to cry during the terrible storm of the day before.

That morning Lawrence Croft was a very much puzzled man. What had happened to Mrs. Keswick

345

he could not divine, and at times he imagined that her changed demeanor was perhaps nothing but an artful cover to some new and more ruthless attack.

Annie took occasion to be with her aunt a good deal during the morning, but she reported to Lawrence that the old lady had said very little, and that little related entirely to household affairs.

Mrs. Keswick ate dinner with them. Her manner was grave and even stern; but she made a few remarks in regard to the weather and some neighborhood matters, and before the end of the meal both Lawrence and Annie fancied that they could see some little signs of a return to her usual humor, which was pleasant enough when nothing happened to make it otherwise. But expectations of an early return to her ordinary manner of life were fallacious. She did not appear at supper, and she spent the evening in her own room. Lawrence and Annie had thus ample opportunity to discuss this novel and most unexpected state of affairs. They did not understand it, but it could not fail to cheer and encourage them. Only one thing they decided upon, and that was that Lawrence could not go away until he had had an opportunity of fully comprehending the position, in relation to Mrs. Keswick, in which he and Annie stood.

About the middle of the evening, as Lawrence was thinking that it was time for him to retire to his room in the little house in the yard, Letty came in with a letter which she said had been brought from Midbranch by a colored man on a horse; the man had said there was no answer, and had gone back to Howlett's, where he belonged.

The letter was for Mr. Croft and from Miss March.

THE LATE MRS. NULL

Very much surprised at receiving such a missive, Lawrence opened the envelope. His letter to Miss March had not yet been sent, for the new state of affairs had not only very much occupied his mind, but it also seemed to render unnecessary any haste in the matter, and he had concluded to mail the letter the next day. This, therefore, was not in answer to anything from him ; and why should she have written ?

It was with a decidedly uneasy sensation that Lawrence began to read the letter, Annie watching him anxiously as he did so. The letter was a somewhat long one, and the purport of it was as follows : The writer stated that, having received a most extraordinary and astounding epistle from old Mrs. Keswick, which had been sent by a special messenger, she had thought it her duty to write immediately on the subject to Mr. Croft, and had detained the man that she might send this letter by him. She did not pretend to understand the full purport of what Mrs. Keswick had written, but it was evident that the old lady believed that an engagement of marriage existed between herself (Miss March) and Mr. Croft. That that gentleman had given such information to Mrs. Keswick she could hardly suppose, but, if he had, it must have been in consequence of a message which, very much to her surprise and grief, had been delivered to Mr. Croft by Mr. Keswick. In order that this message might be understood, Miss March had determined to make a full explanation of her line of conduct towards Mr. Croft.

During the latter part of their pleasant intercourse at Midbranch during the past summer, she had reason to believe that Mr. Croft's intentions in regard to her were becoming serious, but she had also perceived that his impulses, however earnest they might have been, were controlled by an extraordinary caution and prudence, which, although it sometimes amused her, was not in the least degree complimentary to her. She could not prevent herself from resenting this somewhat peculiar action of Mr. Croft, and this resentment grew into a desire, which gradually became a very strong one, that she might have an opportunity of declining a proposal from him. That opportunity came while they were both at Mrs. Keswick's, and she had intended that what she said at her last interview with Mr. Croft should be considered a definite refusal of his suit, but the interview had terminated before she had stated her mind quite as plainly as she had purposed doing. She had not, however, wished to renew the conversation on the subject, and had concluded to content herself with what she had already said, feeling quite sure that her words had been sufficient to satisfy Mr. Croft that it would be useless to make any further proposals.

When, on the eve of her departure from the house, Mr. Keswick had brought her Mr. Croft's message, she was not only amazed, but indignant; not so much at Mr. Croft for sending it as at Mr. Keswick for bringing it. Miss March was not ashamed to confess that she was irritated and incensed to a high degree that a gentleman who had held the position towards her that Mr. Keswick had held should bring her such a message from another man. She was, therefore, seized with a sudden impulse to punish him, and, without in the least expecting that he would carry such an answer, she had given him the one which he had taken to Mr. Croft. Having, until the day on which she was writing, heard nothing further on the subject, she had supposed that her expectations had been realized. But on this day the astonishing letter from Mrs. Keswick had arrived, and it made her understand that not only had her impulsive answer been delivered, but that Mr. Croft had informed other persons that he had been accepted. She wished, therefore, to lose no time in stating to Mr. Croft that what she had said to him with her own lips was to be received as her final resolve, and that the answer given to Mr. Keswick was not intended for Mr. Croft's ears.

Miss March then went on to say that it might be possible that she owed Mr. Croft an apology for the somewhat ungracious manner in which she had treated him at Mrs. Keswick's house; but she assured herself that Mr. Croft owed her an apology, not only for the manner of his attentions, but for the peculiar publicity he had given them. In that case the apologies neutralized each other. Miss March had no intention of answering Mrs. Keswick's letter. Under no circumstances could she have considered, for a moment, its absurd suggestions and recommendations; and it contained allusions to Mr. Croft and another person which, if not founded upon the imagination of Mrs. Keswick, certainly concerned nothing with which Miss March had anything to do.

The proud spirit of Lawrence Croft was a good deal ruffled when he read this letter, but he made no remark about it. "Would you like to read it?" he said to Annie.

She greatly desired to read it, but there was something in her lover's face, and in the tone in which he spoke, which made her suspect that the reading of that letter might be, in some degree, humiliating to him. She was certain, from the expression of his face as he read it, that the letter contained matter very unpleasant to Lawrence, and it might be that it would wound him to have another person, especially herself, read it; and so she said: "I don't care to read it if you will tell me why she wrote to you, and the point of what she says."

"Thank you," said Lawrence. And he crumpled the letter in his hand as he spoke. "She wrote," he continued, "in consequence of a letter she has had from your aunt."

"What!" exclaimed Annie. "Did Aunt Keswick write to her?"

"Yes," said Lawrence, "and sent it by a special messenger. She must have told her all the heinous crimes with which she charged you and me, particularly me; and this must have been the first intimation to Miss March that your cousin had given me the answer she made to him; therefore Miss March writes in haste to let me know that she did not intend that that answer should be given to me, and that she wishes it generally understood that I have no more connection with her than I have with the Queen of Spain. That is the sum and substance of the letter."

"I knew as well as I know anything in the world," said Annie, "that that message Junius brought you meant nothing." And taking the crumpled letter from his hand, she threw it on the few embers that remained in the fireplace, and as it blazed and crumbled into black ashes, she said: "Now that is the end of Roberta March!"

"Yes," said Lawrence, emphasizing his remark with an encircling arm; "so far as we are concerned, that is the end of her."

CHAPTER XXVIII

On the next day old Aunt Patsy was buried. Mrs. Keswick and Annie attended the ceremonies in the cabin, but they did not go to the burial. After a time, it might be in a week or two, or it might be in a year, the funeral sermon would be preached in the church, and they would go to hear that. Aunt Patsy never finished her crazy-quilt, several pieces being wanted to one corner of it; but in the few days preceding her burial two old women of the congregation, with trembling hands and uncertain eyes, sewed in these pieces and finished the quilt, in which the body of the venerable sister was wrapped, according to her well-known wish and desire. It is customary among the negroes to keep the remains of their friends a very short time after death; but Aunt Patsy had lived so long upon this earth that it was generally conceded that her spirit would not object to her body remaining above ground until all necessary arrangements should be completed, and until all people who had known or heard of her had had an opportunity of taking a last look at her. As she had been so very well known to almost everybody's grandparents, a good many people availed themselves of this privilege.

After Mrs. Keswick's return from Aunt Patsy's cabin,

where, according to her custom, she made herself very prominent, it was noticeable that she had dropped some of the grave reserve in which she had wrapped herself during the preceding day. It was impossible for her, at least but for a very short time, to act in a manner unsuited to her nature; and reserve and constraint had never been suited to her nature. She, therefore, began to speak on general subjects in her ordinary free manner to the various persons in her house; but it must not be supposed that she exhibited any contrition for the outrageous way in which she had spoken to Annie and Lawrence, or gave them any reason to suppose that the laceration of their souls on that occasion was a matter which, at present, needed any consideration whatever from her. An angel, born of memory and imagination, might come to her from heaven, and so work upon her superstitious feelings as to induce her to stop short in her course of reckless vengeance; but she would not, on that account, fall upon anybody's neck, or ask forgiveness for anything she had done to anybody. She did not accuse herself, nor repent; she only stopped. "After this," she said, "you all can do as you please. I have no further concern with your affairs. Only don't talk to me about them."

She told Lawrence, in a manner that would seem to indicate a moderate but courteous interest in his welfare, that he must not think of leaving her house until his ankle had fully recovered its strength; and she even went so far as to suggest the use of a patent lotion which she had seen at the store at Howlett's. She resumed her former intercourse with Annie, but it seemed impossible for her to entirely forget the deception which that young lady had practised upon her. The only indication, however, of this resent-ment was the appellation which she now bestowed upon her niece. In speaking of her to Lawrence or any of the household, she invariably called her "the late Mrs. Null"; and this title so pleased the old lady that she soon began to use it in addressing her niece. Annie occasionally remonstrated in a manner which seemed half playful, but was in fact quite earnest; but her aunt paid no manner of attention to her words, and continued to please herself by this half-sarcastic method of alluding to her niece's fictitious matri-monial state.

Letty and the other servants were at first much astonished by the new title given to Miss Annie, and the only way in which they could explain it was by supposing that Mr. Null had gone off somewhere and died; and although they could not understand why Miss Annie should show so little grief in the matter, and why she had not put on mourning, they imagined that these were customs which she had learned in the North.

Lawrence advised Annie to pay no attention to this whim of her aunt. "It don't hurt either of us," he said, "and we ought to be very glad that she has let us off so easily. But there is one thing I think you ought to do: you should write to your cousin Junius and tell him of our engagement; but I would not refer at all to the other matter; you are not supposed to have anything to do with it, and Miss March can tell him as much about it as she chooses. Mr. Keswick wrote me that he was going to Midbranch, and that he would communicate with me while there; but as I have not since heard from him, I presume he is still in Washington."

A letter was, therefore, written by Annie, and addressed to Junius in Washington, and Lawrence drove her to the railroad station in the spring-wagon, where it was posted. The family mail came bi-weekly to Howlett's, as the post-office at the railroad-station was entirely too distant for convenience ; and as Saturday approached it was evident, from Mrs. Keswick's occasional remarks and questions, that she expected a letter. It was quite natural for Lawrence and Annie to surmise that this letter was expected from Miss March, for Mrs. Keswick had not heard of any rejoinder having been made to her epistle to that lady. When, late on Saturday afternoon, the boy Plez returned from Howlett's, Mrs. Keswick eagerly took from him the well-worn letter-bag, and looked over its contents. There was a letter for her, and from Midbranch ; but the address was written by Junius, not by Miss March. There was another in the same handwriting for Annie. As the old lady looked at the address on her letter, and then on its postmark, she was evidently disappointed and displeased.; but she said nothing, and went away with it to her room.

Annie's letter was in answer to the one she had sent to Washington, which had been promptly forwarded to Midbranch, where Junius had been for some days. It began by expressing much surprise at the information his cousin had given him in regard to her assumption of a married title ; and although she had assured him she had very good reasons, he could not admit that it was right and proper for her to deceive his aunt and himself in this way. If it were indeed necessary that other persons should suppose that she were a married woman, her nearest relatives, at least, should have been told the truth.

At this passage, Annie, who was reading the letter aloud, and Lawrence, who was listening, both laughed. But they made no remarks, and the reading proceeded.

Junius next alluded to the news of his cousin's engagement to Mr. Croft. His guarded remarks on this subject showed the kindness of his heart. He did not allude to the suddenness of the engagement, nor to the very peculiar events that had so recently preceded it; but, reading between the lines, both Annie and Lawrence thought that the writer had probably given these points a good deal of consideration. In a general way, however, it was impossible for him to see any objection to such a match for his cousin, and this was the impression he endeavored to give, in a very kindly way, in his congratulations. But, even here, there seemed to be indications of a hope, on the part of the writer, that Mr. Croft would not see fit to make another short tack in his course of love.

Like the polite gentleman he was, Mr. Keswick allowed his own affairs to come in at the end of the letter. Here he informed his cousin that his engagement with Miss March had been renewed, and that they were to be married shortly after Christmas. As it must have been very plain to those who were present when Miss March left his aunt's house that she left in anger with him, he felt impelled to say that he had explained to her the course of action to which she had taken exception, and although she had not admitted that that course had been a justifiable one, she had forgiven him. He wished also to say at this point that he himself was not at all proud of what he had done.

"That was intended for me," interrupted Lawrence.

"Well, if you understand it, it is all right," said Annie.

Junius went on to say that the renewal of his engagement was due, in great part, to Miss March's visit to his aunt, and to a letter she had received from her. A few days of intercourse with Mrs. Keswick, whom she had never before seen, and the tenor and purpose of that letter, had persuaded Miss March that his aunt was a person whose mind had passed into a condition when its opposition or its action ought not to be considered by persons who were intent upon their own welfare. His own arrival at Midbranch at this juncture had resulted in the happy renewal of their engagement.

"I don't know Junius half as well as I wish I did," said Annie, as she finished the letter, "but I am very sure indeed that he will make a good husband, and I am glad he has got Roberta March—as he wants her."

"Did you emphasize 'he'?" asked Lawrence.

"I will emphasize it, if you would like to hear me do it," said she.

"It's very queer," remarked Annie, after a little pause, "that I should have been so anxious to preserve poor Junius from your clutches, and that, after all I did to save him, I should fall into those clutches myself."

Whereupon Lawrence, much to her delight, told her the story of the anti-detective.

Mrs. Keswick sat down in her room and read her

letter. She had no intention of abandoning her reso-
lution to let things go as they would, and therefore
did not expect to follow up, with further words or
actions, anything she had written in her letter to
Roberta March. But she had had a very strong curiosity to know what that lady would say in answer to
said letter, and she was therefore disappointed and
displeased that the missive she had received was from
her nephew, and not from Miss March. She did not
wish to have a letter from Junius. She knew, or
rather very much feared, that it would contain news
which would be bad news to her, and although she
was sure that such news would come to her sooner or
later, she was very much averse to receiving it.

His letter to her merely touched upon the points of
Mrs. Null, and his cousin's engagement to Mr. Croft;
but it was almost entirely filled with the announcement, and most earnest defence, of his own engagement to Roberta March. He said a great deal upon
this subject, and he said it well. But it is doubtful
if his fervid, and often affectionate, expressions made
much impression upon his aunt. Nothing could make
the old lady like this engagement, but she had made
up her mind that he might do as he pleased, and it
didn't matter what he said about it; he had done it,
and there was an end of it.

But there was one thing that did matter: that unprincipled and iniquitous old man Brandon had had
his own way at last, and she and her way had been
set aside. This was the last of a series of injuries to
her and her family with which she charged Mr. Brandon and his family; but it was the crowning wrong.
The injury itself she did not so much deplore as that

the injurer would profit by it. Arrested in her course of raging passion by a sudden flood of warm and irresistible emotion, she had resigned, as impetuously as she had taken them up, her purposes of vengeance, and, consequently, her plans for her nephew and niece. But she was a keen-minded as well as passionate old woman, and when she had considered the altered state of affairs, she was able to see in it advantages as well as disappointment and defeat. From what she had learned of Lawrence Croft's circumstances and position,—and she had made a good many inquiries on this subject of Roberta March,—he was certainly a good match for Annie; and although she hated to have anything to do with Midbranch, it could not be a bad thing for Junius to be master of that large estate, and that Mr. Brandon had repeatedly declared he would be if he married Roberta. Thus, in the midst of these reverses, there was something to comfort her and reconcile her to them. But there was no balm for the wound caused by Mr. Brandon's success and her failure.

With the letter of Junius open in her hand, she sat, for a long time, in bitter meditation. At length a light gradually spread itself over her gloomy countenance; her eyes sparkled; she sat up straight in her chair, and a broad smile changed the course of the wrinkles on her cheeks. She rose to her feet; she gave her head a quick jerk of affirmation; she clapped one hand upon the other; and she said aloud: "I will bless, not curse!"

And with that she went happy to bed.

CHAPTER XXIX

ON the following Monday, Lawrence announced that his ankle was now quite well enough for him to go to New York, where his affairs required his presence. Neither he nor the late Mrs. Null regarded this parting with any satisfaction, but their very natural regrets at the necessary termination of these happy autumn days were a good deal tempered by the fact that Lawrence intended to return in a few weeks, and that then the final arrangements would be made for their marriage. It was not easy to decide what these arrangements would be, for, in spite of the many wrongnesses of the old lady's head and heart, Annie had conceived a good deal of affection for her aunt, and felt a strong disinclination to abandon her to her lonely life, which would be more lonely than before, now that Junius was to be married. On the other hand, Lawrence, although he had discovered some estimable points in the very peculiar character of Mrs. Keswick, had no intention of living in the same house with her. This whole matter, therefore, was left in abeyance until the lovers should meet again, some time in December.

Lawrence and Annie had desired very much that Junius should visit them before Mr. Croft's departure for the North, for they both had a high esteem for him, and both felt a desire that he should be as well satisfied with their matrimonial project as they were with his. But they need not have expected him. Junius had conceived a dislike for Mr. Croft, which was based in great part upon disapprobation of what he himself had done in connection with that gentleman; and this manner of dislike is not easily set aside. The time would come when he would take Lawrence Croft and Annie by the hand, and honestly congratulate them, but for that time they must wait.

Lawrence departed in the afternoon; and the next day Mrs. Keswick set about that general renovation and rearrangement of her establishment which many good housewives consider necessary at certain epochs, such as the departure of guests, the coming in of spring, or the advent of winter. These arrangements occupied two days, and on the evening that they were finished to her satisfaction, the old lady informed her niece that early the next morning she was going to start for Midbranch, and that it was possible, nay, quite probable, that she would stay there over a night. "I might go and come back the same day," she said, "but thirty miles a day is too much for Billy; and besides, I am not sure I could get through what I have to do if I do not stay over. I would take you with me, but this is not to be a mere visit; I have important things to attend to, and you would be in the way. You got along so well without me when you first came here that I have no doubt you will do very well for one night. I shall drive myself, and take Plez along with me, and leave Uncle Isham and Letty to take care of you."

THE LATE MRS. NULL

Under ordinary circumstances Annie would have been delighted to go to Midbranch, a place she had never seen, and of which she had heard so much; but she had no present desire to see Roberta March, and said so, further remarking that she was very willing to stay by herself for a night. She hoped much that her aunt would proceed with the conversation, and tell her why she had determined upon such an extraordinary thing as a visit to Midbranch, where she knew the old lady had not been for many, many years. But Mrs. Keswick had nothing further to say upon this subject, and began to talk of other matters.

After a very early breakfast, next morning, Mrs. Keswick set out upon her journey, driving the sorrel horse with much steadiness, intermingled with severity whenever he allowed himself to drop out of his usual jogging pace. Plez sat in the back part of the spring-wagon, and whenever the old lady saw an unusually large stone lying in the track of the road, she would stop, and make him get out and throw it to one side.

"I believe," she said, on one of these occasions, "that a thousand men in buggies might pass along this road thrice a day for a year, and never think of stopping to throw that rock out of the way of people's wheels. They would steer around it every time, or bump over it; but such a thing as moving it would never enter their heads."

The morning was somewhat cool, but fine, and the smile which occasionally flitted over the corrugated countenance of Mrs. Keswick seemed to indicate that she was in a pleasant state of mind, which might have been occasioned by the fine weather and the good con-

dition of the roads, or by cheerful anticipations connected with her visit.

It was not very long after noonday that, with a
stifled remark of disapprobation upon her lips, she
drew up at the foot of the broad flight of steps by
which one crossed the fence into the Midbranch yard.
Giving Billy into the charge of Plez, with directions
to take him round to the stables and tell somebody to
put him up and feed him, she mounted the steps, and
stopped for a minute or so on the broad platform at
the top, looking about her as she stood. Everything
—the house, the yard, the row of elms along the fence,
the wide-spreading fields, and the farm buildings and
cabins, some of which she could see around the end of
the house—was all on a scale so much larger and more
imposing than those of her own little estate that, although nothing had changed for the better since the
days when she was familiar with Midbranch, she was
struck with the general superiority of the Brandon
possessions to her own. Her eyes twinkled, and she
smiled; but there did not appear to be anything
envious about her.

She presented a rather remarkable figure as she
stood in this conspicuous position. Annie had insisted,
when she was helping her aunt to array herself for
the journey, that she should wear a bonnet which for
many years had been her head-gear on Sundays and
important occasions. But to this the old lady positively
objected. She was not going on a mere visit of state
or ceremony; her visit at Midbranch would require
her whole attention, and she did not wish to distract
her mind by wondering whether her bonnet was
straight on her head or not, and she was so unaccustomed to the feel of it that she would never know if

it got turned hind part foremost. She could not be at her ease, nor say freely what she wished to say, if she were dressed in clothes to which she was not accustomed. She was perfectly accustomed to her sunbonnet, and she intended to wear that. Of course she carried her purple umbrella, and she wore a plain calico dress, blue spotted with white, which was very narrow and short in the skirt, barely touching the tops of her shoes, the stoutest and most serviceable that could be procured in the store at Howlett's. She covered her shoulders with a small red shawl, which, much to Annie's surprise, she fastened with a large and somewhat tarnished silver brooch, an ornament her niece had never before seen. Attired thus, she certainly would have attracted attention, had there been any one there to see; but the yard was empty, and the house door closed. She descended the steps, crossed the yard with what might be termed a buoyant gait, and, mounting the porch, knocked on the door with the handle of her umbrella. After some delay, a colored woman appeared, and as soon as the door was opened, Mrs. Keswick walked in.

"Where is your master?" said she, forgetting all about the Emancipation Act.

"Mahs' Robert is in the lib'ery," said the woman.

"And where are Miss Roberta March and Master Junius Keswick?"

"Miss Rob went Norf day 'fore yestiddy," was the answer, "an' Mahs' Junius done gone 'long to wait on her. Who shall I tell Mahs' Robert is come?"

"There is no need to tell him who I am," said Mrs. Keswick. "Just take me in to him. That's all you have to do."

A good deal doubtful of the propriety of this pro-

ceeding, but more doubtful of the propriety of oppos-
ing the wishes of such a determined-looking visitor,
the woman stepped to the back part of the hall, and
opened the door. The moment she did so, Mrs. Keswick entered, and closed the door behind her.

Mr. Brandon was seated in an arm-chair by a table,
and not very far from a wood fire of a size suited to
the season. His slippered feet were on a cushioned
stool; his eye-glasses were carefully adjusted on the
capacious bridge of his nose; and, intent upon a news-
paper which had arrived by that morning's mail, he
presented the appearance of a very well satisfied old
gentleman in very comfortable circumstances. But
when he turned his head and saw the widow Keswick close the door behind her, every idea of satisfaction or comfort seemed to vanish from his mind. He
dropped the paper; he rose to his feet; he took off
his eyeglasses; he turned somewhat red in the face;
and he ejaculated: "What, madam! So it is you,
Mrs. Keswick?"

The old lady did not immediately answer. Her
head dropped a little on one side, a broad smile be-
wrinkled the lower part of her well-worn visage, and,
with her eyes half closed behind her heavy spectacles,
she held out both her hands, the purple umbrella in
one of them, and exclaimed in a voice of happy fervor:
"Robert! I am yours!"

Mr. Brandon, recovered from his first surprise, had
made a step forward to go round the table and greet
his visitor; but at these words he stopped as if he had
been shot. Perception, understanding, and even animation, seemed to have left him as he vacantly stared
at the elderly female with purple-sunbonnet and um-

brella, blue calico gown, red shawl, and coarse boots, who held out her arms towards him, and who gazed upon him with an air of tender, though decrepit, fondness.

"Don't you understand me, Robert?" she continued. "Don't you remember the day, many a good long year ago, it is true, when we walked together down there by the branch, and you asked me to be yours? I refused you, Robert, and although you went down on your knees in the damp grass and besought me to give you my heart, I would not do it. But I did not know you then as I know you now, Robert, and the words of true love which you spoke to me that morning come to me now with a sweetness which I was too young and trifling to notice then. That heart is yours now, Robert. *I* am yours." And with these words she made a step forward.

At this demonstration Mr. Brandon appeared suddenly to recover his consciousness, and he precipitately made two steps backward, just missing tumbling over his footstool into the fireplace.

"Madam!" he exclaimed, "what are you talking about?"

"Of the days of our courtship and your love, Robert," she said. "My love did not come then, but it is here now—here now," she repeated, putting the hand with the umbrella in it on her breast.

"Madam," exclaimed the old gentleman, "you must be raving crazy! Those things to which you allude happened nearly half a century ago; and since that you have been married and settled, and—"

"Robert," interrupted the widow Keswick, "you are mistaken. It is not quite forty-five years since that morning, and why should hearts like ours allow the passage of time, or the mere circumstance of what might be called an outside marriage, but now extinct, to come between them? There is many a spring, Robert, which does not show when a man first begins to dig, but it will bubble up in time. And, Robert, it bubbles now." And with her head bent a little downward, although her eyes were still fixed upon him, she made another step in his direction.

Mr. Brandon now backed himself flat against some book-shelves in his rear. The perspiration began to roll from his face, and his whole form trembled. "Mrs. Keswick! Madam!" he exclaimed, "you will drive me mad!"

The old lady dropped the end of her umbrella on the floor, rested her two hands on the head of it, settled herself into an easy position to speak, and, with her head thrown back, fixed a steady gaze upon the trembling old gentleman. "Robert," she said, "do not try to crush emotions which always were a credit to you, although in those days gone by I didn't tell you so. Your hair was black then, Robert, and you looked taller, for you hadn't a stoop; and your face was very smooth, and so was mine; and I remember I had on a white dress with a broad ribbon around the waist; and neither of us wore specs. What you said to me was very fresh and sweet, Robert, and it all comes to me now as it never came before. You have never loved another, Robert, and you don't know how happy it makes me to think that, and to know that I can come to you and find you the same true and constant lover that you were when, forty-five years ago, you went down on your knees to me by the branch.

THE LATE MRS. NULL

We can't stifle those feelings of bygone days which well up in our bosoms, Robert. After all these years I have learned what a prize your true love is, and I return it. I am yours."

At this Mr. Brandon opened his mouth with a spasmodic gasp, but no word came from him. He looked to the right and left, and then made a lunge to one side, as if he would run around the old lady and gain the door. But Mrs. Keswick was too quick for him. With two sudden springs she reached the door and put her back against it.

"Don't leave me, Robert," she said, "I have not told you all. Don't you remember this breastpin?" unfastening the large silver brooch from her shawl and holding it out to him. "You gave it to me, Robert; there were almost tears of joy in your eyes on the first day I wore it, although I was careful to let you know it meant nothing. Where are those tears to-day, Robert? It means something now. I have kept it all these years, although in the lifetime of Mr. Keswick it was never cleaned; and I wore it to-day, Robert, that your eyes might rest upon it once again, and that you might speak to me the words you spoke to me the day after I let you pin it on my white neckerchief. You waited then, Robert, a whole day before you spoke; but you needn't wait now. Let your heart speak out, dear Robert."

But dear Robert appeared to have no power to speak, on this or any other subject. He was half sitting, half leaning on the corner of a table which stood by a window, out of which he gave sudden agonized and longing glances, as if, had he strength enough, he would raise the sash and leap out.

367

THE LATE MRS. NULL

The old lady, however, had speech enough for two. "Robert," she exclaimed, "how happy may we be, yet! If you wish to give up to a younger couple this spacious mansion, these fine grounds and noble elms, and come to my humble home, I shall only say to you, 'Robert, come!' I shall be alone there, Robert, and shall welcome you with joy. I have nobody now to give anything to. The late Mrs. Null, by which I mean my niece, will marry a man who, if reports don't lie, is rich enough to make her want nothing that I have; and as for Junius, he is to have your property, as we all know. So all I have is yours, if you choose to come to me, Robert. But if you would rather live here, I will come to you, and the young people can board with us until your decease; after that I'll board with them. And I'm not sure, Robert, but I like the plan of coming here best. There are lots of improvements we could make on this place, with you to furnish the money, and me to advise and direct. The first thing I'd do would be to have down those abominable steps over the front fence, and put a decent gate in its place; and then we would have a gravelled walk across the yard to the porch, wide enough for you and me, Robert, to walk together arm in arm when we would go out to look over the plantation, or stroll down to that spot on the branch, Robert, where the first plightings of our troth began."

The words of tender reminiscence, and of fond, though rather late devotion, with which Mrs. Keswick had stabbed and gashed the soul of the poor old gentleman had at first deranged his senses, and then driven him into a state of abject despair; but the practical remarks which succeeded seemed to have a more direful effect upon him. The idea of the being with the sunbonnet and the umbrella entering into his life at Midbranch, tearing down the broad steps which his honored father had built, cutting a gravelled path across the green turf which had been the pride of generations, and doing no man could say what else of advice and direction, seemed to strike a chill of terror into his very bones.

The quick perception of Mrs. Keswick told her that it was time to terminate the interview. "I will not say anything more to you now, Robert," she said. "Of course you have been surprised at my coming to you to-day and accepting your offer of marriage, and you must have time to quiet your mind and think it over. I don't doubt your affection, Robert, and I don't want to hurry you. I am going to stay here to-night, so that we can have plenty of time to settle everything comfortably. I'll go now and get one of the servants to show me to a room where I can take off my things. I'll see you again at dinner."

And, with a smile of antiquated coyness, she left the room.

CHAPTER XXX

MR. BRANDON was not a weak man, nor one very susceptible to outside influences ; but, in the whole course
of his life, nothing so extraordinarily nerve-stirring
had occurred to him as this visit of old Mrs. Keswick
endeavoring to appear in the character of the young
creature he had wooed some forty-five years before.
For a long time Mrs. Keswick had been the enemy of
himself and his family, and many a bitter onslaught
she had made upon him, both by letter and by word
of mouth. These he had borne with the utmost bravery and coolness, and there were times when they
even afforded him entertainment.   But this most
astounding attack was something against which no
man could have been prepared ; and Mr. Brandon,
suddenly pounced upon in the midst of his comfortable bachelordom by a malevolent sorceress, and
hurled back to the days of his youth, was shown himself
kneeling, not at the feet of a fair young girl, but before
a horrible old woman.

This amazing and startling state of affairs was
too much for him immediately to comprehend. It
stunned and bewildered him. Such, indeed, was the
effect upon him that the first act of his mind, when
he was left alone and it began to act, was to ask of

itself if there were really any grounds upon which Mrs. Keswick could, with any reason, take up her position? The absolute absurdity of her position, however, became more and more evident as Mr. Brandon's mind began to straighten itself and stand up. And now he grew angry. Anger was a passion with which he was not at all unfamiliar, and the exercise of it seemed to do him good. When he had walked up and down his library for a quarter of an hour he felt almost like his natural self; and with many nods of his head and shakes of his fist, he declared that the old woman was crazy, and that he would bundle her home just as soon as he could.

By dinner-time he had cooled down a good deal, and he resolved to treat her with the respect due to her age and former condition of sanity, but to take care that she should not again be alone with him, and to arrange that she should return to her home that day.

Mrs. Keswick came to the table with a smiling face, and wearing a close-fitting white cap, which looked like a portion of her night-gear, tied under her chin with broad, stiff strings. In this she appeared to her host far more hideous than when wearing her sun-bonnet. Mr. Brandon had arranged that two servants should wait upon the table, so that one of them should always be in the room; but in his supposition that the presence of a third person would have any effect upon the expression of Mrs. Keswick's fond regard he was mistaken. The meal had scarcely begun when she looked around the room with wide-open eyes, and exclaimed : "Robert, if we should conclude to remain here, I think we will have this room repapered with some light-colored paper. I like a light dining-room. This is entirely too dark."

The two servants, one of whom was our old friend Peggy, actually stopped short in their duties at this remark ; and as for Mr. Brandon, his appetite immediately left him, to return no more during that meal.

He was obliged to make some answer to this speech, and so he briefly remarked that he had no desire to alter the appearance of his dining-room, and then hastened to change the conversation by making some inquiries about that interesting young woman, her niece, who, he had been informed, was not a married lady, as he had supposed her to be.

At this intelligence Peggy dropped two spoons and a fork ; she had never heard it before.

"The late Mrs. Null," said Mrs. Keswick, "is a young woman who likes to cut her clothes after her own patterns. They may be becoming to her when they are made up, or they may not be. But I am inclined to think she has got a pretty good head on her shoulders, and perhaps she knows what suits her as well as any of us. I can't say it was easy to forgive the trick she played on me, her own aunt, and just the same, in fact, as her mother. But, Robert,"—and as she said this the old lady laid down her knife and fork and looked tenderly at Mr. Brandon—"I have determined to forgive everybody and to overlook everything, and I do this as much for your sake, dear Robert, as for my own. It wouldn't do for a couple of our age to be keeping up grudges against the young people for their ways of getting out of marriages or getting into them. We will have my niece and her husband here sometimes, won't we, Robert?"

THE LATE MRS. NULL

Mr. Brandon straightened himself and remarked: "Mr. Croft, whom I have heard your niece is to marry, will be quite welcome here, with his wife." Then, putting his napkin on the table, and pushing back his chair, he said: "Now, madam, you must excuse me, for I have orders to give to some of my people which I had forgotten until this moment. But do not let me interfere with your dinner. Pray continue your meal."

Never before had Mr. Brandon been known to leave his dinner until he had finished it, and he was not at all accustomed to give such a poor reason for his actions as the one he gave now; but it was simply impossible for him to sit any longer at table and have that old woman talk in that shocking manner before the servants.

"Robert," cried Mrs. Keswick, as he left the room, "I'll save some dessert for you, and we'll eat it together."

Mr. Brandon's first impulse, when he found himself out of the dining-room, was to mount his horse and ride away; but there was no place to which he wished to ride, and he was a man who was very loath to leave the comforts of his home. "No," he said. "She must go, and not I." And then he went into his parlor, and strode up and down. As soon as Mrs. Keswick had finished her dinner, he would see her there and speak his mind to her. He had determined that he would not again be alone with her, but since the presence of others was no restraint whatever upon her, it had become absolutely necessary that he should speak with her alone.

It was not long before the widow Keswick, with

a brisk, blithe step, entered the parlor. "I couldn't eat without you, Robert," she cried, "and so I really haven't half finished my dinner. Did you have to come in here to speak to your people?"

Mr. Brandon stepped to the door and closed it. "Madam," he said, "it will be impossible for me, in the absence of my niece, to entertain you here to-night, and so it would be prudent for you to start for home as soon as possible, as the days are short. It would be too much of a journey for your horse to go back again to-day, and your vehicle is an open one; therefore I have ordered my carriage to be prepared, and you may trust my driver to take you safely home, even if it should be dark before you get there. If you desire it, there is a young maid-servant here who will go with you."

"Robert," said Mrs. Keswick, approaching the old gentleman and gazing fondly upward at him, "you are so good and thoughtful and sweet. But you need not put yourself to all that trouble for me. I shall stay here to-night, and in your house, dear Robert, I can take care of myself a great deal better than any lady could take care of me."

"Madam," exclaimed Mr. Brandon, "I want you to stop calling me by my first name! You have no right to do so, and I won't stand it."

"Robert," said the old lady, looking at him with an air of tender upbraiding, "you forget that I am yours, now and forever."

Never since he had arrived at man's estate, and probably not before, had Mr. Brandon spoken in improper language to a lady, but now it was all he could do to restrain himself from the ejaculation of an oath;

but he did restrain himself, and only exclaimed : "Confound it, madam, I cannot stand this ! Why do you come here, to drive me crazy with your senseless ravings ?"

"Robert," said Mrs. Keswick, very composedly, "I do not wonder that my coming to you and accepting the proposals which you once so heartily made to me, and from which you have never gone back, should work a good deal upon your feelings. It is quite natural, and I expected it. Therefore don't hesitate about speaking out your mind ; I shall not be offended. So that we belong to each other for the rest of our days, I don't mind what you say now, when it is all new and unexpected to you. You and I have had many a difference of opinion, Robert, and your plans were not my plans. But things have turned out as you wished, and you have what you have always wanted ; and with the other good things, Robert, you can take me." And, as she finished speaking, she held out both hands to her companion.

With a stamp of his foot and a kick at a chair which stood in his way, Mr. Brandon precipitately left the room, and slammed the door after him ; and if Peggy had not nimbly sprung to one side, he would have stumbled over her, and have had a very bad fall for a man of his age.

It was not ten minutes after this that, looking out of a window, Mrs. Keswick saw a saddled horse brought into the back yard. She hastened into the hall, and found Peggy. "Run to Mr. Brandon," she said, "and bid him good-by for me. I am going upstairs to get ready to go home, and haven't time to speak to him myself before he starts on his ride."

THE LATE MRS. NULL

At the receipt of this message the heart of Mr. Brandon gave a bound which actually helped him to get into the saddle; but he did not hesitate in his purpose of instant departure. If he stayed but for a moment, she might come out to him and change her mind; so he put spurs to his horse and galloped away, merely stopping long enough, as he passed the stables, to give orders that the carriage be prepared for Mrs. Keswick, and taken round to the front.

As he rode through the cool air of that fine November afternoon, the spirits of Mr. Brandon rose. He felt a serene satisfaction in assuring himself that although he had been very angry indeed with Mrs. Keswick, on account of her most unheard-of and outrageous conduct, yet he had not allowed his indignation to burst out against her in any way of which he would afterwards be ashamed. Some hasty words had escaped him, but they were of no importance, and, under the circumstances, no one could have avoided speaking them. But when he had addressed her at any length he had spoken dispassionately and practically, and she, being at bottom a practical woman, had seen the sense of his advice, and had gone home comfortably in his carriage. Whether she took her insane fancies home with her or dropped them on the road, it mattered very little to him, so that he never saw her again; and he did not intend to see her again. If she came again to his house, he would leave it and not return until she had gone; but he had no reason to suppose that he would be forced into any such exceedingly disagreeable action as this. He did not believe she would ever come back. For, unless she were really crazy,—and in that case she ought to be put in the lunatic asylum,—she could not keep up, for any length of time, the extraordinary and outrageous delusion that he would be willing to renew the feelings that he had entertained for her in her youth.

Mr. Brandon rode until nearly dark, for it took a good while to free his mind from the effects of the excitements and torments of that day; but when he entered the house and took his seat in his library chair by the fire, he had almost regained his usual composed and well-satisfied frame of mind.

Then, through the quietly opened door, came Mrs. Keswick, and stealthily stepping towards him in the fitful light of the blazing logs, she put her hand on his arm and said: "Dear Robert, how glad I am to see you back!"

The next morning, about ten o'clock, Mrs. Keswick sent her eighteenth or twentieth message to Mr. Brandon, who had shut himself up in his room since a little before supper-time on the previous evening. The message was sent by Peggy, and she was instructed to shout it outside of her master's door until he took notice of it. Its purport was that it was necessary that Mrs. Keswick should go home to-day, and that her horse was harnessed and she was now ready to go, but that she could not think of leaving until she had seen Mr. Brandon again. She would therefore wait until he was ready to come down.

Mr. Brandon looked out of the window and saw the spring-wagon at the outside of the broad stile, with Plez standing at the sorrel's head. He remembered that the venerable demon had said, at the first, that she intended to stay but one night, and he could but believe that she was now really going. Knowing her as he did, however, he was very well aware that if she had said she would not leave until she had seen him, she would stay in his house for a year unless he sooner went down to her ; therefore he opened his door and slowly and feebly descended the stairs.

"My dear, dear Robert!" exclaimed Mrs. Keswick, totally regardless of the fact that Peggy was standing at the front door with her valise in her hand, and that there was another servant in the hall, "how pale and haggard and worn you look! You must be quite unwell, and I don't know but that I ought to stay here and take care of you."

At these words a look of agony passed over the old man's face, but he said nothing.

"But I am afraid I cannot stay any longer this time," continued the widow Keswick, "for my niece would not know what had become of me, and there are things at home that I must attend to. But I will come again. Don't think I intend to desert you, dear Robert. You shall see me soon again. But while I am gone," she said, turning to the two servants, "I want you maids to take good care of your master. You must do it for his sake, for he has always been kind to you ; but I also want you to do it for my sake. Don't you forget that. And now, dear Robert, good-by." As she spoke she extended her hand towards the old gentleman.

Without a word, but with a good deal of apparent reluctance, he took the long, bony hand in his, and probably would have instantly dropped it again, had not Mrs. Keswick given him a most hearty clutch and a vigorous and long-continued shake.

THE LATE MRS. NULL

"It is hard, dear Robert," she said, "for us to part with nothing but a hand-shake, but there are people about, and this will have to do." And then, after urging him to take good care of his health, so valuable to them both, and assuring him that he would soon see her again, she gave his hand a final shake, and left him. Accompanied by Peggy, she went out to the spring-wagon and clambered into it. It almost surpasses belief that Mr. Brandon, a Virginia gentleman of the old school, should have stood in his hall and have seen an old lady leave his house and get into a vehicle without accompanying and assisting her; but such was the case on this occasion. He seemed to have forgotten his traditions and to have lost his impulses. He simply stood where the widow Keswick had left him, and gazed at her.

When she was seated and ready to start, the old lady turned towards him, called out to him in a cheery voice, "Good-by, Robert!" and kissed her hand to him.

Mrs. Keswick slowly drove away, and Mr. Brandon stood at his hall door gazing after her until she was entirely out of sight. Then he ejaculated: "The devil's daughter!" and went into his library.

"I wonders," said Peggy, when she returned to the kitchen, "how you-all's gwine to like habin' dat ole Miss Keswick libin' h'yar as you-all's mistiss?"

"Who's gwine to hab her?" growled Aunt Judy.

"You-all is," sturdily retorted Peggy. "Dar ain't no use tryin' to git out ob dat. Dat old Miss Keswick done gone an' kunjered Mahs' Robert, an' dey's boun' to git mar'ed. I done heared all 'bout it, an' she's comin' h'yar to lib wid Mahs' Robert. But dat don' make no dif'rence to me. I'se gwine to lib wid Mahs' Junius an' Miss Rob in New York, I is. But I'se mighty sorry for you-all."

"You Peggy," shouted the irate Aunt Judy, "shut up wid your fool talk! When Mahs' Robert marry dat ole jimpsun-weed, de angel Gabr'el blow his hohn, shuh."

Slowly driving along the road to her home, the widow Keswick gazed cheerfully at the blue sky above her and the pleasant autumn scenery around her, sniffed the fine fresh air, delicately scented with the odor of falling leaves, and settling herself into a more comfortable position on her seat, she complacently said to herself: "Well, I reckon dear Robert is about as happy as I can make him."

CHAPTER XXXI

THERE were two reasons why Peggy could not go to live with "Mahs' Junius and Miss Rob" in New York. In the first place, this couple had no intention of setting up an establishment in that city; and secondly, Peggy, as Roberta well knew, was not adapted by nature to be her maid, or the maid of any one else. Peggy's true vocation in life was to throw her far-away gaze into futurity, and, as far as in her lay, to adapt present circumstances to what she supposed was going to happen. It would have delighted her soul if she could have been the adept in conjuring which she firmly believed the widow Keswick to be; but as she possessed no such gift, she made up the deficiency, as well as she could, by mixing up her mind, her soul, and her desires into a sort of witch's hodge-podge, which she thrust as a spell into the affairs of other people. Twice had the devices of this stupid-looking wooden peg of a negro girl stopped Lawrence Croft in the path he was following in his pursuit of Roberta March. If Lawrence had known, at the time, what Peggy was doing, he would have considered her an unmitigated little demon; but afterwards, if he could have known of it, he would have thought her a very unprepossessing and conscienceless guardian angel.

THE LATE MRS. NULL

As it was, he knew not what she had done, and did not consider her at all.

Junius Keswick took much more delight in farming than he did in the practice of the law, and it was only because he had felt himself obliged to do so that he had adopted the legal profession. To be a farmer, one must have a farm; but a lawyer can frequently make a living from the lands of other men. He was very willing, therefore, to agree to the plan which for years had been Mr. Brandon's most cherished scheme: that he and Roberta should make their home at Midbranch, and that he should take charge of the estate, which would be his wife's property after the old gentleman's decease. Roberta was as fond of the country as was Junius, but she was also a city woman; and it was arranged that the couple should spend a portion of each winter in New York, at the house of Mr. March.

Junius and Roberta, as well as her father, hoped very much that they might be able to induce Mr. Brandon to come to New York to attend the wedding, which was to take place the middle of January; but they were not confident of success, for they knew the old gentleman disliked very much to travel, especially in winter. Three very pressing letters were therefore written to Mr. Brandon; and the writers were much surprised to receive, in a short time, a collective answer, in which he stated that he would not only be present at the wedding, but that he thought of spending several months in New York. It would be very lonely at Midbranch, he wrote, without Roberta,— though why it should be more so this year than during preceding winters he did not explain,—and he felt a desire to see the changes that had taken place in the metropolis since he had visited it, years ago.

They would not have been so much surprised had they known that Mr. Brandon did not feel himself safe in his own home, by night or by day. Frequently had he gazed out of a window at the point in the road on which the first sight of an approaching spring-wagon could have been caught, and had said to himself: "If only Roberta were here, that old hag would not dare to speak a word to me! I don't want to go away, but, by George! I don't see how I can stay here without Rob."

There was a short, very black, and somewhat bow-legged negro man on the place, named Israel Bonaparte, who lived in a little cabin by himself, and was noted for his unsocial disposition and his taciturnity. To him Mr. Brandon went one day, and said: "Israel, I want you to go to work on the fence-rows on my side of the road to Howlett's. Grub up the bushes, clear out the vines and weeds, and see that the rails and posts are all in order. That will be a job that I expect will last you until the roads begin to get heavy. And, by the way, Israel, while you are at work I want you to keep a lookout for any visitors that may turn into our road, especially if they happen to be ladies. Now that Miss Rob is away, I am very particular about knowing beforehand when ladies are coming to visit me; and when you see any wagon or carriage turn in, I want you to make a short cut across the fields, and let me know it, and I will give you a quarter of a dollar every time you do so." This was a very pleasant job of work for the meditative Israel. He was not very fond of grubbing, but he earned the

greater part of his ten dollars a month and rations by
sitting on the fence, smoking a corn-cob pipe, and
attending to the second division of the work which
his employer had set him to do.

Lawrence Croft was in New York at this time, a
very busy man, arranging his affairs in that city so
that they would not need his personal attention for
some time to come; he sublet, for the remainder of
his lease, the suite of bachelor apartments he had occupied, and he stored his furniture and books. One
might have imagined that he was taking in all possible sails, close reefing the others, battening down
the hatches, and preparing to run before a storm; and
yet his demeanor did not indicate that he expected
any violent commotion of the elements. On the contrary, his friends and acquaintances thought him particularly blithe and gay. He told them he was going
to be married.

"To that Virginia lady, I suppose," said one. "I
remember her very well, and consider you fortunate."

"I don't think you ever met her," said Mr. Croft.
"She is a Miss Peyton, from King Thomas County."

"Ah!" remarked his interlocutor.

Lawrence walked to the window of the club-room,
and stood there, slowly puffing his cigar. Had anybody met this one? he thought. He knew she had
seen but little company during her father's life, but
was it likely that any of his acquaintances had had
business at Candy's Information Shop? As this idea
came into his mind, there seemed to be something
unpleasant in the taste of his cigar, and he threw it
into the fire. A few turns, however, up and down the
now almost deserted rooms restored his tone. He

384

lighted another cigar; and now there came up before him a vision of the girl who, from loyalty to her dead father, preferred to sit all day behind Candy's money-desk rather than go to a relative who had not been his friend. And then he saw the young girl who took up so courageously the cause of one of her own blood —the boy cousin of her childhood; and with a lover's pride, Lawrence thought of the dash, the spirit, and the bravery with which she had done it.

"By George!" he said to himself, his eyes sparkling and his step quickening, "she has more in her than all the rest of them put together!"

Who were included in "the rest of them" Lawrence was not prepared just then to say, but the expression was intended to have a very wide range.

It was about the middle of December when Lawrence paid another visit to Mrs. Keswick's house. The day was cold but clear, and as he drove up to the outer gate, he saw the old lady returning from a walk to Howlett's. She stepped along briskly, and was in a very good humor, for she had just posted a carefully concocted letter to Mr. Brandon, in which she had expatiated, in her peculiar style, on the pleasure which she expected from an early visit to Midbranch. She had not the slightest idea of going there at present, but she thought it quite time to freshen up the old gentleman's anticipations.

Descending from his carriage to meet her, Lawrence was very warmly greeted, and the two went up to the house together.

"I expect the late Mrs. Null will be very glad to see you," said Mrs. Keswick. "I think she has burnt up all her widow's weeds."

THE LATE MRS. NULL

"You should be very much obliged to your niece," said Mr. Croft, "for so delicately ridding you of that dreadful fertilizer man."

"Humph!" said the old lady. "She cheated me out of the pleasure of telling him what I thought of him, and I shall never forgive her for that."

As Lawrence and Annie sat together in the parlor that evening, he told her what he had been doing in New York, and this brought to her lips a question which she was very anxious to have answered. She knew that Lawrence was rich; that his methods of life and thought made him a man of the cities; and she felt quite certain that the position to which he would conduct her was that of the mistress of a handsome town house, and the wife of a man of society. She liked handsome town houses, and she was sure she would like society; but it would all be very new and strange to her, and although she was a brave girl at heart, she shrank from making such a plunge as this.

"How are we going to live?" repeated Lawrence. "That, of course, is to be as you shall choose; but I have a plan to propose to you, and I want very much to hear what you think about it. And the plan is that we shall not live anywhere for a year or two, but wander, fancy-free, over as much of the world as pleases us, and then decide where we shall settle down, and how we shall like to do it."

If Annie's answer had been expressed in words, it might have been given here. It may be said, however, that it was very quick, very affirmative, and, in more ways than one, highly satisfactory to Lawrence.

"Is it London, and a landlady, and tea?" she presently asked.

THE LATE MRS. NULL

"Yes, it is that," he said.

"Is it the shops on the Boulevards?"

"Yes," said Lawrence.

"And the Appian Way? and the island of Capri? and snow mountains in the distance?" she asked.

"In their turn, most certainly," said her lover, "and it shall be the midnight sun, and the Nile, if you like."

"Freddy," exclaimed the late Mrs. Null, "I thank thee for what thou hast given me!" And she clasped the hand of Lawrence in both her own.

CHAPTER XXXII

THE marriage of Junius Keswick and Roberta March was appointed for the 15th of January, and Mr. Brandon had arranged to be in New York a few days before the event. He intended, however, to leave Midbranch soon after the first of the year, and to spend a week with some of his friends in Richmond.

It was on the afternoon of New Year's Day, and Mr. Brandon was sitting in his library with Colonel Pinckney Macon, an elderly gentleman of social habits and genial temper whom Mr. Brandon had invited to Midbranch to spend the holidays, and who was afterwards to be his travelling companion as far as Richmond. The two had had a very good dinner, and were now sitting before the fire smoking their pipes, and paying occasional attention to two tumblers of egg-nog which stood on a small table between them. They were telling anecdotes of olden times, and were in very good humor indeed, when a servant came in with a note which had just been brought for Mr. Brandon. The old gentleman took the missive, and put on his eyeglasses; but the moment he read the address, he let his hand fall on his knee, and gave vent to an angry ejaculation.

"It's from that rabid old witch, the widow Keswick!" he exclaimed. "I've a great mind to throw it into the fire without reading it."

"Don't do that!" cried Colonel Macon. "It is a New Year present she is sending you. Read it, sir; read it, by all means."

Mr. Brandon had given his friend an account of his unexampled and astounding persecutions by the widow Keswick, and the old colonel had been much interested thereby, and it would have greatly grieved his soul not to become acquainted with this new feature of the affair. "Read it, sir," he cried; "I would like to know what sort of New Year congratulations she offers you."

"Congratulations, indeed!" said Mr. Brandon, "you needn't expect anything of that kind." But he opened the note, and, turning so that he could get a good light upon it, began to read aloud as follows:

"MY DEAREST ROBERT,"

"Confound it, sir!" exclaimed the reader, "did you ever hear of such a piece of impertinence as that?"

Colonel Pinckney Macon leaned back in his chair and laughed aloud. "It is impertinent," he cried, "but it's confoundedly jolly! Go on, sir. Go on, I beg of you."

Mr. Brandon continued—

"It is not for me to suggest anything of the kind, but I write this note simply to ask you what you would think of a triple wedding? There would certainly be something very touching about it, and it would be very satisfactory and comforting, I am sure, to our nieces and their husbands to know that they were not leaving either of us to a lonely life. Would we not make three happy pairs, dear Robert? Remember, I do not propose this; I only lay it before your kindly and affectionate heart.

"Your own

"MARTHA ANN KESWICK."

Colonel Macon, who, with much difficulty and redness of face, had restrained himself during the reading of this note, now burst into a shout of laughter, while Mr. Brandon sprang to his feet, and, crumpling the note in his hand, threw it into the fire; and then, turning around, he exclaimed: "Did the world ever hear anything like that! Triple wedding, indeed! Does the pestiferous old shrew imagine that anything in this world would induce me to marry her?"

"Why, my dear sir," cried Colonel Macon, "of course she don't. I know the widow Keswick as well as you do. She wouldn't marry you to save your soul, sir. All she wants to do is to worry and persecute you, and to torment your senses out of you, in revenge for your having got the better of her. Now, take my advice, sir, and don't let her do it."

"I'd like to know how I am going to hinder her," said Mr. Brandon.

"Hinder her!" exclaimed Colonel Macon. "Nothing easier in this world, sir! Just you turn right square round and face her, sir, and you'll see that she'll stop short, sir; and, what's more, she'll run, sir!"

"How am I to face her?" asked Mr. Brandon. "I have faced her, and I assure you, sir, she didn't run."

"That was because you did not go to work in the right way," said the colonel. "Now, if I were in your place, sir, this is what I would do: I'd turn on her and I'd scare her out of all the wits she has left. I'd say to her: 'Madam, I think your proposition is an excellent one. I am ready to marry you to-day, or, at the very latest, to-morrow morning. I'll come to your house, and bring a clergyman and some of my friends. Don't let there be the least delay, for I desire to start immediately for New York, and to take you with me.' Now, sir, a note like that would frighten that old woman so that she would leave her house, and wouldn't come back for six weeks; and the letter you have just burnt would be the last attack she would make on you. Now, sir, that is what I would do if I were in your place."

Mr. Brandon sat down, drained his tumbler of egg-nog, and began to think of what his friend had said. And as he thought of it, the conviction forced itself upon him that this idea of Colonel Macon's was a good one—in fact, a splendid one. Now that he came to look upon the matter more clearly than he had done before, he saw that this persecution on the part of the widow Keswick was not only base, but cowardly. He had been entirely too yielding, had given way too much. Yes, he would face her! By George, that was a royal idea! He would turn round and make a dash at her, and scare her out of her five senses.

Pens, ink, and paper were brought out; more egg-nog was ordered; and Mr. Brandon, aided and abetted by Colonel Macon, wrote a letter to Mrs. Keswick.

This letter took a long time to write, and was very carefully constructed. With outstretched hands, Mr. Brandon met the old lady on the very threshold of her proposition. He stated that nothing would please him better than an immediate wedding, and that he would have proposed it himself had he not feared that the lady would consider him too importunate. (This expression was suggested by Colonel Macon.) In order that they might lose no time in making themselves happy, Mr. Brandon proposed that the marriage should take place in a week, and that the ceremony should be performed in Richmond. (The colonel wished him to say that he would immediately go to her house for the purpose, but Mr. Brandon would not consent to write this. He was afraid that the widow would sit at her front door with a shot-gun and wait for him, and that some damage might thereby come to an unwary neighbor.) Each of them had many old friends in Richmond, and it would be very pleasant to be married there. He intended to start for that city in a day or two, and he would be rejoiced to meet her at eleven o'clock on the morning of the 5th instant, in the corridor or covered bridge connecting the Exchange and Ballard hotels, and there arrange all the details for an immediate marriage. The letter closed with an earnest hope that she would accede to this proposed plan, which would so soon make them the happiest couple upon earth, and was signed "Your devoted Robert."

"By which I mean," said Mr. Brandon, "that I am devoted to her destruction."

The letter was read over by Colonel Macon, and highly approved by him. "If you had met that woman, sir, when she first came to you," he said to Mr. Brandon, "with the spirit that is shown in this letter, you would have put a shiver through her, sir, that would have shaken the bones out of her umbrella, and she would have cut and run, sir, before you knew it."

The messenger from Howlett's was kept at Midbranch all night, and the next morning he was sent back with Mr. Brandon's note. Two days afterwards Colonel Macon and Mr. Brandon started for Richmond, and in the course of a few hours they were comfortably sipping their " peach and honey " at the Exchange and Ballard's.

The next day was most enjoyably spent with a number of old friends; and in reminiscences of the past war, and in discussions of the coming political campaign, Mr. Brandon had thrown off every sign of the annoyance and persecution to which he had lately been subjected.

"By George, sir!" said Colonel Macon to him, the next morning, "do you know that you are a most untrustworthy and perfidious man?"

"Sir!" exclaimed Mr. Brandon, "what do you mean?"

"I mean," replied Colonel Pinckney Macon, with much dignity, "that you promised at eleven o'clock to-day to meet a lady in the corridor connecting these two hotels. It wants three minutes of that time now, sir, and here you are reading the 'Despatch' as if you never made a promise in your life."

"I declare," said Mr. Brandon, rising, "my conduct is indefensible; but I am going to my room, and, on my way, will keep my part of the contract."

"I will go with you," said the colonel.

Together they mounted the stairs and approached the corridor; and as they opened its glass doors they saw, sitting in a chair on one side of the passage, the widow Keswick.

THE LATE MRS. NULL

If Mr. Brandon had not been caught by his friend he would have fallen over backward. Regaining an upright position, he made a frantic turn as if he would fly; but he was not quick enough; Mrs. Keswick had him by the arm.

"Robert!" she exclaimed. "I knew how true and faithful you would be. It has just struck eleven. How do you do, Colonel Macon?" And she extended her hand.

There was no one in the corridor at the time but these three; but the place was much used as a passage-way, and Colonel Macon, who was very pale, but still retained his presence of mind, knew well that if any one were to come along at this moment, it would be decidedly unpleasant, not only for his friend, but himself. "I am glad to meet you again, Mrs. Keswick," he said. "Let us go into one of the parlors. It will be more comfortable."

"How kind," murmured Mrs. Keswick, as she clung to the arm of Mr. Brandon, "for you to bring our good friend, Colonel Macon!"

They went into a parlor, which was empty, and where they were not likely to be disturbed. Mr. Brandon walked there without saying a word. His face was as pallid as its well-seasoned color would allow, and he looked straight before him with an air which seemed to indicate that he was trying to remember something terrible, or else trying to forget it, and that he himself did not know which it was.

Colonel Macon did not stay long in the parlor. There was that in the air of Mrs. Keswick which made him understand that there were other places in Richmond where he would be much more welcome

394

THE LATE MRS. NULL

than in that room. He went down into the large hall where the gentlemen generally congregate, and there, in great distress of mind, he paced up and down the marble floor, exchanging nothing but the briefest salutations and answers with the acquaintances he occasionally encountered. The clerk, behind his desk at one side of the hall, had seen men walking up and down in that way, and he thought that the colonel had probably been speculating in tobacco or wheat; but he knew he was good for the amount of his bill, and he retained his placidity.

In about half an hour, there came down the stairs at one end of the hall an elderly person who somewhat resembled Mr. Brandon of Midbranch. The clothes and the hat were the same that that gentleman wore, and the same heavy gold chain with dangling seal-rings hung across his ample waistcoat; but there was a general air of haggardness and stoop about him which did not in the least suggest the upright and portly gentleman who had written his name in the hotel register the day before yesterday.

Colonel Macon made five strides towards him, and seized his hand. "What," said he, "how—?"

Mr. Brandon did not look at him; he let his eyes fall where they chose,—it mattered not to him what they gazed upon,—and in a low voice he said: "It is all over."

"Over!" repeated the colonel.

Mr. Brandon put a feeble hand on his friend's arm, and together they walked into the reading-room, where they sat down in a corner.

"Have you settled it, then?" asked Colonel Macon, with great anxiety. "Is she gone?"

"It is settled," said Mr. Brandon. "We are to be married."

"Married!" cried Colonel Macon, springing to his feet. "Great heavens, man! What do you mean?"

Not very fluently, and in sentences with a very few words in each of them, but words that sank like hot coals into the soul of his hearer, Mr. Brandon explained what he meant. It had been of no use, he said, to try to get out of it; the old woman had him with the grip of a vise. That letter had done it all. He ought to have known that she was not to be frightened. But it was needless to talk about that. It was all over now, and he was as much bound to her as if he had promised before a magistrate.

"But you don't mean to say," exclaimed the colonel, in a voice of anguish, "that you are really going to marry her?"

"Sir," said Mr. Brandon, solemnly, "there is no way to get out of it. If you think there is, you don't know the woman."

"I would have died first," said the colonel. "I never would have submitted to her!"

"I did not submit," replied Mr. Brandon. "That was done when the letter was written. I roused myself, and I said everything I could say; but it was all useless: she held me to my promise. I told her I would fly to the ends of the earth rather than marry her, and then, sir, she threatened me with a prosecution for breach of promise; and think of the disgrace that that would bring upon me—upon my family name, and on my niece and her young husband! It was a mistake, sir, to suppose that she merely wished to persecute me. She wished to marry me, and she is

going to do it." The colonel bowed his face upon his
hands and groaned. Mr. Brandon looked at him with
a dim compassion in his eyes. "Do not reproach yourself, sir," he said. ' We thought we were acting for
the best."

But little more was said, and two crushed old gentlemen retired to their rooms.

In the days of her youth Mrs Keswick had been
very well known in Richmond, and there were a good
many elderly ladies and gentlemen now living in that
city who remembered her as a handsome, sparkling,
and somewhat eccentric young woman, and who had
since heard of her as a decidedly eccentric old one.
Mr. Brandon also had a large circle of friends and
acquaintances in the city. And when it became known
that these two elderly persons were to be married—and
the news began to spread shortly after Mrs. Keswick
reached the house of the friend with whom she was
staying—it excited a great deal of excusable interest.

Mrs. Keswick, according to her ordinary methods of
action, took all the arrangements into her own hands.
She appointed the wedding for the 8th of January,
in order that the happy pair might go to New York
and be present at the nuptials of Junius and Roberta.
Mr. Brandon had thought of writing to Junius, in the
hope that the young man might do something to avert
his fate; but remembering how utterly unable Junius
had always been to move his aunt one inch, this way
or that, he did not believe that he could be of any
service in this case, in which all the energies of her
mind were evidently engaged, and he readily consented that she should attend to all the correspondence. It would, indeed, have been too hard for him

to break the direful truth to his niece and Junius. He ventured to suggest that Miss Peyton be sent for, having a faint hope that he might in some manner lean upon her; but Mrs. Keswick informed him that her niece must stay at home to take charge of the place. There were two women in the house who were busy sewing for her, and it would be impossible for her to come to Richmond.

Her correspondence kept the widow Keswick very busy. She decided that she would be married in a church which she used to attend in her youth; and to all of her old friends, and to all those of Mr. Brandon whose names she could learn by diligent inquiry, invitations were sent to attend the ceremony; but no one outside of Richmond was invited.

The old lady did not come to the city with a purple sunbonnet and a big umbrella. She wore her best bonnet, which had been used for church-going purposes for many years, and arrayed herself in a travelling suit which was of excellent material, although of most antiquated fashion. She discussed very freely with her friends the arrangements she had made, and protuberant candor being at times one of her most noticeable characteristics, she did not leave it altogether to others to say that the match she was about to make was a most remarkably good one. For years it had been a hard struggle for her to keep up the Keswick farm, but now she had fought a battle and won a victory which ought to make her comfortable and satisfied for the rest of her life. If Mr. Brandon's family had taken a great deal from her, she would more than repay herself by appropriating the old gentleman, together with his possessions.

THE LATE MRS. NULL

After the depression following the first shock, Mr.
Brandon endeavored to stiffen himself. There was a
great deal of pride in him, and if he were obliged to go
to the altar, he did not wish his old friends to suppose
that he was going there to be sacrificed. He had
brought this dreadful thing upon himself, but he
would try to stand up like a man and bear it; and,
after all, it might not be for long : the widow Keswick
was a good deal older than he was. Other thoughts
occasionally came to comfort him : she could not make
him continually live with her, and he had plans for
visits to Richmond, and even to New York; and,
better than that, she might want to spend a good deal
of time at her own farm.

"For the sake of my name and my niece," he said
to himself, "I must bear it like a man."

And, in answer to an earnest adjuration, Colonel
Pinckney Macon solemnly promised that he would
never reveal, to man or woman, that his friend did
not marry the widow Keswick entirely of his own
wish and accord.

It was the desire of Mrs. Keswick that the marriage,
although conducted in church, should be very simple
in its arrangements. There would be no bridesmaids
or groomsmen; no flowers; no breakfast; and the
couple would be dressed in travelling costume. The
friends of the old lady persuaded her to make considerable changes in her attire, and a costume was
speedily prepared, which, while it suggested the fashions of the present day, was also calculated to recall
reminiscences of those of a quarter of a century ago.
This simplicity was the only thing connected with the
affair which satisfied Mr. Brandon, and he would have

been glad to have the marriage entirely private, with no more witnesses than the law demanded. But to this Mrs. Keswick would not consent. She wanted to have her former friends about her. Accordingly, the church was pretty well filled with old colonels, old majors, old generals, and old judges, with their wives and their sisters, and, in a few cases, their daughters. All the elderly people in Richmond who, in the days of their youth, had known the gay Miss Matty Pettigrew and the handsome Bob Brandon felt a certain rejuvenation of spirit as they went to the wedding of the couple who had once been these two.

The old lady looked full of life and vigor, and, despite the circumstances, Mr. Brandon preserved a good deal of his usual manly deportment. But when, in the course of the marriage service, the clergyman came to the question in which the bridegroom was asked if he would have this woman to be his wedded wife, to love and keep her for the rest of their lives, the answer, "I will," came forth in a feeble tone, which was not wholly divested of a tinge of despondency.

With the lady it was quite otherwise. When the like question was put to her, she stepped back, and in a loud, clear voice exclaimed: "Not I ! Marry that man there?" she continued in a higher tone, and pointing her finger at the astounded Mr. Brandon. "Not for the world, sir ! Before he was born, his family defrauded and despoiled my people, and as soon as he took affairs into his own hands, he continued the villainous law robberies until we are poor and he is rich ; and, not content with that, he basely wrecks and destroys the plans I had made for the comfort of my old age, in order that his paltry purposes may be carried out. After all that, does anybody here suppose that I would take him for a husband? Marry him! Not I!" And, with these words, the old lady turned her back on the clergyman and walked rapidly down the centre aisle until she reached the church door. There she stopped, and turning towards the stupefied assemblage, she snapped her bony fingers in the air, and exclaimed: "Now, Mr. Robert Brandon of Midbranch, our account is balanced."

She then went out of the door, and took a street-car for the train that would carry her to her home.